The shining splendor of our Zebra Lovegram logo on the cover reflects the glittering excellence of the story inside. Look fo Lovegram whenever you buy a historical romance. It's a trac guarantees the very best in quality and reading entertainme

★ ★ ★ ★ ★

Judith Hill—
"Best Up and Coming Author of 1991
—*Affaire de Coeur*

"A KNIGHT'S DESIRE . . . a riveting story peopled interesting, vivid characters who will move your emotions. . . . packed with sensual imagery, this novel is a five-star winner which had this reader begging for more. Ms. Hill is certain to become an author whose books you'll want to read again and again. This novel was so well written that I wanted to stand up and clap at the end. Ms. Hill is truly a talented author!"

—GiGi Rounds, reviewer
Affaire de Coeur

PASSION'S CHALLENGE

"Are you a woman who will accept a man's desires?" Garret asked. Softly he stroked her cheek. "Or is your boldness only a pretense?"

Suddenly Taryn was aware that his hands had moved. One had gone to her nape, the other had traveled down to the small of her back. Gently, but firmly, he was drawing her closer to him. Now his lips were at her ear.

"I want you, as a man wants a woman. But are you woman enough to bear all which that entails?" And then his mouth was on hers.

Again she experienced the same feeling that had coursed through her when he had kissed her before . . . yet this time it was stronger. This time he did not push her away. She melted into his embrace, feeling a rising hunger, an aching need, until she was breathless with pleasure . . .

JUDITH HILL

ZEBRA BOOKS
KENSINGTON PUBLISHING CORP.

To Genevieve Feligno, my Aunt Jay:
I didn't tell her I was naming a character in this novel after her because I wanted it to be a surprise. Unfortunately, a month after this went into production, she suffered a massive stroke. Thus far she is partially paralyzed and able to speak only a few words. We continue to hope and pray she will one day be able to pick this up and see her name in print, and know I make this dedication with love.

ZEBRA BOOKS

are published by

Kensington Publishing Corp.
475 Park Avenue South
New York, NY 10016

First printing: September, 1992

Printed in the United States of America

Prologue

Wynshire Castle, England, December 1169

"She be at it again, milord!"

The heavy oak door slammed shut, jolting awake the recumbent form dozing in one of the chamber's three upholstered window seats.

"She?" Charles Maitland, the newly titled Earl of Wynshire, brushed a lock of golden hair from his forehead and yawned. He pushed away from the thick masonry wall he'd been leaning against and glanced out the arched window to the castle's courtyard below—as if expecting to see the source of his steward's irritation.

"Aye, milord. Yer sister." Conar, Wynshire's beefy seneschal, instantly flinched. In his haste the word had slipped out. He knew better than to call the flame-haired wench a sister to the man he now faced! In Charles' eyes the product of his father's scandalous second marriage to a serving maid was no sibling. And that the old earl had frankly favored his daughter above his son and heir had but added jealous hatred to those feelings of contempt.

Quickly, Conar stepped forward and bowed his head. Hoping to avoid an outburst of his lord's notorious temper, he hastened to make an apology. "Yer pardon, milord."

In sadistic satisfaction Charles smiled. He had seen the flicker of fear in his man's eyes. Without reply, he stood. Again Conar flinched, and Charles' enjoyment grew. Beneath his ermine *pelisse* he felt himself becoming hard. He rubbed the thickening shaft surreptitiously. Had he a woman already warming his bed who could provide him release, he would prolong his steward's discomfort—and thereby his own pleasure. For while other men might obtain tumescence with the thought or sight of a comely wench, the Earl of Wynshire had found the possession and exercise of his new powers to deliver the greatest arousal.

Nervously Conar shifted his weight.

The action served to return Charles' attention to the matter at hand. "Well?" he demanded in irritation. "What has she done this time?"

Conar's audible sigh of relief was not lost on him, but his enjoyment of the moment had passed. Charles crossed the room to the opposite wall and straightened the large wooden crucifix which hung there. Beneath it, on a shelf, was a small silver box richly chased with figures of saints and angels. These he lightly caressed as his steward's voice filled the chamber.

"The same. She be knowing naught her place nor business." Conar turned to face him. "Just now she came to me—demanding I have several of the German hirelings flogged. Seems the men carried off a girl from the village and had a bit of fun in the woods. Lady Taryn claims the girl was 'raped.' She wants me to make an example of them. By the saints!" He rolled his eyes upward. "Since when is tossing up the skirts of a peasant maid a crime?"

Silently Charles swore. This time Taryn had gone too far. With each day that passed her actions undermined more of his authority! Peasant women had always been fair game to the noble class, excluded from the protection of the law by virtue of their low rank. Why, even he had availed himself of the base creatures a time or two—

though he preferred the whores of the city who knew their craft. Taryn must be dealt with. "What did you tell her?"

"Told her I'd take it up with ye," Conar answered, his voice weighted with caution. "Didn't like it, she didn't. She's trouble, milord. Got half the village stirred up with her talk of 'justice.' The dumb bastards are loyal to her, they are. 'Tis a right blessing she warn't born a man—"

Conar broke off, seeing the dark scowl twisting his lord's perfect features. Primogeniture aside, it was common knowledge that had the old earl's second issue also been a male, Charles' claim as heir might have been in jeopardy. Still, despite her gender, Lady Taryn's will was one to be reckoned with.

Knowing she would always bear a stigma because of her mother's low birth, her father had instilled within her a singular sense of pride and honor. As a result she repeatedly stepped beyond the place appointed to a woman. The incident of an hour ago was but one of many. It was no wonder her half-brother had been trying to marry her off these past months since their father's death.

Conar secretly frowned, recalling the strange circumstances surrounding the old earl's untimely demise. There were some who believed that the man had been poisoned. Indeed, the illness which had befallen him had been mysterious—and his death undeniably swift.

At once Conar pushed the notion aside. Nothing but trouble would come of such ideas. Charles was his lord now, and he would do well to remember that. "What would you have me do, milord?"

Deep in thought, Charles did not immediately reply. He fingered the lid of the silver box for several moments before finally lifting it. From inside it he withdrew a folded sheet of parchment. "Nothing," he said.

Closing the box, he nodded, a decision made. He had not intended to share the contents of the letter in his hands, but perhaps it would serve his plan better if he did . . .

"Do nothing," he repeated. "'Tis I who am lord and master. I deem that no crime has been committed. And if my half-sister has difficulty in accepting that judgment, she will soon forget it when she learns of my next." Triumphantly he clutched the document in his hand. "I have decided upon her husband. Three weeks hence, at the Christmas Mass, Taryn shall be betrothed by proxy to Baron Lynfyld. They will marry in the spring, at Castle Jaune."

Conar looked upon his lord with dismay. He knew Charles had been having difficulty in arranging a marriage. Though she was by no means hard upon the eyes, the Lady Taryn was considered by all the Earl had contacted to be past a marriageable age. Without benefit of a sizeable dowry, she was surely destined for the nunnery, and if asked, Conar would have wagered the shirt on his back that Charles would never forfeit Wynshire lands for any such purpose as a dowry—not even to rid himself of his half-sister.

Mother of God! he thought suddenly. Baron Lynfyld must have demanded a substantial dowry. Past sixty, the man was one of the wealthiest landholders in England—his fortune not inherited, but amassed through shrewdness and miserliness. Had Charles lost leave of his senses? If he were indeed so desperate to be rid of the wench, why not send her into a convent?

"Which lands will . . . ah . . . be given in dowry?" he asked aloud, cautiously guarding his expression.

To his surprise Charles burst out into laughter. "Therein lies the beauty of this arrangement!" he exclaimed, an indisputable tone of smugness in his voice. "Though he's been thrice married—and widowed, the baron has produced no heir. Since his last wife, but a child of twelve, died in childbirth, he has hence decided to seek a bride of, shall we say, more viable maturity. But she must be a virgin and of the noble class. It would appear, he believes, that only such a womb, fertile yet pure, can bear his seed to fruition. So intent is he upon obtaining this prize that he has agreed to take himself a wife who will bring him no lands—namely, my half-sister."

Charles broke out into a wide grin, no longer able to contain his satisfaction. What he had failed to mention to his seneschal was the vast sum of silver the baron was willing to pay for a chaste, mature bride—silver which would fill Wynshire's coffers and pay for the mercenaries from aboard who were an integral part of its lord's future plans.

He returned his attention to the man before him. "On the morn of the wedding, Taryn will be examined by a midwife. It she fails the test, there will be no marriage. Therefore, we must ensure that my half-sister remains as she is now—unknown to any man. For that I will hold you personally responsible." His voice was clipped. "Should she be found to be unchaste, I will have you and every tenth man on this estate castrated."

He paused to allow the meaning of his words to become quite clear, then continued. "So, you best make sure she neither learns of the baron's requirements, nor does anything which would invalidate this agreement." He held up the parchment in his hand. "Do you understand?"

Conar fought down the taste of bile. "Aye, milord." Careful to conceal any emotion, he stared at Charles. The man was evil, hungry for power. His motive for delivering his sister into such a marriage rather than the convent had to go deeper. There had to be more to the agreement with Lynfyld. But whatever it was, it was not his place to know. "Have you contacted the Earl of Arundel?"

Hearing the name, Charles felt an instant knotting in the pit of his stomach. A knight of exceptional valor, and a favorite of King Henry, the dark and mysterious lord of Castle Jaune was also Charles' seigneur. As such, his permission was needed before Taryn's marriage could take place.

"Aye," he answered, composing himself quickly lest Conar detect his uneasiness. The Great Earl's permission was but a formality which would be granted in the spring. Yet, for a reason he could not fathom, ever since Charles had begun laying the groundwork for his plans, he had had the distinct feeling that Garret d'Aubigny could be a threat to them.

He dismissed the nagging doubt, replacing it in his mind with a much more satisfying thought. In a few months' time he would be rid of Taryn—and the richer for it—and that much closer to his greater goal: the crown of England.

"And when will ye be telling the Lady Taryn of yer plans, milord?" Conar's voice cut into Charles' thoughts.

"This evening," he answered, ". . . at supper."

"Silence! I should like to make an announcement."

Charles' voice rose above the always present din in Wynshire's great hall during meals—for the space was packed with more than a hundred men-at-arms, servants and guests of its lord.

The hall quieted. As he rose slowly from his chair beside hers on the dais, Lady Taryn Maitland looked up at her half-brother. The smile on his bearded face was one she knew too well. Instantly a sense of uneasiness gripped her.

"I bid you all to raise your cups." Lifting his own goblet, Charles continued, his voice ringing out to reach the farthest corners of the vast room. ". . . For on this day I have received joyous news." He turned his golden head with its carefully styled waves toward Taryn. "Three weeks hence, at the Christmas Mass, my sister shall be betrothed."

What? Taryn felt her face drain of color. Through the blood pounding in her ears she could hear the sounds and cheers evoked by Charles' announcement.

Several of her ladies-in-waiting rushed to her side, placing kisses upon her cheeks and gushing words of congratulations.

"Why, we had no idea!"

"Lady, you didn't tell us!"

"Who?"

Indeed, who?

The question exploded in Taryn's mind. *Who?* She looked at Charles and fought to compose herself. Though she had no looking glass to confirm it, she knew her face was as white as the linen tablecloth clutched in her fingers. Fearing she would falter if she attempted to move, she could only mouth the question. *Who?*

Charles' smile seemed to increase in size, slashing his handsome features and turning his face into a grotesque vizard. She squeezed her eyes shut. Immersed in a dizzying darkness, she heard his voice.

"Baron Lynfyld."

The name tugged at the fringes of a forgotten memory. As she struggled to recall it, the voice of one of her former ladies-in-waiting rang in her mind. The girl, who had been called Elizabeth, had had no female kin. As was the custom, she had been sent by her father to Wynshire to learn from its lady the art of managing a household.

Elizabeth had been a giddy thing, prone to gossip, and one of her favorite topics had been her father's liege lord. According to Elizabeth, the old man was hideous to behold. Though infamous for indulgences of the flesh, he had failed to sire a single child. Twice widowed, he had recently taken to wife a child bride in the hope of producing an heir.

Frantically, Taryn sought to remember the man's name. That he had been baron she was sure. Baron . . . Baron Field . . . no, something "field," Baron Lonfield . . . *Dear God, no! No!* The name of her betrothed was one and the same as the lecher in Elizabeth's tales!

Her eyes flew open. In her revulsion, she unwittingly

repeated the words which had been Elizabeth's very own summation of the man. "Lynfyld is a troll!"

Her outburst caused several of those nearest to gasp in shock. One of her ladies giggled nervously.

A dark shadow descended over Charles' face. "Guard well your words, woman," he warned through clenched teeth. With a hasty wave of his hand, he gestured to the half dozen minstrels waiting at the table's edge. "Play!" he hissed.

As he sat, the music of their instruments filled the air—sweet strains of the lute, blended with flute and horn.

Taryn heard none of it. She pushed back her chair and stood. Her mind still reeling, she focused on her half-brother.

In icy calm he unsheathed his knife and applied it to the great haunch of stag before him. "Sit down, Taryn."

"Nay." In a gesture left from her childhood days, she flipped back the heavy plait of red hair which hung over her shoulder past her waist. She drew herself up to her full height. When she spoke her voice was strong and even. "Nay. I'll not sit. And I'll not marry a lecherous old man desperate to produce life from his withered loins!"

The great hall fell silent, all eyes turning to view the confrontation of wills.

Charles drove his knife into the table. "Damn you, wench!" In the dead silence his voice resounded like a clap of thunder. "You've defied me once too often!" He stood, toppling his chair, and grabbed her arm. Twisting it cruelly, he pushed her off the dais.

Taryn wrested her arm free and stumbled from him. She knew there was no escaping his fury. Still, she tried. She ran from the hall toward the stairs which led to the upper level. If she could reach her chamber and bolt the portal . . .

But Charles was faster than she. Within a few strides of her door he overtook her. Seizing the end of her braid, he jerked her back. His face was a red mask of rage. "You shall not defy me in this!" he roared.

Taryn whirled. "I will not marry a man I do not love," she spat back at him. "Father gave his word. I would have a love match and not be made to wed against my wish."

"*A love match?*" Charles sneered, repeating her words in sarcastic mimicry. "Such as the one he enjoyed with your mother—a serving wench?" He snorted his disgust and gripped her arm. "My father may have indulged that foolishness, but I shall not. You should have been married off long before your fifteenth birthday. I would have expected these seven fruitless years to have taught you reality, sister. Where is your 'love match?' There is no hope for you save a nunnery."

"Then send me to one! I would prefer it to marriage to a man I did not love—a man all know to be wasted by age and debauchery."

"You have no choice in the matter. My father is dead. You will act according to my desires now."

"And if I do not give my consent?" Taryn lifted her chin defiantly, her gray eyes meeting Charles' icy stare. In confidence she held her ground. She knew the answer, as did her half-brother, for without her free consent there could be no marriage. On this the Church was unyielding. For of its three demands in the matter of matrimony—that a maiden be at least fifteen years of age, that she not be too closely related to the man, and that she give her consent willingly—only the last was never waived. To suit the ambitions of her guardian—be it her father, brother, uncle or king—many a girl of twelve was married off, ofttimes to a man within a forbidden degree of consanguinity. But only if her consent was somehow obtained, at least publicly.

"You *will* give your consent!" Charles' voice, ominous and treatening, sliced through her.

Ignoring it, Taryn plunged recklessly ahead. "There's naught you can do to force me."

"Oh, but there is."

"You would threaten *me?*" In disbelief she looked at

him. Not even from Charles did she expect physical reprisal.

"Nay. I am not so much a fool as to threaten that which holds no importance to you. I know I could have the skin beaten from your back, and you would not relent. The way to obtain what I want from you lies with threatening those you hold dear—the villeins—your mother's kin and ilk. Withhold your consent and I will have fifty men on this manor flogged to within an inch of their lives."

"You would let innocent men suffer?" she cried in a mixture of anger and sudden fear.

"Nay. *You* would let innocent men suffer. If the betrothal does not take place in three weeks' time as agreed upon, I will merely be providing the instrument of their suffering. *You* will be providing the cause." He paused, obviously to allow her time to weigh his words. "Well? What say you?"

Taryn bowed her head. "You leave me no choice," she whispered, her voice quivering in furious resignation.

To her amazement Charles began to laugh. He thrust her from him. "Despite my father's efforts, you remain what you are. Though your spirit is strong—like that of a man's—your emotions are those of a woman."

He reached out and snared her wrist, pulling her forward until their faces were only inches apart. "Emotions make you weak, vulnerable to compassion and pity. Mark my words. As they have this time, they will always lead to your defeat."

Taryn twisted away and watched as he turned on his heel and headed back to rejoin his guests. She could feel the sting of rising tears. Fiercely, she dashed them away. She would not cry—nor would she relent. Somehow she would find a way to defy Charles *and* his plans.

Chapter One

Wynshire Castle, March 1170

On the battlements of the keep a lone figure stood sentinel above the black mass of the castle and the walled bailey before it. The early morning stillness was unmarred. Not even the thrushes and blackbirds in the trees of the garden had begun their cacophony.

The watchman lifted his horn to his lips. The blast shattered the early morning stillness, proclaiming the end of night. Soon the sun would begin its ascent, and another day would commence.

Deep within the castle's thick walls one of its residents had no need for the watchman's announcement. Lady Taryn Maitland had been awake for hours. She paced her chamber, her slippered feet making no noise on the cold, tiled floor. Though the room was dark, she had no need for rushlights. In addition, she pointedly avoided the half dozen iron-bound wooden chests lying about.

Without warning a sob rose in her throat. She bit her lip to hold it back and brought a hand to her breast. She would not cry. But the burning ache within her would not subside. Despite her vow of nearly three months past, she had found no way to escape this day. In a few hours' time she would be leaving all she had ever known to enter into a marriage with an odious man she had never met.

From the stone parapet the watchman sounded his horn once again.

Taryn heard the blast, and the sound ran icy fear through her. Shivering, she wrapped her arms about herself. The effort was wasted. The chill was one from within, and could not be staved off.

"My lady, are you awake?"

The sudden voice outside her chamber door was followed by a knock.

Though it had been muffled by the heavy oaken planks, Taryn recognized the voice as that of her childhood nurse. Quickly she sought to compose herself. It would not do for the older woman to see her teary-eyed and irresolute—not on this, the morn of her departure. She drew a deep breath and called out, "Come in, Moira."

The portal swung open and a heavyset woman wearing the close coif of a matron entered.

Despite Taryn's efforts, the sight of Moira brought an instant tightness of her throat. She tried to ignore it. "You rise early these days, Nana," she stated softly. "But not early enough. Celia has already helped me to dress and plaited my hair."

The cheerful smile she wanted to offer refused to form. Her lips felt stiff and wooden. Fortunately, Moira appeared not to notice.

Placing her hands on her wide hips, the woman directed her attentions to Taryn's hair and dress. The woolen gown, a rust color with an overtunic of saffron, apparently met her approval. But as her gaze went to the fiery hair, braided in a single plait, a brow lifted in critical appraisal.

"I've seen better effort by a stable boy on a palfrey's mane," she muttered with an accompanying sniff of disdain. She walked to the small dressing table in the room's center and picked up a comb. "Come here and sit. Let me do a proper job. An hour in the saddle and that tangle will be undone and flying in the wind."

Taryn suppressed her amusement. She knew there was

nothing wrong in the braiding of her hair. Nevertheless, she obediently moved to sit upon the stool Moira indicated.

She was barely seated before she felt the older woman's fingers deftly working to undo the heavy braid, allowing the tresses to fall to their full length. Taryn watched her in the looking glass set upon the table. She studied the face whose every line and plane were as familiar to her as her own.

For as long as she could remember, Moira had been a part of her life—the mother whom fate had denied her. It had been she who had taken Taryn from Kate Maitland's lifeless arms. Hers was the breast at which the orphaned babe had nursed, hers the guidance and love which had brought the waif to the bloom of womanhood.

That Moira was herself of peasant birth had mattered not. Taryn knew the woman had made a deathbed promise. With the fierceness of a peregrine protecting her young, she had demanded a boon of Wynshire's lord. If the great love the earl had born his second wife carried over to the child she died bearing him, he could scarce deny this request. Those who had taunted the mother's lowly station should never have cause to mock the daughter: Kate's girl must not know ridicule or shame.

True to his word, her father made certain that as Taryn grew, she was educated in a manner which rivaled that of her half-brother, his son and heir.

She proved an adept pupil, strong-willed and stubborn—indeed, much like her father. How Taryn had loved him! His death six months ago had been a horrible blow, unexpected and sudden. He had fallen ill one morning and was dead the next. She had not even had the chance to say goodbye.

Swallowing hard to dislodge the lump that had once again risen to her throat, Taryn forced aside those painful memories. She focused on Moira's face in the looking glass.

The woman's plump cheeks were wet, her soft eyes

filled with tears.

Lest the tears now standing in her own eyes begin to fall, Taryn averted her gaze from the glass. A moment later she felt Moira pat her shoulder.

"There. That be a braid to hold for days." With the pretense of replaiting the hair now done, Moira stepped back. "Up with you now. Come down to the kitchen and have a bite to eat. I'll not have you in the saddle with an empty belly."

Taryn shook her head and stood. "I couldn't eat, Moira. We . . . I . . . I must get on with this. Would you see to these chests? 'Tis time they were brought below and loaded. No doubt Charles will want to ride with first light."

"No doubt," Moira repeated, her voice laced with malice.

Taryn reached out and squeezed her hand. "'Tis not a Christian tone that I hear in your voice, Nana."

"Humpf."

Moira's indignant response to her gentle teasing evoked a soft laugh. "Now what would Father Gregory say should he hear you?"

"The good Father can add it to my sins . . . along with theft," Moira replied evenly. Then, as if having suddenly reconsidered her words, she quickly crossed herself.

The action brought a smile to Taryn's lips. She knew the older woman set little store in the priest's teachings—she viewed much of it as prattle. Still, to deliberately invite divine wrath with blasphemous sarcasm was to risk divine retribution. And the expression on her face was indeed grave.

"Moira, I don't believe for a moment you are capable of sin. What are you talking about? What 'theft?'"

"This." Moira withdrew a folded sheet of parchment from the deep hem of her sleeve. "I took it from Charles' bedchamber this morning after he left."

"What is this?" Taryn took the sheet of parchment she offered.

"'Tis a letter, written, I think, by Baron Lynfyld to Charles."

"But why would you take—"

"I think you should read it, milady." As she had when Taryn was a child, Moira silenced her with a sombre stare. "Last night, Conar had a bit too much wine and began to talk. You know, the way a man will once his tongue has been loosened by drink and he's had himself a romp betwixt the sheets?"

Taryn nodded. But she didn't know, not in the way Moira was inferring. She knew almost nothing about men. At twenty-one, she was as chaste as a girl of seven still in the nursery. Feeling her color rise, she looked to the floor. She knew Moira and Wynshire's steward were intimate—the whole castle did. But to hear her childhood nurse refer to their relationship of the flesh so frankly made her more than slightly uncomfortable.

"Taryn? Are you listening?" Once sure that she had her attention, Moira continued. "On the morn of the day he announced your betrothal, Charles told Conar about his plans. He also told him some things he didn't announce so freely. Milady . . . did you know Charles is giving you no dowry, and that the baron has agreed to it?"

Taryn looked at the older woman in surprise. "Nay," she whispered, her cheeks now flaming. Even a peasant maid was given a dowry—be it only a few chickens or a sack of grain! "Why would the baron agree to forgo a dowry?" Unconsciously she voiced her silent question aloud.

"Because the prize he desired was so rare," Moira stated softly. "You heard Elizabeth's gossip, you know the tales. He's desperate to sire an heir. That last wife he took was a mere child. She got herself a belly all right—then died trying to bring it into the world, along with the babe. Now he's taken it into his head that only a virgin bride in the full bloom of womanhood can nurture his seed and birth a live child."

"Mother of heaven!" Taryn gasped. She had to swallow several times to relieve the feeling of nausea rising within her.

"There's more, milady. You're to be examined by a midwife on the morn of the wedding day. If you're not found to be a virgin, the baron will not proceed with the marriage. Conar was threatened with castration should you have learned of this. Every tenth man on the manor as well. Charles feared you . . . you would—"

"End my chastity," Taryn finished for her.

"Aye. But Conar thought there was more to it than what Charles told him. Conar said the earl took that letter," Moira gestured to the parchment in Taryn's hand, "from a silver box on a shelf and clutched it in his hand—triumphant-like—but also like there was something in it he didn't want known. After he left this morning, I went to his chamber. I found it, just as Conar said, in the silver box under the crucifix. Well—" Impatiently she pointed to the letter. "Will you read it?"

Taryn knew if Moira had been able to read, she would have read it herself. She unfolded the sheet of parchment. Moira had been right. The letter was addressed to Charles, and the seal at its conclusion that of the Baron of Lynfyld.

Quickly she read past the prerequisite formalities. Then, as the meaning of the words before her became clear, she felt her body tighten. "'Tis an outrage!" she cried, lifting her eyes from the page. "He sold me—like a chattel! The baron not only waived a dowry, he paid Charles a king's ransom in silver for the right to . . . to . . ." She looked back down at the script so as to quote it properly. ". . . 'to take himself to wife the Earl of Wynshire's half-sister, known as Taryn, a maid of one and twenty years.'"

"By the saints!" Moira's face, flushed with anger, mirrored Taryn's horror. "I knew it! I knew there was a reason he was forcing you into this marriage."

Numb with shock, Taryn could only stare at the

parchment in her hand. "And there's naught I can do," she whispered, more to herself than to the woman at her side.

"Aye, there is." Moira took her arm and forced her to face her. "Taryn . . . what if you were to . . . lose your maidenhead? Charles told Conar if you failed the midwife's test there would be no marriage."

"Moira!" Taryn looked at the woman in disbelief. "Do you know what you are saying? What you propose is a mortal sin—for a maid to lie with a man not her lawful husband—" Suddenly realizing what she had just said, she broke off. "I'm sorry. I did not mean—"

Moira waved her silent and shrugged callously. "Aye. In the eyes of the Church, 'tis a sin, all right. But in my eyes 'tis the only way you can escape this marriage." Crossing herself again, she then lifted her gaze heavenward. "Lord Jesus, surely *you* can see the injustice being forced upon this child. Help me to make her understand." Her entreaty made, she returned her attention to Taryn. "Milady, listen to me. Your father would ne'er have wanted this."

"My father is dead," Taryn countered. She was unable to prevent the cold emptiness his death had left in her heart from entering her voice. She fought against the torrent of emotions assailing her—grief and anger, fear and helplessness. "I cannot do what you are suggesting. To be tumbled like a dairy maid in a pile of hay . . . I cannot. I will not!"

"Then you do Charles' bidding like a dairy maid—nay, like a whore, a whore who lets herself be sold to whoever presents her bawd the biggest purse! Taryn, I beseech you. Consider my words."

"And do what, Moira? Give myself to whom? Who should be the lucky man? Mayhap I should go down to the stables and wait for the first creature in breeches to come along. 'Your pardon, lowly villein, but your mistress desires to be relieved of her maidenhead. Would you be so kind as to oblige? Oh, there is one thing you should know beforehand, however. My half-brother, the earl, will no doubt have you castrated for your efforts when he learns of this tryst.'"

"It need not be done that way."

"It will not be done in *any* way, Moira," Taryn replied firmly. "'Tis out of the question. I'll not have an innocent man suffer. And what of Charles' threat to Conar? What reprisal do you think my brother will take should this fine purse be lost?" She waved the sheet of parchment still in her hand. "Before the betrothal, when I told him I would ne'er give my consent, he threatened to have fifty men on the manor flogged."

"He told you that to force your consent. He threatened Conar to prevent your chastity from being lost. Both were threats he could later enforce or ignore." Reaching out, Moira touched her cheek gently. Her voice became maternal and patient. "Once your chastity is lost, naught can be done. Threat or nay, 'tis done. To what purpose would he punish innocent men?"

"Charles needs no purpose," Taryn answered bitterly. "I must accept my fate. If it be God's will that I marry Baron Lynfyld, then I will do so. The matter is settled." Despite the flinty determination of her words she was not sure she could keep herself from burying her head on Moira's soft bosom. She pulled away before she weakened. "Would you leave me, please? And take this."

She held out the sheet of parchment, then turned her back to the woman. "You'd best replace it before Charles finds it gone."

Wordlessly Moira took the letter from her hand. A moment later the door closed.

Taryn walked to the room's single window, her steps as leaden as her heart, and looked out. The sky had begun to brighten with the light of dawn. She pressed her cheek to the cold glass pane, soon wet with her tears.

Charles rubbed his hands together briskly and watched

from the steps of the keep as his men loaded the dozen pack horses in the castleyard. He recognized as his own one large mail and leathern portmanteau being tied to a beast's crupper. Might the witless wench who'd packed it have placed his gauntlets in it, he wondered silently. Ten minutes ago, thinking he had left them in his chamber, he had sent a page to fetch them. But the boy was not yet returned.

Again he rubbed his hands together. Perhaps the gauntlets weren't in his chamber to be found. Swearing aloud, he turned and headed up the steps to the keep. If he did find them himself, he'd see that a cane was taken to the negligent page's backside!

Inside the great hall Charles' arrival went unnoticed by the handful of servants bustling about to do the bidding of the twenty or so men seated at the massive trestle tables. These early risers were the men who would be accompanying their lord to Castle Jaune. To make certain the page was not curled in a corner asleep, Charles scanned the room quickly. He then ascended the stairs leading to the sleeping quarters.

Near the top he spied a small form blocking his passage. Given the absence of light, he thought at first it was one the hounds that roamed the castle freely. He prepared to deliver a vicious kick. At the last moment he realized the body was that of his errant page. But the kick was not withheld.

The boy's yelp of pain resounded in the narrow space, echoing off the stone walls.

"Lazy cur!" Charles hissed as the page leapt to his feet.

"Yer pardon, milord," he whimpered, rubbing the site where Charles' boot had connected.

"Is this how you obey my order, boy? I sent you to fetch my gauntlets, not to take a nap."

With practiced skill the child ducked and avoided the hand raised to box his ears. "I warn't sleepin', milord. Honest! Moira tol' me t' wait."

"Moira?"

"Aye, milord. She sent me out, she did. Said she'd look for yer gauntlets herself. I was just waitin', like she said."

Wary of the veracity of the boy's statement, Charles impatiently shoved him aside and made his way down the narrow hallway to his chamber. He flung the portal open. "Explain yourself, woman," he demanded, before he had even lain eyes on the target of his suspicions. His gaze swept the room. Nothing appeared out of order or missing. Partially satisfied, he next looked to the serving woman standing in the room's center.

With hands closed into fists, resting on her hips, Moira drew back her shoulders. Unwaveringly, she met his accusatory glare. "Did you really want that child going through your things?" She inclined her head toward an ornately carved chest at the foot of his bed. "I was passing by and saw him rummaging about in it. When he told me what he sought I sent him out whilst I searched about. Is this what you seek, milord?" She brought forward her right hand. In it was the pair of gauntlets.

Wordlessly Charles reached out and snatched them from her. He clenched his teeth in irritation. Despite her use of the respectful term of address, there had been no respect in the old hag's voice. There never was. She spoke to him in the same manner that she had when he was a small boy.

Without waiting for a reply, she turned and headed for the door.

Charles stiffened as if she had struck him. "Arrogant old witch," he growled at her retreating back. First indulged by his father, and now Taryn, the woman had the airs of the lady of the manor. Certes, she ruled over the servants with an iron hand. Well, he'd see all that changed once he returned from Jaune. She'd learn her place quick enough—or find herself back in the village in a wattle and daub hut!

His anger appeased with that thought, Charles looked about the room. In spite of Moira's explanation, he found it odd she would have sent the page to wait outside.

Unless, of course, she had been doing something more than searching for his gauntlets—something for which she'd wanted no witnesses.

At once his gaze went to the shelf below the crucifix. Was it his imagination, or was the silver box upon it not askew?

In hasty strides Charles crossed over to the wall. He took down the box and lifted its lid. At first glance nothing appeared amiss. He moved over to one of the window seats and sat. Carefully he withdrew the contents of the box: sheets of parchment and vellum bearing broken wax seals, scrolls tied with silk. The letter from Baron Lynfyld and several others were recent, their edges unyellowed by age. Many of the documents, however, were old and brittle. He had found them among his father's possessions after his death.

Sudden and unbidden, spasms of guilt twisted in his gut. *Patricide!* an inner voice shouted. *The sin of son slaying sire. Murderer! For all eternity your immortal soul will burn in the fires of Hell.*

Instantly Charles fought back the voice, the guilt, the religious beliefs designed to keep the masses tranquil. There existed no higher judgement but what a man brought on himself, he told himself fiercely. His father had to be eliminated. The old man would have lived for years. Besides, he had stood in Charles' way. After learning of his son's alliance with the barons plotting against Henry, the earl had threatened to disown him—his only heir! Wynshire was his birthright. He would not see it fall to another!

Charles closed his hand into a fist, crushing the scroll he held. The scroll which had revealed the sins of his self-righteous father, he thought, laughing aloud. He unrolled the document bearing the seal of the Archbishop of Canterbury. Not the present Archbishop, Thomas Becket, who was currently at odds with the King and in exile, but his predecessor, Theobald, the thirty-eighth Archbishop of Canterbury.

Without reading the words before him, Charles silently recited the contents of the decree from memory. *Your request for an annulment of the marriage between a villein known as Miles the Tinker and his lawful wife, Kate, now called by the name Maitland, is denied. Abandonment, even for a period of ten years, does not in the eyes of the Holy Mother Church constitute grounds for the dissolution of a union entered into and blessed in the presence of God and witnesses. Should you continue to live with this woman as man and wife, you will be guilty of the sin of adultery, and she the crime of bigamy. For the sakes of both your souls and eternal salvations, you must end this immoral relationship. Know, too, that any children born of this union will be regarded by the laws of man and God to be illegitimate.*

Charles smiled. "Illegitimate," he whispered aloud. According to the document he held in his hand, Taryn was illegitimate, bastard-born of the woman his father had taken to wife—a woman already wedded to another.

Charles looked at the date upon the archbishop's decree, the twenty-ninth of June in the year 1144. By that date his father had already been married to the whore for three years. He set down the document and sorted through the remaining contents of the box, pushing aside various land grants, harvest records and tax accounts. The one he sought lay at the very bottom of the pile.

He took it up to read. It was a certificate of marriage, dated November twenty-eighth in the year eleven forty-seven, just two days before Kate Maitland's death and Taryn's birth.

Charles rubbed his chin, lost in thought. When he'd first found the documents, he'd sought to unravel the mystery they created. Part of the puzzle was not difficult to explain. It had been no secret that the woman his father wedded had been married in her youth. Most knew the story. The man, a scoundrel of sorts and a stranger without roots in the village, had disappeared. After a decade had passed with no word of him, she had begun to call herself a widow. It was at that time she had come into service at Wynshire Castle. Its lord, also widowed, had fallen in love with her, and they had married.

Here was where the story gapped. Charles was fairly certain that his father had somehow learned that his bride's first husband was still alive. It would have been then that he had petitioned the Church for an annulment of that marriage. Of course his request had been denied. But he had not obeyed Theobald's orders. He had continued to call the whore wife, keeping their sin a secret from all. Then, at some point, Kate's lawful husband must have died—hence the necessity of a second certificate of marriage. The first, from their illegal marriage, would have been kept by Wynshire's priest with all the other official records of the manor's marriages, deaths and births. And thus the lie—that their marriage was not three days old, but three years—continued to be perpetuated to all who did not know the truth.

Charles looked at the bottom of the yellowed sheet of parchment, to the two places where the required witnesess to the marriage would have signed their names. Both were marked with an X. Beside the marks, written in the hand of the priest who had performed the ceremony, were the names of those said witnesses. One of the names he recognized was that of the midwife who had later delivered Taryn. The woman had been dead for better than fifteen years. The other name, however, was illegible, the ink having blurred and faded over the years.

Charles held the document up to the window in an attempt to make better use of the morning light. There was no point; there was no deciphering the name. But given that all known parties involved, including the priest, were now dead, it only made sense to assume that whoever the second witness had been was also long since in his grave.

With the certificate still in hand, Charles stood and walked over to the large hearth which dominated one side of the chamber. He picked up an iron rod resting against the stone wall and poked at the embers of the dying fire. As small flames shot upward, he tossed the document upon them. The brittle parchment caught fire at once, and the only evidence of his father's legal marriage quickly blackened into ash.

Charles smiled in complacent satisfaction at the leverage he now possessed against his half-sister—leverage which might prove invaluable in the days to come. He knew Taryn. He knew her well. His threats against Wynshire's villeins had been successful in forcing her to proceed with the betrothal. But she had not yet set eyes upon her future husband. Charles, on the other hand, had met with Baron Lynfyld on several occasions. Taryn's description of him as "troll" was indeed accurate, and once she saw that for herself, her half-brother might very well need more than threats to force her into marriage.

Chapter Two

Taryn passed through the deserted great hall. The scent of rosemary wafted to her nostrils.

It was a small thing, but she had always taken pride that Wynshire's hall had never borne the stench of decayed food and animal feces commonplace in most keeps. She had insisted that the carpeting of rushes spread over the vast room's stone floor be changed often to rid it of food dropped from the tables to the score of scavenging hounds always underfoot. Moreover, she personally saw to the blending of herbs used to perfume the dried grasses.

Knowing she would never again smell that particular aroma (for it would belong forever to Wynshire alone) threatened to provoke a return of the tears she had shed in her chamber. In an effort to stanch their flow she lifted her head, fixing her gaze instead upon the room's thick walls.

A long, deep crack in the masonry captured her attention at once. Months ago she had ordered a linen panel made—both to conceal the fissure and to halt the cold draft it let in from the outside—never thinking she'd not be in residence to see it hung.

Again she felt the back of her throat burn with swallowed tears. She would not cry.

Crying is a sign of weakness, Taryn. Her father's voice

echoed in her mind. *A woman's weakness. And if you must succumb to it . . . well, you'd best be sure 'tis done in private!*

"Milady." A stoop-shouldered, gray-haired servant waiting by the keep's massive portal quietly stepped forward.

At the sight of him, Taryn's tenuous hold on her emotions broke. Her father's admonition was gone. In its place rang her own cry of anguish. "Oh, John!" she wailed.

As the old man opened his arms, she went to him and laid her head upon his chest. Gentle hands that had once woven her daisy chains, removed bee stingers and dried a pool of tears moved to embrace her.

For the briefest of moments time reverted. She was a child again and the fingers now stroking her hair were ungnarled.

John would make it right. He always did. Hadn't he just yesterday set the broken wing of that sparrow she'd rescued from a cat in the garden?

"Now, now, milady. 'Twill be aright. I promise ye. And Old John has never lied to ye, has he?"

Once more in the present, Taryn shook her head in silent response. How desperately a part of her wanted to believe him! But a part of her also knew there was nothing the faithful servant could do. For his sake as much as her own, she lifted her head and forced a brave smile. "'Tis just that I'll miss you so."

"And I ye," John replied, his voice thick with anger and sadness. "If yer father, the earl, was still alive, this marriage would ne'er be taking place!"

"But he isn't alive," she scolded gently, stepping back. "And you have a new earl now, John. Charles will have you in the stocks if he hears what I hear in your voice. You must promise me that you will speak of him with respect."

"T'would be a promise I couldn't keep, milady. I've no respect for the whelp. Far as I'm concerned, Wynshire *has* no lord. But for yer sake, Old John will hold his tongue."

"For that I thank you. Now . . . if you would open the door . . ." Under the pretense of donning her cloak, Taryn bowed her head. Taking more care than was needed, she arranged the folds over her gown, hastily brushing the remainder of any tears from her cheeks before settling the hood in place. She heard the tell-tale creak of iron hinges. An instant later the gray light of early morning streamed through the doorway.

In spite of the cloak's sable lining, she shivered. The castleyard below was bathed in a fine mist, damp and cold, not unlike the feeling now residing in her heart.

Turning quickly she kissed John's wizened cheek.

"God speed, milady."

With his hand at her back providing gentle reassurance, she stepped forward to descend the steep stairs which led to the bailey and offered the only entrance to the keep. Made of wood, the steps could be easily snatched up or set afire in case of attack. Though she knew their number, she found herself counting off each one. It gave her something on which to concentrate besides the assembled and waiting retinue of men and horses.

Without looking, she knew the party traveling to Castle Jaune would be considerable, the reasons for its size twofold. In addition to Charles' need to flaunt his wealth and power, the threat of attack by robbers was real. Even the best of lords refused any responsibility for the fate of travelers who passed through their lands by night, while the worst of them had quiet understandings with those outlaws who lurked in their forests. Provided the brigands refrained from outrages upon important people, and gifted them generously at Christmas and Easter, the lords gave them free hand.

Taryn had always suspected Charles of the latter type of behavior. She found it both ironic and fitting that he should now be on the receiving end. That her brother was concerned with the possibility of being set upon by bandits was obvious. She counted no less than fifty knights in the bailey. With the exception of perhaps a dozen, all were the foreign German mercenaries who had been arriving at Wynshire over the past few months in growing numbers.

Weeks ago she had made the mistake of questioning Charles as to the reason he continued to take more men into service. Wynshire suffered no shortage of its own men-at-arms, nor was its lord at war. Under those circumstances this additional employment seemed pointless—a foolish depletion of the manor's stores. When she'd attempted to explain the cost of merely feeding what was rapidly becoming a small army, Charles had become furious. Callously he had pointed out that the state of Wynshire's stores would soon be of no concern to her.

"*Frouwe.*" A knight clothed in *hauberk* stepped to her side. Like all of the men assembled, he was helmed and fully armed, carrying his shield suspended round his neck from a broad leather strap. He gestured to a saddled palfrey several paces away.

Taryn dipped her head in acknowledgement and followed him to the horse. Wordlessly the man grasped her waist in his mail-gloved hands, lifting her to the saddle. With practiced ease she flung her cloak across the horse's back as she set her knee firmly into place over the pommel of the sidesaddle. Once mounted, she tucked her skirt over her kid boot before leaning back against the cantle. Silently, the man handed her the reins, then withdrew to join his companions.

From atop her mount Taryn possessed a clear view of the entire yard. She noted the string of sumpter beasts already loaded with provisions and supplies. The journey to Castle Jaune would take several days. If no quarters were available they would be forced to make camp en route—hence the need for tinder and flint and steel for making fires, bedding, tents, and, of course, food.

Again she thought of the outlaw bands that might be encountered, and found herself half hoping an attack *would* occur. Certes, capture by cutthroats could be no worse a fate than that which awaited her!

With Elizabeth's words as guide she pictured the face of the man who would soon become her husband. The grotesque image she conjured brought an acrid taste to her mouth. She lifted her head and took in great gulps of the crisp air—to little avail. Coupled with what she had read in Lynfyld's letter not an hour ago, the inevitability of her fate was undeniable. To serve the greed of one man and the bestial desires of another, her life had been sold for a purse of silver.

Across the yard she spotted her half-brother's fair head. Intent on giving Conar last minute orders to be carried out in his absence, Charles did not appear to have noticed her. Though nothing she might tell him could change what would happen, she was suddenly compelled to confront him.

The temper which was her father's legacy rose, bringing a warmth no fur-lined cloak could induce. She set her heel to her horse's flank and rode up to the pair of men deep in conversation. "I would have a word with you, Charles." Ignoring Conar's gape-mouthed response to her interruption, she added a final syllable. "Now."

With patent fury in every movement, Charles dismissed his steward and gestured to the squire waiting some distance away with his lord's palfrey. Another squire would lead the earl's destrier. Unless contact were made with an enemy, the great war-horse would not be ridden on the journey. His energies were too valuable to be wasted for mere transport.

"Be quick about it," Charles snapped. "I want to get under way—now that you have finally seen fit to honor us with your presence."

"You sold me! The baron bargained with you for a virgin bride!" The words escaped her lips in a rush, half accusation, half statement of fact.

The expression of Charles' face was unmistakably one of surprise, but he recovered quickly. "What of it?" he replied evenly.

Throwing back his cloak, he pulled on his gauntlets and stepped into the stirrup of his mount. Setting himself into the saddle, he looked at her coldly. "If you know that much, then you should know this as well. If you are thinking of voiding my contract with Lynfyld by spreading your legs for one of these men, don't bother. There isn't one amongst them who will relieve you of your condition. Every cock in this party has been threatened with castration should your maidenhead be breached between now and our arrival at Castle Jaune. Your betrothed contracted for a virgin bride, and a virgin bride he shall have!"

Taryn stared at him in outrage. "You *are* a bastard!" she cried.

"No, dear sister." Charles smiled a slow, cruel smile. "*That* distinction belongs entirely to you. Betwixt my father and your mother there was ne'er a legal union, for she was already married—to a man of the same peasant stock as she. And despite my father's wealth and power, the Church refused to annul that marriage."

"You're lying!" she gasped, his statement having slammed into her like a fist. "I don't believe you!"

"Believe what you will," he responded. "But I speak the truth and I have the documents to prove it. After my father's death I found a letter amongst his papers, written by the former Archbishop of Canterbury. In it he rejects my father's request for an annulment of your mother's first marriage. Apparently she was not widowed as claimed, but merely abandoned."

"Why then was I not told of this?" Fiercely she struggled to keep her wits. She must not let the pain and confusion flooding her heart be revealed and betray her. She could not give Charles that satisfaction.

"At the time, it would not have served my objectives," he answered with brutal candor.

"And now it does?"

"Aye. You see . . . your mother died an adultress, giving birth to a bastard. Hence, you are entitled to nothing. I could have cast you out, but did not. Instead I arranged for you a marriage which will one day leave you a wealthy widow."

"To no gain of your own?" she replied bitterly, outraged that he should attempt to wrap his deeds in the mantle of kindness and generosity.

He smiled. "As I said, I had objectives—to be rid of you with minimum effort and maximum gain. Lynfyld offered a sizeable purse and his only requirements were that his bride be chaste and of noble blood."

"And if I were to tell him he has purchased instead a bride of 'peasant stock'?" Carefully she watched for a sign that her threat might carry weight.

Charles laughed. "He knows. Think you the old miser would have waived a dowry, if he believed you had claim to one? For his purposes . . ." Again he laughed, an evil, malicious laugh. ". . . It suffices merely that my father's blood flows through your veins. In fact, your illegitimacy suits him rather well. You have no place to go *except* into this marriage. After all . . . who else would take you to wife under these conditions?"

Suddenly Taryn felt drained and lost, as if all the strength to deny her half-brother's charges had ebbed away. Somehow she knew Charles spoke the truth about the circumstances of her parents' marriage. His revelations stripped her of her identity and her birthright. The product of her mother's adultery, she had not even the claim to the name Maitland. She was like a ship with neither anchor nor home port. Forsaken, damned by sins of the past, she had been set adrift.

"No one."

Charles' cold voice cut through her thoughts. Startled, she realized he was answering the question he had posed to her.

"Lynfyld knows it. I know it. And now . . ." his voice softened ". . . you know it."

In confusion she looked at him—then realized his victory accorded him the ability to be, if not kind, then at least civil.

"Find your place in line, Taryn."

In numb obedience she guided her horse into the midst of the procession exiting beneath Wynshire's portcullis.

She never glanced back, riding as if in a trance.

They rode for hours. The sun crested, and finally the physical ache of her body intruded upon and overwhelmed her emotional pain.

She looked up at the gray sky in an attempt to gauge the time travelled. Through the lattice-like canopy of the winter-bare trees that touched and joined above them, she noted the noon position of the sun.

Why had Charles not yet stopped? Did he intend to travel as if on campaign, without rest? The silent questions served to break the spell which had descended upon her.

She looked to the men riding on either side of her. The portion of their faces left uncovered by their helms revealed nothing, but that meant little. They had been trained to endure rigor, as had their mounts.

The thought that she could be keeping her saddle for hours yet angered her. She reckoned the road they travelled in the manner as would a knight the strength of a challenger—with heedful hostility. Like most highways in England, it was an abomination, a muddy trail riddled with ruts. The old Anglo-Saxon law which decreed woods and undergrowth to be cleared to a depth of ten feet from the main road had long been abandoned by the country's Norman conquerors. A century after William—a century of neglect—had resulted in what she now beheld: woods that extended right to the edge of the roadway, giving easy hiding to robbers and beggars.

A quick and furtive glance at the small army in whose company she rode quickly erased the fringes of hope for attack that she'd earlier entertained. To challenge such a party would be madness.

Her earlier despair returned.

Suddenly, the air resounded with the cry of a child.

Taryn rose in her saddle to look down the procession of knights riding behind her.

They had been joined along the way by several merchants, packmen and other humble travelers, including a family of peasants. The father staggered under a great sack, the lead rope of a donkey clutched in his hand.

Upon the scrawny beast was balanced the remainder of his household gear and two young children. At his side trudged his wife, wearily carrying their youngest, an infant.

Taryn slowed her horse's pace. Her heart went out to the woman. In all likelihood younger in years than Taryn, the peasant's body was bent from toil like that of an old woman. Her skirts dragged in the mud, weighing her down further. She stumbled and nearly dropped her precious burden.

At once Taryn turned her mount and rode to the end of the line, indifferent to the startled gazes of the men she passed.

Seeing her approach, the woman stared up at her in a mixture of awe and fear. "Milady," she murmured, quickly dropping her eyes.

"Might you allow me to carry the child?" As the woman stepped back in surprise, Taryn smiled gently in an attempt to put her at ease. She stretched out her arms. "Please."

"Oh no, milady. I couldn't." The mother looked fearful.

"Please," Taryn repeated softly. She leaned from the saddle so that she might whisper to the woman. "I have a great love for children. To cradle your babe would give me joy. Surely you would not refuse me such a small request?"

"Oh no, milady!" the woman exclaimed, her eyes widening clearly in realization of her fate—and her babe's too, perhaps—if she offended this lady. "T'would be an honor." Hastily she lifted the sleeping infant to Taryn's outstretched hands.

Unmindful of the filthy rag wrapped about its tiny body, Taryn drew the child close. She heard a horse approaching and knew its rider before he spoke.

"Water seeks its own level. So too, does blood, I see."

Taryn lifted her gaze and met Charles' furious glare. Her gray eyes held his firmly, undaunted.

As if knowing argument would be futile and clearly

unwilling to call greater attention to his half-sister's debasing actions, he jerked his mount around to return to the procession's head.

The merchants and other travelers bowed their heads in respect as he passed. Glad to travel in his formidable company, several voiced aloud their gratitude for his protection.

Watching him, Taryn sniffed in derision. The Earl of Wynshire protected them merely for the reason that it would add to his prestige to approach Castle Jaune with a great following.

Just as Charles resumed his place at the head, a throng of beggars materialized from the woods. "Alms, Messire, alms," they chorused, their whining cry gaining strength as he neared their ranks.

Taryn knew the beggar's disguise was a favorite for robbers. Still, she stiffened in dismay as Charles spurred his horse forward, knocking down two of the more persistent wretches who had dared to lay hands upon his mount's bridle. One held up a wrist minus the hand. Another pointed to where an eye had been gouged out. The sight of their deformities filled her with anguish and she grimaced.

"Don't waste your compassion on the likes of them, milady."

Taryn looked at the knight riding beside her and recognized him as one who had long been in her father's service.

He gestured to the objects of her pity and smiled almost paternally. "They've no doubt suffered just punishments for crimes committed. I hear tell, too, some even mutilate themselves merely to work on the sympathies of the gullible."

Astonished that he had dared speak to her, Taryn barely heard his words. Not a single retainer had addressed her since they had left Wynshire Castle. Clearly, her half-brother's threat had been taken to heart by his men.

With her thought barely formed, she heard Charles' voice ring out, delivering a sharp command. The knight, who had done nothing but offer a kind word, complied immediately and spurred his horse a safe distance ahead of hers.

In a mixture of anger and resignation, Taryn turned her attention to the now awakened infant in her arms. For several moments she tried to soothe the squalling babe, but her efforts were in vain. He was no doubt hungry.

She pulled her horse up to wait for the mother, who with her family, had fallen behind the pace of those on horseback. As the wretched churls approached, she tucked several coins taken from the purse at her waist into the infant's swaddling.

"He's a bit damp," she stated evenly for the benefit of those within hearing distance. Then, with a conspiratorial wink, she surrendered the child to its mother.

By late afternoon the heavily wooded area they travelled had given way to tilled fields and pastures dotted with grazing cattle and sheep.

Taryn knew they were still on Wynshire lands, so there would be no local lord's castle over the next slope, no keep where travelers might arrange shelter and a meal. How she craved a bed and a crackling fire!

A fine rain had been falling for almost an hour. She was wet and cold; her body ached with fatigue and hunger. Charles had not let up their pace. Following her confrontation with him, he had in fact increased it. She was sure he had done it out of spite—for only the merchants on horseback had been able to match it. Those on foot, including the peasant family, had been left far behind by the time the entourage finally did stop to rest and eat. The repast had been meager—soldier's rations of hard bread, cheese and sour wine. Even now the few mouthfuls she had managed to choke down lay like lead in her stomach.

Wearily she tugged the hood of her cloak farther down to shield her face from the rain, thus she did not see the village they approached until they were almost upon it. Convenient to the highway, the hamlet contained a few dozen structures, mostly small hut-like houses of wattle and daub. The largest had two stories. It was to this that Charles led his party.

They entered its yard to the accompaniment of honking geese fluttering from under their horses' hooves.

Taryn focused upon the weathered board hanging over the cottage door. "The saints be praised!" she whispered aloud. The sign proclaimed the structure to be an inn.

Its owner, a smooth, smirking man who had no doubt heard the clamor, appeared hastily in the doorway. Obviously he was shrewd enough to know a fine purse when he saw it. Oblivious to the rain now falling heavily, he stepped outside and began to praise his hostelry. "Welcome, milord." He bowed and gestured to the open half-door at his back. "I bid ye to partake of my humble establishment. Within are all manner of comforts. Soft beds packed high with white straw. A hearty meal to fill the belly and home brewed barley beer to ease the aches of a long journey. And if it be wine that ye desire, a barrel of the finest vintage—"

Charles silenced the man with a haughty wave of his hand. "And what ask you for these 'comforts,' innkeeper?"

"Oh, but a paltry sum, milord, a paltry sum."

As Charles haggled with the man over payment, one of his men moved to help Taryn dismount. Her knees nearly buckled, and had it not been for the arm he placed about her waist, she would have collapsed into the mud. But when the words of appreciation she offered were met with a cold, mute stare, she turned away from his rebuff, disheartened anew.

Suddenly too tired to care any longer how he or his companions viewed her, she lifted her skirts out of the muck and advanced to the tavern door.

With the price now settled, Charles dismounted, handing over the reins of his palfrey to the inn's owner.

Discernibly insulted by the action which served to lower him to the status of a mere stable boy, the man nevertheless bowed in unctuous compliance.

"Taryn." Charles turned toward her.

Dimly aware she was behaving no less obsequiously than the innkeeper, she obligingly placed her hand atop her brother's, allowing him to guide her inside. She was greeted at once with the stench of stale wine, poor cooking and unwashed bodies too long confined in an unaired space. She felt her stomach lurch.

The inn was a dark, noisome hole, crowded with men and women alike, drinking and dicing around bare oaken tables. The public room was long, but low. Though not inordinately tall, Charles was forced to bend his head to clear the crossbeams of the ceiling and avoid the numerous smoking oil lamps hanging on chains. Their murky light was aided by a roaring fire burning in a wide hearth at one end of the room.

Taryn eyed the settles before it.

"Milord, milady! You do this roof honor!" A heavy-set matron in a stained smock and kirtle pushed her way through the crowd. Nervously, the woman—no doubt the owner's wife—wiped her hands on the filthy rags of an apron knotted about her thick waist and bade them follow her away from the fireplace toward the opposite side of the room. "Come, please."

Taryn's hopes of resting before the fire died.

The woman led them to a far corner where a carven screen afforded a degree of privacy for the high born patrons of the tavern. There was a single trestle table flanked by benches, similar to those in the common room. But that this was reserved for high blood was clear. Upon its worn top burned tallow candles, providing a more even light for those privileged to use this space.

"Yer pardon, Sir Knight." With a hasty apology to the table's only occupant for the interruption of his meal, the innkeeper's wife jerked off her shawl and used it to wipe clean a few feet of board. "Sit, please, milady."

The knight looked up, standing immediately as Taryn moved to the table. He pulled out the bench to afford her easier access and bowed. "You do a humble knight honor, lady."

His voice was young, and even in the low light it was easy to see something of unformed youth still in his face. Despite her fatigue, Taryn smiled. She unfastened her cloak, anxious to be free of its damp weight.

At once he was at her back lifting the wrap from her shoulders.

She felt a rush of pleasure—more warming than the fire's heat. So long in the company of Charles and his mercenaries, she'd forgotten the simple courtesies of chivalry.

As she sat, the knight carefully folded her cloak, draping it over the bench beside her.

Charles stalked to the far side of the table and planted himself squarely across from her.

Retaking his seat on her right, the young knight smiled in boyish nervousness. "Might you do me the honor of sharing my trencher, lady?" He moved the wooden dish which had been before him so that it lay between them. "'Tis a mutton stew of sorts, blandly spiced and overcooked, but hot and filling."

From the corner of her eye Taryn saw Charles scowl. His displeasure—wrought by the young man's attention—pleased her more than the attention itself. She fixed her gaze on the knight with a secret smile.

Within minutes she learned his name, Bernard of Girart; his home, a small barony on the western coast; and his quest. As the third born son, he had inherited nothing upon his father's death. Having chosen not to serve his oldest brother, he was now seeking employment.

". . . with a lord who might one day reward me my loyalty and bravery with a small fief of my own," he explained with a grin.

Taryn wished him good fortune, and between mouthfuls of the stew (which was indeed as Sir Bernard had described, bland and overcooked), she plied him with questions about his homeland. She had never seen the sea, and her curiosity was one he seemed more than willing to satisfy.

"Fill!"

Charles' sudden shout to a passing serving maid startled Taryn from her conversation with Sir Bernard. She looked across at her half-brother, now flanked by several of his higher ranking men.

"Fill, wench!" he repeated, this time pounding his tankard on the table top with such force that the candles shook, spattering hot grease.

"Take care, my lady." Sir Bernard's voice was calm and reassuring. As she returned her gaze to him, he wiped up a spot of tallow near her sleeve with the hem of his tabbard.

Carefully Taryn cast a sidelong glance at Charles. The young knight's efforts had earned a scowl from her half-brother, who was now studying them both intently. She recognized the look in his narrowed stare at once. It was akin to the tone she had heard in his voice when he'd ordered his man away from her on the road.

The arrival of the owner's wife carrying a tray laden with freshly filled tankards momentarily distracted Charles. Breaking his stare, he reached for the ale and the men on either side of him grabbed for the remainder. One bellowed an oath as his companion jostled his arm, causing him to slosh the drink down his front.

Taryn pushed back from the table. She had no wish to witness the scene played out each night at Wynshire Castle. In this inn, just as they were wont to do in his great hall, Charles and his men would drink themselves sodden—as would the others in the public room. Already she could hear their drunken voices. Within a few hours they would be slumped over the wooden tables, their faces in a pool of spilled ale. Those who remained conscious would be urged to the yard behind the inn to relieve their strained bladders or to carouse with the unsavory females who haunted such establishments.

"I'm for bed," she stated firmly, rising.

Charles lifted his head. "The road this day was long," he agreed, narrowing his gaze anew.

"Please . . . allow me to escort you." Sir Bernard moved to stand.

But before the young man could swing his leg over the bench, Charles nodded his head in silent command to one of his men standing behind Sir Bernard.

The knight seized the younger man's shoulder, aborting his leave. "The Earl of Wynshire desires that you stay," he ordered, his voice thick with drink.

Taryn realized what was happening and choked back her outrage. "I thank you, Sir Bernard." She managed a tight smile. "But I need not trouble you. I am sure the proprietress can show me the way." She sought out the innkeeper's wife, still keeping one eye on the table of men. Sir Bernard was not going anywhere. The shoulder hold was maintained while others in the party quickly moved to flank him on the bench.

"To bed, milady?" The matron approached, wiping her hands on her apron. "I've had the finest room prepared for ye, a fire on the hearth as well. Come, I'll show the way."

Taryn followed the woman in silence. She led her up a narrow flight of stairs and down an even narrower hall, opening its last door with a flourish. "Here it be, milady."

The room so proudly displayed was a cramped slit of a space with a single window covered by a shutter. There was a litter of dried rushes on the floor and a rough bed frame on which lay a pile of bedding. From it Taryn could detect the faintest odor of herbs. At least there would be no vermin, she thought in relief, looking about.

The promised hearth fire did not exist. But there was a legged brazier with some glowing coals. A stool beside the bed did service as a table. The woman set the candle she carried upon it and then withdrew with the promise of water for washing.

At her departure Taryn moved to the window. The air within the room was more stale and stifling than that of the lower floor. She worked at the shutter's fastenings. Encrusted with rust, they gave proof to her suspicions—the window had not been opened in years.

At last the warped wood yielded, grating open. The night chill entered, making her instantly conscious of just how foul the inner air was.

Setting aside her cloak, she leaned out to breathe deeply of the crisp freshness. Her gaze fell upon the courtyard below, where several figures moved about in the darkness. Taryn continued to watch. There were perhaps four or five men stumbling about, apparently kicking something on the ground.

A knock at the door diverted her attention from the window. She went to the portal and opened it for the matron's entrance.

"Water for washing, milady," the woman proclaimed, lifting into view the covered kettle she carried. At Taryn's nod she entered. Seeing the opened window, she instantly frowned. Wisely, she held her tongue as she set the kettle down beside the candle.

"What is happening in the yard?" Taryn asked.

The woman shrugged. "Seems yer men-at-arms took offense at the young knight's behavior. Yer brother ordered them to teach him some manners."

Taryn felt an immediate tightening in the pit of her stomach. "What . . . what was it that he did?"

The woman grinned, revealing black and broken teeth. "T'would seem he took a bit too much interest in yer ladyship."

Taryn squeezed her eyes shut and turned away. "Thanks given for the water," she whispered, sick at the realization of what the young knight's simple courtesies had cost him.

Chapter Three

Taryn watched the shadowy form emerge from the inn and cross the yard toward her through the morning blanket of fog. Though his features were obscured by the swirling mist, his gait was most recognizable. She leveled a narrowed gaze, greeting his arrival with quiet fury. "Was it really so necessary to have set your dogs upon him?"

Charles met her verbal attack with complacent ease. "You were warned I would take no chance of losing Lynfyld his prize."

And you your purse, Taryn thought furiously. Even after having learned from the innkeeper's wife that Sir Bernard's injuries had not been so severe as to prevent his leaving before dawn, outrage over the attack of Charles' men upon the young knight still seethed within her. Now, his callous retort served to release that emotional dam already straining.

"You bastard! He was scarce more than a boy!" Without conscious thought her hand shot up from her side, its target the sneering face before her.

Charles seized her wrist in mid-air and cruelly twisted it behind her back. Ignoring her cry of pain, he increased the pressure until she was sure he would wrench her arm from her shoulder. "That *boy* was man enough to foil my plans!" He maintained his hold a moment longer, then released her.

For a brief instant she could concentrate on nothing but the burning sensation radiating from her shoulder. As it subsided, reason returned. She reined in her raging emotions. There was no point—not in striking out physically, nor in verbally protesting his actions. Still, she was compelled to deny his charge, to refute his accusation. "You know I would ne'er have taken him into my bed."

"No matter." Charles shrugged. "Be assured though, you'll not be getting another opportunity. Tonight we set up the tents and make camp in the woods. Tomorrow night I shall ask for shelter at the monastery at St. Swithin's at Winchester."

A bitter laugh parted Taryn's lips, followed by a scornful observation as to the clear motive behind his itinerary. "Certes, my chastity will be safe enough with the good monks. Their vows include one of celibacy, do they not?"

Without response Charles turned from her and gave the awaited signal to his men to draw their saddled horses into riding order. Suddenly, the tens of men who had been standing stiffly about leaped into motion, filling the yard with a flurry of activity and sound. Horses neighed, harnesses creaked, and voices shouted orders. Charles' squire appeared at his side, the reins of his palfrey servilely extended.

Charles snatched them from his hand and mounted, sneering down at her. "We ride."

And ride they did, at an unrelenting pace. By the time the order to camp was finally issued, exhaustion such as Taryn had never known had robbed her of any thought save sleep.

Long before dawn her foreboding that the second day would be no different proved accurate. With first light still hours away, the camp was astir, making ready for the day's march. Now even Charles' battle-hardened mercenaries exhibited signs of fatigue. They took to their mounts in grudging obedience. But only when the man who was paying their wages was not within earshot did they venture to voice their grumbled complaints.

Just before noon a heavy rain began to fall, and at last their pace was eased. The road, by royal decree wide enough for sixteen armed knights to ride side by side, rapidly turned into a river of mud. To avoid the low center and the deepest muck, the party now kept to the berms, riding in pairs.

Taryn rode alone until they were but a few miles from Winchester. Charles dispatched several men ahead to arrange shelter at the monastery located conveniently upon a hill outside the city, then took up a position at her side.

Unlike their arrival at the inn two days earlier, this time he remained with her, helping her to dismount and leading her forward to greet the black-robed abbot waiting to welcome them. Acting every bit the role of devoted brother, he escorted her through the cloistered halls.

Taryn nearly choked on the nausea his solicitous behavior evoked. Desperate to distance herself from the outrageous charade, she declined to partake of the abbot's offered meal and retired to the tiny, austere cell provided her. Despite her exhaustion she slept fitfully, tossing and turning on the narrow pallet. A single thought haunted her. By this same time tomorrow they would have reached their destination. She would have met the man destined to be her husband.

In contrast to the dark despair weighing her heart, Taryn awoke the next morning to a day that was bright with promise, hope and sunshine. The rains were gone, the sky clear. The irony depressed her all the more. It was as if God were signaling his approval of her plight.

Indeed, that thought was echoed by St. Swithin's abbot as he stood in the cobbled courtyard of the monastery and bade them farewell. "God be with you, Lady, and may the Lord grant you a marriage long and happy—for surely this fine weather is a sign of His favour."

Taryn looked upon the man's face, kind and sincere. No doubt, the abbot quite logically assumed she looked forward to the life which awaited her.

Before she could offer differently, Charles stepped forward. At the touch of his hand upon her back, placed, she knew, in tacit warning, she stiffened instantly. Still, her half-brother's action scarce surprised her. He had come too far and was too close to the achievement of his insidious goal to brook the chance she might say something which could give the churchman cause to wonder if the bride-to-be's consent might not have been obtained under duress.

"My sister and I thank you for your blessing and your hospitality, Abbot. But if we are to reach Castle Jaune by nightfall, we must be underway. Taryn . . ."

His arm now firmly locked about her waist, Charles guided her in silence toward her saddled palfrey. Then, just as he set her into the saddle, he spoke under his breath. "I am heartened to see that the inevitability of your fate has at least taught you prudence."

"Do not mistake discretion for defeat," she countered coldly. "All I have learned is the depth of the evil in your soul. Until this marriage takes place, you have not yet won."

Even as she heard his contemptuous laugh, she saw in his eyes the slightest flicker of misgiving. Seeing it filled her with a curious sense of hope. She set her heel to her horse's flank, sending the animal bounding forward.

By midday, however, that hope had melted away as the morning mist before the sun. She looked up at that bright orb and saw in it a foe. Its steady path across the sky heralded both hours passed and distance covered. Her dreaded fate ever neared.

* * *

"There it be, milord! Over the rise!"

The sudden shout roused Taryn from the state of half-sleep in which she had been riding for the last several hours. She straightened in her saddle to view the object of the forward rider's excitement.

Looming ahead in the southern sky were the battlements of a mighty fortress. In clear contrast against the azure heavens she could see the sharp lines and angular indentations of its parapets' crenellation. From atop the highest point the standard of its lord proudly whipped in the wind.

Taryn's heart pounded in her chest and her fatigue vanished. Though they were still too far away for her to discern the pattern upon the rectangular banner, its colors were distinct—red upon a field of yellow—the colors of Garret d'Aubigny, Great Earl of Arundel and holder of its royal castle, Jaune.

She fixed her gaze on the flag. The pattern upon it soon came into focus—a crimson falcon in flight against a jonquil sky. She lowered her gaze and her attention to the fortress itself. Flanking towers protected the approach to its gateway. Abutting those towers was a stone curtain wall which surrounded the bailey and keep within. She noted the keep was taller than Wynshire's—four stories instead of three. The moat they neared appeared wider, too. Clearely this was no castle easily besieged. King Henry believed the chain of royal castles formed "the bones of his kingdom". At Jaune he had obviously set his beliefs into practice.

The forward riders reached the lowered drawbridge and the noise of their horses' hooves upon the timbered span now resounded. Taryn, lagging as far to the rear as possible without drawing attention, followed their progress and saw a small party of men coming into view just within the gateway.

Logic told her that since Charles had dispatched an

advance rider to announce their arrival, these men were no doubt a welcoming party. Among them would be Jaune's lord, his steward, or a captain of his men-at-arms—and her betrothed.

That thought sent her blood, already quickened, racing. In an effort to maintain at least an outward calm, she tried to concentrate on the whitewashed walls of the fortress, estimating their height and thickness, and counting the scores of arrow slits covering each stage of their approach.

The effort was futile. While she could lock her eyes on the heights of stone, she could not force her thoughts away from the group waiting below. As her horse passed through the portcullis, she gave up the struggle and returned her attention to them.

Without warning one broke ranks and shuffled toward Charles' horse.

At once her half-brother reined in his palfrey. Signaling his men to ride on to the inner bailey, he then dismounted.

Taryn watched as he moved to embrace the man. The breath she had unconsciously been holding was let out in a half-sob.

Elizabeth's description left no doubt. There was no mistaking the man's identity. Her betrothed was much shorter than Charles, possessing by nature a squatty, fleshy stature which had obviously been unable to absorb decades of indulgence—for in old age he had become grotesquely bloated.

As if in a dream she saw Charles detach himself from the baron and move across the yard toward her. She barely felt his hands encircle her waist and lift her from the saddle. Still without a sense of reality, she saw the man lumbering in their direction. She was reminded instantly of the trained bears she had seen at market fairs, forced to walk upon their hind legs in a stumbling, clumsy gait.

"My dear."

The raspy voice sent a cold ripple of disgust through her. There was no way she could guard her expression. Glad for the hood set over her hair, she quickly lowered her head, knowing her face would thus be concealed. "My lord, Baron."

"She is a prize, Charles! A jewel!"

Her head still bowed, Taryn heard the crunch of dried leaves and knew Lynfyld had stepped back. A moment later she sensed his gaze slithering down the length of her. She bit her lip to keep from screaming. She wanted to bolt, to run and escape the humiliating inspection she must now endure. She did not, but instead forced herself to stand mute under his scrutiny.

"Slender, but not too. Wide of hip. Firm breasts by the look of it. A woman's breasts, I'm pleased to note. My last wife was but a child, you know, Charles. With breasts barely budded."

Sure Lynfyld's attention was now turned to her half-brother, Taryn risked an upward glance.

Lynfyld had stepped close to Charles and was whispering in his ear. Suddenly the old man burst into phlegmatic laughter and slapped his listener resoundly on the back. "Aye, they provided no pleasure in fondling. T'was naught to grab hold of! Not like your sister here, I'd wager!"

Behind the concealing hood Taryn's face burned with humiliation. At least Jaune's men were out of earshot. Still, she could not bear the foul man's ribald observations a moment longer. She was certain with his next wheezing breath he would stagger forward to sample his purchase. "The ride was long, Charles," she offered abruptly. "Might we not greet our host and be shown our quarters?"

"Where the devil *is* d'Aubigny?" Charles' fair head snapped from side to side, as if he had suddenly realized with her words that Jaune's lord was indeed absent.

"Ah . . . the Great Earl was called away . . . on urgent business." One of the men who had been standing, waiting respectfully at a distance while Charles and the Baron conversed, now quickly stepped forward. "I'm Richard, steward of Arundel. My lord asked that I . . . ah . . . offer his apologies and greet you in his stead."

"When will he return?" Charles' question clearly carried a tone of annoyance.

"I couldn't say, milord," the man replied, stiffening visibly in response to the harsh quality in Charles' voice. "The Great Earl answers to few men. He'll return when he decides to return, and not before. Now, if you and the lady will follow me, I'll show you to your quarters."

Taryn cast a quick glance at her half-brother. His displeasure at both the Earl of Arundel's absence and with the steward's curt reply was unmistakeable. She found herself smiling as she lifted her skirts to follow Jaune's seneschal across the outer bailey.

Charles and the Baron lagged behind, apparently discussing the untoward behavior of their host, for she overheard such phrases as "damned inexcusable" and "malapert bastard."

She passed through the fortified gateway of the inner curtain wall, replete with watch towers, and entered the inner bailey. She found her thoughts on their absent host.

One of only twelve men in England to bear the title of "Great Earl," Garret d'Aubigny was known to be a knight of exceptional courage and valour, a particular favorite of King Henry. Yet rumors abounded that as a man he was the Devil incarnate. More than an occasional visiting cleric had fled Castle Jaune with tales of its arrogant lord's blasphemous disregard for the holy teachings of the Church. Gossips at court recounted no tale more fondly than that of his youthful marriage to a maiden driven insane by his insatiable appetites.

"Taryn."

Charles' voice, coupled with his tight and sudden grip upon her arm, jolted Taryn from her silent deliberations. She looked at her half-brother questioningly over her shoulder, noticing that Lynfyld was now a few paces behind them.

"The baron has expressed a desire to pay the local inn a visit. There seems little point in taking the evening meal here. Without d'Aubigny's presence there will be neither entertainment nor a suitable fare."

No whores or free flow of drink, you mean. Careful to keep her expression from revealing the disdain she felt, she forced a civil reply. "As you wish."

"You will take your meal this evening in your room. If questioned, you will claim fatigue from the journey."

Taryn nodded, relieved. There certainly was truth in such an excuse, for she felt nauseated and drained. She stood for a moment and watched as Charles rejoined the baron. They retreated across the bailey in the direction of a two-storied, half-timbered structure which probably housed both the garrison's men-at-arms and its stables.

"Milady? Shall we go?"

Focusing her attention on Jaune's steward, Taryn again nodded. "Aye. Lead the way, Richard—it *was* Richard, was it not?"

The man's face brightened instantly. "Aye, milady. Richard it is, at your service." Extending his arm, he grinned. "You'll pardon me for saying so, milady . . . but your brother there is an ass."

A giggle rose in Taryn's throat. Though she succeeded in smothering its sound, she was helpless to stop her lips from forming a smile. "You have the gift of understatement, Richard."

"Nay, milady. I just say what I see."

Still smiling, Taryn placed her hand upon the man's outstretched arm and allowed him to guide her toward the keep.

Strangely, the feeling of amusement did not leave her as she ascended the broad flight of steps leading to the second story entrance to the round tower. Intrigued, she studied the unusual configuration.

She had heard of King Henry's abandonment of the

standard design of a square tower, the corners of which rendered a keep more vulnerable during a siege. Also, a round tower enabled the keep's water supply to be safeguarded during attack because the design called for the castle to be constructed around an existing well. Henry's efforts to raze, rebuild or renovate the older castles in his kingdom were well known; his methods were extreme, but effective.

In the early months of his reign he had ordered all royal castles surrendered, to be granted back to those lords with a "proper attitude." As that had been nearly seventeen years ago, the man who had relinquished his holdings must have been the present earl's father. After demonstrasting his fealty, he had been accorded once again the honor and title of Arundel, along with its castle.

"Lady Taryn?"

The sound of her name startled Taryn. She halted her speculations and looked about to see the source of the female voice.

Standing just inside the building's entrance was a tiny old woman, no bigger than a child of ten.

"I am Maite," the woman continued, her strong, firm voice belying her appearance. "If you'll follow me, I'll show you to your room." Without waiting for a reply from Taryn, or a response from Richard, she turned and entered the keep.

"You'll have to forgive her," Richard stated softly. "She's been here since before there was a single stone laid. She delivered Arundel's last two earls into this world and swears she'll live to see a third christened. Probably will, too. Don't let her size or age fool you, milady."

"You prattle on worse than a woman, Richard!" Maite's voice drifted through the doorway. "Leave off with your featherheaded stories and bring the lady inside."

Taryn looked at Richard in amazement. That the old woman could have heard his words seemed hardly possible, yet creeping up the steward's thick neck was a bright flush of embarrassment.

Like a child who had just been scolded by his nurse, the man, who had only moments ago faced Charles' haughtiness without so much as a flinch, slumped his shoulders. "I didn't say anything, Maite," he murmured in feeble denial to the unseen woman. With a hand at Taryn's back, he urged her inside.

Taryn stopped short at the doorway. The huge room before her, clearly Jaune's great hall, had to comprise at least two thirds of the circular keep. It was a hall unlike any she had ever seen. She could not see across to the far side of the tower, as she had expected to, because of a curving inner wall which formed a circle in the middle of the room. Set in this wall at regular intervals were windows into the open aired space at the very core of the tower. These apertures allowed light to enter the room, revealing to Taryn the fact that this inner shaft must be open to the sky two stories above her.

Directly before her was a raised dais with its back circling halfway around the inner shaft. Cutting off her view on both sides of the dais were two walls which intersected the circle at angles, partitioning the remaining space on this floor.

Swiftly padding toward a door in the partition wall to the left was Taryn's diminutive guide.

"Lady Taryn, will you come, please," she stated somewhat impatiently.

Though she would have liked time to appraise the great hall more thoroughly, Taryn moved quickly to follow the tiny figure disappearing through the doorway. There would be time enough later, she reasoned. Time to take in the room's massive hearths, the elegant wall hangings, even to count the numerous tables and benches—if she so desired. Sitting down to sup beside the baron would surely rob her of any possible appetite! Thinking of the ordeal she would have to endure, if not this evening, then the next, she experienced a sudden shudder.

"This way, Lady Taryn."

Maite's voice reached her as she passed through the doorway into a much smaller room, an anteroom which served as a place for waiting and also as a transit area between the hall and the inner stairwell which led to the floors above.

"The third floor has been set aside for the Great Earl's guests," the woman offered as she took the first step.

Taryn had no need to ask the occupant of the keep's fourth and uppermost floor. Skirts in hand, she followed Maite up the spiral staircase and wondered anew about the woman's mysterious lord.

Was it desire for privacy, eccentrism or mere arrogance which provoked Garret d'Aubigny's behavior? She had heard Charles vilify his seigneur often enough to know there was no love lost between liegeman and lord. Certainly a shared enmity would explain the Great Earl's seemingly deliberate failure to present himself at their arrival.

She pondered the question as she ascended the stairs, which rose past the dizzying height of the great hall to reach the third floor. The spiral ended at a landing. This time, instead of an open room, she was confronted by a narrow passageway leading to the same inner wall. To her left another flight of stairs continued up to the next floor.

The lord's chambers, she thought, both intrigued and suspect of the man she had yet to meet.

"This way, Lady Taryn." Maite gestured to the corridor.

They passed down a dark hallway which grew progressively brighter as they neared its end. There, the hall opened on to a passage which circled to the right, skirting the tower's inner well wall.

On her left Taryn passed several windows similar to the ones in the great hall. The light they afforded the cold stone walls surrounding her served to ease the sensation she felt of being unable to breathe.

Maite passed two doors on the outer wall of the

corridor before finally stopping at a third. She fumbled with the large ring of keys hanging from the girdle about her waist until she found the proper one, and fitted it into the lock.

Taryn heard the click of the latch releasing. Maite pushed and the heavy portal creaked open.

"This will be your room, Lady Taryn."

Taryn started at the sound of the woman's voice. It suddenly seemed strained, containing a peculiar, almost sharp edge. She looked at the old woman in confusion, but the deeply lined features betrayed no trace of accompanying emotion. Wondering if fatigue and the beleaguered state of her own emotions might not have made her unduly sensitive, Taryn dismissed the observation as imagined.

At Maite's gesture she entered the crescent-shaped chamber. As happened below, she stopped short, a gasp of awe escaping. The room before her was truly breathtaking.

Generous of size, its outer, curved wall was nearly entirely taken up with a window embrasure. With two steps leading up to it, the alcove-like space, indeed the size of a small room itself, contained built-in window seats along each side. Though protected by an iron grille and wooden shutters which could be closed, the large stone window frame had been carefully cut and fitted with pieces of colorful stained glass.

It was more beautiful even than Wynshire's chapel apse, Taryn thought. She forced her attention from the window recess to the rest of the room. Its plastered walls and ceiling had been made more cheerful by paintings of flowers, vines and leaves. The colors of red and blue and yellow were carried out in the numerous linen wall panels. Richly dyed and embroidered, they bespoke of countless hours of meticulous labor. The room's furnishings consisted of a bed, gilded and inlaid with ivory, covered in red silk and trimmed with gold fringe; a handsomely carved chest at its foot and a leather-covered smaller one for jewels, and a prayer stool.

Clearly the room had been furnished and decorated to a particular taste—a woman's. Perhaps the sister of her absent host?

"The room is lovely," Taryn whispered. She felt as though the sound of her voice would somehow compromise the sanctity of the space. "It must have been difficult for its original occupant to leave."

Maite stared at her with the strangest of expressions. Then, without reply, she moved to the bed and turned down its silken coverlet. "I will bring you water for washing," she finally spoke, ". . . and a tray. You must be wanting of food and rest after your long journey."

At once Taryn realized she had been politely chastised, but for what? She lowered her head in confused embarrassment as the woman slipped wordlessly past her.

Now alone, she removed her cloak, walked to the chest and hesitantly lifted its lid. She was half surprised to find it empty. Everything about the room seemed to be in such proper order—as if its occupant would return at any moment. She went to the prayer stool and picked up one of the several books of devotion it contained. Thinking the leather-covered missal might bear a clue as to its former owner, she opened it.

Upon its inside cover, scratched in a childish scrawl, was a name: *Clarissa.*

"Clarissa," Taryn repeated softly. Who had she been? And what had become of her? Had she been a sister to Garret d'Aubigny—married off in her youth? Or had she died before her hand could be given in marriage? Certainly that explanation would account for Maite's strange reaction to Taryn's statement. Did Jaune still mourn the death of its daughter?

Hearing Maite's return, Taryn quickly replaced the book and retreated the room's center.

Maite entered and placed the covered kettle she carried upon a small table in the room's corner. "The kitchen is preparing a tray. It will be brought up directly."

Taryn shook her head. "You need not bother. I am not hungry. It is only sleep that I desire."

"As you wish then. Would you be wanting anything else?"

"Nay, thank you." Taryn turned toward the window, softly aglow with the last light of day. The sun was setting.

"Lady Taryn?"

In surprise Taryn glanced back at the old woman.

"This room belonged to the last Countess of Arundel."

"The Countess?" Taryn repeated the words, her mind racing. *Not the sister of Garret d'Aubigny, but his wife—the maiden said to have been driven insane!*

"Aye. She and the Great Earl were betrothed as children. Ten years ago this summer she came to this keep a bride of sixteen."

"What . . . what happened to her?" Taryn asked hesitantly. All the ugly rumors she had heard swirled in her brain.

"She died." Maite's curt, flat reply left no doubt that the subject was not one to be addressed further.

"I . . . I'm sorry," Taryn murmured, empathizing with the old woman's grief at the loss of a loved one. But the pain she suddenly saw reflected in the weary eyes did not seem to be one of grief. It was one of sadness and sorrow—sorrow not for the dead, but for the living.

She shook off the strange feeling enveloping her and realized how very tired she was.

Maite departed and she gratefully turned toward the bed.

She had scarce lain down when sleep took hold.

Chapter Four

Garret d'Aubigny watched as the dark head that had a moment ago been resting upon his chest moved down the length of his bare torso. He curled his fingers in the tangled hair to check its descent.

The woman in his arms mewled in protest.

"Still unsated, wench?" Husky from sleep, his voice carried no trace of either gentleness or affection. Their heated coupling upon awaking only minutes ago meant nothing to him. And with his physical need for her fulfilled, he had no desire to now engage in playful lovers' games—even if time permitted, which it did not. Were he to leave this instant, and ride hard, he still would not reach Jaune before nightfall. Maite would have his head if he snubbed his guests a second night.

Thinking of the old woman who had raised him, he smiled. In his mind he pictured her scolding him, raised on tiptoe, gnarled finger wagging in his face. Softly, he laughed aloud.

Seemingly encouraged by his laughter and obviously mistaking its cause, the woman at his side stirred again. Pressing her silken length closer, she slowly slid a hand up his thigh. Tracing with her fingertips a teasing pattern over the naked flesh, she sought the source of her earlier pleasure.

But his shaft lay unresponsive to her touch, flaccid in

its nesting of damp hair.

Undaunted, she nipped at the taut skin of his belly.

Deciding he could attemper both Maite and her anger, Garret contemplated lifting his restraining hand. He knew where the moist, warm mouth would fare. Why not partake, if the wench was willing?

He released his fingers' clasp, and the woman resumed her gambit.

She flicked her tongue in taunting temptation, first over the hood and then down the length, before taking him in fully.

Garret felt himself stir in response to the skillful assault, growing hard as her fingers stroked him in an accompanying rhythm.

Suddenly she stopped and lifted her head to eye the result of her efforts. The full lips turned down into a pouting frown. "Certes, the Great Earl can offer better," she teased.

"His response is only as good as his enticement," Garret countered, amused by her change in tactic. Instead of stimulating him to performance, she would goad him. "You have demonstrated well enough your skill in arousing the giver of pleasure. Might you be equally deft in arousing the recipient?"

He grasped her slender shoulders and lifted her so that she sat straddling his thighs. Now at arm's length, her full, high breasts proved a most tempting display. "Show me what *you* offer, Madame Flambard."

A pink tinge appeared on the woman's cheeks. She made a move to get off, but he held her fast. "Show me, Geneviève," he pressed, his voice cool and controlled. "You are no chaste maid and the pretense suits you poorly. You have had more men to your bed than there are hairs on your beautiful head."

Flushing fiercely, the woman licked her lips, and Garret knew the heightened color was brought by passion. Her breathing had quickened and her brown eyes had taken on a glassy appearance.

Slowly and hesitantly she brought a tapered finger to her mouth, licked its tip, then lowered it to one naked breast. Languidly she traced a wet path around the erect nipple. The hand dropped away and she repeated the action, this time sucking on her finger before bringing it to the other breast.

Lost in the wicked sensation the touching of her own body elicited, Geneviève Flambard whimpered in pleasure. She beheld the man lying beneath her, watching her in silent command. His muscled body, sleek and hard, still glistened with the perspiration of their earlier lovemaking. Between them, swollen and rigid, his complete erection pulsated in promise of further pleasures. "Does what I offer entice you, milord?" she whispered.

Without reply, he released one hand's grasp and brought its forefinger to her lips.

Obligingly, she took the finger into her mouth, wetting it thoroughly.

He removed it and imitated her action, circling the rosy peaks.

The fact that his eyes were cold went unnoticed by the woman now trembling in anticipation. She knew that when of a mind, the Great Earl of Arundel could pleasure a woman as few could.

Garret rolled one hard nub between his forefinger and thumb, evoking an instant cry from the lips breathlessly parted. He took his hand from her shoulder. Clutching a fistful of hair at the nape of her neck, he pulled her to him. Still tormenting her nipple, he followed the outline of her mouth with his tongue, then plunged it inside.

The sweet mixture of pain and pleasure washed over Geneviève like a molten wave. She tasted him hungrily and reveled in the sensations assailing her—his hot, punishing mouth, the hand at her neck which kept her where he wanted her as his fingers kneaded her breast. All the while she could feel the burning length of him, assuring her of the delightful fulfillment to come . . .

* * *

"'Tis high time you returned! Did I not give you a better upbringing, boy? Two days 'tis, since you rode out—with naught said to a soul of your plans."

Garret dismounted, smiling at the disembodied voice besetting him. He gestured to a waiting stable boy to lead away his destrier, then searched the dark corners of the yard with his eyes. "And how long have you been out here, waiting to deliver this tongue-lashing, Maite?"

"Too long," the woman retorted, stepping out of the night into the flickering torchlight at the stables' entrance. "Chilled to the bone, I am, waiting for your backside to ride through that gate. Certes, the Great Earl would not be so rude as to twice insult his guests, I'm thinking, and all the while the sun sets lower and the shadows grow longer. By the saints! Where *have* you been? You knew the Earl of Wynshire was scheduled to arrive yesterday."

"Aye, I knew," Garret answered flatly. "And *you* knew I did not care a whit for welcoming that coxcomb. I cannot abide Charles Maitland and shall not pretend otherwise. 'Twas a sad day Wynshire fell into his hands. If it truly is the old earl's blood which runs through his veins, then surely it has soured. And if the truth be told, it would scarce surprise me to learn that the greedy whelp had a hand in his father's sudden death last summer."

Garret pulled off his gauntlets and shoved them beneath the belt about his waist. "Enough of Maitland." Stepping forward, he unfastened his mantle and removed the marten skin from his shoulders. "Come here, old woman. Let me wrap this around you." He held the mantle open.

Maite remained where she stood.

Amused by her stubbornness Garret smiled silently. He stepped behind her to tenderly place the fur over her frail form. Upon his own frame the garment was knee-length. On Maite it trailed on the ground. He draped an end up over her shoulder to prevent her from tripping upon it. "Now, to answer your earlier question . . ." He smiled knowing the reaction his next words would provoke. ". . . I was in Kirdford."

"As if I had to ask!" Maite snorted in disgust, crooking her head back over her shoulder to view him. "And how *is* merchant Flambard's wife?"

Garret smiled. Despite her years, little escaped Maite. "Madame Flambard is quite well. Thank you for asking." Then, because he knew nothing would incense the old woman more, he manufactured a flippant lie. "She inquired about your health as well, and sends her regards." He set his arm about the bony shoulders and playfully kissed the wrinkled cheek. "Now, let's get you out of the cold."

"Argh!" The woman shrieked at his caress and pushed at him with more strength than one would have thought possible for the tiny body to possess. "I can still smell the odor of your coupling! I'll not have you near me til you bathe!"

Garret laughed at her pointed exaggeration. "I am heartened to see that age has not robbed you of your sense of smell," he teased, stepping back with a deep mocking bow. "It must compensate for your failing eyesight, hum?"

"There is naught wrong with my eyesight, you insolent pup!" Maite lifted her chin and leveled one of her sternest glares. Such looks from the old woman had been known to set the boldest of knights in their place. "I see just fine. And what I see is a lord who shirks his responsibilities, a guilt-ridden knave masquerading in a man's body whilst he seeks the spousal pleasures of marriage from another man's wife."

"You *are* in a fine humor tonight," Garret replied quietly.

Maite flinched at the level tone of his voice. She recognized it and knew the forced control was far more dangerous than had he shouted. As a wound which would not heal, the events of the past festered still within his soul. Like all her others, this attempt to make him confront it had also been futile.

"Do you intend to berate me further, or am I now free to greet my guests?" His voice still measured, he lifted a brow. "After all . . . I should not wish to *shirk* my responsibilities." Without waiting for a reply he started forward in the direction of the keep and then stopped abruptly, turning his head. "They have all arrived?"

"Aye, arrived and already seated to sup. Baron Lynfyld, the earl, and his sister, the baron's betrothed." Carefully Maite studied his face in the torchlight. She might as well make known the real reason she had been awaiting his return. She set her shoulders. "You should not give your consent, Garret."

"What?" He turned to face her fully.

"'Tis a foul match. He's a lecherous old fool and she's an innocent young girl. I believe she's being forced into this marriage."

"And upon what do you make this claim?"

Maite smiled gently. "You know I can see what others can't. I can see through the cloaks of deception and pretense people don. I know here . . ." she gestured to her heart ". . . that what I say is true. To give your consent would be to sentence this child to a hellish fate."

Garret knew better than to question the old woman's words. From personal experience he knew how accurate her observations could be. Since her childhood she had possessed the ability to see into a person's soul. "The gift of sight," the villeins called it. And that "gift," coupled with her diminutive stature, had led most to believe she was endowed with unearthly powers—a descendant of the ancient fairy folk who, according to legend, had dwelt upon the isle of Britain centuries before its Roman conquest.

Still, he could not refuse to grant his consent based upon his former wetnurse's intuitive talents, no matter how accurate he might think them. "The arrangements of the marriage have been made. My consent is a mere formality. I cannot withhold it.'

"But you can!", Maite insisted. "You are the earl's seigneur. The baron's as well. You possess the authority to do as you will, without explanation."

"Without explanation, aye. But not without cause."

"I have given you cause!"

"Nay, you have given me your suspicions, Maite. I cannot, and I will not, act upon mere feelings. Now, will you come, or remain here in the cold?"

Maite recognized defeat. She knew further discussion would be pointless. The words spoken by the tall man now headed toward the torchlit steps of the keep resounded hauntingly in her mind: *I cannot, and I will not, act upon mere feelings.* Because you have lost the ability to do so, she thought.

Bloodied in battle at the age of sixteen, Garret d'Aubigny had learned early to sever himself from his youthful emotions. The man and the warrior had become inseparable, controlled and implacable, able to fight, kill or whore with the same degree of detachment. Only once, for a short time, had the innocence of first love slackened the tight rein he held on his emotions. But after that horrible night ten years ago the control had become complete and constant.

Maite shook her head sadly. And as she stepped forward to follow her lord, her shoulders were hunched, her gait suddenly that of an old woman.

Taryn struggled to endure the presence of the man seated between her and Charles at Jaune's high table.

Clearly drunk, her betrothed leered at her openly, fairly licking his thick lips in anticipation. "Merely laying eyes upon you causes my loins to stir, lady. I will plant my seed deep and it will grow." He reached out and placed a meaty hand over her small one. "I feel it. You shall be the one to bear me an heir. A strong healthy son."

He laughed, and she fought a violent urge to gag. In addition to his grotesque physical appearance, Baron Lynfyld possessed a breath more putrid than the stagnant moat about Wynshire Castle.

The realization that she would soon have that mouth pressed to hers, to be forced to endure its owner's intimacies, rendered her nauseous. Whether it would offer offense or not, she had to leave. She leaned forward, looking past the baron, to make her request of her half-brother.

Tossing down yet another tankard, Charles appeared no less drunk than Lynfyld—the only difference was that while Lynfyld betrayed his state with raucous laughter and words, Charles sat in stony silence. Slouched in his chair, he stared at the vacant seat to his right—the mocking evidence of their host's continued absence. He ignored the men seated left of the chair; Richard, the steward, and others who held positions of high rank at Jaune.

That their lord had not yet presented himself Taryn found unconscionable. For better than an hour they had sat, until the hall had filled with men and the serving of food had begun. With no appetite of her own, she had occupied her attention with sneaking chunks of meat from her trencher to a bay-colored hound that had settled at her feet. Once fed, the animal seemed content to sit by her side, his head docilely nestled in her lap.

Now, beneath the din of men shouting and eating, she heard the rhythmic thumping of its tail against the rush-strewn floor. With the wave of nausea passed, she leaned back and stroked the soft, furred head.

Suddenly the dog shook off her hand. He stood and turned to look out upon the gathering of men. His tail wagged so furiously that his hindquarters swayed from side to side.

From her vantage point at the table's end Taryn

possessed an unobstructed view of the great hall. She looked past the score of tables hers faced, in the direction of the animal's obvious excitement, to the keep's double portals, and saw one of the doors open. Maite entered, her tiny frame engulfed in a fur mantle. She was followed by a tall man dressed in *hauberk* and mail hood. He pulled off the coif, handed it to the woman, then turned, surveying the hall's occupants.

Taryn looked to the dog. Its entire body now quivered in anticipation. Then, seemingly in response to a signal unintelligible to her, he bounded toward the newcomer.

He looked to be one of Jaune's men-at-arms, and wore a knight's spurs. That the hound was his was clear.

With interest she watched the ensuing greeting of master and beast. Kneeling on one knee, he took the animal's head into his hands, scratching behind its erect ears. An instant later she heard a shrill whistle leave his lips. In immediate obedience the half dozen other dogs that had been foraging among the tables went to him.

Perhaps he was the master of hounds, she thought. But that position was rarely held by a knight. Her curiosity piqued, she continued to watch the man as he rose to his feet.

He dismissed the dogs, except for the bay hound who remained at his heel, and moved into the main body of the hall. At several tables he stopped to speak to their occupants, once even sitting down to a tankard of ale. Steadily, he moved nearer to the high table.

With a critical eye Taryn took in the details of his appearance.

His dark hair was long, tied back from his face in a fashion which made his square jaw seem cut from stone. His *hauberk* was simple in cut and looked to be well worn. The sword at his side was plain as well. Hanging in a scarred scabbard which spoke of long and hard use, its metal hilt was wrapped with leather to make a good grip which would not turn in a sweating hand.

Looking upon him, she sensed the power of one

accustomed to command. Despite his appearance, she was almost certain this man was no mere knight.

At length he approached the far end of the dais, the end where Jaune's men sat.

No doubt he must offer up his respect to them, she thought. Then, bewildered, she watched him mount the platform.

With the air of one who sat at high tables by right of blood, he passed behind the men, greeting each in turn.

Suddenly, from the corner of her eye Taryn noted Charles' reaction to the man's presence. Her half-brother sat rigid, his eyes locked on the interloper now at the table's center. Unaware, or simply indifferent to the attention focused upon him, the man pulled out the vacant chair and dropped into it.

Blessed Mother! she silently exclaimed, realizing at once the man's identity. Stunned, she sat back in her chair. The arrogance of Garret d'Aubigny surpassed any she had ever seen! Surely he had known his guests were arrived. Maite would have informed him. And certainly upon entering he had seen them seated at his own table. But instead of hurrying forward to make an apology for his tardiness, he had meandered among his men, taking the time to drink a tankard—why, he had even taken the time to greet his hounds!

She sat forward and looked sideways at her half-brother. Charles' initial annoyance with his host's absence upon their arrival had only increased during this, their second day at Jaune. By the time they had entered the great hall for the evening meal his mood had been black indeed. This final affront would surely send him into a livid rage. Yet despite his fury, she doubted he would risk endangering his plans with a voiced protest that might anger his arrogant lord into withholding his consent.

Her suspicion proved sound as she watched Charles swallow his indignation and rise to greet the man with forced civility. To achieve his goal he would suffer the insult in silence.

Taryn slumped back, the spark of hope extinguished, truly before it had been fired. Through the desolation of despair descending upon her, she heard Lynfyld's voice make his own greeting.

As neither man bothered to present her to their host, she sat mute as they resumed their seats.

Relieved to be done with the requisite formalities, Garret leaned back. His empty belly rumbled with the need to be filled. His hunger, together with the fatigue of his hard ride, had given him a pounding head. He would sit with his "guests" for no longer than it would take him to eat. Responsibilities and courtesies be hanged! He was for bed.

He beckoned a passing serving maid to fetch him a trencher. As the girl, a buxom flaxen-haired wench with a ready smile, hastened to do his bidding, he returned his attention to the occupants of his table. Looking past Charles Maitland and the baron, he fixed his gaze upon the woman seated to the old man's right. When he had entered the hall he had paid the slender feminine form no heed. He now took a moment to appraise the object of Maite's concern.

Though she kept her head bowed, the little he could see of her face seemed pleasing enough. Certainly her fiery hair, impossible to overlook, provided a change from the blond ideal of femininity he found enticing. Complimenting the flame-colored tresses, she wore a gown of saffron. Looking upon her he was struck with the thought of rich, fragrant spices. He shifted his gaze to the baron. The peculiarity of their match did indeed spark his curiosity. It was odd her brother had been unable to arrange better for her, odder still that she would be agreeable to his choice.

Sudden and unbidden, Maite's claim returned to nag at his conscience. Could the old woman be correct? Was the Earl of Wynshire somehow forcing his sister into this marriage? There was only one way he would know.

"Mistress Maitland."

Taryn started at the sound of her name spoken by an unfamiliar masculine voice. She looked down the table. The Earl of Arundel stared directly at her.

"Come here." Again he spoke, this time summoning her with a wave of his hand.

Feeling like one of his hounds, she rose and made her way behind the baron and Charles, both of whom were watching her intently.

Eyes lowered, she presented herself to him. "My lord."

Garret tipped back his head to view her. Meekly, the lady kept her own bowed. "Your brother seeks my consent to your marriage with Baron Lynfyld. Ere I grant it, I would know that you are a willing party to this match. Do you enter into this union willingly and do you give your consent freely?"

Willingly, no! she silently screamed. But the words which finally passed her lips were others. "Aye, my lord. I have given my consent."

To her own ears her voice sounded weak, carrying no conviction. *Please, sainted Mother, let him hear it and know I am being forced.*

"Look at me, Mistress."

The harsh command cut through her silent prayer and she flinched instinctively. Still, she raised her eyes to behold the face of the man in whose hands her fate lay.

He was perhaps thirty, far younger than she would have thought for the position he held. And while there was no denying the rough-hewn handsomeness of the man, it was his eyes which kept her spellbound. Pale green, their intensity transfixed her.

"What is the purpose of this?" Loud and rife with indignation, Charles' voice resounded down the table. He shoved back his chair as if to stand, but apparently reconsidered. "My sister is already betrothed. Thus her consent *has* been given. Why do you question her now?"

"Because she scarce gives the appearance of a blushing bride."

Jaune's lord turned his full attention on Charles, and Taryn felt as if she had ceased to exist. For the second time in as many days she found herself being discussed in her presence, by a man who acted as if she could not hear what was being said—by a man who did not care to spare her feelings.

"She stands before me ill at ease and subdued, her eyes lowered," Arundel's earl continued, the probing celadon stare now fixed upon her half-brother. "Then, when I demand she look at me, I see only sadness and dread mirrored there."

"This is absurd!" Charles cried out. He jerked his head upward to look at her. "Taryn, tell the earl what he wants to hear."

His eyes narrowed, and she suddenly realized that if she did not acquiesce to this marriage, she would be of no value whatsoever to her half-brother. His threat of days past echoed hauntingly in her mind: *You have no place to go except into this marriage.* She shivered at the prospect of his savage retribution. Charles' cruelty would know no bounds.

"My consent has been given," she repeated softly.

A grin of satisfaction broke out across Charles' face, and he returned his gaze to his doubting seigneur. "There, you see, my lord? 'Tis assuredly pre-wedding nerves that you detect. Why, I'd wager there's not a maid in England who has not had such a case on the eve of her marriage."

"Mayhap 'tis not pre-wedding nerves, but wedding *night!*" Lynfyld's laughter rang out. All eyes now upon him, he raised his tankard. "To the consummation of this marriage!"

As Charles lifted his own tankard, Taryn looked to the man on her left. Garret d'Aubigny had stiffened visibly. An unfathomable look darkened his features. His eyes seemed to drift away momentarily, focusing on some invisible spot—a place of private pain. Then it was gone—so quickly she thought she must have imagined it.

"My consent is granted," he stated flatly.

Taryn squeezed her eyes shut. His words were a death sentence. Suddenly, her earlier nausea returned, and she feared she would be ill where she stood. She opened her eyes. "Please, might I be excused?"

Garret nodded. Moving only his eyes, he followed the progress of the woman departing the dais. This time Maite had been wrong. Twice he had heard it from the lady's own lips. She might not be altogether pleased with her intended, but she *had* given her consent. Besides, what concern was it of his whom she married? The sooner he was done with the Maitlands, the better.

Aware of the eyes watching her, Taryn stepped from the dais. She forced herself to hold her head high and to walk steadily to the door which would take her from the hall to the anteroom. Once through it, however, her reserve of control was drained. She dropped her head, lifted her skirts and dashed for the refuge of the stairwell.

Too late she saw the buxom serving maid, hands laden with a filled platter and pitcher of ale, who blocked her path. Taryn ran straight into her, nearly toppling her and sending ale sloshing over the both of them.

Gasping in shock, the maid glared at her.

Taryn saw the flicker of recognition enter her eyes and knew whatever reproach the girl might otherwise have delivered would be now withheld. She murmured an apology—which went unacknowledged—and stumbled to the spiral staircase. Her foot had taken barely three or four treads when she heard the maid at last give vent to her suppressed anger.

"Did ye see that, Mary? She near knocked me flat!"

Taryn wilted against the wall, suddenly bereft of either the energy or will to take another step. Assuming that the "Mary" the maid addressed was the Virgin, she was startled to hear a feminine voice actually respond.

"Aye, I saw. Came out of the kitchen just in time I did

to see yer ale bath!" A high-pitched cackle sounded. "Ye can't be too 'ard on 'er though, Bess. The poor thing's prob'ly beside 'erself. And do ye blame 'er? Did ye 'appen to git a good look at 'er intended?"

The women's voices joined in snickers.

Then the first spoke again. "That ol' pock-marked and bloated goat's a real catch, eh? Imagine, 'avin' saved 'erself for that! 'Tis no wonder she 'ad to run up to 'er chamber. I'd wager she's tossin' up 'er supper right now!"

Crouched in the darkness of the stairwell, Taryn cringed in shame. There was no doubt who they were discussing.

"'Tis a right shame Lord Garret don't take 'is due," the woman called Mary continued. "At least then she'd be knowin' *one* night of pleasure in a man's bed. Judgin' from the way ye was limpin' about last week, I'd say our Great Earl was *great* indeed!"

The serving maid tittered. "Couldn't sit proper fer days—not that I be complainin', mind ye. But what's this 'due' yer talkin', Mary?"

"The lady, of course." Again the older woman broke into her high cackle. "'Twas right common in my mother's day, the ol' Saxon custom of a lord beddin' 'is vassal's bride on 'er weddin' night. In fact, 'twas high praise to their choosin' of a bride. Of course, the Church frowns on such, but some of the ol' lords still keep the practice. Even gave it a fancy soundin' Norman name. Can't recall it, though."

Droit du seigneur. The words leaped into Taryn's mind and her heart began to swell with the seed of a desperate hope.

Chapter Five

Within the firelit sanctuary of her chamber Taryn paced. For better than an hour she had traced and retraced the same path, from the door to the window embrasure and back. Her turbulent emotions and thoughts would not be quelled. Elusive and conflicting, they defied comprehension.

Droit du seigneur. The right of the lord. Over and over the words repeated themselves, and the components of the desperate plan born in the stairwell of the anteroom surfaced anew.

Having seen her betrothed, having suffered the repugnance of his company for but one evening, only a single thought remained. She must stop from happening the wedding which would make her his wife and send her to his bed. She had to fail the midwife's exam in the morning. She must lose her chastity this night.

But could she do it? Could she offer herself to the one man who possessed the legal right to take it? And if she were to go to him, would he even act upon the shameless proposition?

She thought back upon the stories she had heard—the rumors of Garret d'Aubigny's apparently indiscriminate and ofttimes indiscreet liaisons at court. His own serving women supported the truth of the tales. Their ribald comments as to his skill and physical endowments left little room for doubt that the man's reputation for wenching was one rightly deserved.

The facts seemed indisputable. The man shared his bed freely and without reservation. But in this instance, where he had already granted his consent for a marriage to take place, might he not be uncharacteristically discriminating? Legal right aside, what she wanted of him was to commit an act of dishonor.

At once she dismissed the thought. She had seen or heard nothing which could possibly lead her to think that honor was any more a trait of Jaune's arrogant lord than courtesy. He would act accordingly.

That conviction brought her back once more to her original question. Could *she* do it? And did she have any other choice? This night, or the next, her maidenhead would be breached. At least with the lord of Jaune she would gain her freedom. The consequences of that freedom, the risk of defying God's will, of committing a mortal sin, all faded in the face of self-preservation. So too, did the fear about her future position once she had foiled Charles' plan.

That her half-brother would cast her out, she was sure. But against his liege lord neither he, nor Lynfyld either for that matter, would be able to take issue. She was equally sure that in bearing responsibility for her altered state, Garret d'Aubigny would also have to bear responsibility for her future—if only to send her to a convent—a prospect surely more desirable than the one which awaited her now.

Her decision made and her mind clear, Taryn ended her pacing. She moved to the bed and lay down, to await such time as she would place herself—and her fate—in the hands of Garret d'Aubigny.

But sleep was impossible. She lay there, shifting now and then in the large bed, until the fire which had been banked for the night finally died. It was time.

She rose and stripped off her clothing, the saffron *bliant,* the rust-colored gown, and at last, hesitantly, her chemise. Naked, she shivered as she reached for the robe draped across the foot of the bed.

Meant to be worn for warmth over a *camise*, the woolen garment's only closure was a single tie at the throat. Taryn donned the robe quickly and tied the silken cord. Clutching the sides closed, she moved to the dressing table and sat.

It seemed like a foolish thought, but she suddenly felt she would feel less vulnerable should she wear her hair unbound.

Clumsy and unresponsive, her fingers undid the heavy plait as her mind teemed with questions, doubts and fears. Would she be made to undress, she wondered. Would he take her quickly? She knew there would be pain with his breaching, but not how much. And would she be expected to sleep at his side afterward?

Fool! she chastised herself silently. She was about to commit the most shameful of acts and she sat worrying about decorum, the how and after! What did it matter but that she lost her virginity?

Her task completed, she ran her fingers through her hair, and then stood. Once she left this chamber there could be no turning back. She took a deep breath and reached for the candle burning atop the table. Those passages with windows onto the well wall might be lit with moonlight, but the narrow halls which led to the stairwell, and the stairwell itself, would be engulfed in darkness.

Picturing the path she must take aloft, and concentrating upon it alone, she crossed the room and opened the door. A draft of cold air hit her, sending the flame in her hand dancing wildly. She shivered, steadied her hand and peered out. Silence and darkness greeted her. She took another deep breath, slipped through the door and closed it. Passing Charles' and the baron's doors, she quickly followed the circular hall, not stopping until she reached the narrow passage which led to the stairs.

Empty silence filled the space. Eerie shadows, cast by

the candle, flickered off the walls. She listened for a footstep, a sound which would indicate she was not alone. Hearing nothing except the pounding of her own heart, she made her way to the landing. The stairs below were dark and soundless, as were the ones leading above.

She lifted the hem of her robe and took the first step. The timber creaked under her weight, and she held her breath as the sound echoed in the confines of the stairwell. It died and she continued up.

At last she reached the head of the stairs. Here it was very different than the floor below. Here there was no long passageway to the tower's core, but a hall of only a few paces in length, providing access to two doors, one on the right and one on the left. Beneath the doors only the one on the right displayed light, soft light as from a low burning fire.

Realizing she had reached her goal, she crossed herself and hesitantly approached it. She blew out the candle, then set it on the floor. Her fingers travelled up the rough hewn wood to locate the latch. Feeling the cold iron, she paused. Should she knock? No doubt he was asleep. Perhaps she should just slip inside. And then what? Climb into bed beside him? One thing was certain: she could not stand in the hallway!

She released the latch, freezing as the slight noise resounded loudly in the dark silence. Was it enough to wake a sleeping man? The thought that the honed instincts of a warrior would hear the noise never occurred to her. Nor did the thought that upon entering she could very well encounter a sword point.

She pushed the door open just wide enough to slip inside, then closed it behind her. Again the sound of the latch seemed thunderous in the dead stillness. Setting her back to the door, she scanned the vast chamber. Her attention went immediately to the large bed across from the massive fireplace centered in the wall to her left.

Elevated and draped with curtains that had been left

half drawn, she could not tell if the bed were occupied. She stepped forward, forcing one foot in front of the other. A few paces from the platform she realized the bed was empty.

Awash in a mixture of relief and despair she stared at the unrumpled sheets, the smooth coverlet folded back. The decision had been taken from her! It mattered not if she were willing to sacrifice her chastity. The man was not there. Suddenly her courage left her. She ran to the door, her trembling fingers seeking the latch.

"You give up easily."

Taryn gasped and whirled. Her heart felt as if it had leaped into her throat, and she fought to breathe. *He was here!* She looked in the direction from which the deep masculine voice had sounded.

The settle before the fireplace seemed to come alive as a shadowy figure rose from its seat.

How had she missed seeing him there?

He rounded the bench and stood before her.

For a second time she found herself taking in every detail of Garret d'Aubigny's appearance. Unbound, his hair fell past shoulders which were naked and broad. His smooth chest gleamed in the firelight, and she could see numerous scars, the badges of battles long ago waged and no doubt won. Her eyes darted to the dark line of hair which ran down the flat, muscled belly. At least he wore breeches, she thought in an inane instant of relief—though the cloth molded to his muscled thighs and calves like a second skin.

Through her thoughts she heard a half growl, half chuckle.

"Mistress Maitland."

His greeting was both that and question.

"My lord," she managed to gasp in reply, dropping her gaze to the floor.

"As this chamber is on an entirely different floor than yours, Mistress, I am reluctant to believe you entered it by mistake. And unless you walk in your sleep, you'd best make quick with an explanation as to the purpose of this visit."

The deep voice seemed to echo in the huge room. Spartan in furnishings it contained, unlike her own chamber below, neither tapestries nor floor coverings to absorb the sound. Even the crackling fire seemed abnormally loud.

"My impatience grows, Mistress. The purpose of your presence in my bedchamber—now!"

Taryn fingered the cord at her throat. She could not bring herself to voice the desperate goal of her visit. "My presence is no mistake, my lord. Nor do I walk in my sleep." She whispered the words numbly—far more aware of a secret voice within her, shouting instruction. *Let the robe fall. Offer to him what you desire he take. Make known your availability, your willingness.*

She pulled the knot free, letting the robe slide open over her shoulders and clutching it closed at her hips. Bare from the waist up, she felt the heat of the fire warm her exposed flesh—then realized she was too far from the flames. The fire came from within, from shame. She glanced up.

The expression of the man before her did not change. He made no move to step closer. He did not blink an eye, nor could she even detect the rise and fall of his chest in breathing. Under his bold stare she felt the biting sting of tears and blinked them back.

"Drop the robe and turn around."

"*My lord?*" Taryn gasped and stared at him in shock.

A mocking smile turned up the corners of his mouth. "You heard me, Mistress. 'Tis my desire to view the total offering. I do not purchase a horse without first examining the entire beast. Surely you do not expect me to bed a woman without having first seen the swell of her hips and the roundness of her buttocks. A mere glimpse of breasts is quite insufficient." He returned to the settle and sat down, positioning himself for the best vantage point. "And for my taste they are a little small at that."

Taryn felt the tears well. But the cruel, arrogant man before her was not finished.

"Be quick about it, Mistress. My interest wanes."

Only the sudden image of Lynfyld's leering face gave her the courage to swallow her pride and growing humiliation. All that had been said of Garret d'Aubigny was true! He was a beast without honor! With a smothered cry she let loose her grasp, and the robe dropped to her feet.

She never saw his reaction, his momentary loss of control and surprise. Her eyes were tightly squeezed shut to hold back the tears she refused to let him see.

It seemed like an eternity that she stood there. She could feel his gaze traveling every inch of her body, searing her with shame. She blessed the low light and the distance between them, then remembered how easily she had been able to detect the defined lines of his own body.

"Turn."

Her shame increased, but she did as ordered. In the wake of the total degradation she felt, a new emotion stirred within her—anger. He wanted to debase her. She would not allow him the satisfaction. She straightened her shoulders, silently giving thanks for the unbound tresses sweeping the backs of her thighs. He would see nothing.

"Clothe yourself."

The sudden command caused her to whirl. He had leaned back in the settle, stretching his long legs straight and resting his head against the high back. He yawned. "Mayhap another time, Mistress."

Taryn choked back a cry of rage. Her temper smothered the flames of her humiliation and a shiver coursed through her. She bit her lip to keep from spewing a hateful retort. She mustered as much pride as she could and stooped to retrieve her robe. She pulled it on, her fingers trembling.

Utterly oblivious to her presence now, he stood and stepped to the hearth. Taking up the length of iron resting against the wall, he poked at the glowing logs. The rising flames illuminated his face. It was devoid of any emotion. His task completed, he replaced the iron rod and looked at her, as though bemused by her continued presence. "Return to your bed, Mistress. Mine is not to be shared this night."

Like oil thrown on a fire, his words ignited her smoldering temper. Her tears dried instantly. "I was waiting to offer an apology, my lord." Her voice laced with bitter sarcasm, she stared at him defiantly. "I *did* enter this chamber by mistake. I was under the impression I would find a man within. 'Tis clear I have erred."

The last reaction she expected from him in response to her obvious disaparagement of his manhood was amusement, but his laughter rang out.

"A lesser man would take offense, Mistress." Smiling the same mocking smile, he returned to his seat.

His arrogance was insufferable! Taryn turned on her heel and fled. The sound of his laughter followed her, ringing in her ears even after she had slammed the wooden door shut behind her.

Garret stared at the closed door. Had what just occurred really happened? Had Charles Maitland's sister really stood in front of him, unclothed and offering herself quite undeniably for his taking?

Garret shook his head. There could be no other explanation for her visit than that she had sought to seduce him. But why? And on this, the eve of her marriage to another? Or was that the answer?

Faced with a certain future of unfulfillment, had she, having already known a virile man's lovemaking, come to him for a final indulgence of the flesh?

Or had she sought to seduce him for a purpose more designing than mere pleasure? She had to know of her betrothed's desperate desire to produce an heir. Had she, therefore, come to him in the hope that his seed would get her with child—thereby enabling her in nine months' time to pass off the issue of his loins as that of her husband's?

"Scheming whore!" he exclaimed out loud, laughing again. In a way he admired her daring and audacity, to a point of almost regretting not having obliged her. She was comely enough, certainly willing and clearly not without experience. Indeed, he might have acted in haste in sending her away.

He shrugged off the thought. There was no shortage of women willing to share his bed. But he chose carefully. Women, he had learned, regardless of blood and upbringing, fell into one of two groupings: Those chaste and proper maids who wanted commitment and thus performed the carnal act with the passion of stone out of a sense of duty to bear a son, or those like Geneviève Flambard who wanted and expected no more from a man than physical satisfaction. Only of this latter type did he avail himself. He had learned from the past. He would not be swept again into that whirlpool of emotion, emotion which stripped bare the soul and laid open wounds never to be healed . . .

Memories, guilt and pain—ever just on the fringes of conscious thought—suddenly threatened to rise. Always when he was tired the past returned to haunt him. And he was tired now, his fatigue relaxing the inexorable mental control which kept the demons at bay. Fiercely, he drove them back. His initial reaction to the entire evening was the only logical response. He was for bed.

. . . Cold and rigid she lay beneath him, her eyes wide with fear. She was dry and unready for his assault. But with the inexperience and impatience of youth he plunged himself into her. She screamed in terror and pain . . .

Garret bolted upright, his heart slamming against his ribs. The image before him faded, and the dream died. He was alone in his bed, his body damp with sweat. He closed his eyes and fought the last vestiges of the familiar nightmare.

But suddenly he heard the scream again, this time echoing not from within his mind, but from the floor below.

He sprang from the bed, reaching instinctively for the sword lying upon the carved chest at its foot. Again he heard the cry, a woman's cry. Hilt in hand he raced from his chamber.

"Lackwits! Keep her quiet or her screams will surely have the entire castle upon us!" Charles glared at the two men engaged in a struggle to wrestle Taryn from the corner to which she had fled.

Trapped, his half-sister was nevertheless making the task no easy feat for them. She clawed at the one who held her from behind and kicked at the other. All the while she twisted her head from side to side in an attempt to dislodge the hand now clamped across her mouth. The muffled sounds of her cries mingled with the men's mutterd oaths and heavy breathing.

"Get her to the bed!" Charles ordered, his growing impatience quickly turning to anger. "Carry her if you must."

In immediate compliance to his command, the man whose hand covered her mouth pressed her head to his chest. His other arm wrapped about her slender waist. "Her feet!" he gasped to his partner.

"By the saints, Maitland!'

The raspy voice was accompanied by a pressure upon his arm. Charles turned his attention from the struggle and looked to the man at his side.

Lynfyld, his face red with exasperation, pointed to the trio moving to the bed. "Why does she fight the examination? Can it be that you seek to sell me damaged good?"

"Certes, not!" Desperate to calm the older man,

Charles set his arm about his shoulders and guided him to the foot of the bed. *Damn her!* he silently swore. To the very end she complicated his plans! "You have my word, Baron. The terms of our agreement stand. 'Tis modesty —no more—which prompts her resistance."

"Humpf!" Lynfyld's response carried no conviction. He pulled away from Charles and stared down at the writhing figure on the bed. Clearly there would be no appeasing him now. Only the midwife's findings could do that.

Charles jerked his head to the woman waiting patiently by the window. "Come! Get on with your task!"

His back to the room's door and his attention divided between the midwife and the struggle her approach evoked from his half-sister, he was unaware of the portal's opening.

Standing in the doorway, Garret beheld the bizarre scene before him. Evidently unmindful of his presence, Charles Maitland and Baron Lynfyld watched as two men fought to hold a woman down upon the bed. One of the men, with a hand already pressed to her mouth, grabbed a fistful of red hair to hold her still. The other attempted to capture and part her flailing legs.

An old woman, whom Garret recognized as the village midwife, stepped to the bed's edge. Reaching for the hem of the woman's chemise, she turned to address the two observers. "Shall I proceed, milords?"

Confused, Garret looked to the men for an inkling as to what was happening.

Lynfyld held up his hand and signaled the midwife to wait. Lynfyld turned to the man beside him. "I swear, Maitland, by all that is holy, should she prove to be unchaste there will be no marriage!"

With his words Garret immediately understood not only the scene unfolding, but the purpose of the woman's midnight visit to his chamber. Maite had been right after all! Lynfyld's betrothed *was* being forced into marriage—and had sought last eve to escape it by nullifying what clearly were the terms of it.

Christ's eyes! he muttered silently. Instinctively he knew the course he was about to take was not a wise one. Still, he could not stand by and allow this travesty to proceed. That he could not do and remain a man. He slammed the door shut to make his presence known.

All eyes turned to him.

The desired effect achieved, he spoke. "Release her!"

Garret watched the men at the bed exchange furtive glances. He stepped forward, lifting his sword and advancing its point. "Loose her—now!'

With no belaying order coming from their own lord, the unarmed men responded, if not to the command, then to the threat. They released their holds, slinking away from the bed.

The midwife did likewise, retreating to her position by the window.

"There is no cause for concern, my lord." Charles dismissed his men with a wave and silently cautioned Lynfyld to keep still. In assessing the situation he had quickly realized that to defy their host would be a grave mistake. D'Aubigny's intrusion was untimely and certainly unfortunate, but there was no need to panic. He need only come forth with an explanation. "Actually . . . what is taking place, my lord . . ." He paused, forcing himself to swallow the bitter taste of subservience. ". . . is not your concern. 'Tis a simple family matter."

"It takes place under my roof and rouses me from sleep. It damned well is my *concern!*" Garret replied coldly, his eyes fixed on the pair of men exiting. The door closed and he turned his attention to Maitland's sister.

Whatever doubt still lingered disappeared at the sight of her face. Stained with tears, it begged for deliverance and implored him to act. Knowing he would later regret it, he answered her voiceless call. "I gave you no leave, Mistress. Return to my chamber."

Her gray eyes widened first with shock, and then understanding. She scrambled from the bed, clutching together the thin, torn undergown she wore.

The underlying meaning of his words was lost on neither of the men still by the bed. Maitland stiffened, and Lynfyld's mouth gaped.

"What are you saying?" the latter finally managed to gasp.

Preoccupied with forming his response, Garret did not notice that the woman had stopped a few feet from her brother. Once made, his claim could not be retracted. "I am saying," he stated slowly, "that if her virginity is a prerequisite for marriage, then, indeed, there will be none performed this day."

Lynfyld's face turned a purplish red and he wheeled on the man at his side. "I bargained with you for a *virgin* bride, Maitland! I'll take no other man's leavings! By the terms of our agreement I demand you return the sum paid—in full and within the week—or by God, I shall make known to all your plans for that silver!" Without waiting for a reply he stormed across the room.

Maitland stood as if stunned. Then, the sound of the door slamming at the baron's exit seemed to jolt him to the realization of his own loss.

Before Garret could react, he leaped forward and seized his sister's arm. "You little whore!" He shoved her from him with such force that she lost her balance and fell to the floor. "Whore!" he shouted again and spat.

But the trail of spittle never struck her. In a single movement Garret crossed the distance between them, seized him and slammed him back against the wall.

With his forearm locked across the man's upper chest he kept him immobile and turned to look down at the woman. "Return to my chamber—now!" His voice was soft but utterly commanding.

"Take your hands off me!" Maitland shouted.

Garret's sword hand tightened around the hilt of his blade as he beheld the man in his grasp. From the corner of his eye, he saw the woman rise to her feet, then stumble toward the door. With her out of harm's way he allowed the icy control to surge within him, that dispassionate inner restraint which enabled him to kill without hesitation. "Do you forget to whom you speak, liegeman?" he growled. His wrath now fully aroused, he moved his arm upward to press across his adversary's throat.

Maitland worked his mouth as if he wished to spit again.

Garret brought the point of his sword to the man's chin, and Maitland swallowed.

"I am owed compensation," he whispered hoarsely, his speech affected by the forearm at his throat. "What you took was not yours to take."

"Nor was it yours to sell," Garret answered, his voice complacent and cold. Keeping the sword poised, he released his hold. "Your sister offered herself freely. You are owed naught!"

Coughing and rubbing his throat, Charles glared at the man before him. He was not stupid enough to attack an opponent armed with a sword while he himself had none.

"I want you gone from this keep by noon." He spun on his heel and left the room.

Thought he heard d'Aubigny's command, he refused to acknowledge it. In mute defiance he watched as the man walked through the door.

"My payment, milord?"

"Payment?" Charles spun and glared at the room's only other remaining occupant. He had forgotten all about the midwife. Suddenly, the fury he had not been able to unleash upon his seigneur had a target. "You'll get not a penny, you old hag!" he shouted, giving full vent to his rage. "You performed no service!"

"I had not the chance!" the woman cried. Though she shrank in fear, she did not acquiesce. "'Twas through no fault of mine that Lord Garret interrupted, making his claim that you took so quick as gospel. Tell me, milord . . . if your sister *is* unchaste, why did she fight my examination? 'Twould only have proved what she apparently wanted known!"

The logic of the woman's words hit Charles like a fist. Why *would* Taryn have struggled?

"'Twould be easy enough to verify," the midwife continued. "You would be a fool, milord, not to demand proof of his claim."

Listening outside the door which had failed to swing completely closed behind him, Garret swore. He knew the direction the midwife's goading was headed. Without waiting to hear Maitland's response to it, he hastily made his way back to his own chamber.

Entering, he ignored the figure seated before the hearth and crossed the room to the bed. He tossed down his sword.

Taryn leaped to her feet. But there was no acknowledgement of her presence. She watched in bewilderment as the Great Earl of Arundel felt beneath his pillow, taking up the small dagger he located there.

"You are more trouble than you are worth, Mistress," he finally stated, casting her an icy glower. "But I'll not be exposed as a liar. I assure you, before the sun next rises, what I have told your brother will be truth and fact."

Something in his eyes warned her to keep silent. She watched as he brought the knife to his side. Stretching the taut, bare skin even tighter, he sliced the blade across a rib. The small line turned bright crimson, and as the blood began to flow he pressed his palm to it. A moment later he brought the hand away.

In almost morbid fascination she continued to watch his actions.

He leaned across the bed, cleaning his hand in the center of the snowy-white linens. Then, tossing the coverlet over the stain, he walked to the wash basin in the corner. The wound, skillfully made over bone, had already begun to clot. He washed and dried his hands, and had no sooner donned a shirt than there was a pounding at the door.

"That will be your brother," he stated evenly, moving toward the door. "Not a word from you, do you understand?"

She nodded, but the effort was wasted. His back was already to her.

He opened the door, and with the unconscious haughtiness of one accustomed to command, he addressed the man who stood there. "Your purpose for this intrusion, liegeman?"

Taryn had the distinct impression Garret d'Aubigny knew the answer to his own question. Before her half-brother even spoke, he moved aside as though to invite him in.

"I would see firsthand the evidence of my sister's shame," Charles answered curtly. He strode into the room and headed straight for the bed.

Heart pounding, Taryn looked to Jaune's lord.

There was not the slightest sign that he shared her apprehension. He leaned against the door frame, his arms crossed, his expression blank. Only his eyes gave him away. In shock she realized their pale depths shone with a gleam of satisfaction.

She looked back at Charles as he ripped aside the bed's covering of silk and fur. At the sight of the bloodied sheet, his face went gray.

"You thankless harlot!" he roared, turning to her.

Instinctively she shrank from his fury. But before he could act upon it, a deep voice sounded.

"If are you satisfied, take your leave." With head cocked, Taryn's champion indicated the way, kicking open the door. Though his arms were still crossed there was no mistaking the tension in his body. All amusement was gone from his eyes. They were hooded and veiled with violence. He was poised for attack.

Charles hesitated for only an instant. "I will have naught more to do with you," he growled at her as he retreated. "As you have gone to his bed, go you now into his care. And when he tires of you, let him do with you as he wills! You have no home at Wynshire, whore's daughter!"

Garret watched Maitland's departure with mixed feelings. As much as he enjoyed having bested the man, the fact that he now had to bear responsibility for his sister did not please him. What was he going to do with her?

He looked to the slender form garbed only in her flimsy undergown. At the moment no answer was forthcoming. What had he been thinking when he made his rash and ridiculous claim? Unfortunately, *that* answer came all too readily.

It had been the sight of her tears that had spurred him to act. He never could abide the sight of a woman's tears. Certainly Clarissa had known it, and used weeping to her every advantage. After that first night the mere prospect of her eyes filling with moisture had been enough to dampen his fiercest desires.

He looked at the woman waiting nervously for him to speak, but in her stead he saw his young wife. The painful memories churned, and though he shoved them back, he was helpless to remove the harshness from his voice. "Return to your chamber, Mistress, until you are summoned."

Taryn nodded numbly. She was free! But at what cost did her freedom come—and to what ends?

Chapter Six

Garret entered his chamber. Tired and preoccupied, he threw off his mantle and tossed it upon the bed in disgust. The ceaseless activities which had filled his day had not put from his thoughts—even for an instant—the question hammering in his mind. What was he going to do with the woman now housed within his walls?

For the hundredth time he muttered a silent oath. The answer he had rejected all day was still the only answer he had been able to conjure. Because of his own thoughtlessness as to the consequences, he would have to continue—at least for a short while—the charade that had been set into play. To keep Charles Maitland's sister safe, and his own word of honor unimpugned, she would have to pose as his leman.

"Damn it all," he swore aloud, raking his fingers through the hair that had escaped its leather binding to fall across his forehead. It was the last thing he needed—a virgin under his roof, posing as his mistress!

"My lord?"

The soft whisper intruding on his thoughts sent him whirling, blade drawn. "What are you doing here?" he demanded. The instant the words left his lips, he remembered. He had left orders for Maite to have her brought up to his chamber, that he might speak with the lady in private. He hadn't expected the old woman to have simply abandoned her in his quarters, though.

"I . . . I was told to await your return . . . here." Nervously she made a gesture to indicate the room.

He waved her silent and sheathed his sword. Removing the belt and scabbard, he placed them on the bed atop his discarded mantle. "Let us get on with this."

She could not know he was referring to the agreement he had decided must be reached between them. At once it became evident just what it was that she took his words to mean.

Garret saw her eyes widen and fill with an emotion he recognized too well: fear. Still, she stepped forward, her trembling fingers going to the laces at her throat. Suddenly he became aware of her state of dress—or rather undress. The lady wore no gown and mantle, merely a bedrobe. As that realization dawned, the sides of the wine-colored garment parted to expose first one breast and then the other, each creamy white.

Before he could speak she was completely naked, standing before him, the robe at her feet looking like the petals of a rose from which she had emerged. Quickly he recovered, a raised eyebrow the only indication of his shock. "'Tis twice in as many days you have presented yourself to me in this manner, Mistress. Ne'er have I know a virgin so anxious to lose her maidenhead."

Instead of coloring with shame as a chaste maid should have, she met his gaze straight on. With all the bravado of a whore, he thought, his shock yielding to amazement.

"And how many virgins have you known, my lord?" she then countered.

His reaction to her retort was instant and fierce. Every muscle in his body tensed. The only virgin he had known was Clarissa. Remembrances of their wedding night flashed in his brain, burning like a white-hot iron.

"Enough," he answered tersely, completely unnerved. Whether by the unexpected sight of the woman's unclothed body (far more visible now by waning daylight than it had been the previous night by firelight), or by the sudden resurgence of the past, he wasn't sure. "Clothe yourself," he commanded, fighting for control. "I do not intend to do anything on an empty belly."

Only then did he see the faintest rise of color. But he was too concerned with his own discomfiture to appreciate it. He stormed to the door, flung it open and walked out into the hallway. "Maite!" he roared down the stairwell.

Taryn took advantage of his absence and quickly bent to retrieve her robe. She had just pulled it on when he reappeared in the doorway.

Avoiding her eyes, he crossed the room and dropped into one of the two chairs at a small table by the window. "We will eat here."

She hestitated for a moment, then realized his gruff statement was, in fact, an invitation to be seated. She rounded his chair, taking her seat across from him.

In stony silence he stared past her, unseeing, to the window at her back.

Taryn frowned in consternation. Obviously Jaune's lord was not one for conversation! From beneath a screen of lowered lashes she studied her taciturn host.

As upon his arrival the previous evening, his clothing was commonplace, that of a simple knight—a plain cotton *bliaut*, knee-length, mud brown in color and bearing not a single band of embroidered silk or gold lace.

She glanced over to the bed. His discarded mantle was equally plain, unadorned by fringes or tassels or precious stones. His sword, as she had noted earlier, was no proud lord's weapon with a silvered and jeweled hilt. In fact, in this man before her there was nothing at all of the ostentatious display of wealth Charles so favored. Save an ornate chess board atop a low trestle table by the fireplace, the furnishings of his chamber comprised no more than bare necessities, austere and spartan. Had she now known better, she would have thought herself in the presence of a lowly baron.

Except for his mien, she realized with an icy shiver. In

Garret d'Aubigny's arrogant bearing there was nothing humble. Beyond question or doubt, his demeanor was that of the highest of lords.

She shifted her attention back to him. Still her presence went unacknowledged. Knowing that until he spoke she must remain silent, she lowered her eyes. She did not raise them until she heard footsteps and a familiar voice.

"My lord. Lady Taryn."

Maite stood in the doorway. In her hands she carried a tray laden with several dishes of food, a pitcher and two goblets.

At last the lord of Jaune spoke.

"Enter, old woman, and see that you keep your tongue still."

To Taryn the harsh reprimand was undue. Yet from the tiny figure approaching the table it merely elicited a soft laugh. Maite set down the tray and distributed the dishes before them.

Taryn paid their contents no heed. Her focus was on the curious and mute exchange which seemed to be taking place between Garret d'Aubigny and his serving woman.

That Maite was somehow amused, or pleased about something, was clear. At what, Taryn could not fathom. She was certain of the old woman's emotions; she was equally sure of his.

The man seated before her was *not* amused. His eyes never left the old woman as he watched her pour dark wine into the goblets and set a cup in front of each of them.

As soon as she was finished, he dismissed her with a curt nod. "That will be all."

"Indeed, my lord." With the tone of her voice the woman made her response a question—a question which evoked an instant scowl on the face of her lord.

"Not another word, Maite," he warned through teeth clenched in restraint.

"Wouldn't think of it, my lord," she replied. But her eyes betrayed her words. As she bowed and withdrew, they crinkled in unabashed triumph.

More puzzled than ever, Taryn looked at her dinner companion.

His face now devoid of emotion, he took from his waist a short, triangular dagger. Spearing one of the half dozen roasted partridges on the platter before him, he lifted the bird and unceremoniously deposited it on her plate. A small round loaf of white bread followed, and she grimaced.

Though clean, the knife's thin blade bore the scratches of frequent use. Reflecting upon the nature of that use—to administer the *coup de grâce* to a fallen foe—Taryn shuddered.

"Again, Mistress? 'Tis twice now you have shivered. Mayhap with dropping your robe everytime I set eyes upon you, you have caught a chill."

Taryn glared at him and struggled for a response. She could sense his silent laughter and the realization that he had been watching her all this time unnerved her more than she wanted to admit. Had he been sizing up what was to be the last course of his meal?

The apprehension she felt in that dreaded knowledge faded in the face of her outrage at being scrutinized as some sort of sweetmeat yet to be savored. She lifted her chin defiantly. "You made quite clear this morning your intent, my lord. I only desired to have the matter dispatched posthaste." She paused and took a deep breath. "I did not expect to be made first to sit and partake of a meal in your saturnine company," she finished coldly.

Lifting an amused brow, he took up his goblet. "Prefer you, then, that we take to my bed?"

"As you wish, my lord." She pushed back from the table, standing before she realized what her defiance had wrought. Her challenge—which was no real challenge, but a childish act of spite—had been taken up! He would have her now.

She froze. The beat of her heart drummed in her ears. Swaying unsteadily, she watched him drain the goblet. Her fingers gripped the table's edge in fearful anticipation.

But he did not move to stand. The brittle silence between them seemed to last an eternity. Finally, he broke it.

"Sit."

Though scarcely above a whisper, his command, harsh and raw, tore through her. As he set his goblet down, she collapsed into the chair.

In fury Garret stared at her. It had been a mistake to have had her brought here, to have had her sit across the small table from him. He was helpless to pull his gaze from the unlaced front of her robe. Beneath the soft fabric the lush curves of her breasts taunted him with a truth he fought to disavow. He wanted her.

Had she been a town whore or a village wench, she'd have been bedded by now, without hesitation. But she was neither whore nor wench. She was a lady, of gentle birth and blood. And though her actions hardly lent credence to the fact—she *was* a virgin. He refilled his goblet and struggled to find an explanation. Perhaps she was a demivirge, as were many of the ladies at court—one whose sexual activities stopped just short of intercourse.

And if that be the case, where did that leave him? Without conscious thought he drained his cup again. Setting it on the table, he stood. His appetite—at least for food—was gone. Ignoring her startled gaze, he moved to the fireplace and set a log upon the low flames. He had to distance himself from the source of his confusion. Where were the instincts which had served him so well last night? Thinking her a lady free with her favours, he had felt no interest. Now, knowing she was virgin, he was fighting arousal. How he woud enjoy this irony—were it not *his* loins afire!

His solitude was short lived. Barely had he seated

himself upon the bench when he sensed her presence and heard her voice.

"My lord."

In disbelief he raised his eyes. She stood before him, his goblet cupped and offered in her hands.

But at last the wine had taken effect, dulling his senses sufficiently that his qualms of conscience now seemed half-witted. He would rethink his position, he decided. He would give her one last chance . . .

He smiled mockingly. "Is it your intent to render me too drunk to perform, Mistress?" With his words he felt his blood stir and knew if she responded with her characteristic shamelessness he would act.

"Nay, my lord."

But her face belied her answer. Drained of all color, it was as white as the linens on his bed.

His desire went cold. For in that instant he knew, despite her outward boldness and previous actions, the woman before him was terrified. In a curious mixture of disappointment and relief he looked away.

To have had one sobbing, hysterical virgin lying beneath him was enough for this lifetime. The decision he had made earlier would stand. He sighed and rubbed his hand across his eyes. "You enjoy a unique honor, Mistress," he stated dryly. "On this day you have made of me a liar—not once, but twice. First in my declaration to your brother, and now. I rescind my morning's oath. I would not take you by force or in shame, rifting from you what should be freely given."

"My lord?" She looked at him, bewildered.

Garret groaned in exasperation. Were his words not clear enough? "I possess neither the desire nor the disposition to take your virginity, Mistress."

Her lovely face clouded with deeper confusion, then fear. "If you do not, my brother—"

"Will not find out otherwise," he interrupted sharply. What he was about to propose had been given great thought, and, until he had sat down across from her, had seemed judicious. "As far as your brother knows, you are no virgin. He'll find it no easy task to marry you off—that is, should he decide to take you back into his keep. Even if he does succeed in arranging a marriage, as his seigneur I must approve the match. I will not do so unless you are agreeable to his choice. We will sustain the lie which has been born this day. If it is believed you are now my leman, it will make Charles' task all the more difficult."

He paused for a moment, waiting for an answer. Then, taking her silence for assent, he continued. "In the meantime, as I cannot leave you in unprotected celibacy, I will seek out for you a suitable husband from within my own entourage." He reached out his hand. "Now . . . my cup, and to bed with you."

Wordlessly, she handed him the goblet and took a hesitant step toward the door. Stopping, she turned and looked at him. "My lord?"

"Aye?"

"Thank you . . . for what you did . . . said . . . this morning . . . and for now."

Uncomfortable with her expression of gratitude—for he regretted still his actions—Garret stared into the rising flames. Before this day his words had never contained any falsity. "To bed, Mistress," he replied stiffly. He closed his eyes and listened for the sound of her retreating footsteps.

"My lord?"

"What now?" he growled. He gripped the goblet he held with both hands. By all that was holy! Why did she not leave?

"Might you fancy a game?"

"What?" Garret opened his eyes in utter dismay. Once dismissed, he had expected her to flee from him like a frightened deer. But almost like a knight standing ground, she remained where she was.

"'Tis magnificent." She gestured to the low table

mounted with a massive chessboard of onyx and alabaster which stood a few feet from him. One of Garret's few opulent possessions, the board and its heavy ivory pieces had been a gift from King Henry.

"Might you fancy a game?" she repeated. "I was taught by my father. He always said I played as well as any man. I can offer you a challenge."

Her expectant, almost mischievous smile sent his pulses racing anew. "*That* you have already done, Mistress." Ignoring the sudden inner voice that warned him to send her away, he set the goblet down, reached out and pulled the table nearer. At least the game would give him something to occupy his thoughts—something besides the lithe figure now kneeling before him without invitation. He looked down at her. Though he did not consciously realize that he now saw her differently, his words reflected the change. "Ladies first," he said softly.

A curious smile touched her lips. "I thank you for not addressing me as 'mistress'. Now that I am posing as such, I do not relish the word as a continual form of address. Under these . . . ah . . . unusual circumstances, my lord . . . do you think we might be less formal? I was christened Taryn."

At the sound of her name, a sensation pulsed through him, as uncontrollable as his earlier arousal had been. This feeling was foreign and unnerving as well. He laughed in an effort to dismiss it. "Very well . . . *Taryn*. Hand me that goblet and make your move."

In less than a dozen moves Garret regretted having tossed down the wine. True to her word, Lady Taryn Maitland was as skilled as any man he had played. He had to concentrate fiercely just to stay even. The wine-induced stupor seemed only to blunt his mental senses. Physically he was as alert as ever to her presence.

Her scent, ironically enough—given his earlier impression of her—was one of roses, and it lingered in his nostrils despite the repeated deep breaths he drew to dispel it. Nor could he keep his eyes from returning to the site where two gracefully bent fingers kept her robe closed.

At one point she reached out across the board to capture his knight, and loosed that hold. The left side of the robe slipped from her shoulder. This time he was near enough to her to see clearly the sharp contrast of pale flesh and dusky nipple. His breath became instantly ragged.

Still, the game progressed, but Garret found his attention gone from it completely. He considered putting an end to it. He would ride into the village and avail himself of one of the whores he bedded regularly—easier yet, why not summon up the buxom kitchen wench from below? Quickly he decided against either course of action.

Refusing to acknowledge that there might be another reason for his reluctance, he told himself he dared not risk her brother learning the truth.

The nagging logic which told him that as lord he could do as he pleased—mistress or no—he shunned. As long as this charade was in existence, his would be a celibate life. The prospect was hardly pleasant, and unwittingly, he groaned aloud.

Taryn heard his groan, but took it for a sign of a different frustration. The arrogant lord of Castle Jaune was not pleased with the prospect of losing. She made two foolish moves and the game was soon over, her queen captured.

Thinking he would be appeased with his win, she looked up. Despite the low firelight she could see that his face was hard-set, his eyes cold.

"Do not make that mistake again, Mistress. I will not be given what I cannot take. And if I want it, I *will* take it! Tonight the victory is yours."

Taryn stared at him, speechless at the icy tone of his voice. Then, her temper flared. She flipped back the braid which lay nestled across her shoulder and rose from her sitting position to her knees. She cowered in front of no man's prideful blustering. It was a quality in her Charles could never abide. Whether noble or peasant, women were regarded by her half-brother as being lesser than men in all aspects, base creatures suitable for but a single purpose. Clearly the Great Earl of Arundel was of a like mindset.

So be it—but he would not be taking out on her the anger he felt at his inability to best a believed inferior in a fair contest! "Mayhap we'd best establish the rules of this charade ere we commence to play it, my lord," she stated quietly, firmly. She noted and ignored the look of surprise which appeared in his cold green eyes. "That I am in your debt is a fact I do not dispute. And I *am* grateful for your aid this day. But I'll not be treated as aught less than I am. In spite of my gender, I have intelligence and worth."

Garret clenched his mouth tight and fought a sudden smile. The lady's mettle was worthy of a man. Few of his own vassals would confront him so directly. It was no wonder Charles had been anxious to marry her off. He could well imagine the challenge she must have presented that self-important peacok. Well, one fact was certain. She'd not be creating the same havoc under his roof. The lady had been correct in her declaration. It *was* time to establish the rules. There was but one who wore the breeches in his household.

He stood, careful to guard his expression. "Worth?" he repeated. "Aye, worth you have. And tonight your worth shall be as a bed warmer."

"My lord?"

The panic he heard in her voice nearly provoked him to laughter. Where was her mettle now? It appeared to have fled along with her color. He rubbed a hand across his mouth to conceal the smile he could hold back no longer.

She stumbled to her feet. "I don't understand."

"'Tis simple enough," he answered easily, moving

toward the great canopied bed. "Certes, you did not think to sleep in a bed other than my own? 'Tis a poor mistress who would let her master crawl betwixt cold sheets. And you *did* agree to pose as my mistress, did you not?"

He had to turn away lest he burst out in laughter. However, under the pretense of removing the mantle, sword and scabbard from the bed, he was able to watch her from the corner of his eye.

Although unlike peasants, castlefolk slept naked, he was certain it could not be modestey which kept Taryn Maitland firmly rooted to the spot she occupied. Having twice dropped her robe in front of him, it was clear the lady possessed little of that virtue. Her pride had to be battling her fear.

Suddenly Garret recalled his own earlier reaction to the sight of her partial undress as she had sat across from him. Even now his blood stirred at the mere thought of her naked body beside his. His intent was to show the sharp-tongued wench her place—not to mete himself punishment!

"You may keep the robe, Mistress," he offered, hoping the mockery he'd forced into his voice would conceal his rising uneasiness.

Her sigh of relief went unheard—lost in his own.

Taryn forced herself to lie still. She didn't want to risk her restless movements waking the man beside her. More importantly, she didn't want the Great Earl of Arundel to know she was unable to sleep. But how *was* she supposed to sleep—with his unclothed body not a foot from her! The bed was wide enough; did he have to lie so close she could feel the warmth of him?

In the same silent breath she bemoaned her plight and berated herself. Why hadn't she left well enough alone—thanking him and leaving when she'd had the chance? Instead, because she had for some unfathomable reason wanted to stay, she had offered the chess game as an excuse.

That, too, had been a mistake. Her forfeiture of the game had angered him more than her certain victory would have. And his resultant indignation had done nothing but worsen the situation by igniting her own stubborn pride. Would she ever learn to curb her tongue, to learn her place?

Moira's voice echoed in her mind. How often her nurse had spoken those words! She'd always said too, though, that the fault was not Taryn's. The late Earl of Wynshire had indulged his second born, filling her head with foolish ideas. Hence she had never learned—or even learned to feign—that role of subservience most women seemingly acquired at birth.

But the thought was of no comfort to his daughter now. Whether innate or taught, Taryn's refusal to accept that lesser station which was her woman's due had landed her just where she was—in the bed of a man who intended to teach it to her by humiliating her!

She tensed in anger. Of Garret d'Aubigny's motive she was sure, as sure as she was that he would also keep his word. He would not touch her. So what was this strange sense of frustration and fear she was feeling? Her honor was safe.

Suddenly she felt the toes of her left foot curl. An instant later the muscles in her calf contracted. She tried to flex her ankle, but the effort was futile. It was as though there were a steel rod running the length of her lower leg. She gritted her teeth and stifled a cry of distress. Every muscle in her body screamed in protest now. She had to walk—and to walk she would have to stand.

Silently calling forth every oath she had ever heard, she slowly edged to the side of the bed. Senses tuned, alert for a change in his breathing which would indicate she had awakened the man asleep beside her, she sat up. With a sigh of half pain, half relief, she placed her feet upon the cold floor.

"I gave you no leave, Mistress."

Taryn gasped at the sound of his voice. At some unconscious level she noted that it contained not the barest trace of sleepiness. He had been awake the entire time!

"I've a cramp in my leg," she snapped. "I need to walk."

She slid off the bed—and promptly cried out in agony as her full weight was put upon the affected limb.

"Sit down."

She obeyed. Not because she wanted to, but because she had to. If she hadn't, she'd have collapsed to the floor. She felt his weight leave the bed. A moment later she saw his shadowy form moving toward her. Silently she gave thanks for the darkness.

"Right or left?"

"Left."

Without another word he knelt before her, taking her ankle into his large hands and bracing her foot against his bare thigh.

Taryn closed her eyes, darkness aside. No man had ever touched her in such a manner. The intimacy was unnerving, somehow frightening, threatening . . .

Beginning at a place just above her ankle, he began to massage her leg, slowly moving upward to her knee. The warmth of his hands, intensified by the friction he created rubbing the cramped muscle, soon became a soothing heat. She could feel the tightness abating. But before she could truly appreciate the feeling, the heat was no longer soothing. Suddenly more intense, it seemed to be creeping up her thigh.

A low moan bubbled up in her throat—a moan which had nothing to do with the pain his skillful ministrations had eased. "'Tis all right now," she proclaimed, her voice quivering. She wanted to pull her leg away, but could not.

He ignored her and continued. His fingers, working the muscle, never ventured past her knee. Yet she could feel a peculiar, tingling sensation between her thighs as the heat became greater, higher and deeper.

Completely unnerved, confused by what she was feeling, Taryn cried out in fear. "My lord, please!"

He threw off her foot and stood.

Feeling his anger, knowing he had taken umbrage with her, she could only whisper a tremulous, feeble apology. "I'm sorry."

"Leave."

"My lord?"

"Leave. Now." His cold voice was without inflection, ringing with command.

She stood hesitantly, expecting him to say more, to vent his anger. Her fear and confusion only grew when he did not.

Suddenly she felt lost in his silence. And though she had done nothing wrong, she felt shamed. Inexplicable tears welled in her eyes. For the first time in her adult life she had no whetted words to disguise and shield her emotions. Like a child running to its room to cry itself to sleep after a beating, she fled from the man before her.

Chapter Seven

Taryn stood in the window embrasure of her chamber. Bathed in the glorious early morning light which entered in rainbow hues through the stained glass, she was, nevertheless, oblivious to the serene beauty of the apse-like alcove. Within her a silent storm raged.

A week had passed since the night she had fled in tears from Garret d'Aubigny. In that time she had known nothing but idleness and isolation, and virtual silence from the man who had ordered her to keep to her chamber save for the taking of meals.

Even now she bristled in remembering his command, and the manner in which he had issued it.

Still shaken by the events of the previous night, she had entered the great hall for the day's first meal, hoping to make amends with him. It had taken but one look at his face to tell her it was not to be.

His cold, mute stare had said more to her than words ever could. Without bothering to stand, he had gestured that she was to take the chair directly to his left. They had eaten in silence. When he had finished, he stood.

"Upon entering this hall you shall take only that chair. Except to eat, and unless otherwise summoned, you shall stay in your chamber."

So shocked had she been by his order, Taryn had been able only to nod. Then he had left.

In the following days scarcely a dozen words had passed between them. At first she had tried to remain indifferent to his behavior, reminding herself of the debt she owed him. Were it not for his intervention, she would be Lynfyld's wife. Nor could she forget the payment he could have taken in return. But as the week wore on, her grateful attitude toward him became less so. She had not asked for aid, nor asked him to give his word falsely. If he felt trapped, it was in a trap of his own making. That she should suffer for his poor judgment infuriated her.

"Enough!" she suddenly shouted, whirling from the colored panes. She would endure not another moment of this exile. If he regretted his decision, then let him make another. Let him send her away—to a nunnery. How much worse could that cloistered existence be from that which she now knew?

She crossed the room, stopping long enough to snatch up her cloak. Tossing it around her shoulders, she headed for the door. At least it was not yet kept locked, she thought, her anger rising still more.

She entered the corridor and made her way to the stairwell. She didn't know where he could be found, but she would find him. She would seek him out and confront him. One way or another, her imprisonment would end this day!

"Lady Taryn."

Maite's familiar form stood poised on the landing. Her arms laden with fresh bedding, the old woman looked at her, surprise evident in her eyes.

Taryn tensed, fully expecting the woman to send her back to her chamber.

Instead, Maite inclined her head in greeting. A slight smile touched her lips. "Didn't think 'twould take this long. You near disappointed me."

Taryn stared at her in confusion. But there was no further explanation of the strange comment. Maite shifted the linens in her arms to a more comfortable position and headed up the stairs to her lord's chamber above.

Taryn watched the tiny form until it had disappeared. Then, as she took the first stair downward, she heard Maite's voice once more.

"You'll find him out in the yard, by the stables."

Taryn turned. Even as she peered into the darkness, she knew the woman was gone. How had she known Taryn's intent? Pushing the question aside, she descended the staircase, quickly passing from the anteroom through the great hall.

There she found the room's massive portals open to the morning air. Two serfs carrying in a large log for one of the hall's two fireplaces stepped aside to let her pass. She dipped her head in acknowledgement and proceeded through the doorway. Abruptly she stopped, blinking to adjust her eyes to their first exposure to direct sunlight in better than a week. Reveling in the rays' warmth, she found her resolve strengthened further. Garret d'Aubigny be damned! She would be shut up within the damp, cold stone walls of his prison tower no longer.

She descended the stairs to the bailey and crossed the yard, headed for the outer ward and the stables she remembered seeing upon her arrival.

The clang of metal striking metal, at first faint, grew in strength as she neared her goal. She knew the sound well. It was the sound of knights training, of sword meeting sword as they practiced and honed their deadly battlefield art.

Her step quickened, and she soon found herself overly warm. Though it was only late March, the sun shone with the intensity of summer. With little need for the heavy woolen cloak upon her shoulders, she shrugged it off. Draping the garment over her arm, she approached the stables and paused to get her bearings.

Save a couple of serfs cleaning the stalls, the area was deserted, yet the sound of clanging metal was louder than ever, and clearly punctuated with the shouts of many men. Focusing on the clamor, she realized its source came from the direction of an open gate in the curtain wall.

She walked to the gate and found herself at the entrance of a third bailey. The absence of structures made clear the function of this area, that of an exercise yard for both man and beast. Here a score of men were gathered about a dozen fully armored pairs, who went at each other with sword and ax. The clunking of steel weapon meeting wooden shield was rivaled only by the shouts of the onlookers. She scanned the men gathered, but did not see the one she sought. A few of the men, however, noticed her.

Almost at once the air became still. Those engaged in combat stopped in mid-swing to see the reason for their audience's sudden disinterest. Setting eyes upon her, they all, to a man, bowed.

"I seek your lord," Taryn stated, painfully aware of the covert looks now being exchanged and the whisper of voices which had replaced the shouts of only moments earlier.

"Then you've come to the proper place, lady." One man, his bearded face flushed and streaming with sweat, stepped forward. He sheathed his sword and bowed. "Sir Ronald, milady, at your service. Lord Garret is there . . ." He gestured to the far side of yard which contained several tilting paths, replete with quintains. "He's attempting to instruct a couple of squires in the art of sitting a horse. If you'll follow me, I'll take you to him."

A ripple of soft laughter rose from the men's ranks, and Taryn felt her color rise in response. She had forgotten her role to these men, that of their lord's leman. No doubt they figured her wanting of his attention and hence arrived in pursuit of it. "Thank you, Sir Ronald," she managed to reply.

She followed him across the yard to one of the sand-covered lanes set at regular intervals with bales of hay. Around the bales raced a huge black horse. Low in the saddle, its rider guided the animal at near breakneck speed through the maze-like pattern.

Intrigued with the skill of both rider and mount, Taryn paused to watch.

"There's not a man in England who sits a horse better than our lord," Sir Ronald stated, his voice lowered, clearly in awe.

Our lord. With the man's words Taryn's gaze shot back to the rider, now dismounting at the far end of the list. There was no doubt as to his identity. The proud carriage of his head, the set of his wide shoulders would have been recognizable to her at twice the distance. She watched as he handed the reins to a waiting youth and stepped aside.

The boy mounted and set his heels to the horse's flanks. The first turns he took with relative ease, though at nowhere near the speed of his instructor. With these first successful maneuvers his confidence seemed to grow, however, and he increased his horse's pace.

"Milady."

Sir Ronald propelled her forward, but her attention remained on the boy.

Several more turns were taken, then, suddenly, the horse seemed to balk. Fighting his rider's control, he shied from a turn and the boy went flying.

Taryn gasped and stepped forward.

"Nay, milady." Sir Ronald set a restraining hand upon her arm. "You'll only embarrass the boy more. All 'tis hurt is his pride."

True to the man's words, the boy stumbled to his feet.

She smiled, seeing him struggle bravely against the tears that rolled down his dusty cheeks, leaving a dirty trail in their wake.

"'Tis all right, boy. You merely turned him too hard."

Taryn froze at the sound of the familiar voice.

Clearly, her presence had not yet been noticed by Garret d'Aubigny, as he strode forward and clapped the boy reassuringly on the back, raising a cloud of dust. "A man must handle his horse as he makes love to his woman—firmly, so there's no doubt who holds the reins, but gently, too."

Taryn heard the man beside her fight to stifle a chuckle, and her earlier embarrassment returned, this time even deeper.

But the arrogant lord of Jaune was not yet finished with his debasing analogy. "Like making love, Tom, remember. Just as a woman is apt to do, a horse only lets you *think* you are master. Treat him harshly and he will quick enough prove to you the true order of things."

The man beside Taryn burst out into laughter. "Mayhap you should wait 'til the boy has been with a woman, milord. From the look on his face I fear you make a comparison beyond the realm of his experiences."

Garret looked up. The smile on his face died at once as he saw her.

She bristled at his naked hostility, and her temper flared. Unable to halt her words, she spewed forth a week's worth of frustration and anger. "Mayhap you should wait 'til you know yourself how a woman thinks and acts. In your dealings with the one who stands before you, milord, 'tis most clear you are no more skilled than the boy you attempt to teach."

Garret d'Aubigny's reaction was immediate and furious. He grabbed her arm and jerked her from his man's side. "*If and when* you have a complaint, Mistress, I'll thank you to make it in private!"

"And how might I accomplish that, milord," she countered hotly, "when you have avoided me at every turn since sending me from your bed?" She fought to disengage herself from his grasp and succeeded only in compelling him to tighten it. Her cloak fell to the ground.

"Leave off with your struggle, wench," he snarled, "and we will discuss your grievance." Without waiting for a reply, he pulled her toward the privacy and shade offered by the dark shadows of the outer curtain wall and released her.

"Now speak, ere I forget your station and administer

the beating your actions rightly deserve."

Taryn lifted her chin and took a deep breath. She must keep both her temper in check and her wits sharp. "I'll not be treated as a prisoner, locked away save for the taking of meals." Despite her silent resolve, the fingers which moved to smooth and straight her gown trembled. "'Tis bad enough you accord me the respect of a scullery maid . . ."

He raised a brow, yet remained silent. But had he spoken his thoughts, she would have known them no less clearly. Her outburst of minutes ago *was* undeserving of a lady.

"I offer an apology," she murmured somewhat begrudgingly, "to have confronted you before your man was unseemly. But surely you must understand what life has become for me here."

If possible, the brow arched higher. His cold green stare impaled her. "Is it so insufferable, Mistress? Are you not clothed and fed, given a roof over your head?"

"'Tis not enough!" she cried in exasperation. "I am accustomed to running a keep, accustomed to activity, ofttimes ceaseless, from sunup to sundown. Here—" She swept her arm in a gesture that encompassed their surroundings. "Here I have naught but idleness and loneliness to fill my day. My lord, I beseech you. I don't know what I have done to evoke your disfavor, but 'tis clear I have, and yet I appeal to you. I cannot continue as I have."

"Desire you then to be released from our agreement?"

Taryn heard a curious rise and fall in the tone of his voice, as if an initial lilt of excitement were then tempered by reflective disappointment. "Nay, my lord," she replied. This time it was she who lifted a brow, but in bewilderment. "I desire only the opportunity to be useful."

She was almost certain she heard a sigh of relief. But as he had turned to signal Sir Ronald forward, she couldn't verify the thought by looking upon his face.

"See Maite," he stated, returning his attention to her. "She will readily enough find aught for you to do."

From the corner of her eye Taryn saw Sir Ronald's approach. Hastily she made her second request. "And your command that I remain shut away in my chamber?"

This time there was no mistaking the sound he expelled. The blasphemous oath muttered under his breath caused her to cringe, and she fought the urge to cross herself.

"You can scarce be of use to Maite *and* remain shut away, now can you, Mistress?" He raked his hair from his forehead with an angry, stabbing motion. "I rescind my order. 'Tis something I seem to do often enough"—again his eyes bored into her—"of late."

"Milord?" Pausing at a respectable distance, Sir Ronald bowed.

"Escort the Lady Taryn back to the hall."

"At once, milord. Lady?" He held open her cloak, chivalrously retrieved and shaken free of dust.

Taryn stepped forward, turning that he might set the wrap upon her shoulders. Any thought she might have entertained of thanking Garret d'Aubigny vanished as he wheeled without another word and headed back to the waiting squires and horses. Suddenly chilled, she gathered the folds to her.

Garret entered his chamber and stripped off his *bliaut.* His shirt, tugged up and over his head, followed. Instead of tossing it to the floor as he had his tunic, he balled the fine linen and rubbed it down his torso, wiping away the sweat trickling down his chest.

"Do you know how difficult 'tis to remove such stains?" A towel sailed through the air toward him, launched from behind a carven screen in the room's corner. "If 'twas *your* shoulders that ached from pounding the wash in a trough filled with wood ashes and lime, you'd quick enough stop that habit!"

Garret glowered at the parclose. "I'm not of a mind this morning to tolerate your nagging, old woman."

Smiling, Maite rounded the screen, wiping her hands on the apron knotted about her waist. "I gather then, from your foul mood, that she talked to you?"

Garret tossed the shirt to the floor and wiped his face with the towel. "Aye." He knew better than to bother asking how she knew of his conversation with the fiery-haired wench. Maite always knew. And what little she didn't know by virtue of her special "gift," she gleaned through castle gossip. Though it had occurred only an hour ago, he had no doubt the entire keep was now abuzz with talk of the confrontation in the exercise yard.

He kept his expression blank and glanced toward the screen.

"Aye, your bath is ready," Maite answered in response to his unvoiced question. "Though I'm at a loss to understand this peculiar habit of yours to bathe at mid-morning."

"Because now is when I desire it. The sweat and dust are as a second skin after the morning's training." With his words he instantly realized the opportunity he'd given her to broach the very subject he did not want to discuss. He sat on the bed to remove his boots and grinned. With Maite, as with warfare, he had learned the best defense was an offensive maneuver. "Besides, what is this propensity of yours of late? You've not bathed me so much since I was a babe in arms. Do we suddenly suffer a shortage of serving maids?"

He stood, and without bothering first to undo the thongs which attached his hose to the breech-girdle, untied the cord at his waist. Indifferent to the presence of the tiny woman, he then peeled off *braies* and hose together.

"Nay, we've no shortage of wenches, mouths fair watering at the prospect of bathing their lord in the hope of then sharing his bed that night." Maite signified her opinion on the matter with a sniff of disdain. "'Tis another habit of yours known well enough. Have no fear. You're not losing your appeal. But whilst you have the Lady Taryn in your care, 'twould serve you well to exercise a bit of restraint."

At the mention of the lady's name his grin turned to a frown. He stepped into the waiting wooden tub with an oath on his lips.

"Well?"

"Well what?" He sat and set about locating the cake of soap sunk to the tub's floor.

"What happened this morning?"

"What do you think happened, Maite?" he answered curtly, knowing the battle was lost. His fingers closed around the soap. "I relented—as it seems I must do every time her will opposes mine."

Silently Maite smiled at his choice of words. Her proud lord did not say he had yielded, capitulated, or acquiesced to the lady's demands. Nor would he have. Such words would imply defeat. Instead, he had selected a word which suggested the choice had been his.

His choice, she mused. He'd had the choice all right—as much choice as ice had whether or not to melt under the summer sun!

Suddenly the air rang with her laughter. She liked the image playing in her mind, an image of her lord's cold control dissolving as it was now confronted with the fiery will of the flame-haired woman now under his protection.

"She wants to be useful." Garret cast her a scathing look and continued. "'Twould seem a life of leisure is not to the lady's liking. I told her to talk to you. Find something to keep her occupied—and out of my sight."

"As you wish, my lord." Maite composed herself and approached the tub, washing cloth in hand.

"'Tis not as *I* wish, but as she wishes." Angrily he grabbed for the cloth, snatching it from her grasp. "She has also been accorded the freedom to go as she pleases."

"And?" Maite fought another spurt of laughter.

"And what? She made only those requests."

"Then I make a third, on her behalf, and for your own."

"You speak in riddles, old woman."

Maite sighed. How could what was so obvious to her be so unrecognizable to others? "As the lady did not bring up the subject of your treatment of her, I shall. You cannot continue to ignore her as you have—not if you hope this deception of yours to go undiscovered. Who will believe you took the baron's betrothed as mistress, only now to pay her no heed?"

He looked at her in surprise. Clearly the concern she voiced had not occurred to him.

"I know you didn't take her chastity," she stated gently, knowing she treaded dangerous ground. "Thus far, I am the only one who knows. But unless you begin to treat her in a manner befitting a man who desired her enough to steal her from another on her wedding eve, your secret will soon be known to all."

"As much as I am loathe to admit it . . . what you say has merit and bears heeding," he conceded slowly. "Very well. I shall cease to ignore her. Now . . . go to her. I have no wish that this morning's antics be repeated. And if the insolent chit thinks I have not acted quickly enough, 'tis sure to be another public scene."

Maite smiled and withdrew. Truly in his "mistress" Garret d'Aubigny had met his match. Now all she had to do was somehow arrange it so that there would sufficient contact between them. She took the stairs to the floor directly below with a spring in her step.

Taryn glanced up at the sun, now nearly centered in the azure sky. She closed her eyes and offered a silent prayer of thanksgiving. For the first time since Charles' announcement of her impending betrothal she felt a sense of well-being. She had escaped his loathesome plans. Once again she could look forward to the future and whatever it might hold.

And what might her future hold, she wondered suddenly. The life she had known at Wynshire was ended. She could no longer lay lawful claim to that which had been hers. She was now in strange and unfamiliar surroundings, alone, separated from loved ones . . .

Her eyes filled with tears, and like a cloud moving in front of the sun, sadness at the loss of those she had once held so dear threatened to darken the bright promise of hope which had shone only a moment before.

She lowered her gaze and blinked back her tears. There was as much to celebrate as to mourn. The victory achieved this morning had been no small feat. She must not let the concessions won become less meaningful because of self-pity. Already she had exercised her regained freedom, exploring her new home in preparation for her new life.

The tour of Jaune had been Maite's idea. After Taryn had been returned to the great hall by Sir Ronald, she had retired to her chamber, giddy with her triumph and yet uncertain as to what to do with it. She then remembered Garret's instruction. But before she could seek Maite out, the woman had come to her.

She offered no immediate instructions, suggesting instead that by acquainting herself with the operation of Jaune, Taryn might find a task which suited her. Richard's competence as steward aside, on a manor the size of Jaune there were sure to be duties better suited to a woman's hand.

Taryn had followed the old woman's advice. Departing the keep, she had first wandered the inner bailey, then the outer, and had learned much of this place. Jaune's inner court, site of the keep's outside kitchen and granary, was large enough to also contain a formal garden, a vegetable garden, a poultry yard and a small fish pond. Almost like a village in and of itself, the outer yard possessed a forge, carpenter's shop, brewhouse, and falconry. In addition to the stables and more than a dozen small thatch-roofed cottages of wattle and daub which provided housing for the keep's servants, there was also a chapel.

To see it all had taken her the better part of an hour. But despite it all, no idea had been born as to what role she might fulfill.

Discouraged, she cast a final glance about her, then looked up once more to the sun. The morning meal would be served soon. She turned in the direction of the keep, shaking her head.

Though she had been at Jaune for a week, she still could not reconcile herself to this odd, and to her way of thinking, late, meal hour. Instead of nine or ten, the first meal was served near noon—by order of its lord, who believed his men trained better on empty bellies. Whether they did or not was irrelevant, for, as with all aspects of life at Jaune, Garret d'Aubigny's will was law.

Returning to the keep, Taryn found Maite in the great hall, seemingly awaiting her arrival.

"Well, Lady Taryn, have you found the answer to your idleness?"

Taryn shook her head. "I think not, Maite. 'Tis a well-run manor. Richard is to be commended. I saw naught which cried out for a woman's hand."

"Indeed?"

The old woman looked at her intently and Taryn had the distinct feeling Maite was attempting somehow to convey without words a specific thought.

"There was one thing, though," she replied slowly, as a realization not formerly made suddenly *did* come to mind. "I saw no woolhouse. Surely Jaune possesses a place reserved for spinning and weaving?"

"In an earlier time, aye," Maite replied. "When my lord's mother was alive she oversaw those tasks and Jaune possessed a woolhouse to rival any. But after her death it gradually fell to disorder. With no firm hand and watchful eye to prevent it, more wool and flax were lost than were produced. There were thefts and underhanded deals made with the cloth and wool merchants, poor quality and prices . . ." she broke off and shrugged. "The village women spin and weave in their homes now."

"What of Jaune's needs? A manor of this size should have at least a half dozen looms in constant use."

"What is needed is purchased," Maite replied. "After Lord Garret became earl he closed the woolhouse and made instead arrangements with several merchants in Kirdford. Jaune's wool and flax are now sold, in exchange for an agreed upon number of cloth-yards."

"'Tis a poor system," Taryn grumbled, beneath her breath. She little trusted tradesmen, experience at Wynshire having taught her that theirs was more times than not a product of doubtful quality and high price.

"Aye. But with no one trained to oversee a woolhouse, 'tis the best that can be done." Again Maite shrugged and turned away. She need not have bothered, however. The gleam in her eye went unnoticed by Taryn.

Deep in thought, she mulled over the idea she was about to propose and could find no fault with it. "Maite?"

"Aye?" The woman turned.

"Might our lord be convinced to entrust me with that task?"

Maite allowed herself a slight smile. She was well-pleased with this morning's happenings. "You ask much, Lady Taryn," she answered, careful to guard her expression. "'Twould be a large undertaking. I can only make the request; the decision is his, but I will do what I can."

"Maite spoke to me."

Taryn looked up from her trencher to the man seating himself beside her. She had wondered if his absence were due to Maite's promise to speak to him as soon as possible. The noise of the hall faded. She was unaware of the better than a hundred men talking, eating and drinking. Her every sense was riveted on Garret d'Aubigny.

"I agree with you," he continued, reaching to fill his plate from the various dishes laid out before him. "It makes little sense for Jaune to buy what it can produce. Not when the wool and flax are available, grown here on the land. As Maite told you, when I was a boy my mother oversaw the spinning and weaving. Since her death, however, there has been no Countess of Arundel to take over those duties."

The tightness in his voice was unmistakable and Taryn wondered as to the cause. But as he continued to speak, she could not stop to speculate upon it.

"Before I consider reestablishing a woolhouse, I would first see that you can run a wool 'room.' You claim to be able to train and oversee what would be a major operation. Prove it to me first, on a smaller scale. I will provide you with the chamber across from my own. 'Twas my mother's. Though it hasn't been used for years, there are still looms within, and they should suit your needs."

"And help?" Taryn strove to keep the excitement she was feeling from being heard in her voice. "Might I have . . ." Mentally she counted the number needed to clean, card and comb, and spin for a single loom. ". . . nine or ten girls from the village to train?"

He raised a brow, as if irked by the forwardness of her request. "You are fortunate to be getting the chamber, Mistress. Not to mention the opportunity to prove yourself."

"I need help," she stated firmly, chafing at his persistent use of the word "mistress" as a term of address.

"Very well. The room and a couple of village maids—young ones, too young to work the field."

"Five," she quickly countered, though she knew she bore the risk of losing all. "And I need at least two of them older, with nimble fingers and the wits to learn a loom."

"Four. Four and the chamber. 'Tis all you'll get. Accept it now, Mistress, or I will rescind the entire offer."

Taryn smiled. "Four it is. Thank you, my lord."

He acknowledged her gratitude with a grunting sound.

Too delighted with her victory to be offended by his rudeness, she returned to eating. Suddenly, though, she felt a childish urge to gloat. She shifted her gaze from her trencher to the man at her side. "I would have been satisfied with only one," she murmured softly.

Above the rim of the cup he had raised to his lips, he stared at her. The pale hard eyes suddenly seemed to brighter. "'Tis base to boast, Mistress," he stated quite matter-of-factly. "Especially when there is naught of which to brag." He took a long swallow and set the cup down. All the while his eyes held hers. Then without warning, he smiled, and she felt her heart flutter in a way she had never before experienced.

"I would have given you twenty . . . Taryn."

Chapter Eight

Garret awoke with a start. Again he heard the thunderous crashing and pounding which had pulled him across sleep's threshold. Raw instinct surged and a single thought choked his mind: Jaune was under siege!

He ripped the bed's coverings from his body and swung his legs to the floor. Two separate actions became one as he jerked on his *braies* and took up his sword. He whirled toward the chamber door—and stopped short.

The banging was not the reverberating pounding of a battering ram, but hammering. And the voices he suddenly registered were not the cries made by men in battle, but simple shouting, beneath which rippled the laughter and chattering of women.

Relief in the realization that the clamor came not from an attack quickly crested, and then washed away. In its place a seething anger rose.

He crossed the room in heated strides, giving rein to his fury with a silent vow: By the powers in Heaven *and* Hell, the person responsible for this tumult would be paying the stocks a visit! He swung open the door, and stepped out into the corridor—just as two serfs exited the room across from his. Between them they struggled with the unwieldy weight and awkward size of a huge mattress.

"Yer pardon, Lord Garret." One of the men—the more fortunate of the pair since he walked forward and was hence able to see what lay in his path—dipped his head in greeting.

Garret somehow doubted the acknowledgment was made either out of respect or as an apology for his interrupted sleep.

And indeed his suspicion proved valid with the man's next utterance. "Ah . . . might yer lordship step to the side? 'Tis a sharp turn."

Nonplussed at the request, Garret complied. He flattened his back to the wall, thereby allowing the men to navigate the turn which would place them in a position to take the stairs. Over their heads he looked toward the room. From within a racket to rival Armageddon could be heard.

Suddenly the forward man's elbow connected sharply with his belly.

He winced and gritted his teeth. The serf groaned aloud.

Turning his head, he offered a sheepish smile. "Sorry, milord. Thought I had it."

Garret grunted. *The stocks were too lenient! He'd have the culprit in irons!*

"Be sure you burn it, do you hear?"

The sound of a female voice from inside the room cut short his rumination. Recognizing it, he stiffened immediately.

"Aye, milady," the man closest to the door answered. "'Tis good as ash." He looked at Garret, and for the briefest of moments the division of their stations ceased to exist. They were not serf and master, but men—and the expresison in the eyes of the first for the second was unmistakably one of commiseration.

In acknowledgment of the churl's silent message Garret's lips twisted into a wry smile. He waved the man forward and crossed the corridor to the room's entrance. The blistering castigation he intended to deliver died on his lips at the sight of the chaos before him.

There were no less than twenty people in the chamber.

Men on ladders stripped panels from the walls as others pried off boards nailed over the shutters of the room's three windows. Still more shoved or carried furniture to a pile.

Awaiting transport below, he guessed, noting the heap's collective state of disrepair as he stepped around it. After all, for twenty years the room's only function had been that of storage.

The floor space cleared was being scrubbed by a half dozen women on hands and knees wielding stiff-bristled brushes and wooden buckets. The odor of lye reached his nostrils. Unaccustomed to the smells of drudgery, he coughed violently.

"If the fumes are making you faint, step outside for a few minutes. See that you don't go empty-handed, though. Take those cushions next to you. They're as vermin-infested as everything else in this room."

Garret stared at the back of the feminine form issuing the order from the chamber's center. Her head tilted back, hands on rounded hips, she watched as two men ripped a tattered panel from the wall directly opposite the doorway. A rag wrapped about her hair concealed the fiery tresses and the shift she wore was the coarse-spun wool of a servant, but that was where all similarity ended. In Lady Taryn Maitland's tone and demeanor there was noting servile. She was clearly in charge.

Without turning, she seemed to know whomever she had addressed had not moved to obey. "Go on. Be quick about it!" she snapped, sharp irritation rising in her voice.

Garret stood, stunned. It made no matter that she knew not whom she had addressed—a dozen pair of eyes were now trained upon him, awaiting his reaction.

"'Tis not the sort of service I am accustomed to performing for you, Mistress." He dragged out his words for their fullest effect. "Add the word 'please,' however, and I *might* be inclined to comply."

It was not his imagination that he heard her gasp.

Within the chamber all work ceased. A dead silence descended.

She spun around and he reveled in the sight of her face flushed to a deep crimson. Satisfied he had re-established his position—and hers—he turned to leave before her sharp tongue could form a retort.

But he was not quick enough.

"*Please.*" Clear and even her voice shattered the silence.

He whirled and their gazes locked. He had lost and he knew it. With a single thrust of his sword he impaled one of the ragged cushions lying at his feet, turned and exited the room.

Once in the hallway, however, he stood and glared at the speared cushion. He'd be damned if he was going to actually take it below!

"Allow me, milord."

Garret looked up from his curious trophy to the tiny form waiting quite patiently at his door.

With a soft laugh Maite stepped forward and reached out to remove the cushion from his blade. "I hope this hapless pillow is all you gutted. Blood is such a nasty stain to clean. We've enough work to do setting that room to rights."

"Then you knew? You had a hand in this?"

"I knew. But I had no part." Maite tugged the cushion free and tucked it under her arm. "'Twas the Lady Taryn that organized it after talking to you. 'Twould appear she's got a talent—don't you think?"

For creating havoc in my life, he mused but did not voice the thought. "I might have been given warning," he grumbled aloud.

"What? I didn't tell you?" Maite brought a wrinkled hand to her chest in a gesture of dismay. "My apologies, milord. I was to tell you last night at supper and forgot all about it. 'Tis my age creeping up, no doubt."

Garret leveled a narrowed gaze. Despite her assertion, Maite was not prone to absent-mindedness. She was still as sharp as steel. Yet to accuse her of lying would accomplish nothing. What was done, was done. "How much longer must I endure this disturbance of the regular course and order of my life?" he asked instead.

At once a curious smile appeared on the lined face. "The chamber shall be ready within the week. Lady Taryn promises 'twill not take more than three days."

"See that it doesn't, old woman." Garret walked to the doorway of his room, entered and then turned. "And give her a message for me. Tell her I am keeping score. 'Tis three and one—and I am a poor loser."

"Then you'd best learn different, Garret." Maite met his cold stare with one of equal intensity. "And you'd best begin to heed my advice—unless you desire your secret revealed."

Inwardly he winced at the truth of her words. Yet he would not give her the satisfaction of knowing the blow had struck home. He shut the door with a definitive slam.

"*Score?*" Taryn turned her head to look at the woman lacing the right side of her *bliaut*. An instant ago she was so tired she could barely stand, much less hold this uncomfortable position of arms extended straight out. The last thing she'd wanted to do was wash and dress to go below for supper. But now with Maite's words ringing in her ears, her fatigue vanished. "He's keeping score?"

"'Tis what he said, Lady Taryn. Now, might you try to stand still? I've enough difficulty with these stiff fingers of mine without you jumping about like a cat with fleas. And hold your arm a mite higher."

"I'm sorry." Taryn lifted her arm and forced herself to stare straight ahead. As loath as she was to admit it, this revelation of Maite's filled her with a peculiar sense of elation. Surely if Jaune's lord felt himself in a contest of wills with her—to a point of tallying each's victories—then he was not as indifferent to her as he would have her believe!

She did not bother to consider why that realization should make her happy. Instead her thoughts turned in a different direction. Was this ongoing battle with Garret d'Aubigny of her doing, or to her liking? Did she really want to remain in the household of a man with whom her every contact became an encounter?

"You know, Lady Taryn . . . if you are not satisfied with what exists between you and Lord Garret, you *could* change it."

Taryn dropped her arms and looked incredulously at the old woman now stepping back. Was Maite capable of reading minds? Or had she unwittingly voiced her thoughts aloud?

Maite's expression provided no clue. "Let him know you desire otherwise."

Taryn shook her head. "I tried that yesterday morning. True enough, he gave me the wool room, but I think 'twas just to appease me. Naught would make him happier than ne'er to have to look upon me again—" She stopped abruptly, realizing what she had said. She was supposed to be the man's mistress. Quickly she made an attempt to right her inadvertent slip.

"—save those times when he . . . he desires . . ." Frantically she searched her memory for the words Moira had so often used. ". . . a romp betwixt the sheets," she finished.

So pleased was she that she had remembered, she did not see Maite's brow rise in amusement.

"Well then . . ." The old woman stepped around to her left that she might complete the task of lacing the tunic's opposite side. "'Tis a matter of showing him."

"How do I do that?" Taryn asked, obligingly lifting her arm. "How do I show him that I am not at war with him? Especially after what happened this morning. He's sure to be in a foul mood."

"Do not let his mood dictate yours. When he is brusque, respond with gentleness. Greet rudeness with civility, anger with composure. There can be no war, be it of wills, words or weapons, without combatants. There now . . . 'tis done." With a final tug Maite stepped back. "Look at me."

Taryn obediently turned.

Maite nodded in satisfaction. "There's not a soul that looking at you now would see the scullery maid you were an hour ago."

Taryn looked down at the tight-fitting tunic she wore. A deep sapphire blue in color, with long, wide sleeves, the garment fell to the ground in close folds. Only when she moved and the sides parted was the garnet kirtle beneath revealed. She turned back the hem of the sleeves to expose their rich lining of embroidered silk. In the two weeks she had been at Jaune she had paid her appearance little heed. It had, in fact, been Maite who had selected this gown—despite Taryn's protests it was too fine for a simple supper.

"Well?"

Taryn met the older woman's questioning gaze and smiled. "Do you think *he* will note the difference?"

"Unless he's been struck blind in the last hour." Maite grinned slyly. "But just to be sure, let us unplait your hair. Tonight you shall wear it flowing . . . with a veil, I think."

A quarter of an hour later Taryn entered the great hall. Despite Maite's assurances that she looked as regal as a queen, she felt nervous and unsure. She tentatively touched the edge of the thin linen veil overhanging her forehead. Reassured that the confining circlet atop her head had not slipped, she took a deep breath and lifted her chin. Her gaze went instantly to the dais.

In a departure from his normal habit of entering the hall after the serving of the meal had begun, Jaune's lord was already arrived. Standing behind his chair, he was washing his hands in a silver bowl held by one of his pages. Another boy waited patiently at his side, holding out the towel for him to use.

He took the towel and as he dried his hands, he nodded.

This gesture seemed to serve as a silent signal. The men who had been milling about the lower tables now began to sit.

Taryn set her shoulders and mounted the platform. She had taken only a few steps when she sensed that her presence had been noted. She forced a nonchalance she did not feel and continued to the table's center.

The pages greeted her with shy smiles and stiff bows. "Good evening, lady," they chorused in unison.

As the first extended the bowl that she might wash her hands, the second moved to pull out her chair.

"Leave it."

The sound of their lord's voice caused both youths to freeze.

"I will seat the lady." Garret stepped forward, laying his hands on the chair's high back as if to dispel any doubt the page might have that his assistance was still required.

Remembering Maite's words, Taryn smiled at the boys, letting her smile include their lord.

It was not, however, returned.

She dipped her fingers into the warm scented water, then wiped them dry on the offered towel. With another bow the boys withdrew to attend to the other guests and she had no choice but to turn her attention the man still standing behind her chair.

Sharp and assessing, almost daring her to object, his eyes slowly travelled the length of her. When he'd completed his scrutiny he pulled out her chair, bidding her with a curt nod to take it.

Taryn was not sure if the warm flush she felt ascending was from embarrassment or anger. His arrogance was insufferable! Still, she held her tongue and took her seat. She might very well burst from the effort, but she would heed Maite's counsel. This night she would not lose her temper, nor provide him with any excuse or means by which to perpetuate the tension between them.

She heard the scraping sound of his chair on the

wooden platform and knew without lifting her head he had taken his seat beside her. She reached for her wine goblet. "I owe you an apology for this morning, my lord. I did not know 'twas you when I ordered you from the chamber."

His grunted reply held a myriad of possibilities, none of which seemed destined for elaboration. She raised her eyes to see him staring at her.

"You . . . you have done something different . . . to your appearance?"

"Nay, my lord. I think 'tis merely the contrast to how I was this morning."

Again, he favored her with the same grunting response. "This wool room of yours, Maite tells me you have promised to have it in working order by week's end."

"Aye. Today 'twas stripped and cleaned. The furniture which was deemed salvageable has been taken to the carpenter's shop for repair. Those pieces which were in good condition have already been inspected, cleaned and rubbed with beeswax—" She broke off, realizing she'd been babbling. Surely the man did not care about such details! "Your pardon. I did not mean to—"

"Continue. What progress do you anticipate tomorrow?"

"The walls shall be whitewashed, my lord," she replied, concealing her surprise by turning her attention to the food now set before her. This initiation of conversation was most uncharacteristic. "New doors leading out to the room's balcony will be hung and broken panes of glass in the windows replaced."

"And the looms? They have also been inspected? After two decades of neglect the cords of the heddles are sure to require replacement."

This time she could not disguise her surprise. She looked at him in wide-eyed perplexity. The workings of a loom was hardly a matter with which she'd have expected him to be familiar. She nodded numbly. "The work shall be done tomorrow."

"Then I shall make my inspection the day following. If there is aught which is needed and cannot be taken from the guest rooms below, tell Richard. I will see that he purchases it when next he goes to Kirdford."

"Thank you, my lord." Taryn felt a sudden urge to shake her head, to reassure herself she was not dreaming. Never had so many words been civilly exchanged between them. Surely the secret to winning his good graces could not be so simple as a demure demeanor and a change in hair style? Yet the results were indisputable.

The feeling of relief and accomplishment did not leave her as the remainder of the meal passed with polite dialogue. When he stood, thereby signaling the meal's conclusion, she did not hesitate to take his offered arm.

He led her from the dais to one of the hall's two massive hearths. There the pages and squires had arranged chairs around a half dozen low tables. Several chessboards had been set up and a game of backgammon had already commenced between Jaune's steward and the captain of the men-at-arms.

If either man felt surprise at her presence, they did not show it. Each bowed in greeting as she took the chair Garret indicated—opposite his own across a chessboard.

"You will favor me with a game, Lady Taryn."

As his statement was that and not a question, she nodded in acknowledgment rather than reply.

He gestured that she was to make the first move, then turned his attention to the several hounds that had settled themselves at his feet.

Taryn smiled, noting that the one with its head upon his knee was bay in color. "That first night I sat at your table, he honored me with such attention. That is, until he heard your arrival."

Garret laughed and in that instant he seemed another man, one younger, less hardened not by time, but by deeds. "Do not feel slighted. In fact, you were paid a great compliment. Becket does not make friends easily."

"Becket? You have named a dog after the Archbishop of Canterbury?" Taryn gasped in shock. Surely it was a calculated insult to call Thomas of London by the middle class name of his father?

The smile which had come with Garret's laughter widened. He was clearly amused by her reaction. "It seemed fitting at the time. Becket was a gift from King Henry and our sovereign's feelings about the Archbishop currently in exile are no secret. Actually, he appreciated the humor and expressed the hope that Becket would serve me more loyally than his namesake had him. Besides, as I am sure you have heard, I am not known as a particularly pious and reverent man."

His mocking tone held a hint of defiance—as if he dared her to find fault with that which he was. She chose to ignore each—his sarcasm and his challenge. She had made too much progress this evening to allow the man's darker side to daunt her. She focused her thoughts instead upon the game, but found in a relatively short time she was about to be checkmated.

He appeared to realize it as well and regarded her with narrowed eyes, his mouth set tight. "Do you let me win, Mistress?"

"Nay, my lord. I fear I am too tired to concentrate. Tonight the victory is yours." As she heard herself repeating the very words he had spoken to her the first time they had played, she cringed. Despite her resolve to the contrary she had just reaffirmed the existence of the contest between them. Yet he did not appear to be bothered by her statement.

He stood and offered his arm. "Come. 'Tis time we were for bed."

She breathed a silent sigh of relief and rose, taking his arm. She bade good night to the men still playing backgammon.

Noting their sly exchange of knowing glances, Garret smiled in secret satisfaction. It had not been so very difficult after all to accord the wench courtesy. But he certainly wasn't going to let Maite know that fact. He would escort his "mistress" to her bed, then take to his own—and no one need be the wiser.

Two days later, true to Taryn's word, the wool room was completed, and Garret made his promised inspection.

Standing in the doorway, he looked upon the chamber in amazement. He could see no resemblance to the boarded up, dank and dark space it had been. Traces of a brilliant sunset streamed in through the windows. From the open balcony doors a crisp breeze wafted, rustling the curtains of the bed located in an alcove set apart from the main body of the room.

He entered, nodding his head in satisfaction. Though he was reluctant to admit it, the results of her labor were indisputable. Not only had the chamber been restored to its former state, the work had been done in a most timely and organized fashion—a detail Richard had made a point of stressing to him last evening.

According to Jaune's steward, the serfs rarely worked so cohesively and unbegrudgingly as they had under her direction. Even the women, who certainly had reason to resent the Great Earl's "ward," appeared to accept her position and authority.

"In fact," he had said, laughing, "Lady Taryn could pose a threat to my own position—if you should ever decide to avail yourself of these other 'talents' of hers."

Garret had felt a decidedly mixed reaction to the man's remark. On the one hand he was heartened to know his charade was believed. Yet, on the other, the reference to a nonexistent intimacy between them had served to remind him of the true state of things. Not since he'd been a bare-faced youth had he gone so long without a woman, and the frustration was taking its toll. Even now the muscles in his belly tightened, as they did each night as he lay alone in his bed.

He forced his thoughts from the subject. There was

nothing to be gained by dwelling on his newly celibate life. The decision had been his and his alone. As long as she was in his care, he was honor-bound to protect her—and that protection meant perpetuating the lie.

Garret turned his attentions back to the chamber, and found his eyes drawn to the pair of looms set back to back, dominating the room's center.

He stared at the one closest to him, and suddenly the room seemed filled with the faint echo of women's voices. The long, late afternoon shadows took on soft, hazy shapes, and the time was no longer the present.

He saw a small boy standing beside the high-backed chair, head nestled in his mother's lap. Seated before the loom, her feet on the treadles, she tossed her shuttle of wool back and forth between the rising and falling heddles. To the rhythm of the shuttle and the clanking of the loom, she sang a song to ease a sleepy child into slumber.

Then, as quickly and unbidden as the image had appeared, it slipped away. Yet the damage had been wrought. The door to the past had been opened, and from the recesses of his mind, its demons released. He stepped forward, drawn by a will not his own.

Trembling, his hand reached out and he touched the vacant chair, the silent loom. "Some day my son was to have been lulled to sleep by your music," he whispered. "Now you stand ready. But the boy who was to have been your audience lies buried in a convent courtyard, murdered in his first breath by the woman who gave him life."

He turned from the loom, fists clenched in silent anguish. It was a mistake to have opened this room! It should have remained sealed.

He stumbled toward the door, one lucid thought driving him: He had to distance himself from this place, from the memories somehow brought to life, memories of the past and memories of what was once to have been the future.

Moments later, with no recollection of how, he found himself at the stables.

The squire ordered to saddle his destrier did so without question, and Garret flung himself onto the stallion's back. He took up the reins and set his heel to the animal's flanks.

The huge war horse bounded forward heedless of all that lay in its path. In the yard frantic geese took flight to escape its slashing hooves. Several chickens, not as fortunate, were ground into the mud beneath the beast's weight.

Garret paid the bloodied carcasses no heed, urging the stallion forward toward the outer curtain wall.

He did not return until nightfall. Exhausted, he entered the great hall.

Ignoring the curious stares of those men who had no doubt witnessed his mad flight, he took his seat. The chair on his left was empty. He sighed in relief. Though the demons which had driven him out were now once again leashed, he was in no state to discuss with his "mistress" the very thing which had freed them.

He reached for the flagon of ale before him. He rinsed his mouth, spat, then drained the flagon in a single long draught. In his mind a silent vow was made: he would have nothing more to do with her wool room.

Chapter Nine

"Wool?"

"Aye, milord. Wool."

Garret forced himself to turn his aching head and look at the man seated on his right. The ale of last night had left his senses dulled, his head pounding. He had heard nothing of Richard's words save that one he had repeated hoarsely.

"Jaune has none." His steward, knowing better than to reveal by either tone or expression any impatience he might feel at his lord's inattentiveness, merely continued —or perhaps restated—his disclosure. "Last year's crop was sold and 'twill be another month yet before the flocks are ready for this spring's shearing. In the meantime, the lady—"

"Has naught to card, spin or weave."

Garret flinched at the sound of the female voice on his left. The higher pitched tones seemed to slice through his brain. Ignoring their speaker and fighting the urge to cradle his head in his hands, he addressed his steward. "Then go to Kirdford and purchase what is needed from Flambard."

"I cannot, milord. There is too much here which demands my attention. The villeins are sowing their plots, and yours as well. The gardens are being planted. The cows are again in milk. Cheese has begun to be made.

Because of the heavy rains this spring the drainage ditches require repair. All must be tallied, accounted for and supervised or the wretches will steal you blind."

Wincing with the effort, Garret turned to the woman now sitting in silence at his side. When he'd entered the hall and seen her red head bent in conversation with his steward, he should have known trouble was brewing. "You heard Richard. You will have to wait for your wool, Mistress."

Taryn bowed her head demurely. She had no intention of waiting. Taking care to keep any curtness from her voice, she cast him an innocent sideways glance—one which belied her true feelings. Very likely he would be no more receptive to her idea than had been his steward moments ago. "I should like to go to Kirdford myself, my lord."

"Without a proper escort? 'Tis out of the question. You just heard the man. He is too busy."

His voice was firm, but so was her determination. She drew a deep breath. "There is no reason *you* could not act as that escort."

His handsome features darkened with an emotion she was at a loss to understand. "'Tis out of the question, Mistress," he repeated.

"Why?"

His gaze shifted for a brief instant to the man seated beside him.

"Ah . . . your leave, milord?" Hastily Richard rose to his feet, the unspoken command understood.

Garret nodded, and his steward quickly departed the dais.

Once he was out of hearing distance, Taryn repeated her question. "Why? Certes, there is naught here which would suffer should you take a day to escort me to Kirdford."

"'Tis not a journey which can be undertaken in a day."

"So?"

"So we would have to overnight in Kirdford."

His reasoning was lost on her. "I still do not see how that would present a problem."

"You do not see how that would present a problem?" He turned in his chair to face her. "You, and I, away for a night . . ."

Suddenly she understood—or at least thought she did. "My lord, is it not a little late to worry about my honor? Need I remind you . . . I am already playing the role of your leman."

"That is just it. You are *playing* the role. And thus far 'tis one performed in name only. We have shared no bed—save for a brief incident better forgotten—but were we to travel together 'twould be expected, by my men and by others."

That was it! He worried about accommodations. Silently Taryn smiled as a plan of attack took form in her mind. "Forgive me, my lord. I did not understand. I thought the reputation you sought to protect was mine. I now realize 'twas yours." She shrugged resignedly for added effect. "Odd . . . I did not realize your manhood was so fragile a thing as to come into question should we take separate rooms at an inn."

His eyes narrowed and the hard line of his jaw grew more so. "You goad me, Mistress."

"Nay. I seek only to understand your logic."

He raised a brow. Clearly he did not believe her. Neither did he seem ready to relent. He sat back in his chair. "Are you not concerned that the charade in which we are engaged will become suspect, were we *not* to share a room and bed?"

"That again hangs on your reputation. You have openly proclaimed an intimacy betwixt us. Are you known as a man who gives his word falsely? Or is your reputation as a wencher so insubstantial that others would immediately suspect our relationship is but staged?"

It never occurred to her to wonder why he simply did

not choose the truly logical solution, and insist that if she wanted to make the journey she would sleep in the same room, if not bed, as he.

"Then too . . ." Now she made no attempt to conceal her smile. Victory was within her grasp. "I should think an unwillingness for us to travel together would be far more suspect behavior than our sleeping apart."

She was not sure if she heard his groan or merely imagined it. "I will know no peace if I refuse, will I, Mistress?"

Taryn lowered her eyes. She had won! "You *did* promise to provide me with what was needed."

This time his groan was clear. "And so I did. Very well. Let us be done with this folly quickly. We will make the journey on the morrow. But I warn you, Mistress, I have an uneasy sense this will not proceed as you expect."

Rejecting his premonition as absurd, Taryn stood. Confident and absorbed in her triumph, she did not see the way his face contorted with pain as her chair scraped the wooden platform.

Through narrowed slits Garret watched her exit. Once she had disappeared through the doorway, he finally allowed himself to drop his throbbing head into his hands.

In the wake of the pain assailing him, his vow of less than a day lay forgotten. He reveled in the blessed silence, but it was short-lived. Soft footsteps approached the dais, then ceased.

Without lifting his gaze he knew their owner. "What is it, old woman? What does she want of me now?"

Maite laughed softly. "Naught, my lord. Lady Taryn is most delighted with your decision to accompany her to Kirdford. I'm afraid 'tis on my own behalf that I intrude upon your, er . . . solitude. Might I ask to what merchant's shop you intend to take her?"

The question seemed innocent enough, but Garret knew that with Maite nothing was ever as it appeared. He lifted his head from his hands. "I have not given the matter thought. But Jaune has always patronized Eduard Flambard's establishment."

She looked at him as if he had taken leave of his senses. "Are you mad? You cannot take her to Flambard's!"

"And why not?" Immediately he was on the defensive. "True, I do not trust the monger as far as I can spit. However, over the years we *have* reached an understanding."

She hissed between her teeth, the derisive sound saying far more than any words could. "An understanding? In exchange for your patronage, he looks the other way whilst you bed his wife?"

Garret smiled wryly. "Thus far it *has* been an arrangement from which all parties have benefited."

"That is precisely my point, boy. Is it your intent to 'benefit' on this trip, or merely to flaunt your sordid 'arrangement' in front of the Lady Taryn?"

Garret's temper was at last crossed. "This is a trip whose only purpose is business, old woman. In fact, 'tis a trip I would prefer *not* to make. But since that choice now seems out of my hands, I will at least have the final say in with whom I shall conduct my transactions! The matter is settled. We go to Flambard's—or we go not at all."

He shoved back from the table and stood. But as he glared down at the petite form before him, his anger seemed suddenly to abate. When he spoke he found his voice calm. "I will not vaunt what I am, Maite. Neither will I conceal it. If the Lady Taryn sees aught which offends her, so be it."

So be it. Guarding her expression, Maite watched as he stepped from the platform. Only after he had disappeared through the doorway leading to the anteroom did she permit herself a complacent smile. She had counted on his pride to overrule his judgment. But it never hurt to take precautions. Tell a man he could not have something, and he would quick enough want it. Tell him he could not do a thing—and no power on earth could stop him from doing it.

Garret would take Taryn to Flambard's. Fate and feminine jealousies would take care of the rest. For now her work was done.

"Once we are over the next rise you will be able to see Kirdford's walls."

Taryn lifted her gaze to the man riding at her side. Since leaving Jaune Garret had spoken scarcely a dozen words to her—not that his silence had been unexpected. In fact, it was this initiation of conversation which now surprised her. "Is it a large town?" she asked, hoping to continue the dialogue.

"Not large and not small." He rose up in his saddle, turning to look behind him. The three men riding as rear guard had apparently lagged too far behind for his taste, and he now signaled them forward.

Upon departing Jaune, Taryn had wondered if their escort of only a half-dozen men was adequate. She could not help thinking of the large entourage Charles had assembled. Warily, she eyed the underbrush and thickets lining the road. It was a frightening thought to consider that in every copse danger might lurk. Thankfully, the groves of trees had been thinning and growing more scattered, giving way to small hamlets and villages—a sure sign their destination was near.

She shifted her weight in an attempt to ease her tired back. She had not been atop a horse since that journey from Wynshire, and her muscles were unaccustomed to the strain of riding hour upon hour.

"I would have expected complaint." Garret settled back against the cantle. "For a woman, you keep your saddle well."

With his comment Taryn realized he had been watching her. Somewhat uncomfortable in that knowledge and unsure how to respond, she bowed her head. "I shall take that as a compliment, my lord."

"As it was meant, lady."

For a brief instant she thought he might smile. But the chiseled face outlined in mail never softened. He stared at her a moment longer, then turned his gaze to the hard-packed roadbed before them.

In frustration she directed her eyes forward as well, noting how the traffic on the dusty thoroughfare seemed to have increased. It was quite considerable now—far more than she would have expected given Garret's characterization of Kirdford's size.

There were peddlers returning from the villages to replenish their saddlebags, rich merchants on horseback, and ragged serfs afoot. Wagons laden with merchandise vied for space on the rutted highway with great two-wheeled carts hauling produce to town. Destined for that same market were peasants driving livestock. To the sounds of creaking axles, rumbling wheels and shouting men, the clanking and banging of a tinker's pots could be heard. Immediately ahead of their own forward guard rode a priest; the jingling bells on his horse's halter proclaimed his calling, yet added to the clamor.

Pilgrims all, she thought. All drifting through the countryside, travelling in the same direction as they, toward the city in the distance.

Abruptly, as if in response to her silent musings, the horizon dipped. Taryn had her first glimpse of Kirdford, rising above the floor of the shallow valley in which it nestled. It seemed no different than any other town—high encircling walls of stone, surmounted by towers, very much like those of a castle.

Beyond the fortified walls she could see a tumbled mass of roofs, sloping at every imaginable angle. In the very center rose the thin spires of a church. At sunset its bells would ring, warning the citizens that the town gates were about to be shut. Travellers who arrived too late would have to stay outside until dawn, when once again the gates would be opened.

"There is no need for concern. We will be at Flambard's establishment long before the gates close."

This time Garret's comments unnerved her completely. It was bad enough that he watched her, but this? Were her thoughts and emotions so clear that he could read them? Indeed, she had been contemplating the distance yet to be covered and the time remaining. Less than half of the sun still showed above the rooftops.

"Once we enter the city, I will send two of the men ahead to arrange for lodgings," he continued, seemingly unaware of her discomfiture. "We will ride on to the merchant's. I will have this wool business transacted today, that we may depart the city with first light."

"After all, we must be done with this folly quickly." Taryn mumbled his words beneath her breath sarcastically. But what had she expected? Pleasant company and a gracious escort? From Garret d'Aubigny? A rather unladylike sound erupted from the back of her throat. 'Twould be a far more likely occurrence that the Devil would regain lost grace and enter Heaven!

Father Gregory's face came to mind at once. She laughed aloud at the thought of his horror. The simple village priest would surely postulate that Satan had found a foothold in her soul, for what else could possibly possess her to even consider such a blasphemous analogy.

"There is something which amuses you, lady?"

Garret's cool and disapproving gaze was like a bucket of cold water splashed upon a fire. The light-heartedness which had barely taken hold was quashed. "Naught which I would care to share, my lord."

With effort she smiled sweetly, then focused her eyes on the city looming ahead. *Arrogant lout! Mannerless caitiff!*

Her mental compilation of epithets continued until they entered Kirdford. Once they were through the massive gates, however, the intense excitement of the city instantly consumed her thoughts.

Wherever she looked, she saw people. At every corner jugglers and fortune tellers gathered crowds about them and collected a few pennies. Hawkers and peddlers, strolling among them, added to the noise and bustle. Their raucous cries competed with those of the merchants, who also conducted their business practically on the street, displaying their wares upon counters which spanned the eight-foot width of their open shop fronts.

Taryn could not absorb the sights and sounds rapidly enough. She had not been in a city since before her father's death, and even then, the towns near Wynshire were but villages compared to Kirdford's teeming activity.

She glanced hopefully over to the man riding beside her. Might he be convinced to stop at the marketplace just ahead? How she would relish the opportunity to wander about the stalls!

Seeming to know her question before she posed it, Garret shook his head. "Our purpose is wool, lady—and it grows late." With a wave of his hand he dispatched two of his men down a narrow side street, then brought his mount in closer to hers.

She bristled at the unspoken message his action conveyed. If she did not follow his lead, he would be near enough to grab her horse's reins. She shot him an icy glare, but the effort was wasted. He had already dismissed her and turned his attention to the task of skirting the throngs streaming toward the open square in the heart of the city.

He led them from the main thoroughfare onto a progression of narrow side streets. Taryn's initial fascination began to wane. The odor of filth surrounded her, and the congestion now made her feel as if she could not breathe.

Here there was no open space at all. Too valuable to waste, every inch was usurped by houses and their ground-floor shops. Since each successive story of the tall wooden structures jutted out beyond the one below, the eaves of opposing buildings almost touched over the street.

No sunlight could enter, and these twisting alleys were dark and airless, ankle deep in mire, befouled by the accumulation of garbage and refuse thrown out from the houses above and the shops below. Butchers slaughtered animals at their shop fronts and allowed the blood run into the ditch which ran in the center of the street. Into the same *kennel* dyers released noisome waters from their vats and poulterers flung chicken heads and feathers. The task of clearing away what waste did not run off was left to the pigs that wandered freely.

It was no easy feat to avoid the small razor-backed scavengers. Accustomed to traffic both mounted and on foot the long-snouted animals moved only when physically threatened—and often not quickly enough. Their heartrending squeals of pain echoed eerily in the dim alleyways.

Instinctively Taryn edged her palfrey closer to the huge destrier.

From the corner of his eye Garret noted the action and was amused by it. In the square she had resented his protective gesture. But now that she felt somehow menaced, it did not bother her to seek that at which she had earlier chafed.

He shook his head. No matter. They had reached their destination—the street of wool merchants and weavers. He reined in his horse in front of the tallest of the dozen houses which lined the crooked alley. It was an impressive structure, five storied, covered in red paint, with black shutters and doors.

Garret dismounted, as did his men. He signaled them to wait, then walked over to aid Taryn from her horse. In spite of himself, he smiled when he saw her eyes. Wide and filled with awe, they were fixed upon the shop.

Silently, grudgingly, Garret gave the proprietor his due. Eduard Flambard was a shrewd man and one not free from vanity. He would have it known his establishment was the largest and finest in Kirdford. Here there was no simple counter for a meager display of goods. The whole front of the building was open to the street, providing an enticing view to curious passersby and inviting patrons to enter.

"Taryn."

At first Garret was not sure she had heard him. She seemed unaware of his presence. Then, wordlessly, she leaned toward him and placed her hands upon his shoulders. He lifted her from the saddle and had scarcely placed her upon the ground before she started forward.

He followed, pausing just inside the door to watch her reaction.

She set the hood of her cloak from her head, revealing her face. He was not disappointed. Like a child's, it was lit with excitement at the sight of the magnificent display. Save a curtain at the shop's rear, every inch of the three interior walls was lined with shelves. These were crammed with bolts of rich cloth of every color and weave imaginable—from wools and silks to priceless oriental textures.

Entertained by her childlike delight, he watched in enjoyment as she walked along one of the walls. From time to time a particular bolt seemed to catch her eye, and she would stop to tentatively run her fingertips across it. She was in no hurry—not that it mattered. As it was near sunset and closing time, there was but a single journeyman present. Standing to one side, he was elsewhere occupied, holding up folds of cloth for the inspection of the shop's only other customer. He nodded in greeting to Taryn and turned to the curtain at his back. "Master. A customer."

Almost at once the drape parted and a finely dressed, overfed man entered from the workshop which was hidden behind the cloth screen.

"Lady." He attempted a bow, but was thwarted in his efforts by his girth. "Welcome. I am Eduard Flambard. How might I be of service this day?"

"Master Flambard." Taryn acknowledged the introduction with a polite nod. "I should like to purchase wool."

"Certes. Serge, worsted or shag?" He stepped over to the wall on his right and gestured to the row of shelves. "Did your ladyship have a specific color in mind?" He reached for a bolt of violet shag. "This is a particularly fine weave—"

"Mayhap I misspoke, Master Flambard," Taryn interrupted. "'Tis not woolen cloth I would purchase, but wool. Raw wool. Unwashed, uncombed and unspun."

Frowning, Flambard replaced the bolt. "I fear you have been misdirected, lady. True, I am a wool merchant, but I buy wool. I do not sell it. I sell cloth; fabrics of the finest quality. Such as this *candal* . . . here, allow me to show you." He tugged free a bolt of peacock blue silk and unrolled a length of the shimmering stuff. This he laid over his forearm. "'Tis the perfect color to compliment your ladyship's hair and complexion." He raised a hopeful brow. "'Twould make a fine gown."

Hesitantly she reached out a hand. As she touched the fabric, Garret noted how her lips parted in a wistful smile.

"'Tis lovely," she agreed, retracting her hand. "But I have come for wool."

Flambard sighed quite audibly, his frustration at having lost a sale clear. He turned to replace the cloth bolt. "Then I fear I can be of no assistance."

With the man's words Garret knew the scene had been played out. Reluctantly he stepped forward from the darkened doorway which had effectively concealed his presence, into the shop's lamplight. "Mayhap you would reconsider?"

"Lord Garret!" Flambard whirled to face him. In his haste to bow he nearly fell over. Righting himself, he quickly moved forward. "Forgive me, my lord. I did not see you. My humble shop is indeed honored. Please—please, enter. In what manner might I serve?"

A muscle in Garret's cheek twitched. The merchant's bowing and scraping had always annoyed him. "You can sell the lady what she desires to buy."

Flambard's gaze darted to Taryn. He looked upon her as if for the first time. Slowly his eyes widened in understanding. "Certes, my lord. I did not realize . . ." With an unctuous bow he turned to her. "What quantity did you desire to purchase, Lady Taryn?"

As the man addressed her by name, Garret noted the appearance of a slight blush on her cheeks. To her credit, however, she handled the awkward moment well, responding to the merchant's question with no hesitation.

Nevertheless, Garret bristled at Flambard's lack of tact. The man might at least have waited for a formal introduction. By speaking her name he had acknowledged that he knew far more than her identity.

Garret felt the surge of an old and familiar resentment. Gossip's capacity to travel knew neither walls nor distance. And while he was long accustomed to being the subject of wagging tongues, that she had become prey to their malicious speculations now raised his ire.

Unaware that he was doing so, he moved protectively to her side. With half an ear he listened as she proceeded to barter with Flambard over price. It did not take long for him to realize she was making the merchant pay—literally—for his *faux pas.*

Taryn held firm to the price she would meet, and when Flambard looked to him to intercede, Garret took satisfaction in ignoring the silent entreaty.

Finally, unwilling to lose the sale, Flambard conceded. With a smile that was clearly forced, he lauded her efforts. "You have a shrewd head for business, lady. Would that my wife were so gifted. But then . . ." He shifted his gaze to Garret. "Geneviève is not without her own talents."

Unflinching, Garret met the man's hooded stare. "Tally your bill," he stated flatly, "and I will pay you now . . . for *all* that you are owed." He reached for the purse at his waist. The resultant sound of tinkling silver brought an instant and genuine smile to the man's face.

"At once, my lord." With yet another bow, he withdrew behind the drape, returning a moment later with a wax tablet in hand. Mumbling to himself, he made a great show of working the figures. Finished, he presented the tablet with a flourish.

Garret glanced only at the total. He could read numbers well enough, cipher if required, but words were so much scribble. As a boy there had been no one in the household to instruct him. Once grown, he had never regarded the shortcoming a failing. It was considered no disgrace to a knight if he did not know his letters. As his father had before him, to keep his accounts he relied upon his steward and occasionally engaged the services of scriveners. He did not worry he might be cheated. A man with wits enough to read and write would not be fool enough to risk the Earl of Arundel's retribution should he ever learn of any deceit.

He tugged off his gauntlet and was prepared to count out the needed number of coins when Taryn coughed softly.

Garret looked down at her questioningly. She stood at his side, her eyes fixed upon the table in Flambard's hand.

"Maybe you would like to check your figures once more, Master Flambard?" she offered, her voice unaccusing, but firm.

Garret watched as the man scanned the tablet. Suddenly his mouth dropped open. He looked up at her in seemingly utter astonishment. "You are right, my lady. I *have* made an error." Hastily he adjusted the figures, then displayed the change to Taryn.

A small smile of satisfaction touched her lips and she nodded.

Flambard looked to Garret. "Shall there be aught else, my lord?"

Garret knew precisely to what he referred. The error Taryn had detected had been intentional, an inflation of the wool's price designed to cover the cost of what

Arundel's earl took from him which was not to be counted from among his inventories. The merchant was still owed. "Add the bolt of blue silk," he answered.

Flambard's face broke into a satisfied smile. "At once, my lord." He crossed over to the wall and removed the bolt of cloth. "Will you take it now, or shall I have it sent with the wool?"

Garret glanced at Taryn. Seeing the expression of unabashed delight on her face, he realized his costly purchase had done more than appease the merchant. He felt an unexpected sense of pleasure. "Taryn?"

"Might we take it?"

Garret found himself smiling. "As you wish." He turned to Flambard. "You heard the lady. We will take it."

"Very good, my lord. Mayhap whilst I have it wrapped, you and the lady would permit me to extend the hospitality of my home? A tankard of ale to wash away the dust of your journey?"

Garret shook his head. "There is no need. I have dispatched some of my men to arrange for lodgings at an inn. Once they are returned, we shall be on our way."

"You did not make prior arrangements?" The merchant looked at him aghast. "My lord, 'tis Holy Week! There's not a room to be found—save mayhap in one of the crude ale houses in the squalid part of the city. And with the Lady Taryn . . ."

He shook his head and proceeded to wring his hands dramatically. "Why, only this morning I had a customer cursing the conditions he was forced to endure. Fleas so thick in the dust under the rushes that the poor man professed to have scratched until blood flowed. I implore you not to submit her to such horrors. Please permit me to extend this night the hospitality of my humble home. In fact . . . I insist you and your lady take my own bed."

Chapter Ten

Taryn felt as if the walls of the shop were suddenly closing in. She struggled for a breath, avoiding the eyes she knew were upon her. She dared not risk even a covert glance in Garret's direction. His warning rang in her ears: *I have the uneasy sense this will not proceed as you expect.*

"Your offer is most generous, Master Flambard, but unnecessary." Garret's voice cut through her thoughts. "I am confident my men will locate suitable lodgings."

"My lord, mayhap you did not hear me aright. 'Tis Holy Week. Every inn will be full. Did you not notice the crowds upon entering the city?"

And the traffic on the highway outside it, Taryn thought. She felt no sense of satisfaction in realizing her impressions had been correct. Given Kirdford's size there had been inordinate congestion upon the road.

Unable to bear it any longer, she cast a sideways glance at Garret. There was no vestige in the hard-set face of the amicable mood which had existed just moments ago. His jaw was clenched, his mouth pressed into a tight line.

"My lord?" Flambard looked at him questioningly.

Garrett blinked and focused on the merchant. "If my men return, and their words bear out what you have said, I shall be in your debt. But I will not put you from your bed. A simple pallet before the hearth will suffice."

"Nonsense! My wife and I will take the servant's room

and I will see that your men are put up in the apartments above, with my apprentices and journeymen." Without waiting for reply, Flambard turned to the man still occupied with the customer. "Joseph, you will see to the Great Earl's men?"

Joseph nodded.

"There. 'Tis done, then." Smiling, Flambard walked to the curtain at the rear of the shop. He drew back the panel and gestured to the stairs thus revealed. "Please, my lord, lady. Come."

Taryn hesitated. Suddenly she felt Garret's hand upon the small of her back. It was not her imagination that the push he gave to propel her onward was nearer a shove. She stumbled forward, lifting her skirts with as much dignity as she could muster.

Garret followed close behind her. His sinister whisper reached her ear alone. "By Christ's blood, Mistress . . . you'll rue this day."

Taryn stiffened her back and made for the stairs. Once atop, she found the steep flight abruptly gave way to a landing, and yet another curtain confronted her. She paused and Garret took her arm, pulling her aside to let the merchant, who had trailed behind, enter first.

"There is no need for ceremony, my lord." Flambard laughed as he mounted the final stair. He walked forward and drew aside this second panel. "Certes, you are no stranger to these walls."

Garret's eyes narrowed, and the look then exchanged by the men left Taryn shrouded in confusion. In the shop below she had twice seen that same look—as if more were being said between them than what their words conveyed.

"Lady Taryn." The merchant made a sweeping motion with his arm. "I bid you welcome to my home."

Taryn stepped through the doorway and into a large square room which clearly served as an area to receive guests and to dine. Eight high-backed chairs stood around the parlor's main feature, a broad oaken table long enough to seat more than a dozen. Before the large fireplace that stretched half the length of the room stood two more chairs. These were richly upholstered in an oriental fabric which matched the cushioned window seats centered upon the adjacent wall. She noted the window was set with crystal plates—an obvious indication of wealth, for only the well-to-do could afford glass panes. The remaining walls were lined with cabinets and chests, each a work of fine craftsmanship. Atop one of the cupboards were displayed plates of hammered silver, upon another an ewer of gilt bronze embellished with silver.

Obviously with Flambard the beliefs of the Church held no sway: because greed was wicked, a man should make a reasonable living by working—and no more.

"My lord, lady, please make yourselves comfortable." Flambard gestured to the chairs before the fireplace. "If you will excuse me, I will see to my wife's whereabouts."

Garret nodded, and Flambard withdrew through a narrow doorway which Taryn guessed led into an anteroom between parlor and kitchen.

Now alone with Garret, she cast a nervous glance in his direction.

The scowl that had hovered ever since Flambard's mention of the state of Kirdford's inns had finally settled across his face. Wordlessly he walked to the window and swung open its wooden shutter.

She moved to one of the chairs and sat. Clasping her hands in her lap, she stared at them for what seemed like an eternity of silence. Finally, she looked up.

He had not moved. He still stared out the window to the street below.

Taryn knew he was watching for his men. "Mayhap Master Flambard is uninformed . . ." she stated hesitantly, ". . . or rather misinformed, about the inns being filled."

He turned to look at her, a mocking half-smile on his lips. "The man is many things, Mistress, but uninformed is not one of them. You have seen his shop. Look about you now. This opulence is more than show. Eduard Flambard has reached the aim of every tradesman. He has attained the position of independent master, with a dozen apprentices and journeymen in his employ. He is a city magistrate and sits on the council which supervises Kirdford's market and the collection of its tolls. This is not done without capital *and* influence. If he says the inns are full, they are full."

"I had no idea he was such a powerful man."

"That is your problem in everything, Mistress." The taunting smile disappeared. "You have no idea, and yet it does not stop you from pursuing what you want, regardless of consequence. I offer our present situation as proof."

Nettled by the tone of censure in his voice, Taryn shot him an icy glare. "You can scarce blame me for our present situation," she whispered.

"And if not you, then who? Who, Mistress, is responsible for the fact we are in Kirdford?"

"I am not responsible for the fact 'tis Holy Week!" Fighting for control, she stood. This was not the time for an argument to ensue. Flambard would be back at any moment. She cast him a second glacial gaze. "Forsooth, 'twill be a most unpleasant night, my lord, if you do not at least *try* to accept the situation with a modicum of grace." Then, tossing back her braid, she crossed the room, feigning an instant and intense interest in the workmanship of the silver plates.

She heard his signature growl. "We will see what grace *you* possess, Mistress, when later we are sharing the same bed."

Before she could reply, Flambard re-entered the room. He looked first at Garret and then at Taryn. "I hope there is not a problem."

Taryn forced herself to smile. "Lord Garret and I were merely discussing the necessity of putting you from your bed, Master Flambard. Surely, there is no need to do so."

"You are gracious indeed, lady. However, I have already broached the subject with my wife. Once I spoke Lord Garret's name, she was most insistent that we extend our fullest hospitality."

"But to give up your bed for the comfort of strangers?" Taryn glanced at Garret from the corner of her eye. She was almost certain she had heard him groan.

"Lord Garret is no stranger."

Taryn turned to look at the owner of the soft feminine voice. She had appeared without warning, an elegantly gowned woman now poised in the doorway. Foregoing a matron's coif, she wore her dark, almost black hair in two long braids entwined with gold thread. Her velvet *bliaut* of red, the most costly of dyes, was trimmed at hem and sleeve with the same gold thread worked into an embroidered design of leaves, vines and flowers. A girdle of woven gold encircled her slim waist.

Taryn could not help but stare. Flambard's wife was quite beautiful, and far younger than he.

"Would you not agree, Eduard?" Favoring her husband with a dulcet smile, she stepped to his side and took his arm. "Now, I think greetings and introductions are in order. Lord Garret . . ." She directed her attention to the man at the window. ". . . as always, your arrival in our home does us honor and . . ." Her sultry voice softened into a breathy whisper ". . . gives us pleasure."

Only with effort could Taryn hear her final words, words that she was sure were meant to convey a more personal welcome.

"Your presence has been sorely missed, my lord."

"Madame Flambard." Garret inclined his head, acknowledging her greeting with a tight smile. "May I present Lady Taryn Maitland."

Slowly the woman turned. Making no attempt to conceal the fact she was doing so, she let her gaze slip over Taryn. "Of course," she murmured, almost as if to herself, "I should have realized . . . Lady Taryn, I bid you welcome."

Taryn offered a tentative smile. Despite the woman's agreeable tone and gracious manner, her arrival had brought an air of undeniable tension into the room. Taryn could feel it emanating from Garret, even from the woman herself. Certainly the warmth present in her eyes as she had greeted Garret was now gone. "I apologize for the inconvenience and intrusion, Madame Flambard."

"There is no need, lady." Again the dark eyes swept over her as though appraising her.

Self-consciously, Taryn brought a hand up to smooth her hair. She suddenly felt as if every mile they had travelled were evident.

Her actions did not escape her host. Flambard turned at once to his wife. "Geneviève, why don't you take Lady Taryn abovestairs that she might refresh herself. I will see to Lord Garret's needs. For the moment, I am sure he is wanting only of food and drink."

"I am sure you are right—for the moment." Flashing him the same winsome smile, she turned to Taryn. "Lady?"

Taryn followed her from the parlor, through the anteroom, then up a flight of stairs which ended with a small hallway.

"This way." Gesturing to the door at the end of the corridor, Madame Flambard led her to their destination.

Any doubt Taryn may have had as to whether or not this was the master chamber was immediately swept away as the woman opened the door.

The room revealed was not only as large as the one below, but also as elegantly furnished. Centered in the space was a massive bed, canopied and curtained against drafts and elevated upon a platform which extended two feet in all directions. A fireplace, twin to the one below, occupied the wall upon the right. Opposite it a dormer window pierced the outer wall.

Madame Flambard followed Taryn into the room, shutting the door behind her. "There is water for washing there in the corner. Do you require assistance—

mayhap in unlacing your gown?"

Taryn shook her head. "This will be fine. Thank you." Hoping the woman would understand a subtle hint and grant her privacy, she removed her cloak. "I'll be but a few moments.

"Take whatever time you need, lady; 'twill give us a chance to get acquainted. I hope you don't mind?"

As the woman moved to the bed and seated herself upon it, Taryn felt a peculiar tightening in the pit of her stomach. Dismissing the sensation as a sign of fatigue, she walked over to the wash basin in the corner. "Of course not," she replied.

She folded back the wide sleeves of her *bliaut* and pushed up those of her undergown. All the while she could feel the woman watching her.

"You know, lady, you are not at all what I expected."

"Expected?" Taryn froze, her face poised just inches from the water.

The merchant's wife laughed. "Jaune is not so far that gossip does not travel."

Feeling her color rise, Taryn quickly splashed her face. "Most times there is little truth to be found in gossip, Madame." Struggling to maintain an even countenance, she reached for the towel beside the basin. "I would prefer, though, that we found another topic of conversation."

"So you do have a temper to go with that hair! I wondered." She laughed again, only this time it was a brittle laugh, without humor. "I meant no offense, lady. Indeed, I find the story of your and Garret's meeting quite romantic—the great lord rescuing the chaste maid from the clutches of another—your betrothed, I believe? Why, 'tis the stuff of which minstrels write songs!"

Taryn's discomfort immediately yielded to angry annoyance. The ease with which the merchant's wife had abandoned Garret's title, using his Christian name, had not gone unnoticed, nor had the gradual changes in her tone and demeanor. She grew ever bolder with her remarks and honey-mouthed comments, the last of which were clearly laced with underlying sarcasm.

Taryn tossed down the towel and turned to confront her. "I have no wish to be rude, Madame, but my relationship with *Lord* Garret is a private matter. It does not concern you, and I frankly find your questions intrusive."

"Intrusive?" The woman rose to her feet. Slowly her mouth twisted into a sneer. "What is intrusive, lady, is that Garret has brought *you,* not only into my home, but to the very bed he and I have shared."

Somehow, perhaps instinctively, Taryn had known. Though her heart set to pounding in her ears like a drum, she heard herself respond with an outward calm she would never have thought possible. "Then mayhap you should voice your grievances to the lord himself, Madame. 'Tis clear he does not feel a like sentiment."

The woman's face went white. She had expected shock, outrage, disbelief.

Taryn would give her none of those, but instead continued evenly, "Unless there is aught else you wish to reveal, I should like a bit of privacy."

In a swirl of red the woman swept to the door. There she whirled and faced Taryn. Her dark eyes burned with contempt. "Do not think you have won, for you may yet sleep in that bed alone. There are a dozen wool merchants in Kirdford, but Garret came here. We will know this night if 'twas only the quality of my husband's wool which enticed him."

The door slammed with her exit, and at last Taryn allowed herself to release the maelstrom of emotions raging within her. She leaned against the table, her breath escaping in a long sigh. She knew Garret's reputation, had even taunted him with it to goad him into making this journey. So why should she feel this sense of betrayal? She was not his wife—not even his lover, save in name. The discovery that he was intimate with Geneviève Flambard should mean nothing. *He* should mean nothing.

But it did. *He* did.

And it hurt. It hurt to know he had lain with her in this bed, and had desired her—as he had never desired Taryn.

A sob escaped in a choking cry as Taryn realized what she felt. What twisted inside her like a knife was more than humiliation. It was jealousy—and anger. She was angry at him for having brought her here to be confronted by his indiscretions, and angry at herself. But then, had he not warned her?

The woman's taunting threat held more truth than she knew—and more than Taryn could accept. Surely Garret had brought her here for two purposes: to flaunt before her that which he was, and to avail himself of that which he routinely purchased. For now Taryn understood the strange glances and unspoken words which had passed between him and the merchant. Flambard knew of his wife's harlotry, but for adequate compensation he tolerated her adultery—and even opened his home to her paramour.

Suddenly, in the wake of the pain assailing her, a new emotion arose—pride. She would not let him know that his actions hurt her. Nor would she let Geneviève Flambard have that satisfaction either. Perhaps the only way would be to accept the woman's challenge. That would show them both. But in what way did she proceed? There seemed to be only one course of action to best Geneviève at her own game. Yet how was she to do this? How was she to entice a man into her bed who had twice sent her from his?

"Taryn?"

She gasped in shock and whirled. If he had knocked she had not heard it. "My lord." Nervously she pushed down her sleeves. "I did not hear you enter."

"Obviously." He shut the door and stepped forward, his eyes fixed upon her. "'Twould appear you have learned modesty, Mistress." With a mocking smile he tossed the saddlebags he carried onto the bed. "My men have returned. They have been from one end of the city to the other. Not that I expected different news, but there are no lodgings to be found. They have taken the horses to be stabled at an inn around the corner. 'Twould seem there's room aplenty for patrons willing to eat hay and sleep on straw."

Taryn nodded, only half hearing what he sad. Was there a message in his actions? The saddlebags he had brought contained her change of clothing, and his. Was this room, therefore, where he intended to sleep? Or would he later join his mistress?

"Do you require aught from the bags?"

"The bags?" Taryn looked at him in confusion, then realized he had no doubt noticed her staring at them. "Nay." She shook her head. "I'll leave you to change and meet you downstairs."

"Before you go, would you help me out of this mail?"

Suddenly Taryn could bear it no longer—this polite conversation a few feet from the bed in which he had made love to another woman! Her jealous anger and pain drove away caution. "Mayhap you would prefer instead that I summon Madame Flambard? I am sure she is much better suited to the task of undressing you than I."

"So you know. I thought as much. Tell me, which of you slammed the door?"

Taryn glared at him in disbelief. The only expression on his face was one of amusement. "I shall let you decide, my lord." She crossed the room and opened the door. "Compare that . . . to this!"

The sound echoed in her ears the length of the small hallway. Fiercely she gathered her shattered composure; by the time she entered the parlor her breathing was almost normal.

Garret entered a few minutes later, his mail abandoned. Wearing a belted tunic and his hair unbound, he stepped into the room with the air of a man wanting to be anywhere else.

Madame Flambard, who had been sitting in sullen

silence at the table's end, brightened instantly. She watched as he approached, her hungry eyes travelling the length of his body.

Seeing her actions, Taryn felt her stomach churn. She looked at Flambard. His sleek face was pinched. Had he, too, noticed his wife's behavior? She turned her gaze to Garret, now seating himself across the table from her. "I see that you managed after all, my lord."

Then, ignoring his answering scowl, she returned her attention to Flambard. "I am told you employ a dozen men, Master."

"In my shop, aye, lady. I have many more in my employ."

"Where do they work if not in the shop?"

Obviously pleased with the opportunity to talk about himself, the merchant cast her a wide smile. "In their homes, apartments they rent from me. I own the buildings in which they live, sometimes even the looms they operate. I find that such an arrangement enables me to maintain greater control. I take the work out to the weavers and collect it after each stage is complete, to check the quality. Thereby I also ensure that there has been no substitution of inferior materials—alas, a very likely occurrence in the weaving of rich stuffs involving the use of gold thread."

"You supervise the other stages as well—when the woven cloth is taken to the fullers to be shrunk and cleaned?" Taryn forced herself to keep her eyes on the man. Whatever else was taking place at the table, she did not want to know.

"Aye. To the dyers as well to fix the colors. You are knowledgeable indeed, milady. How is it that you are so informed? Might it have aught to do with the reason for your purchase today?"

Intent on maintaining this topic of conversation, Taryn explained about the wool room at Jaune and her plans to train the village women.

"I feel I should be concerned." He laughed. "If your

efforts are successful, you could steal my business."

"I doubt that shall be the case, Master Flambard. I do not anticipate an operation on so grand a scale."

"How very interesting, lady." From the end of the table Madame Flambard's silky voice sounded. "You arrive at Jaune the betrothed of another man, and yet now act as the first lady of the manor—well, nearly. Forsooth, I believe there have been no vows of marriage exchanged."

Taryn's back stiffened and her temper flared. But before she could say a word, Garret spoke.

"*Taryn.*" He leaned back in his chair, folding his arms across his chest. His look warned her to keep silent.

She choked back her rage, taking small comfort in the fact that the glower he then delivered Geneviève clearly made the woman wish she *had* kept silent.

As her husband chortled at the unspoken reproach, she turned a shade of scarlet which rivaled her gown.

In silence the meal was served and eaten. At its conclusion Taryn excused herself and retreated upstairs.

Garret watched her departure with a mixture of regret and relief.

"An interesting day, eh, milord?"

Garret looked at Flambard. "Aye," he agreed slowly, "and one not yet ended."

A bitter, scornful laugh rose from the man's throat. "You'll forgive me," he drawled, his voice heavy with drink and sarcasm, "if I cannot empathize with your plight." He turned to his wife. "Remove yourself. I am weary of your wanton display."

Geneviève's eyes flew open in false innocence. But if she intended words of denial, they never reached her lips. In aggrieved silence she rose to her feet.

Ignoring her departure, Flambard shoved a flagon of ale toward Garret. "I should like to share a most appropriate toast." He lifted his goblet. "To woman—confounder of man. Her eye is lecherous, her mouth sweet venom, but to lie betwixt her legs is an earthly

Heav'n." In one draught he downed the cup's contents and looked to Garret for a rejoinder.

Garret's goblet remained untouched. He stared at Flambard. A bitterness twisted inside him, and he looked away from the torment on the drunken man's face. He had always justified his actions with the belief that a husband who could not keep his wife's fidelity did not deserve it. Besides, Flambard had never seemed to object—as long as compensation had been generous.

But suddenly he began to see the affair in a new light. He saw Flambard for what he was—an older man bewitched by the beauty of a young wife. And though he was tormented by her infidelity, he was bent on keeping her at all costs, even if that cost was to be stripped of his dignity and pride, rendered no longer a man but an object of pity to his wife's lover.

"Why?" Garret forced himself to look at him. "Why do you allow it?"

"Why?" Flambard echoed. He blinked as if baffled by the question. "Because I love her."

His answer stunned Garret. This was a reason he would not have guessed. Of course, he would have to admit he knew little of love himself. His marriage to Clarissa had been arranged when they were children. And whatever youthful feelings he had borne his child bride had been buried with his son.

Perhaps his ability to love had been buried as well—certainly he had cared for no woman since. Maybe that was just as well. If Flambard were an example of what love made of a man, he wanted no part of it. His manhood would never be held hostage by any woman's faithlessness. No man would ever have cause to look upon him as he now looked upon Flambard, a pitiable cuckold.

Unable to think of any way to right the situation, he pushed back from the table and stood. "I'm for bed."

She was waiting for him at the top of the stairs, as he

knew she would be. Her lips, moist and warm, were instantly upon his.

He tore his mouth from hers and pushed her roughly away. "You grow ever more reckless, Madame Flambard. Or is his knowledge of your actions not enough? Mayhap you now desire to torment your husband with an actual witnessing of your cuckoldry?"

She pressed her body back against his, running a hand down his chest. "Yours are strange words, my lord." Nervously, she laughed low in her throat. "In the past you ne'er cared. He has slept upon sheets still damp with your sweat and bearing your scent."

"Not this night." In icy contempt Garret removed her hand. "Or any other."

Geneviève stepped back. Even in the darkness of the stairwell he could detect the flinty understanding glinting in her eyes.

"So the lady wins? 'Tis to her bed you crawl?" She tossed her head proudly. "She must perform better than she looks. Or have your tastes returned to virgins? By pretending she is your dead wife, do you ease your guilt since this one does not recoil from your touch in horror?"

Cold fury slammed through him, tearing at the fringes of his control. Suddenly Flambard's pathetic declaration of love rang in his ears. Garret turned away from her in disgust. The thankless whore was worth not even his anger. He walked to the end of the corridor and opened the door.

Chapter Eleven

Taryn heard his entrance and whirled from the bed. Before she could stop them, the words reflecting her surprise escaped. "I did not expect you here."

"And where else if not here?" Suddenly, as if understanding the meaning of her comment, Garret glowered at her. "Do you forget the charade we must honor?"

His anger confused her, but his brutal frankness stunned her pride. Obviously he was not in this room with her by choice, but out of the need to sustain the lie which was the only relationship they shared. And it was most clear he did so reluctantly; he wanted to be elsewhere. It required no skill in the art of deduction to know where and with whom.

His eyes raked her coldly, and she remembered she wore only a thin bed rail. She almost reached for her robe upon the bed, but then she recalled his taunting remark earlier when all she had covered was her bare arms. She took a deep breath and tried to force her emotions into order.

Faced with his unexpected anger her resolve wavered. Her earlier vow to take retribution upon him and his mistress seemed more difficult to fulfill, and an entirely new and foreign emotion tempered her anger as well. She *was* glad he was with her. But suddenly she realized she desperately wanted the reason to be different: she wanted him to want her, as he did the merchant's wife.

The pain of Geneviève Flambard's revelation returned, and with it the jealousy she had tried to deny. She squeezed her eyes shut, reeling at the meaning of what she had just acknowledged to herself.

"Take the bed. I will sleep on the floor."

His words seemed to unleash a strange impulse. She ignored the inner voice which warned her to proceed no further. A will not entirely hers had taken control. She was driven by more than the need to prove her rival wrong. She would not sleep in this bed alone!

Coyly she lowered her eyes as she had seen the other woman do and stepped toward him. "You will not be very comfortable." She managed to imitate the breathy whisper as well. She pressed closer and touched his arm, letting her fingertips linger. "'Tis a large bed, with room aplenty for two."

He looked down at her, and she saw something flicker in his eyes—interest? Encouraged, she continued, the words hers, and yet not hers. "The floor is hard and cold. Surely you would not prefer it to the softness and warmth available?"

Immediately his eyes went cold. "What are you doing?"

"Naught," she purred. She let herself brush against him as she turned back toward the bed.

He halted her movement with a firm hand on her arm, then spun her around to face him. Anger blazed in his pale stare. "You are acting like a whore. It neither becomes you nor pleases me."

Her pulse began to beat erratically, yet she forbade herself to tremble. Anger and pride formed her retort. "It pleased you when she did it."

"You are not her." Roughly, almost violently, he pulled her to him. "You are like a child acting a role which you have no idea how to play. Do you really want a man's hands upon you?" In concurrence with his challenge, his hands slid down her buttocks. "Or his mouth pressed to yours?" He grabbed her by the nape of her neck and positioned her mouth to his.

Taryn could feel the whole hard length of his body pushing against her as his tongue forced her lips apart. Her first reaction was to pull away. But she didn't. That was what he wanted, expected, her to do, to prove himself right—that she was not a woman capable of responding to a man.

And as she stood there passive in his arms, a sudden ripple of awareness seemed to run through the secret parts of her. Somehow her body knew what to do. She pressed closer and opened her mouth to his tongue's entrance.

His body went instantly rigid. He shoved her from him with such force that her head snapped backward.

"Take to your virginal bed and leave me in peace!"

She recoiled in horror at the contempt and disgust that flowed from him. She turned away, burning in shame.

Garret tore his eyes from the slender form stumbling toward the bed. *Peace?* The word echoed mockingly in his mind. What peace would he find this night—with his blood afire and his emotions in turmoil? He had meant only to frighten her, to force her to see herself as she was and to end her ridiculous attempt at seduction. He had not counted on his body responding—or hers!

By all that was holy! Could he not control his desires? He could not take this woman. What she offered to him out of some fit of feminine spite she could not possibly deliver. She was a virgin. How could she, with no experience of men, know what she risked?

He walked over to the wash basin in the corner and ripped off his outer tunic. The cool water he splashed on his face did nothing. The fire he sought to douse burned elsewhere. He snatched up a towel and glanced toward the bed.

She sat, her body rigid, staring straight ahead. Her eyes were bordered with moisture, and when she blinked two droplets escaped to slide down her cheek. Quickly she bowed her head and wiped away the tears.

Watching her, Garret silently groaned. Of all that he had witnessed in this world of death and destruction and of man's capacity for evil, nothing affected him as did the sight of a woman's tears. And he had caused these tears because of his anger at the lechery of others. He was wrong to lash out at her. Even though she was of age, she was in many ways younger. She needed to be treated with more understanding. He had done little of that. Perhaps if he did, they would get along better.

"I'm sorry." Belying his charitable thoughts, his voice was sharp and cold.

She started at the sound of it, yet did not look at him.

"I did not mean to speak so harshly . . ." he continued. His words came slowly and with difficulty. ". . . But you do not know what your actions . . . convey."

At last she glanced up at him. Confusion clouded her face.

He stepped forward reluctantly. "I am a man, Taryn. I cannot help but respond to certain . . . signals. When you act and speak in a manner so as to indicate willingness, 'tis a signal—an invitation. And though I know here . . ." he tapped his temple with a forefinger, ". . . that you make this invitation ignorant as to the consequences and hence I should have honor enough not to take advantage, there is a part of me which wants to cast righteousness aside. I am tempted, and thus I am angered that the invitation was given. Do you understand?"

She looked thoughtful for a moment, then sighed. "Nay. Quite obviously I do not understand. Thrice you have refused my invitation—as you call it—and each time I have been left more confused. How is it that you can desire Madame Flambard, yet turn from me? What is wrong with me?"

Hearing her words, Garret's frustration grew. He could

not make himself more clear. "With you I am as a starving peasant shown a feast of which he cannot partake."

His comparison drew a stare even more blank.

He sat beside her. "Taryn. Seduction, without knowing its rules, can be a very dangerous game. Do you know what it means to be with a man? To truly be *with* a man?"

"Truly?" She shook her head. "Nay."

"Then this you must first learn, before you extend the invitation." Satisfied that he had finally made her understand, he stood. Her hand on his arm, however, stopped him from stepping away.

"Teach me."

"What?" He looked down at her in dismay.

"Teach me," she repeated. "Explain to me what happens betwixt a man and a woman."

"Nay. I cannot. 'Tis something you should learn from a woman. When we return, speak to Maite or one of the others."

"That makes little sense, my lord. If I want to know what 'tis like to be with a man, should I not ask a man?"

Garret sighed. From a point of logic she was right. And if he had learned anything by playing chess with her, it was that she was logical. But that she would ask why he could not teach her only proved how little she did know. "I cannot," he insisted. "I do not know the words."

"Would you be able to explain it to one of your squires? Surely men are not born knowing the ways of men and women. If one of the youths I saw in the yard came to you with the desire to understand, to learn, would you then know the words?"

"Aye. But 'tis different."

"I don't understand why. If what you explain is the same, why is the manner by which you do so not also the same?"

There was her logic again, flawless in her naïveté. "Because a man can say things to another man with words he would never use with a woman."

She looked at him as if mulling over what he had said. When she shrugged, he felt relief knowing that she had at least accepted a part of what he had said—or else he had succeeded in confusing her totally.

Suddenly she gave him the strangest of looks. "In that case . . ." A small smile curved her lips. ". . . pretend I am one of your squires." She sat up straighter and set her shoulders, flipping back the braid that had fallen foward.

A sensation of total frustration poured over him. He felt as if he had just declared "check" only to have her immediately counter with "checkmate." Not trusting his voice, he shook his head.

"Try."

Realizing she would not be put off, he searched for a response. At last he shrugged, resigned. If he told her what she wanted to hear, she'd quickly enough grow embarrassed and beg him to stop. "Very well. Have you ever seen a man naked?"

He was purposely blunt, but the tinge of pink he had expected to see was not forthcoming.

"Nay. But I have seen children, boys. I assume 'tis the same—only larger."

He felt as if he'd been punched in the belly. He fought for composure and continued. He was not yet daunted. "And you know how you are . . . different . . . there?"

She nodded. There was still no blush.

"You have seen animals, mayhap horses, breeding?"

Again she nodded.

"Then that is how 'tis done. 'Tis a joining."

An expression of disappointment crossed her face. "Surely a man does not climb on a woman's back and bite her on the neck?"

In spite of himself, he laughed. "Offtimes 'tis little different."

His humor was lost on her, and she glared at him angrily. "What you have told me I know. 'Tis the 'joining' which I do not understand. What happens?"

He raked his fingers through his hair in exasperation. It was not she who now grew uncomfortable, but he. "The pieces fit together. The man and the woman . . . the pieces."

"How?"

"They fit."

"How?"

Garret lost his composure completely. "Trust me, Mistress. They fit!"

"I don't see how," she grumbled as if to herself. "What I have seen of boys, 'tis a limp piece of flesh. How is a man to 'fit' it anywhere?" She looked up at him. "There must be something you have not told me."

As his frustration vented itself in anger, he suddenly lost all desire to be delicate. If she wanted to know, by God, he would tell her! "Arousal, Mistress." He spoke the word through clenched teeth. "The man becomes aroused—hard. The 'limp piece of flesh' increases in size and stiffens. With this he penetrates the woman. He opens her legs and . . . and . . ."

"What does it feel like?" she prompted impatiently.

Her question sent him over the edge. "By the blood of Christ, woman! Have you no sense of shame?"

"I hardly see what shame has to do with it." She stood up and glared at him defiantly. "First you are angry because I do not know. Now you are angry because I am trying to learn." She tossed back the braid that had again fallen over her shoulder. "I would have thought a man with your obvious experience would be better able to discuss the matter. Mayhap I should speak to a woman after all. I'm sure Madame Flambard would have no difficulty in answering my questions."

He had no idea if her threat was empty or not. From the moment he'd met her, Taryn Maitland had been impossible to second-guess. She was a puzzle whose solution defied him; a virgin who had twice now attempted to seduce him. At least the first time he had understood her reason—or thought he had. But this?

He sighed in surrender. "Ideally, 'tis a feeling of pleasure, Mistress."

She nodded, satisfied. "I had thought as much—for when you kissed me I felt such a sensation."

He stared at her, speechless. He did not know how to respond to her admission of taking pleasure in his kiss.

"Does this feeling intensify when the man 'penetrates' the woman?"

He dropped his head into his hands. "Aye."

"When you kissed me, did you become aroused? Was that the reason for your anger?"

He could feel her gaze, lowered to the area between his legs. "Aye, Mistress. And I will save you the effort. I am feeling it now as well." He looked up at her. "But unless you would have me display it for your inspection there is naught more I can offer."

At last she colored in embarrassment. But the triumph he expected to feel evaded him. "Are we finished?" he asked.

"Aye." She turned back to the bed. "Thank you."

"My pleasure," he muttered.

"I think not, my lord."

As her soft laughter filled the room, she dipped her head in a half-hearted gesture of apology and slipped into bed, pulling the coverlet to her chin.

Garret stared at her for a moment more, then moved to put out the candles burning on the mantle.

Once they were extinguished the room was bathed in a pale shrouding of moonlight streaming in through the window.

Taryn watched his shadowy form pace for several minutes. Finally, he pulled a chair from in front of the fireplace over to the window.

"Go to sleep, Taryn," he stated firmly. His tone brooked no further argument or discussion.

She closed her eyes and tried to obey, but, despite her fatigue she could not sleep.

Surely the fault did not lie with the bed upon which

she lay. The high straw mattress beneath and the one of feathers atop were neither hard nor lumpy. The bedding was as fine as any she had slept upon; linen sheets and soft woolen blankets . . .

No. It was not the bed. It was she. Her mind swirled with questions and thoughts. She went over each word that had passed between them, each expression upon his face, trying to understand what had occurred.

She recalled the feeling of being held against his body, the way her own had tingled in response. Unlike that first night when she had gone to him, this time she had been unafraid. And though he had rebuked her, she at last understood why.

Before, she had believed that he found her undesirable, this man whose indulgences of the flesh were so well recounted. Now she knew that he did find her desirable—he had admitted as much. He found her naïve, as well. And because of some sense of honor or code, he would not take such a woman. But was that which had repelled him merely her lack of knowledge—or her lack of experience as well? If she were again to offer herself, *would* he now accept her "invitation"? Or would he again send her back to her "virginal bed"?

She moaned softly. How could she sort these strange feelings within her? The harder she tried to push them aside, the more they persisted. She opened her eyes and stared up at the bed's canopy, then out through the open curtains. She looked to the still figure in the chair before the window.

His feet propped upon the sill, legs crossed, arms hugged to his chest, Garret slumbered as if he had fallen asleep looking out into the night.

She stared at his profile, dark against the moonlight. She sat up and crawled to the foot of the bed, reaching for his cloak draped across the rail. Easing out of the bed, she padded across the wooden floor to stand beside him. She hesitated for a moment, then spread the garment over his prone form, tucking in the edges at his shoulders. In sleep he seemed a different man. The hard lines of his face were relaxed, making him look more youthful and at peace with himself. Awake there was a harshness about him, a distance not to be breached.

She shook off the thought and turned away.

With her back to him she did not see the one eye which opened to watch her return to her bed.

Taryn awoke with a start, at first not knowing where she was. She looked about and the strange room became familiar. She sat up, her gaze darting to the window. The chair before it was empty, shadowy in the predawn grayness.

"Get yourself ready. We leave at first light. I want to be under way and at the city gates as soon as they are opened."

Taryn stared at the man who had appeared before her. Garret was already dressed. Looking upon him, she saw no trace of the man who had slept before the window. His jaw was set, his eyes cold.

"Did you hear me, Mistress?"

She nodded, watching as he belted on sword and scabbard.

"Ready yourself," he repeated. And then he was gone.

Taryn sighed and climbed from the bed. The day had begun on a poor note, and she doubted it would improve. The journey from Juane had been a far from pleasant ordeal. Compared to what now awaited her, though, it had been a frolic!

Quickly she dressed. When she opened the door to go below she found Garret waiting on the landing. Without speaking, he entered the room and retrieved the saddlebags. Then, with a firm hand at her elbow he guided her down the stairs to where Flambard awaited them. There was no sign of his wife.

"Lady Taryn." He bowed in greeting. "I trust you slept well?"

"Aye," she lied. "But 'twould not have been the case without your hospitality. Please extend my gratitude to your wife. I'm sure her night was not spent in such comfort."

A flicker of amusement entered the man's eyes. "There is no cause for your worry, my lady. Come, I shall escort you below."

Once out onto the street, Garret wasted no time in ordering one of his men to set her in her saddle, as if she were so much baggage.

She fought off her resentment as several mumbled comments reached her ears. Clearly his men were less than pleased with the early departure. Several of the six had the look about them of men who had sotted away a goodly portion of their night.

If Garret noted their state, it was not apparent. Donning hood and gauntlets, he was occupied with the merchant in an exchange of farewells.

Suddenly the city's bells sounded. The gates were open.

Garret mounted and signaled his men forward.

Taryn set her heel to her horse's flank and took her place beside the destrier. Tossing his huge head and pawing the muddy ground, the animal fretted at even this small delay. She smiled wanly. At least there was one in their party anxious to undertake the long and assuredly silent journey back to Jaune.

"You return early. Either you rode as if the Devil himself were at your back, or you departed the city at dawn."

Garret dipped his head, half in greeting to the tiny form rounding the stable's corner, half to clear its low lintel. He should have known Maite would not wait to make her inquiry. "We left at dawn," he stated quietly.

At once a concerned frown appeared on the wrinkled brow. Cocking her head, Maite set clenched fists upon her hips. "What happened—and don't tell me naught. A blind man could read your face, boy."

Garret smiled wryly. "You were right, Maite."

"Indeed? Pray tell about what? 'Tis so seldom I hear that admission from your lips."

He ignored the hint of sarcasm. "I should not have taken her to Flambard's."

"Ah." At once a smile broke out across her face. "So the lady has a jealous streak?"

Amazed that she could have gleaned so much from so few words, Garret looked at her in surprise.

" 'Twas to be expected," she offered in reply to the question he did not ask. "After all, you have become her champion, her protector, of sorts. Under such circumstances, 'tis natural that she should come to develop feelings for you."

"I do not want her 'developing feelings' for me!" He glared at the old woman, furious that she had put into words what he knew and did not want to acknowledge. Was the situation not complicated enough that he should now have to deal with emotions—hers *and* his? Since the first night she had come to him, he had struggled to curtail his physical attraction. Knowledge of her chastity had made it easier, and as the weeks had passed he had been successful in his efforts to see her only as a responsibility. But after what had occurred last night . . .

"Well, whether you do or do not wish it," Maite's voice interrupted his thoughts, "she has." She shrugged. "For the present, however, I think *this* should probably be of more concern to you. It arrived by messenger this noon."

Garret took the folded sheet of parchment she removed from the hem of her sleeve. He recognized its seal at once. " 'Tis from Henry."

"Aye, even *I* can recognize the king's signet when I see it."

Garret raised a brow, yet let the surly comment pass for he knew well its cause. After his mother's death Maite had convinced his father to engage the services of a tutor for a short time. But Garret had lacked the temperament and discipline needed to be a scholar. He had hated the hours of being shut up. His mind was always on the hunt he was missing, the training field exercises he had to forego. Finally, after weeks of rebellion, his father had dismissed the tutor. Maite had never forgiven Garret, and in the twenty-plus years since no opportunity to remind him of his shortcoming was ever overlooked.

He tucked the letter beneath his belt. "Where is Richard?"

She shrugged. "He rode out this morning, saying only he would be back by nightfall."

Garret frowned. His steward could be anywhere, mediating a land dispute between neighbors, investigating a villein's petition for wood and straw to repair a roof that had fallen in, imposing a fine upon a tenant who was idle and hence owed work days. The possibilities were as endless as his duties. To track him down could take hours. But how else was he to learn the contents of Henry's letter? At the present time there was no *scrivener* at Jaune. Richard handled all the records, legal and financial.

Suddenly he thought of Taryn. Had she not been able to read Flambard's bill of sale? "Where is Lady Taryn?"

Maite lifted a brow. It was quite clear she found his question without logic, given his declaration of a moment ago.

"The lady knows how to read," he supplied in annoyance.

"Indeed?" This time she limited her sarcasm to a single word. "She's in her chamber, bathing away two days' worth of dust would be my guess—as she requested water to be heated and brought up."

"Send her to me when she is finished."

"As you wish. Maite turned to leave, then stopped abruptly. "By the way, there's a bath prepared and waiting for you as well."

Garret grinned. "Do you mean to tell me that after all these years you have at last learned to anticipate my needs? Your thoughtfulness is acknowledged—and appreciated."

His mocking bow evoked an immediate huff of defiance. "Save your appreciation. 'Twas not my doing, but the lady's." She wrinkled her nose and sniffed. "And I do not believe thoughtfulness was her prime consideration."

He waited until she had begun to walk away before lifting an arm to make his own tentative appraisal.

Taryn paused at the oaken door. Balancing the towels she held in one hand, she lifted the other and nervously smoothed back the damp tendrils that curled at her temples. Maite had provided no explanation for Garret's summons, only the instructions that Taryn was to go above to his chamber at once. And, too, since she was headed in that direction, she might as well save Maite a trip and deliver his clean laundry.

Left with a stack of towels and her curiosity, Taryn had watched the woman's exit, wondering as to the cause for the strange twinkle she was certain she had seen in the old servant's eyes. Perhaps now she would find out . . .

Squaring her shoulders, she knocked on the heavy door before her. Upon Garret's command she opened the portal and entered. The main body of the room was unoccupied, and her eyes darted to the corners. "My lord?"

"Here."

She followed the sound of his voice, walking over to a wooden parclose that appeared to wall off a small alcove. "You sent for—" Her question ended in midstatement as she stepped around the screen.

There seated in the wooden tub waist-high in bath water, was Garret. From the look on his face it was clear he was as surprised by her presence on his side of the screen as she was upon realizing what the thing concealed.

Stunned, she could only stare.

He recovered more quickly, looking blankly at the towels she carried. "You are able to read, are you not?"

She nodded, confused by his question.

"Very well then. I received a letter today. As Richard is not here, I should like you to read it."

"But why—" She clamped her mouth shut. Suddenly she realized why he had not noticed the mistake in Flambard's shop himself. The Great Earl could not read! "Of course, my lord," she murmured.

Hoping he had not discerned the surprise she must have revealed, she dropped her eyes from his. In so doing her gaze fell upon his naked chest, wet and glistening. She stared in fascination as converging beads of water bypassed the raised scars that marred the smooth skin.

"Ahem."

His cough jolted her from her study of the rivulets' path. She lifted her gaze to find him watching her with equal intensity.

"I should like to get out," he stated flatly. "Will you hand me one of those towels you are clutching and turn your gaze?"

She flushed and tossed him a towel. Turning, she heard him stand and step out of the tub. A moment later he spoke.

"You may turn around."

He had donned braies and hose, but had taken little care in first drying the water from his body. Dampness was causing the cloth to cling to his thighs and to cloy about the area between them. She stared at what was clearly outlined by the damp fabric.

"Is this going to become habit, Mistress?" His tone suggested annoyance tinged with amusement.

"Nay, my lord," she whispered, feeling the heat in her cheeks rise as she averted her eyes.

"Good." He walked over to the table by the window

and picked up a folded sheet of parchment lying there. "Here. Tell me what it says."

Taryn stepped forward and took the letter from his hand. Its seal was unbroken, the impression in the wax clear. "'Tis from His Majesty," she offered hesitantly, not sure if he had been able to recognize the royal seal.

"That much I already know," he growled. "Open it and read it."

She fumbled for an instant to break the seal, then unfolded the single sheet. "Henry, King of England, Duke of Normandy and Aquitaine, and Count of Anjou, To Garret d'Aubigny, Great Earl of Arundel and keeper of its royal castle, Jaune, Greeting—"

"Skip all that blather, Mistress. Read it and just tell me what the damned thing says!" He dropped into one of the chairs at the table and reached for the flagon of spiced wine Taryn had ordered brought up along with the heated water for his bath. She had hoped the refreshment might do for his mood what a hot bath could for a saddle-weary body. Obviously, the first half of her efforts had been wasted.

She quickly scanned the letter.

"Well?" he demanded.

Hesitantly, she looked up and met his questioning stare. She had no idea how he would react to what she had just read. For some reason, however, she doubted he would be pleased. "His Majesty is coming here. From Winchester. In two days."

"Here?" He sat up and slammed down the goblet all in one motion.

"Aye." She watched the spilled wine drip to the floor, then forced her gaze to return to him. "His Majesty is holding Easter at Winchester and will pass through Arundel on his way back to London. He requests your hospitality for a night."

Garret slumped back in his chair and let out a loud, audible breath. He knew Henry's habits as well as his own. Each year he held three great feasts: Christmas at

Gloucester, Whitsuntide at Westminster and Easter at Winchester. There he met with certain chief earls and barons. While he watched them, they took a good look at him. The peace of England depended on what they all saw. Any lack of strength and determination on his part and their loyalties might be swayed. And he, in turn, took their measure. There could be only one reason Henry would be stopping at Jaune. He must have seen or learned something at Winchester.

"Damn!" he swore softly. The rumors of unrest which had been circulating for weeks were apparently more than rumor.

"My lord?"

At the sound of Taryn's voice he forced a false calm and looked at her. "'Twould appear 'tis time for you to earn your keep, Mistress."

The question leaping immediately into her eyes amused him. "You are the closest thing Jaune has to a first lady," he offered by way of an explanation. He took up the goblet and raised it to his lips. "Therefore, I am entrusting you with the task of making the necessary preparations."

Chapter Twelve

Like fire through a droughted field, news of the royal visit spread. By day's end there was not a soul, castlefolk or villein, who did not know of the impending event.

Taryn left Garret's chamber and went to work straightaway. She summoned the butler and cellarer to make an inventory of the food, ale and wine stored away in the great vaults beneath the keep. Next she sent for the chief huntsman and ordered him to muster beaters and course the forests. Castlemen were sent to fish in the river that flowed through the hills above the keep. The catch would be placed in holding pools in the kitchen garden until needed.

She had no idea the number Jaune would be called upon to feed. She had heard stories of the king's retinue numbering up to three hundred. Two days was simply not sufficient time to prepare food for such a throng!

That evening she approached Garret with her concerns.

He seemed somewhat amused by her vexation. "You take this task too much to heart, Mistress," he chided, almost gently. "Henry is but a man. His needs are not so complex. See that his belly and cup are filled—and his bed if he so desires—and he will be satisfied."

She gasped, shocked at the irreverence of his tone. "You speak of the King of England!"

Garret smiled. "I gather you have never met His Majesty?"

She shook her head.

"Then you shall indeed be surprised."

"How so?"

"I doubt he will fit the image you seem to have formed of him. Henry is no polished son of a cultured court. He dresses shabbily, bites his nails, and commonly uses coarse and blasphemous language. In fact, courtiers rail at his foul table manners, and I have seen Queen Eleanor quite irked by his ways. His moods are always unpredictable, and his temper often uncontrollable. Legend even has it that he is of diabolic descent, for one of his ancestors of the courts of Anjou is said to have married a fairy, a daughter of the Devil."

Taryn was not sure if he teased or not. Certainly he spoke in a casual, jesting way. "Save the table manners and bitten nails, he sounds very much like another I know," she murmured under her breath. It was no wonder the Great Earl of Arundel was so favored in the king's eye—the two were kindred spirits, as like as horns on the same goat!

Other than a slightly elevated brow, Garret gave no indication of having heard her deliberately muffled observation. He pushed away from the table and rose, extending his hand. "To answer your original question, though, I doubt he will arrive with any more than thirty or forty in his party. After all, he is not moving court. Make your preparations accordingly. Now, might you favor me with a game of chess?"

Though she would have preferred to decline, Taryn did not. She placed her hand atop his and followed him to the hearth where the boards had already been set up.

Despite her fatigue from the journey and her mental preoccupation with the details of what needed to be done in the next two days, she was able to best him two of three games. She had the feeling, in spite of his words to the contrary, that he *was* concerned about the impending visit.

Finally she excused herself, citing her need to rise early.

She did not lie. Hours before dawn she was dressed and giving orders. Fires were built out in the garden. All day perspiring varlets would be adding great logs over which would roast long spits of geese, drake, and pheasant. Over other fires cauldrons of meat would boil and over yet another—depending upon the luck and skill of the hunting parties soon to depart from Jaune's walls—a whole stag would roast.

And the cooking was not confined to the garden. In the bailey cookhouse and in the keep's kitchen servants had already been assembled to clean, mince, blanch, parboil and crush herbs in preparation for a meal designed to tempt the royal palate.

Elsewhere, other essential preparations had begun. Daily tasks assumed new import and were performed with added effort and ardor. Covers, cushions and wall hangings were taken out and shaken. The great hall was swept, its floor washed and laid with fresh rushes. The long tabletops were scrubbed and extra boards laid upon trestles to provide seating for the influx of guests.

The enormous tablecloths to be used and the bed linens destined for the guest rooms were put into wooden troughs, soaked in wood ashes and caustic soda, then pounded, rinsed and dried in the sun. Even the candle stubs were removed from the iron sconces and replaced. Every silver goblet, plate, platter, pitcher and flagon was polished, either for use or for display upon the open shelves of the hall's two cupboards. Finally, a table was brought in to serve as a staging area, where the foods would be brought for final preparation, decoration or saucing before they were served.

At last the day of the royal visit arrived. In the early afternoon Taryn met with Richard to discuss the final details for accommodations. Henry would, of course, take Garret's chamber. His chancellor and chamberlain would be provided mattresses that they might be near him should he have need of their services. Others of high rank would be given the guest rooms while remaining servants and attendants would bed down upon pallets in the hall.

Taryn had not seen Garret since the evening they had played chess. He had ridden out with the hunting parties that would supply the fresh meat for the feast and was not yet returned. Hence she was unsure what her role was to be. While she doubted Henry was uninformed as to her presence at Jaune, she was more than a little uncomfortable with the prospect of being presented to the King of England as the Great Earl's leman.

As she spoke to Richard about the seating arrangements, she tried tactfully to determine if Garret's steward might know more than she. "Space at the high table will be limited," she began. "Without knowing the exact number in the king's party we cannot yet know who from Jaune will be seated upon the dais."

"Never fear, milady. I have sat at sideboards before." He smiled. "The only two that need to be seated at the high table are you and Lord Garret."

"I?" Taryn tried to keep her voice level. "Are you certain Lord Garret desires that I be in attendance?"

Richard looked at her in surprise. Clearly, Garret had not said so much to him in words, yet until she had questioned him, he had felt no qualms. "I can only assume, lady, that he would want to present you."

"Mayhap we should not make that assumption," she replied gently, noting the man's obvious embarrassment.

At that moment she heard the keep's doors open. Garret entered the hall. That he had just returned with the remaining hunting party was clear. He bore all the signs of hard riding. His mantle was gray with dust, his unshaven face streaked with dirt and sweat.

From across the great hall his eyes locked upon her.

"You are not dressed?"

His question was more a statement of fact. In confusion Taryn glanced down at the simple gown she wore, covered by an apron. Did he mistake the pale-colored shift for a chemise? "Forsooth, my lord, I *am* dressed."

"As a serving wench," he answered brusquely, crossing the hall toward her. "Go and dress yourself accordingly. I'll not be presenting a scullery maid to His Majesty."

"I think you have your answer, lady." Smiling, Richard bowed and withdrew.

"What is he talking about?" Garret gestured to the departing back of his steward.

Taryn lowered her gaze nervously. "We were discussing whether or not I was to be in attendance this evening."

"And why would you not be?"

Seeing that his confusion was genuine made her all the more uncomfortable. "The circumstances are somewhat . . . unusual," she offered hesitantly.

Suddenly he smiled in understanding. "And so you were not sure if I would be presenting to His Majesty the woman I am supposed to be bedding?"

"That was my thought," she answered, feeling a rising warmth.

Garret laughed. "I can assure you, Taryn, for those accustomed to life at court, immorality and scandal are quite commonplace. A mistress hardly causes a raised brow. Henry will not think twice about your . . . ah . . . position at Jaune."

His words, designed to reassure her, succeeded only in intensifying the heat in her cheeks.

"I hope you will be better able to conceal your embarrassment in his presence," he stated, half-mockingly and half in exasperation, "else this chaste maid's blush of yours will surely expose our charade."

"You can scarce expect me to be what I am not," she

retorted angrily. She lifted her eyes and was sure she saw something flash in his. Sorrow? Regret? It was gone before she could identify it.

"Go and dress," he commanded. His gruff tone belied no emotion other than annoyance.

Taryn was still in her chamber when she heard the watchman's horn proclaiming the sighting of riders upon the horizon. Unable to see through the panes of stained glass, she hurried from her room down the corridor to one of the guest chambers whose window she knew faced out upon the entrance to Jaune.

From there she could see down to both the inner and outer baileys below. Armed men scrambled to positions atop the walls while others mounted and rode out through the portcullis and across the drawbridge. How they confronted the approaching party would depend upon its identity as friend or foe.

Before Taryn was able to recognize the standard borne by the score of riders coming into view, the faint flourish of trumpets was heard. No war party would announce itself with such fanfare. Despite the unexpectedly early hour of its arrival, the procession nearing Jaune's walls was clearly the royal retinue.

Taryn dashed from the room, returning to her own to finish dressing. Over her pleated undergown of cream-colored linen she donned a knee-length *bliaut* of rich saffron. Embroidered around its wide sleeves and neck with gold thread and pearls, it was the finest garment she owned. Wide in cut, the overtunic relied not upon laces for fit, but a girdle.

She reached for the one laid out upon the bed. It was her greatest luxury, a belt of plaited cords of black silk held together by gold rings into which were set pearls and emeralds. She clasped the belt loosely around her waist, adjusting it so that it sagged down in a "v" in front to below the level of her hips. When she walked, its trailing ends would sway gracefully just above her knee.

Finally she placed a square veil of sheer white silk over her unbound hair followed by the confining circlet of gold she had worn previously at Maite's insistence. After a quick glance in the looking glass to make sure the veil fell evenly across her forehead, she headed for the door.

On the stairs going down she encountered a man who was on his way up. Something seemed familiar in his silhouette, but the dimly lit stairwell cast his face in shadows. She paused on the landing to let him pass. Not until he stopped several steps below her and spoke did she recognize him.

"I was coming to fetch you. Did you not hear the trumpets?"

"My lord," she gasped, startled to realize his identity—though it was no wonder that she had not. The elegantly cut *bliaut* he wore was far different from his usual attire of scuffed tabard or *hauberk*. Gone, too, were the high boots he wore for riding. In their stead he appeared to be wearing fine silk hose and shoes of appliquéd leather.

Wordlessly Garret took her arm and led her down the stairs into the anteroom.

Now, in more lighted quarters, her eyes took in the length of him. The *bliaut* of blue-green silk, a perfect color match to his eyes, was decorated at the neck and sleeves with bands of embroidery. Draped across his right shoulder was a furred mantle, long and trailing, held in place with a jeweled brooch.

"I shall take your staring to be a compliment," he stated evenly, casting a look at her from the corner of his eye as he led her toward the entrance to the great hall.

"As it was meant," she replied, still somewhat in awe of his appearance. Indeed, he presented a most dignified and magnificent figure.

He shook his head. "I do not know if your unabashed honesty is to be admired, lady—or reprimanded." He guided her into the hall to where the highborn of Jaune had assembled themselves into a receiving line. Placing her in Richard's care, he exited the keep to greet his guests.

"He looks every inch the Great Earl, does he not, lady?"

Taryn looked at the steward whose words echoed her very thoughts. "Aye," she agreed. "'Tis a shame Jaune does not have royal visitors more often."

"And why is that?"

Taryn smiled and gestured to the doors through which Garret had disappeared. "I was speaking in terms of your lord's appearance, his clothing. 'Tis a shame he only dresses so when he is host to the King."

Clearly bemused, Richard rubbed his chin. "Actually, my lady, Henry has visited Jaune often, thrice in the past year alone, and on none of those occasions did Lord Garret look as he does now."

"Indeed?" As Taryn realized the import of what Richard had unknowingly revealed, she smiled in secret pleasure. Then, feeling Richard's eyes upon her and not wishing to discuss the matter further, she turned her attention to the tables set in preparation for the feast soon to commence.

Upon the sparkling white tablecloths stood goblets and shallow plates of silver at each place. This day there would be no pewter tankards or wooden trenchers.

With a silent prayer that all would proceed smoothly and that no food would be overcooked, burned or otherwise spoiled, she looked back to the open doors.

There was the sound of voices, the thudding of footsteps and suddenly the doorway was filled with men. Heading the procession was Garret. At his side walked a man of medium stature, broad-built and bull-necked, with long arms and bow legs. His hair was a flaming red, and the eyes which looked out of the freckled, weather-beaten face were dove gray, eager and questing. They darted about the hall, travelled the length of the reception line and settled promptly upon Taryn.

She felt her heartbeat quicken and her color rise. Casting her gaze to the floor, her uneasiness only increased with each approaching footstep.

"So this is the maid who has captured your fancy, Garret. I compliment you upon your taste and now understand why you were compelled to take her from another."

Through the roar of blood pounding in her ears Taryn heard Garret's voice—somewhat strained and tense.

"Sire, may I present Lady Taryn Maitland."

Taryn forced herself to lift her gaze. The smile which awaited her was kind and engaging.

"Lady Taryn, I am Henry of Anjou, King of England."

"Sire." She dropped into a curtsy, and as she rose Henry extended his hand. She smiled. *Dirty and callused, the nails are indeed bitten.* "'Tis a great honor, Majesty."

"The honor is mine, lady. May I present my chancellor . . ."

The ensuing line of faces, names and titles seemed endless. Taryn soon gave up the effort to remember who was who, or serving in what capacity. In addition to Henry's chancellor, there were chamberlains and personal attendants, his royal secretary, chaplain, marshal and constable.

After being introduced to her, the men proceeded down the line, greeting the assembled parties. The entire process took nearly an hour and in that time the hall steadily filled with Jaune's soldiers. She was sure the walls could hold no more, especially when no less than thirty of Henry's knights entered to join the press of humanity.

At last a fanfare of trumpets signaled all to sit.

Henry, as the honored guest, took Garret's center chair. As host, Garret sat upon his right. Taryn, the only woman present save serving maids, was seated next, also to the right. Beside her were Richard and two other men of Jaune. Upon Henry's left sat his chancellor, chaplain, chamberlain and marshal. The others in his retinue sat among Jaune's people in descending order of social rank on benches at the trestle tables, which were perpendicular to the platform.

Prayers at the high table came next, led by the royal chaplain, a small bird-like man with a pinched face. He took great delight in the obvious discomfort of those who, having ridden long, now fidgeted. At last Henry silenced him with a stern stare. Amens quickly followed and the pages appeared with towels and bowls filled with warm water fragrant with herbs.

As was custom, the first to wash his hands was Henry, followed by Garret, then the others seated at the high table. At Garret's nod, and to the accompaniment of another flourish of trumpets, the servers began to bring in the large silver platters and covered tureens.

The first course began with roasted birds, presented in order of size, the largest to the smallest: swan, goose, duck, then peacock, partridge and pigeon.

A new fanfare signaled that eating might now commence.

Succeeding the course of fowl was one of roasted meats, including venison, beef and pork; and stews, well-seasoned and rich, some in steaming pastry. Following that were the fish dishes, some also baked in pastry or grilled on embers, others prepared in piquant spiced stews or cunningly wrought sauces.

When conferring with Jaune's cook about the menu, Taryn had been amazed at the man's repertoire of recipes and even more surprised to learn he had once worked at the royal court. Garret's fondness for simplicity in his attire and in the furnishings of his castle had obviously dictated a similar constraint to the daily fare. But now given the opportunity, together with her direction and encouragement, the cook's efforts far surpassed her expectations.

Henry constantly and courteously insisted it was as fine a feast as ever he had eaten. Taryn colored with pleasure at each compliment. She knew the importance was not in the quantity served—though Henry was served double portions—but in the profusion of choice.

Food after food was served until it soon became difficult to find places on the tables to set the platters. Each pair of guests had no less than twelve dishes between them, in addition to goblets filled with wine, ale and mulled cider.

At last the final course of fruits and wafers was served. Taryn sat back in her chair and breathed a sigh of relief. Looking down the table, she saw only sated and jovial men.

Garret was involved in a discussion of hunting with Henry. The others seemed equally involved in topics singularly male. Once the last dishes were carried away and the extra tables cleared from the hall, they would drink and game for hours. Despite the fact that she had felt quite comfortable during the meal (save several less than covert glances from the royal chaplain), she knew her presence would afterward be unwelcome.

Waiting for a break in his conversation, she lightly touched Garret's arm.

Understanding her silent request, Garret nodded and stood. "Sire, if you have no objection, I believe Lady Taryn would like to retire."

"Of course." Henry stood, bowing gallantly. "Lady, it has been a pleasure."

"Your Majesty." Taryn curtsied and turned to leave, but stopped short in surprise as Garret moved forward to lead her from the dais.

At the doorway of the anteroom he suddenly lifted her hand to his lips, kissing it lightly. "Thank you."

Instinctively she shrank back as she might have from a threatened blow. She stared at him for a moment, startled not so much by his expression of gratitude, but at the sincerity and gentleness of his voice. Never having heard anything in this tone from him, it gave her a queer feeling.

Garret noted her reaction in confusion. He would have

thought her to be pleased by the compliment.

"You are very welcome," she murmured. Then, gathering her skirts, she hurried toward the stairs.

He shook his head and returned to the dais, noting that the chaplain had exchanged places with the chancellor and was in intense conversation with Henry.

"Sire?" He spoke up instantly the moment Garret set foot upon the platform. "I believe the time has come to make your position known to Lord Garret."

Garret stared at the priest, whose stark black robe and white surplice of the Augustinian order stood in such vivid contrast to the colorful finery of the others seated at the table, as did the severe expression of his countenance compared to the good humor of the rest of the guests.

"Very well, Nigel. I said I would and I shall." Henry sighed, looking away from the man and turning his attention to Garret. "Come and sit down, Garret. We must talk."

"Have I missed something?"

"Quite obviously the meaning of God's Holy Scripture—His commandment regarding fornication in particular!" the priest answered, his voice laden with righteous indignation. "Your loose living is an affront to our Blessed Savior who died that mortal man might know salvation. Before you face the Almighty's judgment you must denounce this brazen vice with compunction and repentance."

Garret bristled at the unprovoked attack. Still, Nigel de Sackville was known to be a prig. "For my 'loose living' I have naught that I wish to repent. To enjoy the caresses of a woman is a totally insignificant sin. And as far as *your* 'judgment' goes, priest, there is none but the Holy Judgment, and that a man brings upon himself—by the way he addresses himself to issues which are truly important in God's eyes."

Above the snowy vestment the man's face turned a vivid hue. "I would advise you to select your words more carefully, my lord. Your remarks might be considered by some to be blasphemous."

"'Twould be naught of which I have not been accused before, priest." Garret reached for his goblet, but angrily spat out the mouthful of wine he took. "You are not the first to attempt to show me the error of my ways."

"Mayhap not. But I do not concede failure as easily as might my fellow brethren. In addition to your lechery, you live by war and rapine; yet you arrogantly proclaim to have naught for which to repent! Such pride alone is a sin."

"I am a knight. I go about my business—which is warfare—in the name of and in service to my king. To take me to task is to take His Majesty to task for waging war."

Henry burst out in laughter. His eyes flashed with the love of a good argument. "Enough, Nigel. There is no man who serves me better. You will not insult him in his own home."

"Forgive me, Sire." De Sackville bowed his head for a moment, then continued in a more placating tone. "I know the esteem in which you hold our host. Upon my holy vows, 'tis not my intent to insult him. Indeed, 'tis because he *is* so valued in your eyes that I strive to save his immortal soul."

"Leave my soul, priest," Garret growled. "I am content with its mortality."

"And what of *her* soul—this woman who shares your bed and your sin?" The priest's quick retort belied the conciliatory tone of only a moment ago. "Do you speak for her as well, damning her as heedlessly as you damn yourself?"

"She is here by choice."

"Living in open sin!" The priest turned to Henry. "Sire, you must act!"

"And do what? Force him to marry his mistress?"

"Indeed!"

"Absolutely not!" Garret roared, slamming down his

goblet. "I'll not be forced to wed in order to appease your priest!"

Immediate silence descended over the hall. All eyes seemed focused upon the dais.

"Return to your drink and conversation," Henry promptly commanded, waving a hand to the room and all who occupied it. When the hum of voices resumed, he turned to Garret. "Actually . . ." he stated quietly, "I think Nigel might be right."

Garret glared at him in shock. "What are you saying?"

Henry sat back in his chair. For several moments he sat in silence, as if weighing his thoughts.

Garret felt a sickening feeling in the pit of his stomach. Henry was known for making swift decisions and then pridefully abiding by them regardless of the consequences.

"I am saying," he began anew, "that 'tis time you remarried and produced an heir. After all, what is the main purpose of marriage, if not procreation? You could do worse. Certes, the Lady Taryn is not sore upon the eyes. Obviously, you find her desirable—else you would not have stolen her from Lynfyld. An act which, by the way, proved most troublesome to me. Both he and her brother petitioned me to take action against you. However, I declined, concluding that the lady's gift to you of her chastity was ample proof she had not consented willingly to the arranged marriage."

He sighed. "But enough of that. On to the matter at hand. I think she would make you a fitting wife, Garret. And, frankly, I would prefer to see her lawfully wedded. What say you?"

"Nay." Garret spat out the word.

At once Henry's eyes began to gleam. His spotty red face turned a darker shade. Garret knew there was nothing he resented more than one who opposed his will.

"Do you defy me in this?" Henry snarled.

"Sire." De Sackville spoke softly, calmly. "Lord Garret's is not the only one whose consent is needed. Let not your anger prevail. The maid has a say."

"That is not my concern. I have the right to choose a husband for her and I shall." Immediately Henry turned his wrath upon the priest. "Whether 'tis Garret or another."

"Indeed, Sire you do. But she is not a chattel, a piece of property as a ewe or cow, for whom you can choose a husband as you would choose a ram or a bull with which to mate her."

"For that I am sure she would thank you, priest," Garret growled.

"Your gratitude is premature, Lord Garret," the man sneered. "I agree with His Majesty that you must marry her, though my reasons are quite different and have naught to do with whether or not you produce an heir. You use this woman for your own pleasure. 'Tis an act which violates the very word of God. Naught but marriage and repentance can make atonement for this sin of the flesh."

"I will not be forced into this or any marriage," Garret repeated.

"'Tis no longer a request, Garret." Henry's voice had taken on an ominous quality. "I have admitted you to my favor, making no secret that I love you as a brother, and those I have loved, I rarely cease to love. But do not defy me in this. I have decided. You shall marry her. And if for some reason she does not consent, then I shall give her as wife to another. There *are* other competent—and obedient—liegemen in my realm," he concluded menacingly.

Garret knew he had lost, yet he made one last, desperate attempt. "'Tis my right to run my personal life to suit myself. I do not mistreat either my vassals or villeins. I faithfully discharge all my obligations to my king. Hence, you should have no complaint against me nor reason to force me to wed against my wishes."

"*Reason?*" Henry's eyes narrowed into slits. "I have reason aplenty, liegeman. As a vassal of the Crown, is not loyalty one of the obligations you claim to discharge?"

"Of course. Upon my life I have pledged it."

"Then I ask you this. Without an heir, to whom will your lands go? As part of your loyalty, do you not owe me the assurance that the passage of Arundel will be to one equally loyal to the Crown? Experience had taught me too well the strife a disputed succession can bring. For this very reason I have decided to have my son crowned now as my successor. There shall be no doubt upon my demise who next will sit upon the throne of England."

Instantly Garret knew this casual bit of information was the true purpose behind Henry's visit to Jaune. He pushed aside his personal feelings to concentrate upon this announcement and its import. "Do you plan to die, Sire, or to abdicate?"

"Neither. But I remember that a disputed succession brought nearly twenty years of civil war to Stephen's kingdom, and my own was difficult enough because I was not a blood heir. I will not allow the same to occur upon my death. My realm will know peace and order after I am gone, and to insure this I will see my successor crowned in my lifetime."

"Young Henry is but fifteen years." Garret looked past the priest to Henry's chancellor. Surely his minister could see the flaw in this plan?

"Prince Henry is old enough to bear arms," the chancellor replied. "I have already begun the negotiations which will lead to the crowning. 'Tis a complicated matter. While there are precedents in France, in England such has been attempted only once before, unsuccessfully, with Stephen's son Eustace. Unfortunately, this makes it more difficult than if it had ne'er been tried at all. To secure Young Henry's position every tenant-in-chief of the Crown must be persuaded to swear fealty to the heir."

"Which they are not bound to do by the letter of the law," Henry reminded him.

"So, this was your purpose in Winchester?" Garret

asked, knowing the answer already.

Henry nodded. A hint of a smile returned to his face. "You always did understand me, Garret. Well? Do I have then your word that you will swear an oath of fealty to my son?"

"That you have need even to put this question into words is a grievous insult, Sire. Have I not knelt before you and placed my hands in yours, pledging to you my faith, loyalty and obedience?"

Seeing his opening, De Sackville seized this opportunity to re-enter the conversation. "'Twould seem, however, that your obedience excludes matters personal, Lord Garret," he observed triumphantly.

Garret shot him a scathing look. He had been grateful for the change of topic. Henry's moods were so shifting; if his attention were drawn from a subject for long enough, the topic often lessened in import. Yet now the priest had pointedly reintroduced the matter of marriage.

He returned his gaze to Henry, hoping the next words he spoke would divert the man's focus. "What of Becket? By long tradition only the Archbishop of Canterbury may crown a King of England. Do you intend to end his exile?"

"Certes not!" Again Henry's ruddy face deepened in color. "He has done naught but plague me these six years he's been in exile. Louis continues to harbor him in France, and so I am reduced to driving out of the country his relations and those who support him. Before I'd allow that rebel bishop back into England, I'd see the upstart in Hell!"

"Sire!" De Sackville gasped and hastily crossed himself.

Henry ignored him. "I have persuaded Thomas' old rival, the Archbishop of York, to perform the ceremony. The Bishops of Salisbury and Rochester have promised support. Gilbert Foliot, Bishop of London, has pledged his support as well, though he could scarce refuse since he now—thanks to me—administers the See of Canterbury."

"What of the Bishops of Winchester, Norwich and Exeter?" Desperately Garret sought to stall.

Henry shrugged. "They disapprove and may stay away. But I have the support of the majority—even of Louis. He relishes the idea of his son-in-law as King of England, for that would make his daughter Queen. But enough of this. I know very well what you are attempting to do with your questions, Garret. I have neither forgotten nor changed my decision. I want your answer now. And I remind you that to disobey my command is an act of treason. Will you, or will you not, take this wench to wife?"

"You leave me no choice, Sire." Garret spoke the words through clenched teeth.

"Good!" Henry stood. With his will now vindicated, his mood was once more jovial. "Before you are tempted and mayhap even able to persuade the lady into withholding her consent, I should like to inform her of our decision. You will take me to her now."

Garret could do nothing but stand and escort the man to the chamber above. As they ascended the stairs, his dread that Taryn would give her consent suddenly gave way to a greater one, one he was at a loss to understand. What he feared now was not that she would give her consent—but that she would withhold it.

Chapter Thirteen

The knock was more forceful than Maite's usual pattern of three light taps, but because she often checked in on Taryn before retiring, Taryn opened the door without hesitation. She fully expected to see the old woman's petite form. Instead, her gaze encountered an all too familiar masculine torso. Even that surprise became insignificant, however, as she recognized the stocky, shorter figure at his side.

"Sire!" She gasped in shock and dropped into a curtsy.

"I apologize for the intrusion, Lady Taryn." Henry stepped forward and inclined his head. "I can see that you were preparing for bed, but a matter has arisen which must be attended to, and it cannot wait until morning."

Taryn looked to Garret for an explanation. She could not fathom a single reason for this visit. His face, however, was like stone and his eyes pointedly avoided hers.

"Enter, please." She stepped away from the door, clutching the bed robe she wore tightly to her.

Henry waved her to a chair and she was grateful for the chance to sit. Her legs felt as if they had become water.

Garret remained standing, just inside the door, with his arms folded across his chest. The stoic expression on his face was belied by the tension patent in every muscle.

"Lady Taryn," Henry began, "you are past the age

when your father should have given you to some man. Why he was in that regard negligent is now of little import. But with his untimely death, that responsibility fell to your brother who, unfortunately 'twould seem, sought to marry you off to his own gain. I understand the loathsomeness of the match he arranged—hence I did not intervene when petitioned to do so. I was content to leave matters as they were. However, what I have witnessed since arriving at Jaune compels me now to rethink my position."

If possible, Taryn's heart began to beat faster. Garret had been wrong! Henry *was* outraged at what he perceived to be an intimate relationship between his most trusted vassal and a woman not his lawful wife.

"I have known Garret since his father sent him to squire at my court," Henry continued. "He was a boy of fourteen years and I, at twenty-two, was about to end my first year as England's king. I tell you this so that you know I do not make this decision lightly and without knowledge. I sincerely believe this man is noble and honorable, and thus 'tis my desire, lady, that you accept him as your husband."

"What?" In shock she looked at him—then at Garret. No wonder his face was as carven granite! Clearly, he had already been informed of Henry's decision. She felt her throat tighten so that she could not swallow. "Please, Sire." She was able to muster no more than a hoarse whisper. "Might we speak of this—alone?"

She saw Garret's eyes widen. Though he looked to want to speak, he did not.

Henry, his surprise no less, nodded and gestured to Garret to leave.

When he had, Henry turned to her. "You have pricked my curiosity indeed, lady. What needs to be said that cannot be said in his presence?"

Suddenly Taryn did not know why she had requested the private audience. Had she intended to inform him of the charade? Or did she want to tell him that she could not marry a man who seemed at best only able to tolerate her?

Henry's voice interrupted her frantic thoughts. "I am waiting, lady."

"Sire, these are circumstances which do not lend themselves to an easy explanation." She searched for the words, but could not find them. "Lord Garret does not want a wife!" she burst out at last.

To her chagrin Henry laughed. "Few men do, lady. But they take themselves one for a variety of reasons. Now, whether or not Garret wants a bride is not a matter of consideration here."

"Sire . . ." Taryn felt a helpless sense of inevitability. For whatever reason, Henry was convinced this was a suitable match. Unless . . .

A fragile thought sparked to life. Perhaps she could persuade him differently. "This marriage would be unfair to Lord Garret, Sire. Wedding me he would receive no dower lands."

"You speak of your brother's disowning?"

"Nay. Even without Charles' disavowal, I would bring no man lands." She hesitated before continuing. She had not confronted the circumstance of her birth since learning of it. "My father and mother were ne'er legally married," she stated softly. "I am bastard-born and thus entitled to naught."

"Does Garret know this?"

"Nay. Our . . . ah . . . relationship was such that 'twas not a consideration."

Henry smiled. "If this is your only concern, lady, then there is none. The happenstance of your birth and whether or not you are entitled to dower lands is of no import. I will see that Garret is amply compensated for what is not forthcoming. I ask only for your consent. Do you or do you not agree to marry Garret d'Aubigny?"

Taryn looked to the floor. She could not put from her mind the expression on Garret's face. How could she marry a man who so clearly did not want to marry her?

"I must tell you, lady, that I find your hesitation not only irksome, but peculiar. Certes, I could understand were Garret a man such as your betrothed. But he is young and virile and sought after by maid and married woman alike. A hundred wenches would leap at what I offer. Even a gentlewoman of legitimate birth enjoys naught in her own name. She can expect no greater honor than to be married to a knight. Here I offer a woman, who by her own admission is of questionable blood, one of my noblest knights, a man of wealth and position, and she falters. What is more strange is that she is already intimate with him. Can you explain this to me?"

Taryn could think of only one rejoinder. "I do not desire to be wedded to any man, Sire."

"That is not your choice, lady. You no longer have male kin willing to offer you support and you live in open sin with a man not bound by law to offer you any. I will not have it. Either you agree to marry Garret d'Aubigny or you shall become a royal ward. You will leave Jaune and return with me to London. There I shall find you a husband. But I caution you, this one might not be an earl, or young, handsome and lusty. So—do I have your answer?"

Taryn swallowed hard and squared her shoulders. She heard her voice respond. "I cannot disobey the desires of my king, Majesty."

Charles Maitland let his eyes rove over the rounded pair of buttocks bent over his bed. Even with the aid of the long stick in her hand the girl had difficulty reaching across the vast breadth to straighten the linens.

She was too petite for the task, he thought, though nicely proportioned. He felt a grin slide across his face. The tax accounts could wait. He set down the roll of parchment he had been studying on the table before him.

Unaware of his appraisal, the girl walked around the

bed to attack it from the other side. Now the roundness he eyed spilled over the top of her laced bodice.

"I have not seen you before."

The girl looked up from her task with a shy smile. "Nay, milord. 'Tis my first day. I've just come from the village."

"What is your name?"

"I'm called Rose, milord."

"Ahh. No doubt for the bloom of your cheeks?"

She colored prettily and dipped her head.

"Come here . . . Rose."

Confusion flashed across her face as she hesitantly stepped away from the bed.

"That's it, set down the stick and come over here." Charles sat back in his chair and watched her approach. "Closer. I'd like to get a good look at you."

Once she was within arm's length, he reached out and captured her hand. He pulled her into the narrow space between his chair and table, positioning her between his knees, with her backside pressed against the table's edge.

He released his hold and fingered the laces across her breasts. "Do you know who I am, Rose?"

"Aye, milord. You be the Earl." The girl attempted to ease away from him, but was thwarted by the table at her back and his knees on either side.

"And do you know what it means to be the Earl of Wynshire?"

She stared blankly at him and shook her head.

"It means . . ." He tugged at the dangling end of one of the laces, undoing the knot. ". . . I own everything . . . and everyone . . . to do with as I please." He lifted his gaze from the soft, bare flesh and searched the girl's face. He found what he was looking for—the slight tremble of her lips and the look of growing understanding. He felt himself stir in response to the girl's fear.

"Do you have a suitor, little flower? A young man who woos your favor and mayhap holds a . . ." He winked. ". . . a special place in your heart?"

The girl blushed a color deserving of her namesake. "Isaac."

"One of my villeins?"

She nodded.

"And this Isaac, has he . . ." Charles leaned forward and slipped a hand up under her skirt. As he sat back his fingertips skimmed the naked flesh of her inner thighs, coming to rest at the downy juncture. He pressed the heel of his palm against her, letting his middle finger enter the slit. "Has Isaac enjoyed your favor?

The girl's face had drained of color. He could feel her fear now. Her entire body trembled with it.

"Aye, milord," she whispered.

"And did you find it pleasurable, coupling with him?" With his free hand he began to undo the laces of her bodice.

"Aye, milord." He barely heard her.

"Do you not think it would be far more pleasurable to couple with an earl than a lowly villein?" He parted the sides of the bodice and released her breasts from the restraining fabric. The firm young flesh sprang free, the rosy peaks jutting forward. With thumb and forefinger he pinched the tips into hardness.

She sobbed softly. "I don't know."

"Think about it." He cupped the breast and lowered his head, flicking his tongue around the erect nipple. "After all, you would not want me to send Isaac away, now would you, little flower?" He sucked the dusky circle and its surrounding creaminess into his mouth and delved the finger inside her deeper.

The girl's cry was lost in a sudden rapping that sounded on the chamber's door.

With an impatient growl Charles removed his hand from between her legs and raised his head. "Enter!"

Upon his command the door creaked open. Conar stepped into view with another man at his side. "Yer pardon, milord. The justice for Northumberland to see you."

From the corner of his eye Charles saw the girl attempt to ease together the sides of her unlaced bodice. "I did not tell you to cover yourself," he snarled, prying open her fingers' grasp. He noted the welling tears of shame in her eyes, and his arousal increased.

Reluctantly he forced himself to turn to the man at his steward's side. "This had better be important, Hugh. Conar, you are dismissed."

Hugh de Moreville grinned. "I've just come from court. I think you'll find what I have to say worthy enough." His eyes darted from Charles to the girl still pinned between him and the table. "Mayhap you'd like to dismiss the slut as well?"

Charles reached out and traced a slow circle around the exposed nipple. "My little flower wouldn't repeat aught she overheard, would you, Rose?" He tweaked the nub hard enough to cause her to cry out.

She shook her head. The tears now rolled freely down her cheeks.

Charles returned his attention to his visitor. "What news have you of Henry's visit to Winchester? Did he ask the attending barons to pledge their fealty to his heir, as we anticipated?"

"Aye, he did."

"And how was this received?"

De Moreville shrugged. "There were no strong objections. Young Henry is a gallant knight and very popular with most of the barons, thus this plan of the King's appears as though 'twill work. We must prevent that from occurring. We have labored too long and hard to create disunity and dissension to have faith restored in the Crown by this. If our cause is to be successful, we must keep the barons discontent and doubtful as to the integrity of Henry's rule."

"Dimwit!" Charles snorted in disgust. "Do you not see how this 'plan' of Henry's aids our cause? Naught would serve our interests more than to allow this coronation to take place—as long as 'tis not performed by the

Archbishop of Canterbury or with Alexander's permission in Rome. For then, when Henry acts in defiance of papal decree, he himself gives our cause the splendid war cry that we fight for the rights of the Church."

"Brilliant!" The baron's face brightened with a wide smile. "Hence when the time comes that we set our plan into action we are not disloyal traitors to the Crown, but noble defenders of Canon Law. How perfect! Unless . . ." His smile suddenly faded. "What if Henry is successful in bringing about a reconciliation with Thomas and brings him back to England to crown his successor?"

"'Twill ne'er happen. Thomas will agree to no reconciliation unless Henry gives the Kiss of Peace, and this our prideful king has pledged ne'er to do. Just look at what occurred this past November, when Henry, taking seriously Thomas' threat to place all England under interdict, at last decided 'twas time to bring their quarrel to an end."

"You speak of their confrontation at Montmartre?"

Charles nodded. "My informants tell me he and the Archbishop were within moments of reconciliation. Thomas had already dismounted and promised to serve him as a loyal baron for the lands of Canterbury and as a faithful friend in his capacity of archbishop. But when Henry dismounted in turn, admitting him to the royal protection and friendship, he refused to grant the Kiss. He swore his conscience would not allow him to break a great oath he had made years earlier in a fit of rage. And though he promised he would conduct himself exactly as though he had kissed him, Thomas knew this was nonsense. He withdrew his own pledge and they parted, still bitter enemies."

Charles yawned and returned his attention to the girl. He took hold of the fabric at her shoulders and slid it down, slowly and completely baring her upper body. "In this matter we are quite safe. Unless you have other news, Hugh, I am busy."

"I do have other news, of your seigneur, Garret d'Aubigny."

"There is naught regarding that bastard which interests me!" Charles snapped, turning his head to glare at the man.

"Not even that he will wed your sister in a fortnight?"

"*What?*" Immediately Charles forgot the girl. "How do you come by this information?"

"'Tis common knowledge in Arundel. The bans have been posted and twice already read. On the return journey from Westchester to London, Henry stopped at Jaune and issued the command in person. Rumor has it, however, that 'twas not the Great Earl's choice, but Henry's order. From what I hear, angry words were even exchanged on d'Aubigny's part."

"So . . . he is being forced into this marriage?" Charles was suddenly thoughtful.

"Aye." Hugh laughed. "Quite ironic, don't you think? The Great Earl of Arundel reduced to the position of a lackey?"

"You idiot! Do you not see the possible implications? D'Aubigny is one of Henry's most powerful vassals. If this forced marriage has driven a wedge betwixt them, then it can only aid our cause."

Charles pushed the girl aside and stood. "I must know what goes on at Jaune, how d'Aubigny stands." He stepped away from the table and began to pace. "I cannot rely upon rumor, I must have someone there in that castle."

"Mayhap there is one amongst his soldiers who can be bought?"

Charles shook his head. "I need someone closer to him, one who is privy to his decisions."

"Surely you do not think you can buy a knight of his inner circle?"

"Not one who is there now, you lackwit! But I might just be able to expand that circle . . . by one. One who has foresworn all allegiances save those which can be purchased." Charles whirled. He knew just the man! "Before you return to court I want you to go the Île-de-France. Find Simon d'Orléon and tell him that his services are requested."

"Do you think he'll come?"

"He'll come. Now go, and I do not want to see your face again until d'Orléon's is beside it."

The man bowed and withdrew. As the door closed behind him, Charles faced the girl cowering at the table's edge.

"Now, my little flower . . . where were we before this regrettable, but necessary, interruption?"

From the corner of his eye Garret caught sight of the tiny form entering the training field. Muttering an oath, he returned his full attention to the target before him.

He tightened his grip on the reins in his left hand, leveling the lance couched in his right as he readied himself to charge at the shield mounted upon one end of the quintain's pivoting crossbar. Warily he eyed the heavy sack hanging from the other end. The force of his blow upon the shield would send the quintain spinning in a circle, with the sack landing a blow from the rear. He would have to duck quickly and turn his mount sharply to the side, or be unhorsed.

He spurred the destrier forward.

The lance met its intended mark squarely, and in one practiced motion Garret kneed his horse to the left while throwing himself sideways in the saddle. The animal responded and both escaped.

"Well done."

Maite's voice reached his ears and Garret shot the woman a wry smile. Tossing his lance to a waiting squire, he guided his mount toward her. "Your presence here surprises me, Maite. I thought you hated the training field."

"And so I do." Shading her eyes with her hand against the bright rays of the afternoon sun, she looked up at him. "I have been waiting to see if you were going to talk to Lady Taryn. Instead, you have avoided her these past two weeks. Time has grown short; therefore, I must force the issue."

Garret dismounted and handed over the reins to a squire who appeared almost at once to lead the animal away. "I have not avoided her. I have been otherwise occupied."

Her brow lifted. "No matter. You are not occupied at the moment. You and I must talk, now."

"About?"

"About Lady Taryn."

Garret felt an immediate tensing of his jaw. "There is naught to discuss. In a week she becomes the Countess of Arundel, my lawful wedded wife, by order of His Majesty."

He started to walk away, but her hand shot out and grasped his arm.

"Garret, do you not feel aught for her?"

Despite the unexpected question his answer came easily, almost too easily. "Obligation and responsibility."

Maite shook her head. "I think there is more, more than you are willing to admit, especially to yourself."

"There is no more, other than frustration and resentment that I am being forced to take a wife. I had one, and do not want another." He was unable to keep the old pain from entering his voice.

Maite's look softened. "Clarissa was no wife to you. Nor was what you had a marriage."

"You have that aright," he spat sarcastically.

"Then let it go, this pain and guilt. Is ten years not long enough to punish yourself for what happened? Lady Taryn is not Clarissa, and you are no longer a youth. Why continue to deny yourself a wife who can bear you sons—"

"I had a son!" His head snapped around, and he glared at her.

"Indeed, you did," she replied gently, "but that, too, is in the past. You must bury those memories, as you buried him. For ten years I have watched you avoid any woman for whom you might have felt a fondness—though there were many you bedded. This one is different. An act of fate brought her into your keeping, and in the time she has been here you have come to care for her. I have seen it in your face and in your actions. After all . . ." She smiled. "When you, of all men, choose to sleep alone, there must be a reason."

She looked at him and sighed. "This time you cannot deny your emotions."

"I do not deny them. I control them."

"'Tis the same. All you have done is hide from them. Why? What do you fear?"

He could not answer her. How could he admit to the fear that clutched his heart? Fear not only of what Taryn represented in her chastity—but fear of the demons from his past that now seemed poised to rise again like some beast lurking within him.

"To cling to the past, to keep it festering in heart and mind, is to cripple oneself." Maite's voice intruded into his thoughts. He felt her hand leave his arm. "What happened once does not have to happen again. Think about what I have said." With that she turned and walked away.

Watching her departure, Garret stood thoughtful. Could Maite be right? Mayhap Taryn was different. Indeed, thus far she was as no woman he had ever known. Might this work after all?

Taryn sat on a small stool and watched the girl seated at the loom beside her.

"'Tis fine," she murmured in encouragement, following the movements of the inexperienced fingers as they threaded the bobbin across the rising and falling heddles.

The girl looked up and smiled. Suddenly the smile left her face. Her fingers stilled.

"Proceed, Annie. Do what you have just done."

But the girl did not move. Her eyes remained focused on something behind Taryn.

Taryn turned and started at the tall figure silhouetted in the doorway. "My lord." She forced a nervous smile of welcome. "You do us honor. Please, enter."

Wordlessly Garret stepped across the threshold, but halted as if he wished to go no further. He gazed thoughtfully around the room. "Leave us," he commanded abruptly to the half dozen women and girls who had all paused at his entrance.

Spindles and distaffs were dropped at once as their workers hastened from the room. The girl at the loom rose, her bobbin halfway inserted into the warf threads. She scampered past Garret to the door. He closed it behind her, yet did not advance into the room further.

"Forsooth, there was no need to be so gruff. You frightened them." Taryn lifted and leveled an austere gaze.

"You forget yourself, Mistress."

She would have stood, but pride kept her seated. She would not give him the satisfaction of thinking he had frightened her as well. "Why do you dislike me? What do you find so distasteful? Surely, your actions can have no other cause."

Her question caught Garret completely off guard. Curiously, it even bothered him to think she thought so. "I do not care enough to dislike you, Mistress. Nor do I find you distasteful, though at times I do find your actions and sharp tongue unpalatable." He took a bit of pleasure in seeing a faintness of color seep into her cheeks. But as that was not the purpose for his presence, he continued. "We must discuss what we both have avoided since Henry's departure."

Taryn knew at once to what he referred. She had

wondered when he would broach the subject of their marriage, now but a week away.

"Why did you give your consent?" he asked suddenly.

She was tempted to bend the truth, to say only that she had obeyed the desires of their king. But she did not. If they were to be man and wife, she owed him her honesty. "I could think of no reason not to. His Majesty made his position quite clear. He would see me wedded. My only choice in the matter was whether 'twas to you or not. And I did not escape marriage to one old lecher only to be given to another."

She watched as a half-smile threatened to form on his lips. "So you regard marriage to me as a lesser of evils?"

"I do not regard you as evil, my lord. There are even times when I find you quite civil."

Without reply, he resumed staring at her. She wished he would stop. There was something in his look that made her tremble.

Suddenly he stepped toward her.

Taryn almost cringed at his approach. She looked down at the floor as he strode across the room, stopping only when he stood in front of her.

"I do not know what kind of woman you are."

She looked up at him, startled, not really certain she had heard him correctly. His words made no sense. "What kind of woman I am?" she repeated softly, frightfully aware of the unsteadiness in her voice. She tried to overcome it. "What kinds are there?"

He moved a step closer. He was now only inches away, towering over her.

She tilted her head back to look up at him, forcing herself to meet his cold green stare. A shiver raced down her back, and she sat up straighter, hoping he had not detected it.

"Whatever kinds there are, you do not fit any of them." His even voice had taken on an edge, and his eyes now expressed a distance, as if he were thinking of something of another time or place. He reached down and brushed a wisp of hair from her face. "You confuse me, Taryn. You have since that first night you entered my bedchamber. And even with all that has passed betwixt us, I am no better able to understand you."

Taryn felt another shudder shoot through her. This time she was certain he noticed. A strange look entered his eyes, and it was all she could do to remain seated. She wanted desperately to flee.

Garret reached out again and softly stroked her cheek. He had to know. He had to know if what he sensed in her was fear. And if it was, would she react to his touch as Clarissa had, with revulsion and terror?

Without warning he took hold of her shoulders and pulled her to her feet. "Are you a woman who will accept a man's desires? Or is your boldness only a pretense? Beneath are you still a timid virgin?"

Suddenly Taryn was aware that his hands had moved. One had gone to the nape of her neck, the other had travelled down to the small of her back. Gently, but firmly, he was drawing her closer to him. Now his lips were at her ear.

"I want you, as a man wants a woman. But are you woman enough to bear all which that entails?" And then his mouth was on hers. He kissed her deeply.

Again she experienced the same feeling that had coursed through her when he had kissed her in Kirdford. Yet this time it was stronger. This time he did not push her away. The pressure on her back increased and she yielded to it. She melted into his embrace, feeling a rising hunger, an aching need. She was conscious neither of her small movements to fit her body against his, nor of how her mouth opened under his lips. As his tongue explored her, she hesitantly responded, slipping hers into his mouth.

Abruptly he ended the kiss. She would have stepped back, but he still held her close.

Her whole being reeled in confusion, crying out for the

interrupted pleasure and dizzy with a rush of intense emotions.

Contentedly, as if having proved something to himself, he looked down at her.

A strange sense of disappointment overwhelmed Taryn. She understood the meaning of the satisfaction she saw in his eyes. His desire for her was merely physical.

"I know you had hoped for a love match."

She gasped.

"Your brother made ajoke of it that first night when he and Lynfyld sat at my table. But Henry's decision now precludes that from occurring." He released her and stepped back.

He put his hands gently on her shoulders and looked straight into her eyes. "I think we could walk the same road, Taryn, if we are now truthful. I cannot offer you love, for I do not love you. But this I *can* offer; to honor you always as my lady wife, to respect you and to treat you kindly."

Taryn blinked back sudden, inexplicable tears. Though she did not know why, his brutal honesty pained her—as had the realization that there had been nothing but lustful need in his kiss.

She forced herself to smile. "This I can accept."

Chapter Fourteen

Was it possible for such a simple band of gold to weigh so much?

Taryn twisted the ring on her fourth finger, easing it up toward the knuckle, but not over. Garret had placed it there, and she would not remove it. To do so would be a bad omen. It was a silly peasant superstition, she knew, but one she was not brash enough to test.

"May God bless your lives with love, joy and devotion, and may you live in happiness as one." So the priest had said. But surely only a fool could believe in the future of a marriage entered into under such circumstances.

She held out her hand and watched, as in her pacing, the polished metal caught and reflected the candlelight. Actually, the ring was not heavy at all. It was what it represented which encumbered her. By the laws of man and God she was now bound to him, sworn to be "blithe and obedient in bed and at board," until death them departed.

Taryn looked across the room to that which had been blessed by the priest after he had escorted them from the church to the conjugal abode. Their nuptial bed seemed suddenly to dominate the entire chamber. At least in the morning there would be no public display of its sheets!

Despite the nervous churning in her stomach, she felt a wry smile tug at the corners of her mouth. Mayhap there was something to be said for losing one's chastity before marriage? Certes, it nullified the humiliating custom of presenting for the inspection of the curious the linens which gave evidence to the groom's manhood and his bride's virginity.

The very thought of a score of strangers examining the stains of her virginal blood evoked a sense of disgust. To know that such would have been the case she had only to remember the number of onlookers who had crowded into the village's small wooden church. The attendance had far exceeded that which was normal for a Sunday morning. The pious and the curious had vied for space in the nave to hear the Mass and to view their lord's wedding.

Even the priest had not been above an affected display. For the occasion he had donned a fine embroidered vestment over his grubby cassock. From the chancel his voice had rung with enthusiasm and passion, the likes of which had rarely been heard. And surely the topic of his homily had been no coincidence—the Book of Ruth. The final passage he had quoted still echoed in her mind: "May the Lord make this woman, who has now come into your home, as fertile as Rachel and Leah." And had she and Garret not exited the church showered with seeds and accompanied by shouts of "plenty"?

Like a weight she could not lift, the feeling of helplessness and inevitability was almost crushing. Could there be any doubt as to her duty? Especially after what she had overheard only yesterday from two of the serving maids. They had been in the hall the night Henry had made his position known to Garret. According to their recollections of that scene, which centered around a lively speculation regarding Taryn's fruitfulness, it was not moral outrage that had prompted Henry's command, but the desire that his vassal produce an heir.

Taryn looked again to the ring on her hand, then to the bed once more. How long would she have to wait until he arrived and performed *his* duty—begetting the heir his king had demanded?

Almost in response to her silent question a light

tapping sounded at the door, followed by a voice made faint by the wood's thickness.

"'Tis Maite, lady."

"Enter." Chastising herself for the way her heart had leapt at the knock, she turned to face the woman entering. Nervously, she plucked at the silken cord which belted her robe.

"I've brought up a bit of warmed wine. I thought it might help to calm the wedding nerves."

"Is it so obvious?"

"Not to most." Smiling, Maite closed the door behind her. "Why don't you get into bed and drink it? Then I'll rub your back." As if sensing Taryn's hesitation, she stepped forward and handed her the goblet she carried. "'Twill help, I promise."

"There is naught which can help", Taryn answered, fighting a sudden rise of tears. To wash away their bitter taste she raised the cup and took a tentative sip.

"Drink it all," Maite directed, as she went to the bed and turned down its covers. "You know, I put Lord Garret's mother into this very bed on her wedding night, and she was every bit as nervous as you are now. All brides are. 'Tis natural and naught to be ashamed of—or frightened."

Unable to mask her surprise, Taryn looked at the petite form bent over the bed arranging its pillows. "You know, don't you?"

Maite smiled. "I know he cares for you now more than he will admit. And with time, 'tis possible that he can learn to care even more."

Taryn shook her head and drank more of the wine. "I do not believe that. He married me only out of duty and obligation to his king, and to produce an heir. He cares naught for me."

"You are wrong, lady. Tonight you will know that I speak the truth. Of course . . ." She lowered her gaze. "That will depend upon you." Suddenly she looked up from the bed, capturing Taryn's gaze with one of almost hypnotic intensity. "You must do as I say. You must let him know that you welcome him. If he is hesitant, encourage him. Assure him that you give yourself willingly."

Abruptly she broke off the stare and beckoned Taryn to her. "Come. Slip off your robe, and lie down. Let the wine do its work."

In that moment Taryn felt curiously lightheaded. She had scarcely eaten at dinner. Could the wine have such an effect on an empty belly? She stepped forward and found her balance somewhat impaired. She shook her head, but that only made her dizzy. Despite the seriousness of the moment she had the strangest desire to giggle. She waited for the sensation to pass, then walked to the bed.

Nodding her approval, Maite stepped to her side. She took the goblet from her hand, then thoughtfully turned her back as Taryn discarded her robe. While Taryn climbed between the cool linens, she draped the garment across the rail at the bed's foot. "Finish it," she stated, offering once more the wine. "Then turn over and I'll rub your back."

Taryn obeyed, draining the cup in a few long swallows. As Maite took the empty goblet, she stretched out beneath the sheets and rolled over, pillowing her head on her arms. She felt Maite sweep aside her hair and lower the sheet to her waist.

The woman's hands were warm and soothing, skillful in their ministrations. Deftly she kneaded the muscles at the neck. Then, as she ran her thumbs along the backbone, she began to speak. "Tonight, when Garret enters you, there *will* be pain—at the moment the maidenhead is breached—but only for that moment. You must not, however, show that pain—or any fear. 'Tis very important that he think you enjoy it. And you can, if you relax and encourage him to proceed. Do you understand, Lady Taryn? You must not show pain or fear."

Taryn nodded. She was confused by the insistence she heard in the woman's voice. Were these the instructions given to all brides? Yet Maite's words seemed more a warning of what *not* to do. How could she know what to caution her against—unless that knowledge came from the mistakes of another . . . Garret's first wife, perhaps?

In spite of these questions surfacing in her mind Taryn could not muster the energy to contemplate their answers. She felt all tension leave her body and closed her eyes. Maite was silent now, and the soothing touch of her hands, coupled with the wine's effect, lulled Taryn into a rather pleasant half-sleep. So much so, that when Maite patted her shoulder, indicating she was finished, she did not bother to open her eyes or bid her good night.

Feeling as if she were floating, she surrendered to the peaceful sensation, curling up on her side and kicking her legs free of the sheet's restraint.

At the door Maite paused to view her handiwork. The new Countess of Arundel was unaware of the provocative and inviting picture she presented. Her bare body, exposed save a narrow draping across her buttocks, gleamed a flawless ivory in the candlelight, while her hair, fanned out across the pillows, shone with a fire to rival that of the flame in the hearth.

Maite smiled in satisfaction. After more than a month of forced celibacy, the mere sight of his bride would be enough to ignite Garret's desires. With or without demons, no man could possess *that* manner of control.

With a final glance at the recumbent form in the bed she softly closed the door. Her timing was perfect. On the second landing she met the unsuspecting groom. "I did not expect you abovestairs so early, my lord."

Garret ignored the comment. "Is she to bed?"

Only with difficulty did Maite keep her tone even and her expression blank. "Aye."

"And her . . . temper?"

Maite could not prevent a slight smile. A bit of mandrake in his wine as well might not have been a bad idea. "I think that *you* are more nervous than your bride," she replied. "Now go to her. She awaits you."

For an instant Garret tried to decipher the reason behind the woman's expression. Then, discounting it as unimportant, he abandoned the effort and proceeded up the flight of stairs.

Once outside his room he thought to knock, but quickly dismissed the idea. It was, after all, *his* chamber. Then, too, Maite had said she awaited him. He released the door's latch and entered, suddenly wishing he had drunk more than he had. However, unlike that time before, this night he had wanted a clear head and all of his wits about him. He was determined that whatever happened, his actions would not be influenced by lust or directed by drunkenness.

He turned from the door and stared at the sight before him. He could not take his eyes from her. Maite! She had done this—arranged his bride in his bed like a delicacy upon a platter, his for the taking. He felt himself relax somewhat, and even permitted himself a slight smile as he recalled suddenly the expression on Maite's face. In his mind the woman's words resounded: *She awaits you.*

"You old witch," he murmured aloud, stepping into the room. He approached the bed and drew a shallow breath. This was not what he had expected. In her innocence, could Taryn know the temptation she offered? He felt the fire in his veins surge and converge to that part of him he could not control. Logic, which told him that the intensity of his desire was merely a result of his unaccustomed celibacy, was ignored. In this instant he wanted her as he had never before wanted a woman.

He was not sure if she had heard his approach or simply sensed it, but as he stood there, she slowly rolled unto her back. Her eyes fluttered opened.

"Forgive me, my lord," she whispered. "I did not mean to fall asleep."

Garret stared down at her without answering, watching as her effort to understand his presence appeared to drive away the remaining vestiges of sleep.

The dream-like quality in her eyes disappeared, and though she did not move, it became painfully clear to him that she wanted to. He saw her body tense, and noted the hand at her side which reached for the sheet at her bare waist.

To his surprise, however, she did not tug the covering over her. "Come to bed," she whispered.

The soft smile which then touched the corners of her mouth was his utter undoing. The tenuous control for which he had fought now slipped away as his baser instincts reared. He burned with the need to be inside her. Still, he forced himself to undress slowly. Steadily he watched her, looking for the slightest trace of fear or disgust. In spite of his need, if he saw either reaction, he could not—would not—proceed.

Unblinking, she stared up at him. In her eyes he saw uncertainty—but no more. The gray depths did not hold the terror that had long haunted his dreams.

At last he lay down beside her. Propped upon an elbow, he looked at this woman now his wife. She tipped her head back to meet his gaze, the movement emphasizing her throat, long and graceful, and the same creamy color as the rest of her body. His own ached with desire. But he had been fighting his instincts for so long that the denial of his needs now seemed normal, and taking this woman abnormal.

Hesitantly he leaned forward and brushed his lips across hers. Though the entreaty was ever so slight, her mouth parted. He deepened the kiss, letting his tongue tease hers before slipping inside to explore the warm recess.

She responded eagerly, sighing in pleasure as he moved his lips to her neck. Almost without conscious thought his hands caressed her, his fingers stroking her nipples hard. His mouth followed his hands' path. He took a nipple, firm and erect, to suckle, and she moaned aloud. She arched her back and pressed her body closer. When her arms reached for him, he knew she was willing. Still, he lifted his mouth from her breast, looking at her face once more for confirmation.

Her eyes were closed now, but there was no mistaking the breathless contentment that parted her lips. The sight of her desire, coupled with the fire of his own, stripped away his final hesitation. He returned his mouth to hers.

Taryn felt his fingers caress her inner thighs. She moaned softly at the gentleness of his touch. Her dread that he would take her lustfully or merely out of duty vanished. Maite had been right: he did care for her. In every kiss and with every caress she felt his tenderness. Surely such feeling came from more than just physical need or desire! That hopeful belief heated her passion as nothing else could have. Instinctively and without conscious thought she opened her legs in invitation.

Suddenly she felt the fingers exploring the mound between her thighs actually slip inside her. She groaned in response to this new, unfamiliar feeling building deep inside her. He lowered his mouth to her breast again and the sweet sensation intensified until she was certain she couldn't bear it. Desperately she tried to concentrate on something else, on his body pressing close to hers.

She could feel where he leaned against her, hot against her thigh. She realized the length of him and shivered in sudden fear. *Dear God, he would tear her asunder!*

But he seemed to misread her reaction, taking it to be a shudder of anticipation. He raised his head and kissed her gently. "You are ready?"

Taryn remembered Maite's words and nodded.

He positioned himself between her thighs and raised up to give her a clear look at him. "Taryn . . . do you trust me?"

She found his question strange, but did not hesitate in her answer. "Aye," she whispered. And though she wanted to shut her eyes, she did not. She met his gaze unwaveringly, smiling and then encircling his neck with her arms.

Garret entered her slowly, easing into her, and remaining still, allowing her to grow accustomed to his presence. Then he withdrew and made a second tentative entry. This time he could feel the barrier. But with a gentle pressure in her embrace she urged him on. He moved his mouth to cover hers, to muffle her outcry of pain. He could not bear to hear it, yet there was no other way. He drove himself into her. One thrust deep and straight. He felt her rip and open around him. She jerked beneath him, and he froze. But after a long agonizing moment the terror he so feared had not burst forth.

Instead, she kissed him, then freed her mouth from his. "'Tis fine," she whispered.

He withdrew slowly, with care, knowing his withdrawal was hurting her, yet fearing, too, that if he did not initiate a rhythm she would feel only pain. He entered her again. This time his passage was made easier with the lubrication of her blood.

As he began to move within her, she relaxed beneath him. Soon he felt her begin to follow him, rising to meet his entry, riding him. With even, rhythmic thrusts he penetrated her, feeling her passion soar, but restraining himself, still afraid to trust her response.

But under the growing fire of her need his resolve soon melted away. Her response to him was just that—a response *to* him. This was no whore's practiced skill. The woman beneath him was responding by pure instinct. He began to thrust into her wildly, losing the careful pounding rhythm he had set. As fast and as deep as he could, he drove himself into her.

Taryn was sure the world had ended. She threaded her fingers into his hair as she sought to hold on, to brace herself. Suddenly he shifted position slightly, burying himself within her more deeply. But instead of thrusting, he remained deep, grinding himself into her as though to wring every drop of sweet ecstasy from her. And then it started—the white-hot, spiraling sensation . . .

Garret felt her tighten about him and he could hold back no longer. In the echo of her shuddering sob he heard his own hoarse groan.

Asleep, Garret ran his hand along the curve of her buttocks.

Awake, Taryn realized an instant tingle of pleasure at his touch.

Wanting to explore his body as he had hers, she let her fingertips travel down his muscled chest. When she reached his flat belly, however, she hesitated. In Kirdford he had called it arousal. But what did "arousal" look like, or feel like to the touch? She remembered the heated length of him, the pleasure he had given her, and curiosity spurred her on.

She was mystified at what she felt. In no way did the soft, lifeless flesh beneath her fingertips resemble the hard shaft which had first frightened, then filled her the night before.

"Take care, madam, or you will waken the sleeping beast."

Taryn started at the sound of Garret's voice, raspy still with sleep. "And if he wakens?" she asked, genuinely curious. She was not sure if he referred to himself, or to that part of him which she now cradled in her palm.

His answer came in the movement and change she felt in her hand. Fascinated, she ran her fingers the length of his thickening shaft, unwittingly aiding its tumescence.

Suddenly he caught her hand, stilling it and then removing it. "Do not arouse me, Taryn, unless you are prepared to offer relief." His voice was ragged, harsh with stern reproach.

By means of a reply she returned her hand to its former position. He was even more "aroused." She giggled in delight, like a child who had just learned the secret of a new toy. "I believe your warning has come too late, my lord. The beast is more than wakened." She lifted herself up on one elbow and looked down at him. He was scowling, but she did not think he was angry. "I am however, prepared to offer relief," she whispered, playfully nipping at his lower lip.

He turned his head away. "'Tis too soon. You must allow a day or so for healing. Or have you forgotten the pain of my breaching? The blood that was shed?"

She shook her head. "Nay, I have not forgotten. But

'twas worth the pain. Surely you give me too little credit, my lord." A new thought came to her. "But mayhap 'tis too soon for you?" She looked at him in sudden concern, and lay back upon her pillow.

In one fluid movement he rolled atop her. "You know not what you have started, madam."

"I know now." Taryn giggled again. She wriggled into position beneath him, lifting her hips to meet his entry.

"Without such haste," Garret scolded gently. He knew this time there would be no maidenblood to ease his way. But when he moved to caress her, to stimulate the flow of her body's lubricant, he found her already wet, open for him and ready.

As if having read his surprise, she repeated, "Too little credit." Her voice was now thick with passion.

"Did I not tell you before, 'tis base to boast?"

Despite her bold words and obvious desire, he forced himself to enter her slowly. He heard her gasp and felt her body stiffen. His immediate instinct was to withdraw. In her inexperience, she could not have known better. But he had known, and still he had allowed his lust to overrule his better judgment.

He swore in silent anger and started to withdraw.

At once Taryn encircled his neck with her arms and drew him back to her. Having guessed at his intent, she now sought to dissuade him from it. "Surely the beast does not shrink in fear of a woman, my lord? For his presence is most welcome." To prove her words, she rose up to recapture him. Moving slowly beneath him, she imitated his rhythmic movement of the night before. "Without haste," she whispered, repeating back to him his own words.

Garret followed her lead, and Taryn relaxed. The pain subsided and in its place she could feel the seeds of pleasure being sown. Soon the warmth, the pleasure, was steady, waxing and waning with each withdrawal, but always present. She gave herself to it, letting it grow and increase in intensity. Lost in the wondrous sensations, she did not realize he had abandoned the gentle thrusting movement she'd initiated.

Now driving himself deep within her, Garret had set his own pace, a pace she was able to meet without pain. She marveled at his skill. How could he have known when she was ready to endure it?

She did not know her husband was responding instinctively, to her own body's silent signals. Feeling her swell around him, becoming even wetter, he was merely answering her need.

Lost in passion, Taryn experienced the same delicious ecstasy as before.

With a final thrust Garret joined her. "You have tamed the beast, madam," he murmured into her ear. He kissed her gently, withdrew from her, then left the bed. For a moment he stood there, watching as she arched her back, burrowing her bare body deeper into the bed's warmth and softness. A mewling sound, like that of a contented cat, emanated from her.

A chuckle rose in Garret's throat. He continued to study her, taking in every detail—her hair fanned across the pillows, her eyes half-closed, her mouth open in a breathless sigh of satisfaction. As his gaze went lower, he saw a ripple travel through her slender form. When the same mewling sound escaped her lips, he knew she had just experienced a delayed wave of pleasure.

Knowing it was he who had given it to her warmed his own blood. In his loins he felt a renewed stirring. Had he not promised to meet with Richard, he would have rejoined her immediately. Despite his climax only moments ago, he had no doubt he could be heavy and hard again.

"Do you shiver from the cold, madam?" he teased, forcing himself to begin dressing.

He was rewarded with a tinge of pink on her cheeks. "Nay, my lord. I believe 'tis pleasure."

Taryn sat up and drew her knees to her chin. In her mind a score of questions swirled. Had he felt what she had? And if so, was it any different than what he experienced with the other women he had bedded? Was it more—or less—meaningful than when he had been with Geneviève Flambard? She had to know. "Is it always so . . . betwixt a man and a woman? I mean, does a man feel such pleasure with any woman?" Fearing her intent was too obvious, she quickly added, "and does a woman with any man?"

Garret glared at her. "Only a whore finds pleasure with every man who beds her!" Seeing her face go instantly pale, he realized her question was probably an innocent one. He pulled on his breeches before responding further, allowing himself time to overcome his anger. "For the man—if he releases his seed—there is pleasure, aye," he answered at last, gruffly.

"Of that I was sure." Taryn nodded, the color returning to her cheeks. "Many a night I heard Charles bellow in lust. But for the woman . . ." She broke off and smiled in nervous embarrassment. "Even after you said so in Kirdford, I did not truly believe she felt the same manner of fulfillment. I have heard women say 'tis ne'er pleasureful, at best 'tis a boring, banal part of marriage. Others even professed it to be a terrifying and painful experience, their duty as a wife to be endured at the man's will."

Duty. The word sliced through Garret's subconscious like a blade. Clarissa's voice, shaking with terror, repeated the phrases; . . . *terrifying* . . . *painful* . . . *endured at the man's will* . . .

He tried to push aside the past. But it loomed in his mind, relentless and merciless—his wedding night with Clarissa; her tears and silent sobs; his impatience, fueled by drink. What he had done had been no better than rape, and when he had seen himself crimson with her maidenblood, he had gone numb with shame and guilt. Without speaking he had dressed and left her. After that, each time he touched her, her cowering and her tearful pleas had drained him of desire. Finally she had moved into the chamber below and their marriage had ceased to exist, save in name only. He never went to her again, until that night . . .

Unaware of the memories her innocent comment had triggered, Taryn continued gaily. "I am glad I was proven wrong. I think these must be stories told to keep maids from losing their chastity too lightly, hence keeping them pure for marriage. Or mayhap some women do not experience such pleasure?"

"Do they?" she repeated, her voice drawing him back to the present. "Do women always experience such pleasure?"

"Nay," he answered coldly. "Some women truly find no pleasure in the act, only pain."

She raised an eyebrow. "Then must be 'tis a reflection of the man she's with. If he be not skilled and gentle—"

Her assertion twisted the blade of his guilt. "Nay, 'tis a reflection of the woman," he interrupted, fighting the tide of his rising anger. "One who fears coupling will ne'er find pleasure—with any man."

"But why would a woman fear coupling—unless the man were deliberately cruel? Surely only a man who takes pleasure in inflicting pain could take away the pleasure that should be betwixt a man and a woman."

Garret's control snapped. "You presume too much on too little knowledge, madam!"

He crossed the distance between them so quickly, so effortlessly, Taryn had no chance to react. His face a mask of rage, he grabbed her by the arms and jerked her to her knees. She could feel the barely controlled violence rolling off him and shrank in fear, unable to pull her gaze away, frightened at the change in him. "I only wanted to know—"

He did not let her finish. "You will see that your curiosity *and* your desire both remain in this room!" With an angry shake, he then tossed her back upon the bed and turned.

Hurt by his implication that she might be tempted to seek the ecstasy found in his arms in another's, Taryn turned her face into the pillows.

Suddenly she felt shamed, as if she'd done something wrong. She heard the sounds of his dressing, but kept her face turned. Her tears fell, staining the fine linen.

Garret dressed hurriedly and in stony silence. In the ten years since Clarissa's death he had fled from the very accusations that Taryn had just thrown at him. But if even his unskilled bride could see that Clarissa's pain and suffering must have been willfully caused, then surely the guilt was his. He had been wrong to expect Clarissa to respond to him with pleasure. Because he had taken her anyway, the act had driven her to her death. It was no defense that he had been too young and inexperienced to know that only whores enjoyed being bedded. He should have stopped when she first resisted his embrace or certainly when she cried out in pain at his entry.

And yet Taryn had felt such pain, but responded still with complete abandon and pleasure. How could this be?

The suspicion suddenly gnawing at him was one he could not dismiss. For a virgin, Taryn had found far too much pleasure in their lovemaking. With the physical evidence of her lost chastity still upon his sheets, he could not doubt her innocence. What then? Was she, despite her noble upbringing, innately endowed with a whore's lusts, that quality which would enable her to find such satisfaction with a man? Why else would she have asked if a woman felt pleasure with any who bedded her?

In all his silent castigations, it did not occur to him to consider that it might have been love which had created and fueled his young bride's desire, enhancing her pleasure and enabling her to feel what Clarissa had never known.

Without taking the time to belt on his sword, he grabbed it and his mantle, and stormed from the room.

In the great hall Richard greeted him warmly. The wide smile upon his face quickly disappeared, however, at the sight of the scowl on Garret's.

"I can attend to this matter, my lord," he offered hesitantly, "if you would prefer to . . . to remain here."

Garret leveled an icy glare. Clearly his steward mistook the cause for his foul mood to be a reluctance to leave his new bride. Nothing could be further from the truth. He must escape from the agonies she had resurrected. "We will go," he answered tersely.

He did not speak again, nor did his steward.

In silence they left the hall, mounted the waiting horses and rode into the village.

Garret eyed the crowd already assembled. The weekly holding of the lord's court was a public affair, still he suspected the size of the rather substantial gathering to be a result of curiosity having little to do with jurisprudence. As many had probably come merely to view their newly wedded earl as had come to see his justice rendered.

His foul mood became more so. He detested being a spectacle and loathed this sudden attention surely evoked by interest in his private life. He clenched his jaw and guided his horse through the crowd. His suspicions proved true as several whispered comments reached his ears. The main purport of speculation seemed to be upon his bride's condition, mixed with salacious gossip about his first wife's demise.

"A day standing in the pillory might tighten loose tongues." Richard, riding at his side, broke his silence. "'Tis a good way to handle such mindless, idle prattle."

Garret turned a steely gaze to him. "A deaf ear is a better way." He returned his attention to his horse, spurring the animal forward into the village square where he dismounted.

Jaune's sheriff, who in Garret's absence handled the run of crimes, was already present. This day his role would be limited to detailing the offenses committed and offering whatever evidence or witnesses that existed. When home, Garret always acted as his own judge. He took very seriously one of the greatest duties of a high seigneur—that of rendering justice.

As the Great Earl of Arundel he held that right over his vassals and villeins alike. In the case of persons not of noble birth residing on his lands that right even encompassed the absolute power of life and death. At his court both serious and petty crimes which arose on his personal dominions were dealt with. At his utter discretion he could clap villeins in the stocks, order floggings or imprisonment for minor offenses, or summarily order the execution of robbers caught in the act of a crime on his lands.

With a final glance at the crowd Garret took his seat in the high chair placed under the shade of a great oak tree. Richard sat on a stool at his right. Upon a wax tablet his steward would make a written record of the proceedings, later to be transcribed upon parchment. On Garret's left stood two of his vassals, trusted knights who would act as assessors, for no wise lord acted without counsel. Finally, the village priest stepped forward. In his hands he held a box of holy relics upon which oaths would be administered.

Garret nodded and the sheriff brought forward the first cases—two villeins who disputed the ownership of a yoke of oxen. They were followed by a peddler demanding additional payment of a farmer, a peasant who requested the right to send his son to school at a nearby monastery, and a youth charged with stabbing an old man while in a drunken rage.

Garret decided upon the rightful owner of the oxen, deemed that the peddler had been amply compensated, granted the father's request and ordered the youth to be branded on the forehead with a red-hot iron that all men might be aware of him.

Finally, the last case was presented—that of a trio of unemployed mercenaries who had invaded the village, stolen corn from a shed and then fired the storage structure to conceal the crime.

"And they did not act alone, milord," the sheriff stated. "Two others escaped. These three, however, refuse to betray their comrades' lair." A sinister smile twisted his mouth. "Might I recommend that your lordship command torture?"

Garret contemplated the suggestion in silence. Though torture was often inflicted to obtain a confession of guilt or to extort details about accomplices, he felt the recommendation to be extreme in this instance. He spat to indicate his opinion, then looked to the men in question.

They stood before him in sullen silence. Not one had reacted to the sheriff's proposal, nor did they groan or strain at their fetters. Their eyes revealed no emotion.

He brought up his hand to cover a smile of grudging admiration and looked to his vassals for their opinion.

"Their crime is, of course, serious," the first offered. "But the only harm was to the structure."

"Yet punishment must be meted," his companion swiftly countered. "A crime was committed, and unless they are made an example of, who is to say they and others will not return to steal and burn again?"

"A division of opinion." Garret sat back in his chair. Setting his elbow upon the armrest, he rested his chin in his hand as he studied the men for a moment. "Have you aught to say in your defense?"

Each shook his head.

"My lord, might I speak on their behalf?"

Garret turned his gaze to the direction of the voice.

The crowd parted, and the man who emerged from its midst presented a formidable appearance indeed. Dressed in the finest of mail, he was a large man, as tall as Garret and as wide of shoulder. His face was concealed beneath a helm.

"Come forward," Garret commanded. Cautiously he sat upright.

The stranger complied, respectfully removing both the helm and hood from his head, thereby revealing a shock of the blackest hair Garret had ever seen. The man's lower face was covered by a thick beard which only half concealed an ugly scar that ran from just below his left ear up across his cheek and ended below the leather patch covering his left eye. No doubt the same blow which had left the scar had also taken the eye.

Garret glanced at the sword which hung at his side. Passau steel, he guessed, second only to Toledo. This was no mere knight. Instinctively his right hand went to the hilt of his own blade. "Speak."

The man bowed. "My lord, might I plead for leniency? These men are not much more than youths, with unchanneled energies and loyalties. Yet they are brave and do not fear threats of torture." Out of his good eye he glanced at the sheriff, then spat.

His opinion of the man's suggestion was clearly the same as Garret's and his pointedly imitative expression of it earned him a smile. "Proceed. I am listening." Garret sat back.

"I propose that they are wanting only of discipline and an opportunity for honorable employment. Surely a man of your position could be well served by men who would fain suffer a foretaste of the pangs of Hell rather than betray their comrades. Such loyalty is rare, my lord. I know." He gave a curious smile and bowed again.

Garret resumed his previous relaxed position, returning his chin to his hand. In this stranger he saw more than a knight of courage and experience. He saw a man of wisdom wrought from suffering and tempered by compassion. "You believe these men worthy?"

"Aye, I do."

"So much so that you would offer yourself as their captain?"

"Without hesitation."

"So be it." Garret stood, his decision made. "Might I know the name of the man I have just taken into service?"

The stranger smiled. "Simon d'Orléon, my lord . . . at your service."

Chapter Fifteen

Garret's brow lifted. "Your name *and* your reputation are well known, Simon d'Orléon. You call no man lord. Your sword is sold like a harlot's favor. How is it that you are now prepared to enter into my service—when I have mentioned naught of the silver I know your allegiance costs?"

"You speak of the man who existed before this time, my lord." The man gestured to the scar upon his face and smiled wryly. "In the land of the blind the one-eyed man might be king, but in the business of warfare, a one-eyed warrior possesses little worth. 'Tis true that for nearly fifteen years I have been at the beck of any man offering good enough silver, but now I find myself ill-equipped and disinclined to lead that life. I am weary. Like these men beside me, I desire only the opportunity to serve an honorable lord."

He paused, lifting his gaze with the confidence of a man who needed no other's approval. "If, however, in learning my name you wish to rescind your offer, I shall understand."

"Nay." Garret shook his head slowly. "Nay, I do not rescind it."

From the corner of his eye he noted, and ignored, the uneasy looks exchanged by his vassals. He had learned to trust his instincts, and his instincts told him this stranger was, if not a man of true allegiance, a man of honor.

"My offer stands," he repeated, turning to the sheriff. "Free the prisoners." As the man moved to comply, he beckoned Richard and the priest forward to stand on either side of him.

Richard cleared his throat. When he spoke his voice was loud and clear, carrying to the fringes of the crowd. "Let it be known that in the company of these witnesses these men do homage." He looked to the now freed men. "Will you have Garret d'Aubigny, Great Earl of Arundel, as your present and undoubted lord, serving him faithfully in all manner such acceptance entails?"

"Aye," they answered. In turn, each man then stepped forward and knelt at Garret's feet. Placing his right hand upon the box of relics the priest dutifully extended, he made his solemn pledge: "I swear it."

At last it was d'Orléon's turn. Stepping forward, he went down upon one knee. But when the priest held out the box, he waved it aside, clutching instead the hilt of his sword. "This is the blade which will serve my lord. Upon it I will swear my oath." He looked up at Garret, meeting his gaze squarely. "At hazard of mine, I will defend your life."

"So be it." Garret nodded and signaled all four to rise. He turned to the three who a moment earlier had been prisoners. "You will make restitution out of your pay for what was stolen, and by this day's end the storage cottage which was burned will be rebuilt. Once that task is completed, all further orders will come from your captain." He glanced at the bearded man.

There was no need for words to pass between them. With a barely discernible nod Simon d'Orléon acknowledged and accepted his responsibilities.

Justice now meted, the proceedings were concluded. The crowd began to disperse.

Listening to the hum of voices, Garret smiled tightly. Gossip had found new fodder and the wagging tongues another topic.

His smile became genuine. Already the stranger had rendered him service. He turned to Richard. "See that a place is made for d'Orléon at my table tonight."

Taryn tried to ignore the probing stare she knew was focused upon her. She sank down deeper into the bathtub. Letting the warm water rise over her shoulders, she closed her eyes.

Across the room she could hear the sounds of Maite stripping the bed. Knowing the sheet would be bloodied, she had come herself to remove it, to destroy the evidence of Taryn's virginity and Garret's lie, thereby protecting his honor. If only its stained linens were the cause for her as yet unvoiced query! But Taryn knew better.

Unconsciously she shook her head. She was not skilled at concealing her emotions, especially from Maite. The woman must know something was wrong. Despite her advice, which Taryn had followed, everything had gone awry. Was it not enough that she had been shamed and humiliated? Must she now also feel guilt for having disappointed Maite?

She bit her lower lip and prayed the woman would finish quickly and leave without asking questions she was unprepared to answer. In her heart the fragile hope persisted that somehow everything would work out, that she would not have to admit her failure.

Whether she had sensed Taryn's silent plea, or was more concerned at the moment with the disposal of the sheets, Taryn was not sure. But after asking only if her assistance were further needed, Maite did leave.

Taryn remained in the chamber until it was time to go below for the morning meal. She would have preferred to forego the public appearance, but knew she could not. Instead she found herself fervently hoping that Garret's mysterious anger had passed.

In the hall she found most of Jaune's people assembled and seated. She took her chair, mutely acknowledging the several greetings directed to her. Garret's seat was empty. She looked to Richard, who seemed to understand her unvoiced question.

"There have been reports of robbers in the south woods. Lord Garret has taken a contingent of men to investigate. He probably will not return until day's end."

Taryn did not bother to ask why it was that her husband felt the need to go himself when he had a hundred knights in his command.

Richard, apparently of a like mind, made an effort to divert her attention to conversation, telling her of the morning's events.

"From your description he sounds to be a terrifying man, this mercenary," Taryn replied, once the tale had been told. "Truly, he possesses but one eye?"

"Aye. But I think with one he is still more man than most with two."

"You speak as if you admire him."

"Not admire, lady, but respect. He is a man whose very demeanor commands it. Even Lord Garret felt it."

At the mention of Garret's name Taryn lost all interest in the conversation and in the meal. She ignored Richard's startled expression, pushed aside her trencher and stood. Then, with a polite nod in his direction, she left the dais and retreated abovestairs to the wool room.

She remained there until late afternoon, and though she watched the door and the corridor beyond, she did not hear Garret's return. Hence, when she entered the great hall for the evening meal, she was not surprised to see his chair still unoccupied.

She took her place and nervously drank the wine set before her. She was not sure if she could endure another meal without his attendance. Robbers or no, his absence had elicited a number of sly and curious looks toward the dais. And the fact that Richard's chair was empty, as well, made her uneasiness all the worse. At least at the morning meal she had had his company.

She refilled her goblet and turned her focus to the keep's double portals. Just then they opened, and several men entered. She recognized Richard at once and breathed a sigh of relief. She then looked to the men with him. Three were rather nondescript, no different from any of the scores of men-at-arms already seated at the lower tables. But the fourth man caught and held her attention instantly. He could be no other than the mercenary Richard had told her about.

A head taller than Richard, he walked with the cautious stealth and light-footed tread of one who had spent much of his life in strange and dangerous places. His hair was indeed the color of pitch, and as he and Richard separated from their companions and neared the dais, she could see the disfigurement of which the steward had spoken.

Pity, she thought, for without it and the heavy beard which did not really conceal the ugly scar, he might have been a handsome man.

The men came even closer, and Taryn averted her gaze. She did not want to be caught staring. But when she heard them mount the platform she looked up in surprise.

"My lady, may I present Sir Simon d'Orléon."

Taryn turned and tilted back her head. She found herself staring straight up into the stranger's face.

"Sir Simon, the Countess of Arundel."

The man bowed. "My lady."

"Sir Simon." Taryn offered a hesitant smile. Richard's use of her new title had caught her somewhat off guard. Then, too, d'Orléon's very appearance was cause for caution. He was an imposing figure indeed.

"Lord Garret has asked me to seat Sir Simon at his table, lady," Richard offered, by way of an explanation for the man's presence.

"Then by all means, please be seated."

The stranger pulled out the chair beside her own and

promptly sat down.

Taryn saw Richard wince and realized at once the reason for his reaction. Without Garret's presence at the table it did not look at all proper to have this man at her side. Clearly Richard had intended to seat him further down with Garret's other vassals.

The man seemed to sense her uneasiness and smiled. "Forgive my forwardness, lady, but I favor my right side. I prefer to be able to see those I am seated with."

Though his casual reference to his deformity made her somewhat uncomfortable, it did serve to allay Richard's concern. Nodding to them both, he proceeded to his own place on the other side of Garret's chair.

Which was still unoccupied, she thought, as she watched Richard take his seat.

"Lord Garret has returned, but asked that we begin the meal without him," he stated, thereby providing her with the right to signal the serving of the food.

She did so, and as the servers entered, she looked to the man beside her. She now knew what Richard had meant. The black-haired stranger did evoke respect—and even fear. Suddenly, realizing he was aware of her staring, she made a hasty attempt at polite conversation. "Richard told me what happened in the village today."

"Indeed." His brow lifted in amusement.

"Aye. He . . . he thought your defense of the men to be most noble."

To her surprise the man broke out into laughter. "Noble, my lady, is not a word I often hear in the same breath as my name."

She did not know how to reply to his almost mocking comment, so reached instead for her goblet, looking out as she did so among the lower tables. Her gaze sought out the hounds foraging for scraps. The dogs would be the first to sense Garret's arrival.

"I must be honest, lady."

The man's voice and odd remark drew her gaze back to him. "How so?"

"As you learned something of me this day, so, too, did I learn of you."

"Of me?" She looked at him in confusion.

"Aye. I learned that you are newly wedded. Might I offer my best wishes for your happiness?"

She felt her color rise. Surely he must therefore wonder as to the reason for her husband's absence? "Thank you," she murmured, glancing back to the hounds.

Becket, the bay, had abandoned a bone tossed to him and was standing rigidly, attention focused upon the doors.

They opened, and as Taryn saw Garret enter, she felt a decidedly mixed reaction. She quickly lowered her gaze, feigning an unawareness of his arrival.

Garret crossed the room, making his way to the dais. He marked d'Orléon's position and experienced the faintest prick of irritation in noting the man's closeness to Taryn. Though he tried to shrug off the unnatural feeling of possessiveness, it persisted. When he mounted the platform it was evident in his voice as he addressed his guest. "You have met my wife."

His question was more a statement of fact, and d'Orléon clearly recognized it as such.

His response was not an answer, but a statement as well. "You are a fortunate man, my lord."

Again Garret felt the same prick. He ignored it and took his seat, reaching immediately for his goblet. "Your charges have rebuilt the cottage?"

"Aye, and I might add better than 'twas before."

"That does not make it aright."

"Nay, my lord. It does not. But 'tis a start."

Garret let the comment, which could have been regarded as rather bold, pass. "Why is it that you find the wretches worthy of redemption?"

"Because I see in them myself—the youth I once was. I made mistakes and was often guilty of the poorest of judgment, and innocent people suffered."

In spite of himself Garret smiled. He liked this man. Most men refused even privately to admit to their failings—whether past or present—yet this one did so openly and without reservation. "As have I," he stated softly, looking suddenly at Taryn.

All day he had been unable to leave off thinking about what had occurred that morning. He had not needed to investigate the claim of robbers, which had proved false, but had done so simply to avoid her. Mayhap his temper was more to blame than her curiosity. He should not have let her questions affect him as they had. She could not possibly have known the details of his first marriage. Besides, this was their first public appearance as man and wife. He was not of a mind to let his actions give rise to more gossip.

He made an effort to be attentive, and the meal passed on a rather pleasant and comfortable note. At its conclusion he looked at his guest. "Do you play chess?"

"Aye."

In the man's half smile Garret saw recognition of the motive behind the invitation. Garret could learn much of the way the man thought by the way in which he played the game of skill and strategy. "Then we will play." He stood and extended his hand to Taryn. "Will you watch or find for this evening another partner?"

Taryn could not understand this change in Garret's mood. Despite the confrontation of the morning, since sitting down to sup he had acted every bit the role of a dutiful husband. Thus her desire to stay was twofold. Not only did she want to do nothing which would again displease him, but she had also sensed that more was taking place between him and his newest man-at-arms than a mere game of chess. Whatever it was, she did indeed want to watch. "I shall watch," she replied. Then, realizing her blatent interest might appear bold, she quickly added, "Unless Richard will oblige me?"

She looked at Garret's steward and smiled. She knew he preferred backgammon with its element of chance, and hoped he would decline.

"I would be honored." Richard stood with an easygoing smile. "I fear, however, I will not pose much of a challenge. I have, after all, seen you play, lady."

He did not lie. Garret's steward played a very unimaginative and predictable game. She won the first two games easily and was contemplating a move in the third when she suddenly felt the stranger's gaze upon her.

Once he realized she was aware of his stare, he spoke. "You know, my lady, the Church frowns upon women playing games of chance," he said with a half-concealed smile.

"Chess is not a game of chance, Sir Simon," she replied, "but of skill."

He smiled in amusement. "The priests still warn not to waste too much time at it."

Feeling suddenly very comfortable with him, she returned his smile. "I am not wasting time—I am winning!" To prove her point she reached across the board with a flourish and promptly checked Richard's king.

In doing so she lowered her gaze and hence did not see the scowl which furrowed her husband's brow.

Garret stared at her. He had heard the animated tone in her voice, and he liked it no more than he liked the expression he saw on her face. With d'Orléon's attention she had become like a dairy maid giddy and gushing at a squire's attentions.

For the third time he felt that same sense of irritation, only this time it was clearly with her—his wife—who acted not like a modest wife but more like a woman attempting to provoke interest in what she had to offer. "Mayhap you should be merciful and spare Richard yet another defeat," he growled.

Taryn knew at once the message behind his words. She was being firmly dismissed. "And so I shall," she repeated. She managed to keep her tone light, venting the annoyance she felt by flipping back her braid as she stood.

She bade Richard good night, then turned her gaze—accompanied by a gracious smile—to the man seated across from Garret. In spite of Garret's reversal of mood she would see the evening ended on an affable note. "Sir Simon, 'twas a pleasure to have made your acquaintance. I hope next time you will indulge me in a game . . . or two."

"I shall look forward to it, lady."

With her focus fixed upon the man, she missed the flash of annoyance in Garret's eyes. Then, too, when she addressed her husband, her polite words were returned in kind. Hence, she departed the hall utterly unaware of how the brief exchange between her and Simon had tapped his latent anger and suspicions.

Once abovestairs she undressed quickly and got into bed. Garret's dismissal still stung and she wanted to be asleep when he came in. But despite the wine she had drunk, she found it difficult to sleep. She stared up at the canopy and thought of all that had passed between them this day. Each word she weighed in her mind, trying to determine when he had become angry. The answer always seemed the same—when he had snapped at her, telling her that only a whore found pleasure with any man.

But why had that made him angry with her? He had felt the proof of her virginity and thus could not possibly believe her guilty of prior indiscretion. Surely he did not think that because she had enjoyed their lovemaking, she displayed a whore's disposition? That made no sense at all. He had told her coupling evoked a feeling of pleasure.

At last, weary of thought and finally drowsy, she drifted off, ironically thinking of the pleasures of the night before.

"You are a formidable opponent, my lord." D'Orléon

inclined his head in gracious acknowledgment of his second defeat in as many games.

Garret leaned back in his chair. His victories had not been won easily. "The same can be said of you."

The two men stared at one another in silence, each recognizing much of himself in the man before him.

It was Simon who finally looked away. "I thank you for the games. It has been a long time since I have been so well challenged." He stood and bowed. "I bid you good night, my lord."

Garret watched as he left, then stood as well. By the time he reached his chamber all thoughts of Simon d'Orléon had vanished—replaced by those of the woman who now shared his bed.

As he had anticipated, she was alseep. He undressed and lay down beside her, turning to watch her as she slept. In the light of the several candles which had been left burning he could clearly make out her soft features and the tender curves of her body.

He leaned closer and brushed from her cheek a wave of silken hair. It was a mistake. Touching her unleashed his desire. Aroused, but cautious, he kissed her lips softly.

Still deep in her dreams, she turned her face to his. Never opening her eyes she rolled langorously into his arms.

His kisses became more aggressive. In his mind a thought had formed, and he was ready to test the theory. Would she be equally wanton in her response if his treatment of her were less gentle? Surely that was the true measure of a whore—one who responded as Geneviève did—needing no more than raw physical desire, unaccompanied by tenderness or respect.

And though he knew he risked much, he had to know—especially after what he had witnessed of her behavior with d'Orléon.

Suddenly she threw off her slumber. Now beneath him, she stared up into his face.

Garret watched as understanding filtered into her

eyes. He let his hands caress her roughly and kissed her hard.

She turned her head and tried to push him away.

"Am I hurting you?"

Taryn flinched at the harsh edge in his voice. She did not know how to answer. He did not hurt her, but he did frighten her. So unlike the tenderness he had each time before shown her, his roughness now instilled within her an instinctive urge to resist. Yet she remembered Maite's insistence that she show neither fear nor reluctance. And too, this man was her lawful husband. She did not have the right to resist. "Nay," she whispered.

"Then do not turn away," he growled.

She felt him part her legs with his knee as he pinned her arms. It was as if he wanted to insure that there would be no contact between them but physical; he would not embrace her, nor was she to embrace him—but merely act as the recipient of his passion.

He positioned himself. Then, just as she anticipated his entry, he spoke. "Do you want me to stop?"

His question raised a challenge. But of what? Did he think her still timid, incapable of responding to a man?

Suddenly the words he had spoken in the wool room came to mind: *I want you as a man wants a woman. Are you woman enough to endure all that entails?* Was that it? she wondered. Was he attempting to discover how much of a woman she was?

"Do you," he repeated, his voice ragged and strained.

She shook her head—and fought the cry of pain which threatened to erupt as he thrust into her. Incredibly, however, as he began to move within her, the previous warmth of pleasure returned. Despite his lack of gentleness, his passion still ignited a desire deep within her.

She gave herself to it, relaxing beneath him as Maite had instructed. His penetration became more fevered, and still she felt the pleasure build until once again the earth seemed to fall away.

He jerked inside her and then was still.

She opened her eyes and encountered a look that made the breath leave her body. Her mind swirled in confusion, and through a watery gaze she tried to find in his eyes the cause for his contempt. Had she not acted as he wanted?

"You hold yourself cheap, madam." He withdrew from her and left the bed.

The same sense of shame and confusion she had experienced that morning returned, yet this time anger and frustration surfaced as well. "What do you want of me?" she cried. "Have I not given what you asked? I don't understand. Why do you take me—then act as if you despise me for it?"

"Because you experience pleasure with the fervor of a whore. A wife does not conduct herself in such a wanton manner."

"Wanton?" She struggled to sit up. Her confusion was now greater than ever. "Are you telling me that what I experience is not supposed to be felt—save by a whore? You told me yourself that coupling evokes a sense of pleasure. You said naught that only the man was permitted to feel it."

She threw off the sheet and scrambled to her knees, glaring at him in silent fury. At last she found her speech in a wrath-hot rush of words. "By whose judgment is it unseemly for a woman to enjoy the pleasures of the flesh? If 'tis evil or wrong for a woman, then 'tis evil for a man as well—for I do not believe God intended only men to know passion."

She drew a deep breath and continued. "There is much I do not know of men and women. But of this I am certain. I do not believe that because I have felt pleasure in the arms of the man who is my lawful husband, that I am wanton. Nor will I let you make me feel shame. And if to be your wife means to endure your lust while feeling naught—then I would rather that you did treat me as your whore than as your wife!"

Rigid and silent, he stood beside the bed, looking at her.

Had she not known better she would have thought it to be regret and a sense of loss she saw shadowed in his eyes. She waited for his anger, but it was not forthcoming. "Damn you! Will you not speak?"

Finally his steely voice broke the cold silence between them. "You are my wife—that I cannot change. But from this night forth, know that I will not touch you. This marriage has been consummated according to my king's wishes, hence I am not obliged to you further—or to him."

Taryn's breath escaped in a gasp. She rocked back on her heels, staring up at him as she took in the full import of his announcement. "But what of the heir your king demanded?"

If he was surprised by her knowledge of that fact, he did not show it. "I ne'er wanted an heir," he growled. "If I have already gotten you with child then Henry shall be appeased. If not, I shall attribute this union's lack of issue to your barren womb."

Shaken by the cruelty of his lie, she continued to kneel there. Then her confusion and pain welded together in one last upsurge of venom. "'Tis no wonder your first wife went insane," she hissed, unable to stop her words. "I, too, would choose that path rather than ever to have to lie with you again."

His face went black. He grabbed for his clothes at the foot of the bed and stormed from the room.

Only when she heard the door slam did her fury subside, melting into sorrow and anguish. Tears slid down her cheeks, and as she lay back a single sob broke free. she knew Garret's words had been no idle threat or empty vow made in anger. Where would he go? To a guest room below? To the barracks? Or was the escape he sought more than mere physical distance? Was he even now lying with another?

For hours she lay there, listening for his return.

Finally, sometime before dawn she fell into an exhausted half-sleep.

She was awakened by the sound of the door opening. Feigning sleep, she watched through the lashes of her lowered lids as Garret entered. He wore the shirt and breeches he had left with.

He approached the bed's foot and removed from the chest located there his mail and a leather tunic. Over the breeches he donned *chausses*, then the tunic over his shirt. As he tied the laces across his chest, he glanced to the bed.

Taryn squeezed her eyes shut. After a moment she heard him struggle into his *hauberk*, then belt on his sword. She risked another covert look, but he had already crossed the room. And when he slammed the door shut behind him, she knew he had known she was awake all along.

"Damn you!" she cried, sitting bolt up-right.

Futile and forlorn, the cry echoed in the empty chamber. The tears she thought had dried welled once more in her eyes.

An instant later a light rapping sounded at the door.

Taryn wiped the tears from her cheeks. Maite had wasted little time in coming to her. Probably, too, she had passed Garret on the stairs. This morning there would be no way Taryn could avoid her questions.

She drew a deep breath. "Enter."

The door opened and Maite's familiar silhouette appeared. "Lady Taryn." The woman nodded in greeting as she turned to close the door.

Taryn drew a second steadying breath. In what form would Maite's query come? Certainly the servant had demonstrated the ability to be equally forthright as cryptic.

In silence Maite crossed the room and opened the shutters. The gray light of daybreak entered the chamber. "It looks to be a clear day. Shall I order water to be heated for your bath?"

Taryn nodded, watching as the woman's gaze went from her to the empty place in the bed beside her. Could she tell that Garret had been gone all night? Unable to bear what she might see in her eyes, Taryn looked away.

"'Tis said that when love is strong, a man and a woman can make their bed on the blade of a sword. But if their love is weak, a bed of sixty cubits is not wide enough."

Taryn felt her face burn in response to the gentle reproach. Still, she lifted her chin. "I did everything you said. The fault is not mine."

"What happened?"

Taryn shook her head. "It does not matter, save to know this marriage is a mistake."

"I do not believe that, lady." Maite smiled in confident reassurance. "'Twill just take more time. You must be patient."

Taryn stared at her in disbelief, then realized that in not knowing what had passed between her and Garret, Maite could not comprehend the true breadth of their estrangement. No amount of time would mend this rift or erase the memory of the hateful words spoken. "You speak of love being strong and weak, Maite. Do you forget that this is a marriage made without love?"

"There are many forms of love. Some spring forth seemingly overnight, like a mushroom after a summer rain, but others are as an oak, setting deep and strong roots long before the first evidence of its life breaks through the earth."

"Were that I could believe you, Maite," Taryn whispered. Lowering her gaze, she reached for the robe Maite handed her and steeled herself for what the day would bring.

As she had been certain would be the case, Garret was once again gone from Jaune until very late—setting a pattern which would be assiduously followed.

There was no contact between them save when they could not avoid it. Small, polite exchanges for the benefit of others comprised their speech. Even in these instances

Taryn noted how his eyes refused to meet hers. At night they lay side by side, the physical distance between them measured by inches, yet more impervious than the widest moat.

She languished in the sham. Within the walls of their chamber they were as strangers, beyond them as mummers—actors in a dumb show—each mutely playing his role. Her only source of comfort was that he did not shame her by openly availing himself of other women. He was not gone long enough to travel to Kirdford and Geneviève, and whatever dalliances he might be enjoying with Jaune's serving maids were at least discreet, for no whisper of his transgressions ever reached her ears.

Three weeks passed and even Maite began to privately doubt her own initial confidence. She was at a loss to understand what had caused the rift between them. Her attempts to question Garret were utterly futile. For the first time she could not pierce his silence, or feel the cause for his pain. The demons which haunted him were too deeply entrenched in his own mind.

Taryn was no less close-mouthed. Despite Maite's numerous attempts to broach the subject, Garret's bride gave few details and offered little explanation of the wedding night or thereafter. To Maite's great disappointment Taryn's course of action became one of complete resignation to her fate: She had not wed out of love and hence had no right to expect more than what she had—a marriage in name only.

Chapter Sixteen

"I know this man, my lord." Richard spoke up from his position on the stool beside Garret. "His name is Peter and he has been gone from Jaune many months."

Garret turned his attention from the fettered youth who had just been thrust forward into view by his sheriff. "How long?" he demanded of the steward. According to law, if the serf had been gone for a year and a day, he was to be released upon recapture—a free man.

Richard shrugged. "I am not sure. The records are with the rest, in your chamber. I will have to ride back." He made a move to stand.

Garret promptly gestured for him to remain where he was. "I need you here."

"Shall I go, my lord?" Simon stepped forward from his place beside the priest.

"Nay. I want you here as well, Simon." Garret beckoned to one of his squires who had accompanied them into the village for the holding of the weekly court. Though not yet in his seventeenth year, the lanky youth had proven himself loyal and worthy of greater responsibility. Then, too, Garret had his own reasons for what he was about to do.

"Aye, my lord?" The squire, known as Andrew, bowed.

"Ride back to Jaune." Garret paused. Since their marriage Taryn had begun to keep the household accounts. Because many of her responsibilities revolved around providing food, and because supplies had to be arranged for one year in advance, from time to time she had had to review the records kept from previous years. Garret knew she would be able to locate the needed document. He continued. "Find my wife and tell her that she is instructed to give you the manor records kept from last year."

"Tell the Countess that 'tis the scroll which makes note of the births, deaths and disappearances of Jaune's villeins." Richard interjected.

"At once, my lords." Again, Andrew bowed.

As the youth hastened to his horse, Garret signaled to his sheriff to present the next case.

Taryn knelt before the carved chest and lifted its lid. "What is the name of the serf?"

"My lady?" The youth waiting respectfully just inside the doorway looked at her in surprise.

Taryn smiled. "Lord Garret is holding court, is he not?"

The squire nodded.

"And he requested the scroll which records births, deaths and disappearances?"

Again her question elicited a mute nod.

"Well then, whatever must be verified is either the birth or death, or the disappearance of a serf. In any case a name must be known. There is little point in having you deliver to Lord Garret a document which does not make mention of what he desires to know."

"Aye, my lady." He nodded in understanding. "The serf's name is Peter."

Taryn rifled through the various scrolls and sheets of parchment. "And does my husband desire to know about this Peter's birth, death or disappearance?"

"Disappearance, my lady."

At once Taryn knew why Garret had requested the records. What she did not know, however, was the cause for the strained quality she was certain she heard in the youth's answer. "Did you know this man—Peter?"

He hesitated before replying. "Aye, but he is not really a man. He is mayhap a year or two older than I."

Her curiosity grew, yet she did not immediately question the youth further. For several minutes she searched for the needed scroll. Each sheet of parchment pertaining to a given year had been sewn together and then rolled. To find the proper one she had to unroll each and read the date of its final entry.

At last she located the document. As the squire patiently waited, she read through the names listed—and found the name Peter beside one entry making note of a serf's disappearance. She read the date: the twenty-third day of May, in the year 1169. Mentally she calculated today's date—the nineteenth of May. Peter was but five days from having obtained his freedom! Why had he returned now and not later? Had he miscalculated the days?

She masked her expression and looked up. "I've found it."

The youth's face betrayed disappointment.

Giving no indication that she had seen it, she continued. "Do you know why he ran away?"

"He sought work in the city, my lady." He hesitated before going on. "Peter wanted to make a better life for himself. He did not want to be tied to the land, as his father and his father's father before him." Nervously, he looked away.

Taryn was sure she knew the reason for his discomfort at this disclosure. Classes were clearly ordained by Heaven. For a peasant to repine against his status was not only an act which questioned the justice of providence, it was regarded as an ingratitude toward God. "Why did he return?"

"His mother is ill. He met up with a peddler who had passed through Jaune, and when he asked the man for news, he learned of her illness." The youth looked at her strangely. "She is dying, my lady."

At once Taryn knew that despite the difference in their stations these two boys had been friends. She wondered if Garret knew as well. By sending this particular squire to fetch the records, was he testing the youth? And would the boy, upon an order from his lord act—albeit indirectly—against his friend?

Such a ploy would not be out of character for her husband, she thought in silent anger. Who knew better than she the perverse enjoyment he seemed to obtain by testing others, to see whether or not they lived up to *his* expectations?

She forced her anger aside. He would not miss one villein from among Jaune's hundreds. "Tell Lord Garret . . ." She drew a deep breath. ". . . tell him that the date of the disappearance is recorded as the twenty-third day of *April*, last year."

The youth's face brightened in understanding of what that date meant. "Should I not bring the document?"

"Nay," she replied firmly. "I have told you what it says. Now go."

"At once, my lady."

Taryn watched him dash from the chamber. She was very glad she had lied. But for those few days Peter would have been free anyway. Was not the courage to visit his dying mother worth five days?

She rolled up the scroll and replaced it in the chest. Garret could not read the truth, and she was confident no one would question her word.

She was wrong.

"Andrew, are you sure the Countess said the twenty-third day of *April*?" As the youth reaffirmed his initial answer with an insistent nod, Richard scratched his jaw, searching his memory. Last spring the rains had lasted throughout all of April, with planting not commencing until early May. Yet he was certain he remembered seeing this serf working alongside his father, ploughing and spreading manure in preparation for the sowing. But mayhap he was mistaken . . .

"Is aught wrong?"

Richard lowered his gaze beneath Garret's questioning stare. How could he express his doubt as to the veracity of the youth's information without casting disparagement upon the word of his lord's wife? Without replying, he scratched his jaw again.

Garret's eyes narrowed. He knew this nervous gesture of Richard's. Something was wrong, and his steward was concealing it. "Where is the document you were sent to fetch?" he demanded, turning his gaze to the waiting squire.

"Your lady wife did not give it to me," the boy replied, casting a sudden and pleading look to the tall man standing on the other side of Garret.

At once Simon stepped forward. "My lord, 'tis clear that in reading the records and telling Andrew the information needed, the Countess did not see further necessity to hand over the document." He lowered his voice. "I do not think you should blame the boy if she saw fit to overrule your orders."

Reluctantly Garret conceded to Simon's wisdom. Intent now upon a different course, he returned his attention to the squire. "Did she ask you why the date was needed?"

"Nay, my lord."

"But she knew?"

"Aye."

Of course she would, he thought. Taryn was many things, but dimwitted was not one of them. She would know the law regarding runaways. "Did she question you?"

Andrew nodded.

"About?" Garret prompted him. Secretly he was pleased with the youth's unwillingness to betray more than what was asked. A knight was taught from early on not to ask unnecessary questions or to volunteer information. Yet he could not help but wonder if the boy's reluctance to speak did not stem from a cause other than his training.

"She asked me his name and if I had known him."

"Aught else?"

The boy lowered his gaze. "She asked if I knew why he had left and was now returned."

"Both of which you did, because you and he were friends. Is that not true, Andrew?"

"Aye, my lord." The boy's uneasiness increased markedly.

"My lord," Simon interrupted, his voice once more tactfully low. "This has no bearing on your decision. Under the law you are obligated to release this man. His absence from Jaune clearly exceeds a day and a year—by nearly a month."

Garret looked at his vassal in silence. He could not hold the serf further without outwardly admitting that he did not trust his wife, and hence doubted her word. "Release him," he commanded, turning to Richard. "Make note in your records that from this day forth, the serf aforeknown merely as Peter, shall now be known as Peter Mayfreed, a free man."

The serf, who had stood in frozen silence through the entire proceedings, dropped to his knees the instant his bonds were cut. With tears streaming down his face, he crossed himself, then crawled to Garret's feet. "Thank you, milord. Thank you."

Garret looked down at his tear-streaked cheeks. They sported no more hair than a girl's. "Do not thank me. Were you even one day short of the requirement, you would still be a serf, and I would have ordered you branded on the forehead as befits any runaway. Now stand and do honor to your name. No free man grovels at the feet of another."

From the corner of his eye he saw Simon smile—and knew that even with his impaired sight, the man had seen through the harsh inexorability Garret needed to portray. "You know me too well, Simon," he muttered gruffly, standing.

"Nay, my lord. I know only myself."

"My lord?" Richard stood as well. "Our business this day is concluded. Unless you desire otherwise, I shall see to other matters."

"Nay." Garret pinned his steward with a cool stare. "Our business this day is *not* concluded. You will ride with me back to Jaune—and read yourself the date of Peter Mayfreed's disappearance."

At once Richard stiffened, and Garret knew from the naked look of guilt and dread on his face that his suspicions had been correct. He would wager Jaune's entire worth Taryn had lied. "We go," he commanded, his voice betraying no trace of the fury which had begun to smolder within him.

Taryn heard the pair of footsteps. Her heartbeat quickened, and she struggled against the urge to leap up from her chair and run to the wool room's door. There was no need to verify what she knew: Garret was returning from the village, and with him, Richard. Nor was there cause for the heart-racing sense of dread she felt. Jaune's steward did this often, accompanying his lord abovestairs in order to transcribe the morning's proceedings.

She drew a shallow breath and strove to concentrate on the unfinished tapestry mounted on a frame before her, inserting her needle through the heavy weave.

The footsteps neared, then stopped. She heard the chamber door across the corridor open, but not close—allowing the faint sound of male voices to be heard.

"Milady, is aught wrong? Your face is as white as this here wool." One of the half-dozen girls seated in the room spoke up from her chair by the window. Concern evident on her face, she made a move to set down her distaff and spindle.

Taryn gestured for her to remain seated and mustered a weak smile. "'Tis fine, Nora. Resume your spinning."

Though the girl's eyes mirrored disbelief in her mistress' words, she obeyed.

Taryn tugged the length of colored silk, setting her stitch, then inserted the needle once more.

The point never pierced the fabric—for in that instant a thunderous slam erupted from across the corridor.

Before she looked up, she knew he was there. Still, she forced herself to look to the room's doorway, to the man who stood there. Her eyes froze on the familiar, powerful shoulders. She could feel the barely restrained fury emanating from him, and knew from the collective gasp which echoed in the chamber that every person in the room felt it too, including Richard, who stood beside him.

She lifted her gaze, and a shiver raced down her back. His stare was as ice. She glanced over to Richard, knowing even as Garret stepped forward, his steward would do nothing to stop him.

"You have stepped beyond the place appointed to a woman. How dare you conspire to defy me!"

"I did not defy you, my lord."

Her denial seemed to shatter whatever control he still possessed. His face turned dark with wrath, and his pale eyes flashed a lethal warning. "You will not speak to me in that voice. Your actions have done enough already to hold me up for ridicule."

Without warning he reached out and pulled her to her feet. The large tapestry frame toppled to the floor. Halting all hope of escape with an iron grip on her arm, he dragged her hard against him and drew back his free hand. "Tell me, deceitful wife, how reads the true date on the document—or you shall feel a husband's righteous punishment."

Taryn looked past him to the man standing in horrified silence at the chamber's entrance. In his hand Richard held the scroll.

"Will you disavow your lie?" Garret hissed, tightening his grip. "Or are you insolent enough to challenge to Richard's face his word?"

Though inwardly Taryn cringed in terror, outwardly she refused to show the fear clutching her heart. She lifted her gaze and met his icy glare straight on. "You know the true date," she whispered, instinctively flinching in anticipation of the blow she was sure would follow.

To her surprise, however, it was not forthcoming. Instead of striking, his hand lowered, clenching into a fist at his side.

"At last the lying wife speaks the truth," he stated with a calm she knew was deceptive. He back away a slow half step, then spun her toward the door. Without releasing his hold, he shoved her forward.

At once Richard backed out of her path.

Passing him, Taryn caught a glimpse of his face. While there might have been sympathy for her in his expression, there was also support for his lord. A wife owed her husband unquestioning obedience. What she had done was inexcusable. Hence, whatever punishment Garret now deemed fit would not be questioned by his steward. A husband's right to domination over his wife was God-given, a part of the divine order of things.

At the closed door to their chamber Garret paused, reaching out in front of her to release the latch. As the door opened he shoved her forward with enough force that she stumbled and fell.

Looking over her shoulder, she saw him slam the door shut, then whirl to face her. She struggled to rise, then froze on hands and knees as she saw his hands go to the belt at his waist, unbuckling it and then removing it. He slid the strap free of the scabbard and its sheathed sword, tossing both aside. As the blade clattered to the floor, he folded the length of stout leather.

"Have you aught to say which could possibly justify your actions?"

Sensing a hesitation, Taryn took a dangerous gamble. "Naught but that I would gladly do so again. A beating is a small price to pay for the boy's freedom. Knowing, too, I have spared him from mutilation, I now willingly suffer your punishment."

Garret moved faster than he knew she would anticipate. He grabbed her by the hair and jerked her to her feet. He had given her a chance to plead for mercy—instead she had proudly proclaimed the virtue of her defiance!

He reached for the throat of her gown, feeling the back laces give as he tore the garment open to her waist. He pushed her to the bed and tossed her face down across it.

Taryn squeezed her eyes shut. Her thin chemise would not shield her flesh from the leather's bite. She heard the sound of the strap cutting the air, and braced herself. But with the blow there came no pain. She opened her eyes and turned her head. The strap had wound itself around one of the bedposts, which he had struck instead of her.

Through the roar of blood pounding in her ears she heard his voice.

"In all my life I have ne'er beaten a woman. I cannot start now—even with one as deserving as you!"

She watched, astounded, as he stepped back. Clearly it was only with great effort that he had mastered his fury.

He walked to the door, stopping to retrieve his sword. "You are to remain in this chamber until such time as I order differently. Defy me in this, madam, and I *will* beat you in earnest."

With those words he was gone, the door once more slamming thunderously behind him.

But once outside Garret stopped in his flight. He belted on his sword and tried to rein in his raging emotions. What was it about her which so heated his blood? Whether with passion or fury, the result was ever the same—a lack of control he was unable to prevent, which then turned physical.

"Christ's blood!" he swore, feeling his fury rage once more. He was angry at the circumstance, at her and at himself—at the confusion within him he could not understand. It was as if he were being attacked. But the threat was not physical, coming from an enemy without. He was fencing with an emotional foe, an adversary he had never before encountered, in a battle in which he was yet to be skilled. Until he could understand and control this threat, he could not be around anyone. He fled from the keep and made his way to the stables.

He had just given orders to have his destrier saddled when he heard a rider approach, dismount and enter, leading his horse.

Even in the stable's dim light there was no doubt as to the man's identity. Garret caught sight of the black hair immediately.

"My lord." Simon nodded in greeting, his gaze going to the war horse being led from its stall. Revealing no reaction, he handed over the reins of his own mount to a second stable boy. "Do you desire accompaniment?"

Garret shook his head and turned to the boy who appeared to be having difficulty with the girth strap. "Be quick about it, boy!" he snapped.

"I know the date given was false."

Simon's low voice sliced through Garret like a cold blade. He nodded, not trusting his voice.

"I spoke to young Peter," Simon continued. "He was within days of meeting the requirement."

"Five," Garret amended curtly.

Simon gave no indication of having heard him. His low, even voice resumed. "His mother is dying. For that reason he returned."

This information was new. Garret felt as if a second blow had been dealt. "The law is the law."

"Aye," Simon replied. "But had you been in her place, would you not have done the same?"

Garret whirled in anger. "I would not have lied. I would have presented the circumstances."

"To what end? You could not have made an exception for him. Your position as lord does not accord you that luxury. You would have had to carry out the law."

Garret knew he spoke the truth.

"She did you a service, my lord." Simon spoke once more. "Her actions enabled you to do what the law would not, but what your heart and your personal sense of morality tell you to be just."

Garret glared at him. He was right. The struggle between duty and honor had been no small part of his confusion.

Abruptly Simon turned to walk away, then stopped. He looked at Garret over his shoulder. "If it matters . . . I would have acted no differently. You, on the other hand, must be first an earl, and only secondly a man."

Garret turned to his now saddled horse. He placed his foot in the stirrup and mounted before replying. "Your words of counsel are unneeded this time. You have but told me what I already know."

For three days Taryn remained in her chamber. She saw no one save Maite, who brought her meals. But even in the woman's visits Taryn found no respite from her solitude.

For the first time since Taryn's arrival at Jaune, Maite's reaction to her was one of utter aloofness. In those eyes full of silent accusation the message was clear: The reasons for Taryn's action did not matter—not to Garret—and not to Maite. That Taryn had striven to deceive him was unforgivable.

On the morning of the fourth day Taryn could bear her isolation no longer. When Maite entered with a tray of food and a flagon of wine, she waved both away. "Take it," she stated firmly, as she turned from the window to confront the woman. "If I am to be treated as a prisoner let us do it aright—with scraps from the kitchen and brackish water."

The faintest hint of reproach rose in the woman's eyes. Yet she said nothing as she set the tray down on the table beside her.

"I shall not eat it." Taryn squared her shoulders and flipped back her braid.

"'Tis your choice, lady. But as Lord Garret said naught about starving you before he left, I shall continue to bring your meals."

"Left?" Taryn felt her stomach lurch. "Where did he

go?" She was certain she already knew the answer: *Kirdford.*

But Maite merely shrugged ignorance. "He does not share such things with me."

Taryn turned away and stared out the window. She told herself the moisture suddenly welling in her eyes came from staring at the bright sunlight. Yet even as she tried without success to blink it away, her mind filled with images that only evoked more. And as she thought of Garret in Geneviève's bed, making love to her, the taste of bile rose in her throat. But why would he not go to her? She was what he desired, what he truly wanted.

She spun around. Her anguish was as a torrent desperate for release, and she revenged her pain on the only person available. "'He does not share such things with you'—and yet you still profess to know so much? Meting advice and instructions which have all proved as worthless and false as your claims: foolish rantings of mushrooms and oaks, and growing love! He has ne'er cared aught for me and there is no measure of time which will alter that!"

Maite looked at her in icy silence. At last she spoke. "There is naught which can be grown from distrust and deceit. And those, Countess of Arundel, are the seeds *you* have sown."

Taryn could not bear her recrimination. "I did not deceive him to deceive him! I had reasons—"

"I know your reasons," Maite answered coolly. "And as noble as they might have been, your action was still wrong. You placed your husband in a position where his very manhood was in question. How can a man command other men if it appears that he cannot rule even his own wife?" She turned to leave, then stopped, looking at Taryn over her shoulder. "He could have held the boy and not freed him. All he had do was publicly declare your word false. But he did not. He would not shame you without cause or proof. You, however, did not suffer from such pangs of conscience."

Taryn's eyes filled with stinging tears, and as the

woman exited she knew she had lost her only confidant and ally.

With a trembling hand Taryn reached for the flagon of wine. She filled the cup and had just raised it to her lips when she heard the latch release. She set down the goblet and turned slowly. Only one person would enter without first knocking and gaining admittance.

She bit her lower lip, lifted her chin and watched as Garret strode into the room. She could smell the odor of horses about him and knew he was just returned.

His eyes raked her coldly. "I see your confinement has done little to teach you humility. You are still as brazen as a whore."

His callous and cutting remark snapped the fragile thread of control she had managed to seize. "Speaking of whores, my lord . . . how is Madame Flambard?"

His mouth parted into a slow, cruel smile. It was all the affirmation she needed.

Uncaring as to the consequences, she recklessly plunged ahead with her attack. "Might you tell me how 'tis possible that what you find so objectionable in your own wife, fails to bother you when found in other men's wives?"

His smile vanished. "What I do, madam, is of no concern of yours—just as what you do no longer is of mine—save in one matter. You are to keep a proper household. No more will I expect or want of you—ever. By day's end Maite will remove your belongings into the wool room."

He turned to leave, but her voice stopped him. "Am I to be permitted beyond those walls? Or is *that* chamber to become my prison now?"

"You are permitted wherever you like, madam. I no longer care—as long as discretion is exercised. You will deport yourself with all decorum, as befits my wife, or you shall indeed find that room to be a prison!"

Chapter Seventeen

The instant the door closed behind him Taryn ran to one of the chests which held her clothing. She had to get away from this chamber, outside to where she could breathe.

She grabbed a hooded cloak—not because its warmth was needed on so bright and sunny a summer's day, but to shield her face from the curious and prying stares she knew she would encounter.

She waited until she was sure she would not meet Garret on the stairs, then, with the hood pulled low over her hair, she made her way down to the hall.

In the great room she ignored the dozen servants present, who paused in their housekeeping tasks as she hurried to the keep's exit.

Once outside she drew a deep breath, filling her lungs with the sweet fresh air. She looked out into the yard and noted the various small gatherings of laundresses, kitchen and granary workers and other castlefolk she would have to pass were she to cross the bailey. She did not want to have to speak to anyone. Then, too, she would be far more likely to meet Garret in the area around the stables. That was the last thing she wanted.

She turned to look in the opposite direction, to the area farthest from the stables. Her gaze came to rest upon a site she had not visited since her initial tour of Jaune. Adjacent to the herb and vegetable garden located behind the cookhouse, the private gardens of Jaune were walled from view and accessible only through a small wooden gate. No one save members of the lord's family or his guests was permitted there.

She descended the keep's steps and passed several men-at-arms crossing the yard on their way toward the middle bailey. As they caught sight of her their conversation abruptly ceased.

Knowing she had been recognized, she lowered her head and quickened her step. Suddenly a shadow fell across her path.

She stopped and looked up in trepidation. "Sir Simon!" Her breath escaped in a gasp of relief.

"My lady." The coal-black head dipped graciously. "You are well?"

Taryn was not sure if his question referred to her absences from meals the past several days, to the woolen cloak she wore despite the day's warmth—or to the flush she felt seeping into her cheeks. "Aye," she murmured.

"We have had little opportunity to talk," he continued easily. He smiled and chivalrously extended his arm. "Might I walk with you?"

"I . . . I was headed for the garden." She hesitantly placed her hand atop his and gestured toward the leafy canopy of green visible above the cookhouse roof.

"Lead the way, lady." Simon bowed, and as on that first night she had met him, his accompanying smile set her at ease.

Foolishly discounting the inquisitive stares raised, she allowed herself to be propelled forward. Whatever gossip their chance encounter had provoked would not now be quashed were she to be rude and refuse his offer of companionship. Besides, in view of her isolation of late, she welcomed his company.

They rounded the corner of the cookhouse and made their way toward the beckoning shade and greenery.

Under Simon's push the gate creaked open. When she had first viewed the gardens Taryn had been unimpressed, finding the area to be poorly attended. Seeing them now in full bloom, she truly realized their deplorable state. Fruit fallen since last summer still lay strewn and rotting beneath the crab apple, plum and cherry trees. The stone walkway was overgrown with grass and weeds—though the glorious profusion of flowers seemed unaffected by the neglect. Poppies, foxgloves and marigolds all bloomed without mind of the weeds growing in their midst.

Still, she could not help but think of Wynshire's gardens, lovingly attended by Old John. To see rose bushes growing so, untrimmed and wild, would have outraged him. She must speak to Richard, she decided.

Preoccupied with her thoughts, she did not immediately notice that Simon had left her side. Hearing his footsteps behind her, she turned and watched as he plucked a white rose from a weed-choked bush near the wall.

Returning to her, he held out the delicate flower. "Roses are much like people. Ofttimes, in spite of neglect, they blossom into things of beauty."

Taryn accepted the flower from his hand. Unsure of what his words might mean, she sampled the rose's fragrance to avoid an answer.

Simon stepped back, appearing to study her intently. "You know, lady, there is much we have in common, you and I."

Taryn looked upon the large, powerful man before her, his face disfigured by the violence which was the way of his life, and shook her head. She could not help but smile at the ludicrous comparison. "I think, Sir Simon, that there are not two more *dissimilar* people at Jaune."

"Not even, say, Richard and I?"

Thinking of the contrast between Jaune's somewhat effeminate steward and the stalwart knight before her, Taryn laughed aloud.

"'Tis a lovely sound, lady, your laughter. 'Tis the sound of your smile. You should indulge in both more often."

Before she could react, he continued. "Mayhap the reason you do not, is the very reason that I say we *are* alike. We are both strangers here, who have not yet found acceptance."

His statement took her aback. "But you have found acceptance! You have become one of Garret's most trusted men. Why, you stand at his side when he holds court. There are few in whose wisdom and counsel he holds such value."

"Aye. But 'tis not that acceptance of which I speak. Have you noticed, lady, that otherwise I am not often spoken to? Just now you found me not in the company of others, but alone. I am not the sort of man others find easy to befriend." His mouth formed into a sad smile so out of his character she recognized it only when it had vanished. "Then, too, mayhap the fault is mine. I have lived my life in no place long enough to form friendships . . . or attachments."

"I'm sorry," she whispered softly. She touched his arm gently in an attempt to convey what her words might not.

"Do not be." At once his smile became warm and engaging. "The life I live is by choice, my choice. Still, 'tis not without costs—they being companionship, and erudite conversation. Tell me, lady have you ever attempted to engage Richard in a conversation which did not entail some aspect of Jaune—how many acres should be ploughed or the number of cattle a pasture can support."

Taryn laughed. "You must not take Richard's rejection to heart. Jaune *is* his life." She paused and smiled slyly. "I think, too, that mayhap he fears you—and resents a little the trust Garret has in you."

This time it was she who took him aback. Simon shook his head. "You do not hesitate to speak your mind, do you, lady? Certes, you are like no woman I have ever known. You are as outspoken as any man."

"Ah! And so you have identified my greatest flaw. My nurse, Moira, always said I had ne'er learned my place—a woman's place, that is. She blamed my father for having educated me as a son."

"I would guess you were suited to the task. Upon most women I have known, such an education would have been wasted."

Suddenly Taryn wanted to know more about this man. "You speak of women . . . have you known many? I mean, did you—or do you—have a wife?"

For the briefest of instants a strange look flashed across his face. Had he once known love, but been hurt by it? "Nay," he answered. No trace of the vulnerability she thought she had detected could be heard in his voice. "My life is hardly one suited to such. Home, hearth, wife—they are not for me, nor I for them."

She began to understand. Before his disfigurement, he had assuredly been a man much sought after by women. Certainly his refined manners and speech bespoke time spent at court. But now . . . now he purposely made for himself a life with no room in it for what other men took for granted. She looked away, embarrassed that she had pried.

"So . . . lady . . . might that education with which your father indulged you include some knowledge of Latin?"

"Aye." She glanced up, confused by the intent behind his question. "I was taught to read and write English, French and Latin."

"I know you can read English." He smiled teasingly.

Taryn's confusion developed an instant edge. Simon had to know what had happened with the serf. Did he mock her on purpose?

His soft laughter interrupted her thoughts. "You should learn to guard better your expressions, lady. They reveal too much. And, too, you should learn to recognize humor. I have found that even in the direst of events it exists, and finding it can ease the deepest of pain."

Taryn looked up sharply. Though she was sure there was an underlying and specific message in his words, she was unwilling to ask if it was to this situation with Garret that he referred. Irritated, she deliberately sought to bring their conversation back to the initial question.

"Why do you ask if I know Latin?" she repeated.

He answered her easily, with no evidence of having felt her subtle rebuke. "'Tis one of the things I miss . . . here at Jaune. Few enough people can read, even fewer possess the willingness or ability to appreciate what others have written. Have you ever read any works by the Roman poets—Virgil, Ovid or Lucan?"

She shook her head and tried to keep an even countenance. The names he mentioned must be pagan writers, for she had not heard of them. If so, their writings would be considered heretical by the Church.

"In my profession one travels a great deal," he continued. "In a Turkish city I acquired several volumes. I would relish the opportunity to share them." He looked at her hopefully and smiled. "But for now I must leave you. I am expected elsewhere." He bowed deeply. "I thank you most sincerely, lady, for these pleasant moments."

Taryn watched as he made his way through the gate. He was a difficult man to understand, and yet with him she felt a sense of comfort—of acceptance—the likes of which she had not felt since her father had been alive.

Almost immediately a lump rose in her throat. She swallowed hard to dislodge it. There was no point in dwelling upon the past—not when there were matters more immediate and deserving of her focus.

Reluctant to leave the shady and cool haven the gardens provided, she settled beneath a cherry tree and allowed her thoughts to turn to what had occurred between her and Garret. Her marriage to him had been a mistake, and yet there was no course of escape. She was bound to him by the laws of man and God. Or was she? Marriages *were* dissolved—but for reasons relating only to the three requirements: age, degree of blood relation and free consent.

Suddenly the seed of an idea she had not previously considered began to take root. The prospect was both frightening and irrevocable. Was the dissolution of her marriage what she truly wanted? And what if she failed?

What manner of retaliation would Garret take against a wife deceitful enough to seek an annulment without his knowledge? She could be sent to a convent as his first wife had been. And even if she obtained the annulment, might not her fate be the same? She could not return to Wynshire. Where else could she go? Unless . . . unless the man responsible for her present circumstance accepted responsibility for her . . . She would need a king's weight of influence to override a legate decree or an archbishop's. If Henry spoke to the Archbishop of York on her behalf . . .

With every question which arose an answer followed. Yet to every answer there were but more questions.

If she obtained an annulment, might Henry then carry through with his initial threat? She could find herself next wedded to a man more cruel than Garret! There were many men in England such as Lynfyld, who would take a young wife for the mere purpose of breeding. That she had once belonged to another would have little if any import.

Through all her silent deliberations a single question returned to haunt her. Did she—in spite of all which had passed—want to end this marriage? The harder she tried to push the indisputable truth aside, the more it persisted. Like a gnawing ache in her heart, the answer was constant and undeniable. For whatever reason, she was not yet prepared to take that final step.

At last, weary and bereft, she surrendered herself to the one manner of escape available. Though her mind raced, her body, in an act of preservation, chose sleep.

When she awoke the sun had already fallen and was barely visible through the heavy foliage which surrounded her. The shade which had been so welcome in the heat of midday was now, in the coolness of late afternoon, dank and chilling. She shivered and rose stiffly to her feet. She was sure the horn blast which announced the evening meal would have awakened her. Still, she hurried from the garden, anxious to return to her chamber to freshen up.

To her relief she passed no one in the yard and was able to both enter the keep and go above without notice, but her relief was short-lived. When Taryn entered the hall in what was her first public appearance in four days, she encountered looks ranging from covert glances to gaping curiosity.

Mustering a dignity which was but for show, she took her place. Mute nods were the only greeting she received from the several men already present upon the dais. One of Garret's retainers not only did not react to her presence, he pointedly ignored her. Clearly he had taken his posture from the silent figure in the center chair.

Garret ordered a pitcher of ale, and when it came he filled his cup, downing its contents and refilling it—all without a single glance at her. She could not help but notice the space in front of his trencher already held an empty wine flagon.

It appeared that his way of dealing with their estrangement was to drink himself sodden. Let him! she thought. Deliberately she looked past him to the man at his side.

Richard offered a hesitant smile, yet did not speak.

Taryn bristled and averted her gaze. Obviously the steward dared not risk raising Garret's ire by treating her with anything more than neutral civility and the respect to which her position as his wife entitled her. If it was kindness or friendship she sought, she would clearly have to seek it elsewhere.

Though she was sure he would make no note of it, she cast Garret an icy glare.

He turned his head slowly, his pale stare transfixing her with an equal coldness. "In the future, madam, you will see that your visitations to the garden are made alone."

His voice had been too low to have been overheard by any of the men seated upon the dais; still, her pulse quickened and her color heightened. She was not sure what outraged her more—that he suspected her of impropriety, or that her every move was being reported to him.

As much as she wanted to refute his accusation, she refused to dignify his charge with a profession of her innocence.

Her silence seemed to pierce his complacency. "After you have eaten, you will return to your chamber."

Taryn stared at him in disbelief. "I am not one of your hounds, to be restricted of movement, summoned and dismissed with the mere snap of your fingers."

In reply Garret smiled. But it was a cruel smile, devoid of either amusement or warmth. There was something very mocking in the way he talked at her and looked at her. He seemed almost to revel in his rudeness.

Suddenly his hand left his cup. He snapped his fingers.

Within moments the half-dozen hounds that had been foraging among the lower table were at his chair. Tails wagging, with the bay, Becket, in their midst, they vied for their master's attention with eager whines and sharp barks.

"Like so, madam?"

Taryn's back went rigid with indignation. She laid her palms flat upon the table before her and was prepared to push back, when his hand atop hers abruptly halted her movement. Like talons, his fingers wrapped around her wrist.

"You will sit. I'll have no public scene."

His growl was still low enough that the men engaged in conversation to his right were unaware of what was transpiring. Because she could do nothing else, she sat and attempted to pull her arm free.

He maintained, and even tightened his hold. "Do you stay?"

She knew if she did not give her word he would not release her. "Aye," she whispered, feeling a loathing for him well up within her.

He removed his hand and reached again for his cup.

She pushed up the sleeve of her *bliaut*. The imprint left by his fingers in her flesh was clearly visible.

"My lord, my lady."

Taryn swung her head around to look at the owner of the masculine voice which had sounded at her back without warning.

Garret grunted in reply.

With an ease which came either from ignorance of what he nearly interrupted or incredible arrogance, Simon pulled out the chair beside her and sat. "With your permission, my lord, I should like to present the Countess with a wedding gift."

"I care not," Garret replied, acting as if the very matter bored him.

Simon seemed unconcerned by Garret's reaction. Smiling at Taryn warmly, he pushed aside the trencher and plates before him, making room on the table between them for the book he then laid there. "In light of our conversation today, I have decided to make of this a wedding gift, lady."

Taryn felt the blood drain from her face. How was it possible that Simon remained unaware of that which occupied the tongue of every serving man and kitchen wench at Jaune? Especially after the events of the last several days—if not moments! Hers was a marriage undeserving of either celebration or recognition. "'Tis not necessary," she murmured, helpless to disguise in her voice the resonance of rising tears.

"Mayhap you did not hear me aright, lady." Simon's voice was gentle, yet insistent, and as she looked at him, she realized that he did know—and it did not matter.

"I do not make this gesture because I feel a need to," he continued. "I want to. Now . . ." At once his smile became teasing and playful. "Surely, I would have just cause to be grievously insulted if you were to refuse my gift without at least having seen it."

Taryn hesitated in her response. It was not considered proper for a woman to accept presents from any man not a kinsman or her accepted lover. In spite of her reluctance, however, she felt herself responding to the man's kindness. "You are right, Sir Simon." A smile formed on her lips almost without her knowledge. "'Twould be rude indeed."

"Indeed." He pushed the book toward her.

She noted it was a work by Virgil and opened the volume to its first page. Knowing that what she beheld was unsanctioned by the Church, she was both intrigued and wary. She studied the gilt lettering and illustrations, then read several of the first lines. She was about to proceed further when reason and logic stopped her. Whatever the book's contents, it was too valuable and costly a gift. She shut the book. "I cannot accept this."

"Is your refusal a reflection of the book itself?"

"Aye . . . I mean . . . nay." She laid her hand atop the volume and lightly caressed the intricate designs tooled into its leather covering. "'Tis not its content, but its cost." She glanced at him for a moment, then returned her focus to the book. "Please do not take offense. I am greatly touched by the gesture, but this is simply far too valuable a gift. You must keep it—or sell it."

"Lady, look at me."

She lifted her gaze and reluctantly met his. As hard as she tried, the horrible disfigurement could not be overlooked.

"Books have no value if their ideas cannot be shared and discussed. However, if 'tis the tenets of your faith which compel you to refuse, then I shall not force the issue further. If 'tis aught else though, I ask you to reconsider and merely accept the gift in the spirit 'tis given."

In that moment she saw nothing of the ugly scar and leather patch. His gentle smile bathed her in a sense of warmth and comfort not even the cold, disapproving stare she abruptly felt upon her back could displace. "Then 'tis with heartfelt gratitude that I accept your gift," she replied.

Garret slammed down his goblet. He had sat in furious silence, listening to the exchange between his wife and vassal long enough. Deliberately he had not spoken up or ended the intimate conversation. He had wanted to see what she would do. And now he knew. Taryn's actions proved to him what he had suspected. She possessed the dignity of a tavern wench, reveling in the attentions of a man who was a virtual stranger.

He pushed back from the table and stood, letting his gaze fall briefly upon the man seated beside his wife. He did not blame d'Orléon. A man did not make even the slightest advance without invitation. The fault lay entirely with Taryn.

"The Countess shall be retiring now," he stated tersely. His attention still fixed upon his vassal lest he be fool enough to challenge him, Garret held out his arm stiffly. "Madam."

Helpless to defy his unspoken command, Taryn placed her hand atop his and stood. Then, without a word to the half dozen men seated at his table, Garret led her from the dais.

They had nearly reached the doorway between the great hall and the anteroom when the sound of smothered laughter erupted from one of the lower tables. A male voice followed.

"I've seen that look in 'is lordship's eyes before. The lady's about to get 'er skirts tossed up."

"Aye," a second voice replied. "Naught will make a man claim what's his faster than the thinking it's being lost to another."

Mortified, Taryn cast a sideways glance at Garret. Surely that was not his belief—or intent! But his face was inscrutable to her. His chiseled jaw and rigid profile might as well have been carved from stone for all the emotion they betrayed. She was certain he had to have heard the men's comments, yet he did not react. Neither did he speak, even when they were at the door of her chamber. He released the latch and none too gently pushed her inside.

She stood where his push had placed her and watched as he closed the door and turned to face her. Suddenly, without warning of his intent, his hand snaked out and he seized her wrist, drawing her to him. Before she could act, his mouth slashed across hers. His free hand buried itself into her hair to hold her head rigid as his tongue thrust forcefully between her teeth. Bruising and hard, fraught with anger and aggression, his kiss was one not of desire, but pure possession.

Her mind reeled in confusion. For a reason she could not fathom she tilted her head back to accept his kiss. And when he lustily sucked her tongue into his mouth, she responded, shocked to realize the desire he had ignited within her. She did not care that his kiss was not born of heated passion. Logical thought and prudent reserve vanished. He had vowed never to touch her again, and for that reason alone she welcomed even this punishing caress.

She swayed limply toward him, aware more of the aching in her breasts, pressed against his chest, than the strong arm now wrapped around her. The fingers that had been tangled in her hair released their hold. An instant later she felt them working the back laces of her *bliaut*. Then, and only then, did full comprehension of his intent finally wash over her.

The words of the smirking men below rustled through her mind like dry leaves buffeted by an icy wind: *The lady's about to get her skirts tossed up.*

As pride rallied reason, a gasp left her body. She was no serving wench to tumble when the mood struck! It was bad enough that she suffered his rudeness and blatant indifference. Though he did not banish her to the chamber below, all Jaune knew he no longer shared her bed. But must she, whenever his carnal needs required satisfaction, submit—suffering the public humiliation of being dragged abovestairs if that be his inclination of the moment?

She brought her hands up between their bodies and attempted to pushed herself free of his hold.

Though her strength was not great enough to gain more than an inch, her action did have an effect. The muscles beneath her fingertips tensed instantly.

He tore his mouth from hers and stepped back.

She saw his eyes clear as if from a fever, and though his breathing was still heavy, she knew whatever madness had overcome him was gone.

Their gazes locked for an instant, and then he turned from her. At the door he stopped. "You may lock the door if you feel the need, but I give you my word . . . this will not happen again." Flat and emotionless, his voice continued, "I have been summoned to court. In two weeks' time Henry will see his son crowned his heir and successor."

"When . . . when will you leave?" To her ear her breathing was still shallow and labored. She prayed that if he had noticed, he would attribute it to surprise at his announcement rather than to its true cause. Suddenly her pride did not matter so much. She wanted desperately to run to him, to give herself to him, to beg him to be once again the man who taken her virginity with compassion and tenderness. But that man—if he had ever existed—was not the one who stood with his back to her now.

In agonized silence she awaited his response. She thought at first he would not answer at all.

He pulled the door open, took a single step forward and finally spoke. "Under the circumstances, I think 'tis best that I leave as soon as arrangements can be made."

And then he was gone.

Taryn stared at the closed door. She could no more break through it than she could break through the wall which now existed between them. And while she could not see what lay beyond the heavy oak, she suddenly saw very clearly what lay ahead of her—if she remained in this mockery of a marriage.

She turned on her heel and very slowly walked to a chest which held her possessions brought from Wynshire. From a small wooden box she removed parchment, quill and dye.

When she had finished, she did not bother to read what she had written. The words inked upon the page were burned into her memory. She folded the single sheet and affixed a sealing dab of wax. Methodical and numb, each action seemed performed as if in a trance. The first step was completed. In the morning she would give the letter to the only person she trusted to deliver it. After that, her fate would lie in the hands of her king.

Taryn waited anxiously for the hall to clear. As she had anticipated, Garret had not made an appearance for the morning meal. No doubt his attentions were on the far more pressing matter of preparing for his journey. The few snippets of conversation she had managed to overhear at the table certainly seemed to indicate so. Despite the fact that with its hay harvest, June was the busiest month of the year for him, even Richard seemed more interested in the size of the contingent Garret would take to London.

"Suit to court" was one of the more enjoyable services performed by a vassal to his liegelord. When summoned to attend his lord, the liegeman had to go in person and at his own expense, but once at court he and his retainers could look forward to days and often weeks filled with royal banquets and kingly entertainment. That this summons was for a grand purpose indeed—the crowning of the future king—left most of Jaune's men watering at the mouth in hopes of being among the chosen few to accompany their lord.

From what Taryn could gather, it appeared, too, that Garret intended to make a fine show of force and support for the young king. Rumor had it more than sixty knights would ride at his back.

Nervously she looked to the man seated beside her. Though Simon had greeted her upon her arrival with his usual graciousness, he had not made any attempt to engage her in conversation. She wondered if he was also merely preoccupied with the impending journey—or if Garret might not have issued some sort of warning. Clearly he suspected their innocent friendship to be more than it was.

Even now, thinking of the nature of the transgression

he believed her, if not guilty of than certainly capable of, caused a sickening feeling in the pit of her stomach. What she was prepared to do was right. There was no hope for a marriage in which such distrust existed.

From the corner of her eye she saw Simon drain his goblet. Knowing he was prepared to take his leave, she touched his arm gently. "Might I have a word with you?"

He masked his surprise at her request rather well, refilling his goblet and leisurely sitting back in his chair. Somehow he had guessed that the matter was private. Nodding in response to each man who left the table, he patiently waited until they were the only ones remaining. "And so, lady . . ." He sat forward. "How might I be of service?"

Taryn did not immediately reply. If Garret had spoken to Simon, this conversation could put him at risk of disobeying his lord.

"Lady?" Simon prompted her with gentle insistence.

She forced herself to meet his gaze. "I am loath to place you in a position where you are at odds with your lord," she began hesitantly.

"Lady, do I strike you as a man who would cower—even to his liegelord?"

With his words Taryn realized an immediate sense of relief. She could trust no other as she could him. "Will you be among those to travel to London for the coronation?"

Even as she asked it, she was almost positive her question needed no answer. Instinctively she knew Garret blamed her for any impropriety between her and his vassal. She was certain his faith in Simon's ability to serve him retained intact, and the black-haired knight would be the first chosen to ride at his back, if not his side. And if Garret no longer trusted Simon, he would not be fool enough to leave the man behind.

"Aye." Simon's voice brought her attention back to the present. "Lord Garret has expressed that to be his desire."

"Might you deliver a letter for me then?" Taryn

removed the folded and sealed piece of parchment from the hem of her sleeve.

"Of course." He reached out and took the letter from her hand. "And to whom shall I give this?"

She watched him discreetly tuck the parchment beneath his waist before replying. "To His Majesty, King Henry."

Simon's gaze seemed suddenly to bore through her, as if he were attempting to read her thoughts. "Do I take it that this is a private matter?"

She lowered her eyes, uncomfortable with the knowledge she suddenly saw in his expression. "Aye. 'Twould be best if Lord Garret did not know of it."

"I understand."

But Taryn was not sure that he did. And if he was going to risk Garret's ire to do her bidding, he was entitled to know. "Do you remember when we were in the garden yesterday?"

"Aye."

She stared at her hands folded upon the table before her and slowly finished. "Ofttimes a rose bush is planted where it simply cannot grow. When that realization is made, it must be uprooted and replanted, or it will ne'er bloom."

She heard his quick intake of breath and looked up.

His mouth was clenched tight. For a long moment he studied her before responding. "Are you sure, lady, that you truly desire to do this?"

"Aye . . ." she whispered, blinking back sudden tears as she rose unsteadily to her feet. "I am sure."

Chapter Eighteen

Garret raked his fingers through his hair and resumed his pacing of the small anteroom leading to the king's private chambers. He had already waited the better part of the morning to be received by his liegelord.

Christ's eyes! He was not suited for court life. After nearly three weeks in London he had had his fill of it. The coronation was a week past. Why did Henry not release him and allow him to return to Jaune? With all the unrest and discontent provoked by the unsanctioned crowning of young Henry, troubled times were surely approaching.

Already the rumors were as thick as midsummer midges: The exiled Archbishop of Canterbury was so angered by his rival's performance of the ceremony that he intended not only to excommunicate the Archbishop of York and his supporters but to ask Alexander in Rome to place all of England under an interdict.

If the Pope complied with Becket's request, those barons already opposed to Henry would garner much new support. The threat of closing every church in England was a powerful one. Even those previously loyal to Henry would find that loyalty strained. Many would not continue to stand by their king as would Garret, who held no great regard for the Church. A civil war could break out.

"By the blood of St. Martin!" Garret swore softly

aloud, evoking unwittingly the name of the warrior saint. He needed to be home—not here squandering his time with banquets and royal hunts!

Home! Suddenly and unbidden, the word stirred emotions he had struggled to keep at bay. For in three weeks he had been unable to remove Taryn from his mind. The women at court bored him. And though the change in his marital status had done little to dampen their interest in him, he realized that his blood was heated only by thoughts of her. Since laying eyes on her, he had been as celibate as a monk! All others paled in comparison to her; her beauty, intelligence, even her pride—damn her for it! But this time apart had given him a chance to cool his temper, and to come to grips with his own pride. She was his wife. When he returned, he was determined to make an attempt to mend their rift. Hopefully, that would be soon.

Perhaps the summons this morning was a good sign. Perhaps Henry did intend to release him. Garret had no way of knowing. The king's sharp-tongued clerk, in delivering the order to appear, had refused to give a clue as to the reason for it. Peter of Blois was a brilliant man, but flawed by complacent arrogance. Garret knew the man was privy to the reason for the summons. It simply served his sense of self-importance to withhold that knowledge.

With that thought formed Garret heard the door behind him open. He turned, expecting to see one of Henry's attendants. Instead, it was his king who stood there. "Sire." Garret bowed.

"Garret." Henry beckoned him to enter. "My apologies for your wait."

Garret knew immediately that Henry was in one of his rare moods of good temper. England's king was known to keep men of greater position than Garret waiting days for an audience—with no apology offered. But then, why should he not be in good humor? To his thinking, he had just gotten his way in a difficult and important matter. Young Henry had been crowned his heir and successor.

To emphasize his son's new status Henry had even served him with his own hands at the solemn banquet which had followed the coronation ceremony.

Garret entered the private chamber and respectfully waited for Henry to make his will known.

"You have enjoyed yourself?" Henry asked, walking over to a small table which held a flagon of wine and several goblets.

With a wave of his hand Garret declined the goblet Henry offered. "Aye, Sire, I have. But—"

"But you are anxious to return to Jaune?" Smiling, Henry finished the statement for him. "I figured as much—but in due time." Cup in hand, he crossed the room to a long table laden with scrolls and parchments. "I have received several letters whose contents I wish first to discuss with you."

He searched through the piles and located several documents. "We shall begin with the most pressing issue." He took a drink and set down his goblet.

Immediately Garret noted that his demeanor had changed. His smile had disappeared, and he was markedly less relaxed.

"I am sure you are aware of the rumors of how the events of this past week have raised the hackles of my former friend and servant, the exiled Archbishop of Canterbury." Though he strove not to, the man was helpless to keep the rancor from his voice. "They are true. Already news reaches my ear that Thomas strives to turn the Pope against me."

Suddenly Henry's control was lost. He pounded his fist upon the table, sloshing wine over several of the documents. "This upstart! That I raised from the gutter! Saint Michael and all angels be praised—how Becket has plagued me these six years he's been in exile! Louis continues to harbor him, and so he feels safe as he works against me, excommunicating my supporters. And now, just as I learn that he plans to call upon Alexander to place all England under an interdict, I receive this! His insolence knows no bounds!"

His mottled face twisted with fury, he lifted the letter clutched in his fist. "In this he professes a longing to reconcile. In that I am his lord, he says he owes and offers me his advice and service."

"I do not understand, Sire. If this is the true content of his letter . . ." Garret regarded the man before him in confusion. "Is this not what you have hoped for?"

"Aye, and the damned missive *does* begin well enough." As if to give proof to his words, Henry unfolded the sheet. His voice ringing with heavy sarcasm, he began to read from it. "'In that you are my king, I am bound to respect and admire you.'"

"See you? All is well so far, but then he goes on." Lowering his gaze Henry returned to reading. "'In that you are my spiritual son, I am bound by my post to chasten and correct you. Since it is certain that kings receive their power from the Church, not the Church from them, but from Christ, so you have no power to give rules to bishops, to judge Church matters. Listen to the advice of your subject, to the warnings of your bishop, to the correction of your father. Restore everything that has been forcibly taken from myself or my servants, and allow us a safe and peaceful return. Otherwise you can be sure that you shall feel the full weight of God's severity and punishment.'"

"Hear you what he says, veiled behind these words?" Henry demanded. He was now fairly choking on his rage. "But what is worse is that I have no choice but to bow to his extortion—and the traitorous bastard knows it! I cannot risk an interdict."

"So you will make peace with him?" Garret asked.

"Aye." Henry spat his reply, tossing down the letter and reaching for his goblet. After a long draught he continued, oddly calmer, more composed and resigned. "To do so would actually suit my plans as well, for it appears there is also a problem of etiquette." He laughed dryly. "In addition to everything else, I have heard from my son's father-in-law. Because young Henry's wife was not crowned with her husband, Louis is talking of avenging the slighted honor of his family by ravaging the Vexen."

Garret knew at once to what he referred. For years, and until it was finally made Marguerite's dowry, the borderland between Normandy and the Île-de-France had lain in dispute.

Henry continued. "This problem has a simple solution, however. I shall let my son be crowned again, this time *with* his wife. Not only shall this make his title stronger, but Thomas can perform the second ceremony. That should appease him. As we speak, my messengers travel to France to deliver my proposal to both him and Louis."

With a start Garret realized the man was now smiling. Clearly the satisfaction of ultimately obtaining his goal had dulled the earlier sting of outrage over Becket's letter. Still, Garret failed to see what any of this had to do with him directly. This information should have been shared with all twelve of the Great Earls—unless Henry had heard the same rumors as Garret. If so, his king then had just cause to be close-mouthed with his plans. Certainly, opposition to Henry had grown in strength these past months because of the quarrel with Becket. Were those leading the faction to learn of the intended reconciliation, attempts would surely be made to prevent it.

"Well then . . ." Henry's voice interrupted Garret's silent speculations. "Let us proceed to the next matter." Again, he sifted through the documents, locating a second sheet of parchment. "This one concerns you more directly."

"Indeed?" As Henry was waving the letter in the air, Garret could not recognize its seal.

"Charles Maitland desires to renounce his fealty toward you."

"On what grounds?" It was Garret's turn to feel indignation and anger, and he did not bother to disguise either reaction.

"That you had first broken faith with him by seducing

his sister."

Garret met Henry's gaze. There was no point in denying the charge. Whereas he did not seduce Taryn, he had let the belief stand that he had, thereby voiding her marriage contract with Lynfyld. It was an act of breaking faith, true enough. "Does he plan to renounce his fealty to you as well?"

The meaning behind Garret's unspoken words was not lost upon Henry. That he had allowed the deed to go unpunished could easily be viewed as a breach of faith between lord and vassal as well. His color deepened. "You tread dangerous ground, Garret," he warned, his voice ominously low.

Undaunted, Garret continued. "What else can be concluded from Maitland's actions? From his conspicuous absence here, 'tis clear he has ignored your summons and intends to withhold support of the new king."

"Do not let your personal feelings of animosity for the man cause you to make accusations without proof, Garret. There were many barons who did not attend. Forsooth, the bishops of Winchester, Norwich and Exeter did not have the backbone. They hold more fear of Thomas' threats of excommunication than of any reprisals I might make."

"And so you let their disobedience stand?"

"Absolutely not! But for the present time there are matters of more import than the suspected disloyalty of a few barons."

Garret looked at him in surprise. Henry *did* know more than rumor!

His king's ensuing smile verified the thought at once. "I do not trust Maitland either, Garret," he stated gently, the harsh tone of reproach gone. "He is half the man his father was. Alas, experience has too often proved that trustworthy men might have untrustworthy sons. But thus far, all I have for proof is his absence from court and his request to renounce his oath to you. I have already sent my reply. Contrary to his request that I concede to him as compensation the lands he currently holds as your vassal, I have told him that, if indeed, he desires to renounce, the lands shall be forfeit. Otherwise, he is to go to Jaune and perform homage."

Garret grunted. "Loyalty cannot be assured by compelling a man to perform homage—especially from one who desires to renounce his oath, but does not for fear of losing wealth."

"As well I know it. Still, I have sent the same message to your other vassals. In a week's time they are to travel to Jaune and renew their oaths as well. The more recently done, the better the chance is that the man will honor it. Then, too, 'twill provide me the opportunity to gauge the state of other matters."

"Provide *you?*" Garret looked at him in confusion.

"Aye. I shall be accompanying you to Jaune."

Immediately Garret concealed his surprise. "You do me honor, Sire." He bowed his head. "Might I be permitted to ask the nature of the 'matters' whose state you wish to gauge?"

"Garret, I am not a fool. I know the rumors of unrest and of growing forces working against me. If Maitland refuses this summons, his lands are forfeit. That will weaken him, and no man planning war would willingly decrease the number of knights owing him service. However, on the other hand, if he does not, despite his enmity toward you, renounce his fealty, but rather renew it . . . Well then, I would have cause to wonder, would I not?"

Garret laughed out loud. "You set a trap from which he has no escape! With either course of action he chooses, you weaken him, either in actual strength or in the revealing of his treachery."

Henry smiled without reply.

Thinking their business concluded, Garret made a move toward the door. "With your permission I shall make the preparations for our departure."

"I am not finished, Garret."

Garret looked at him in confusion. Henry's voice had again become strained. "Sire?"

"Before you take your leave, might you favor me with an explanation as to why your wife desires an annulment of your marriage?"

"*What?*" Garret stared at him in shock, watching as he withdrew a folded sheet of parchment from beneath his belt. That fact that it had not been included with those upon the table was not lost to Garret. As his shock yielded to disbelief and then anger, a third emotion emerged—pain, and a sense of loss. For months he had wanted to be rid of her. But now, when faced with the possibility, every fiber in his being seemed rallied to the same desire; he would not have her taken from him!

"Your reaction is honest enough," Henry remarked, his calm a vivid contrast to the fury raging within Garret. He unfolded the sheet and glanced at its contents, as though to refresh his memory of them. "This letter bears your wife's name, and was delivered to my clerk by one of your men. I can only assume 'tis genuine."

"Which man?" Garret demanded. "I will have his name or his description."

Henry shook his head. "Obviously she trusted the man, whoever he was. The letter's seal was unbroken. He could not have known that by delivering it, he acted against you. I will not see him punished for merely fulfilling a request made of him by his lord's wife."

Garret scarcely heard Henry's admonition. His refusal to reveal the man's identity did not matter. Garret knew who had delivered the letter. His feelings of only a moment earlier vanished. Gladly would he be rid of her—and the sooner, the better!

"Well?" Henry prompted. "Why does she desire to end a marriage less than two months old?"

"Does she not say?" Garret asked, his voice layered with black sarcasm. "Knowing my wife, I find it difficult to believe she would not thoroughly outline her grievances."

"She says naught of why, only that her consent was initially obtained under duress. She states she was not of a clear mind. Given her lack of free consent, she seeks upon those grounds an annulment. She requests I intervene on her behalf and wield whatever influence I possess with the Archbishop of York."

He folded the sheet. "Strange. But my recollection of the event holds no memory of the lady being in a befuddled state when she agreed to this marriage." He replaced the letter beneath his belt, then raised his gaze, capturing Garret's. "What have you done?"

It was all Garret could do to stand there. He fought with all his strength against the rage consuming his soul. Were the man before him any other than his king, he would have drawn his sword, and answered the accusation with cold steel.

When he did not answer, Henry merely shrugged. "No matter. Once I am at Jaune I will see for myself."

Taryn paced the master chamber. With each step she took the hem of her bed robe flapped around her bare feet, loosening the belt at her waist. She never noticed. Her limbs shook with anger and fear.

Blessed Mother! She could not erase from her mind the memory of the fury upon Garret's face, the cold rage with which he had greeted her as she had waited that afternoon at Richard's side to welcome Jaune's royal visitor.

They had had less than a day to prepare, word having arrived by messenger only the evening before. Standing there, watching the contingent of mounted men pass through the portcullis, her last thought had been of the letter she had given Simon to deliver. But the instant she caught sight of Garret riding into the lower bailey she knew something was amiss. As he neared, her misgiving became only stronger. The lines etched upon his brow had not been placed there by the strain of the journey from London, nor had the tension in his body come from fatigue.

She knew its cause when he reined in his horse before her and dismounted. Oblivious to his king, still mounted, and the scores of men surrounding them, he had whipped off his coif and glared at her with such disgust she thought her very soul must burn from it.

"Whence you have greeted your king, madam, you shall remove yourself from my sight!"

Without realizing she was doing so, Taryn had looked away from him, instinctively searching the rows of mounted men.

"He still rides in my service," Garret hissed, grasping her arm and forcing her gaze back to him. "Though 'tis only by Henry's intervention that I do not cut from his arm the hand which delivered your letter."

Because he did not mention Simon by name, Taryn was not sure if he knew the identity of her messenger. But that fact seemed scarcely to matter. The deed was done, and clearly Henry had seen fit to inform Garret of her request. Had she really thought it might be otherwise? Surely she had not believed Henry would act upon her request without a word said to his vassal that his wife sought an annulment of their marriage.

Biting her lip to keep it from trembling, she mustered the dignity to greet Henry.

Strangely, as he stepped forward, she had seen compassion in the man's eyes. "We shall deal with this later, Garret." The tone of his voice brooked no argument.

Garret released his hold upon her arm, and she curtsied. "Sire."

"Lady Taryn. Please rise. And as there are matters which need to be discussed that do not lend themselves to a female ear, I respectfully ask that you retire abovestairs to your chamber. I trust 'twould be but a small inconvenience to have a tray delivered."

Taryn hesitated in her response. That Henry excused her from the evening meal was not what troubled her. If he did not know that she and Garret slept apart, he would assume her chamber to be Garret's. Was she, therefore, to go to her room—or his?

Marking her hesitation, but misreading its cause, Henry smiled most mysteriously. "This night I shall not take the master's chamber. I'll make my bed elsewhere, leaving you to yours."

And thus she had found herself in Garret's chamber, pacing, waiting in fearful anticipation, remembering Henry's final declaration: *The matter of your request shall be resolved by morning.*

Suddenly she heard a noise, the unmistakable click of the latch releasing. She whirled to face the door, unmindful that with her action the sides of her robe parted.

The heavy oak creaked open, and her heart jumped in her chest. Standing in the darkened doorway, his face cast in shadow, Garret appeared even more threatening. Fear caused foolish, flippant words to spring to her lips. "I hope the intent of your presence is but to fetch a change of clothing?" she asked, noting that he was clad still in *hauberk* and *chausses.*

His familiar grunt was fully anticipated, and as such, heard practically before uttered. "I can assure you, madam, I am *not* here by choice." He turned to usher into the room a shorter, stouter figure that had lingered in the corridor.

"Your Majesty!" Immediately Taryn clutched the front of her robe closed and dropped into a hasty curtsy.

"Christ's eyes, woman!"

Garret's thunderous roar was followed by Henry's amused chuckle. "Under the circumstances, Lady Taryn, I think that—"

"Cover yourself, wife!" With no mind paid to having interrupted his king, Garret glared at her. In heated displeasure his eyes raked her bowed form.

Taryn followed the direction of his gaze and realized in horror that in executing her curtsy the sides of her robe had split apart. They now lay fanned open in twin semicircles on either side of her bare legs.

Henry's laughter echoed in the large chamber. "As I was about to say, let us dispense with formalities. I do, however, thank you for the pleasing sight, lady, and bid you rise."

Cheeks flaming, Taryn rose from the bow and tried as gracefully as possible to rearrange the folds of her robe. What she needed to do was rewrap the sides of the garment across her breasts and then retie the belt. However, she could not accomplish that feat without first releasing her hold completely.

"By the blood of Christ, madam! Will you cease that squirming." Again, Garret's voice resounded like a clap of thunder.

She glowered at him furiously.

Again, Henry laughed, looking first from one to the other. "'Twould appear that this separation has done naught to lessen your animosity for one another."

"'Tis all that remains of a marriage which should ne'er have been entered into." Garret's bitter candor lashed at her.

"I do not happen to believe that." Silent now, Henry crossed the room to the table at the window. Pulling out one of the chairs there, he turned it to face them. Once his ample form was comfortably settled, he spoke again. "But then, that *is* the purpose for this meeting." He raised his eyes to Garret. "Garret d'Aubigny, your wife has requested an annulment to your marriage. She desires that I speak upon her behalf with the Archbishop of York, garnering his support for this action."

Taryn watched Garret's face. Despite the ceremonious tone of Henry's voice and the nature of his words, his expression revealed no emotion.

"I ask you now, formally, for your response. Do you desire a dissolution of this marriage as well? Or do you contest your wife's petition?"

Taryn held her breath, waiting for Garret's reply. She thought his cold silence interminable.

At last he broke it. "I repeat what I first stated ere this marriage was made. I want no wife."

His words were as a searing pain, confirming all she had suspected and feared. Still, she stifled a sob and held her back rigid. No trace of her anguish would she betray.

"Very well." Henry nodded. "But before I am willing

to present this matter to Roger of York, I must first insist upon proof that this marriage is without all hope of salvability. Offtimes when love is not present, passion can be the tie which binds. And I have seen passion betwixt you—if only the passion of anger. For that reason, I desire indisputable proof there is not more than spark to the flame."

He rose awkwardly, turning his back as he then replaced the chair. "Lady Taryn, please stand in front of your husband."

Taryn took several step forward and when she was a few feet from him, Henry spoke. "'Tis close enough. Now . . . remove your robe."

"Sire?" In a mixture of shock and disbelief she gaped at the back still turned to her.

"Do you refuse an order from your king, lady?" As he did not face her, his voice was somewhat muffled. Yet his words were clear.

"Nay, Majesty," Taryn felt as if she would swoon. "But . . ." She cast a pleading look to Garret. Surely he would speak up and protest this madness?

"Then remove your robe," Henry repeated. Suddenly his solemn tone softened. "But fear not. As enchanting as your earlier display was, I have no intention of engaging in lechery. You have my word."

Taryn looked back to Garret. His gaze was fixed upon the floor. Fingers trembling, she slipped the robe from her shoulders.

True to his promise, Henry's back remained turned. Still, he seemed to know the instant she dropped the garment. "Look at your wife, Garret," he commanded. "I want you to see what you profess no longer to desire."

Slowly Garret lifted his eyes.

With his cold stare fixed upon her, Taryn instantly felt as if the flush in her cheeks had spread down her neck to her breasts. She burned with shame.

Garret tried to block out what he saw. Despite her heightened color of embarrassment, her nipples were erect, as if from cold . . . or passion.

Passion, he thought. Aye, there had been passion betwixt them—the likes of which had heated his blood until it boiled from him his very power of reason, leaving him as confused as an ignorant knave.

He clenched his hands into fists at his side. By all that was holy and unholy! She stood just a few feet from him! He could feel the blood racing in his veins, settling into his loins in a familiar, burning sensation of need and desire. He tried to ignore it, and could not.

He shot Henry a sideways look of raw fury. Damn him! He had to have known all along what the sight of Taryn's naked body would do to him. "Has Your Majesty proved his point?" he asked, his strained voice shattering the dead silence.

"Nay, not yet." Again Henry chuckled. "You may take to your bed, lady."

As she darted across the room and scrambled between the covers, Garret sighed in relief. Surely, Henry would now put an end to this insanity!

Henry waited a respectful moment more, then turned, nodding his approval as he looked at her now modestly covered by the sheet she clutched to her chin. "Garret . . ." He shifted his focus to his vassal. "'Tis your turn."

"What?" Garret glared at him in disbelief. It was one thing for her to have endured *his* scrutiny, but he would be damned if he would submit to like treatment! Beneath a calm tone he attempted to conceal his outrage. "Surely, Sire, you are not serious?"

"I am very serious."

"Sire, I will not—"

"You will." Henry's voice grew harsh. "You will do as ordered, liegeman. Now, strip!"

The reference to his position was far from subtle. As chafing as the command was, Garret knew he had no choice but to obey it. He would make no further protest.

Taryn winced at the sight of the dark scowl which settled across Garret's face as he unbelted the sword at his waist. He dropped the sheathed blade to the floor, then struggled to tug his *hauberk* over his head. Had the circumstances been different, she would have found his clumsy, wriggling movements comical and amusing.

As if having sensed her thought, he glared at her as he tossed the removed *hauberk* on top of his sword and proceeded further. He undid the laces of the leather tunic worn to prevent his shoulders from being rubbed raw by the coat of mail. Once unfastened and removed, the tunic followed the path of his *hauberk*. Still she watched him steadily.

But when he pulled his shirt over his head, Taryn shut her eyes. The sight of the small scar across his rib, left from the cut he had made the morning he had confronted Charles, tugged at her heart.

"Lady, open your eyes." Henry's gentle, but insistent command brought her back to the present. "Except for the scars which bear witness to your husband's prowess as a warrior, he is a fine figure of virile manhood. Would you not agree?"

Taryn stared at Garret's broad, bare chest. In the candlelight each hard muscle was defined clearly with nuances of shadow and light. Her gaze slipped over him. Legs firmly planted apart, fist clenched at his side, he stood defiant and proud, wearing now only breeches and *chausses*. The mail leggings fitted the muscular thighs and calves like a second skin.

As hard as she fought to deny it, the sight of him did something to her. "My husband's body was ne'er a source of discontent, Sire . . ." she whispered, feeling her color rise once more. ". . . only pleasure."

"You forget yourself, madam!" Garret growled in warning.

"Let her be, Garret. I find her forthrightness refreshing. Your wife speaks her mind and has no shame in expressing what are natural desires for a healthy woman."

Henry's chiding tone softened. "That is your trouble, you know. You judge all women by one—and that one gave you a false view of reality you have expected all women since to follow. Ten years you have let her memory torment you. I say 'tis time to bury the past. Clarissa was sick, Garret—sick in mind and body with a madness made worse by her rearing. Since infancy she was raised in a convent, taught by the good sisters that women, as the daughters of Eve, are responsible for the sin in the world. Until she came to Jaune as your bride, she knew no other way. She believed what she had been taught; that only perpetual chastity might save her immortal soul. Thus was it any wonder she looked upon the normal intimacies of man and wife as shameful and wrong? Damn it, Garret! The fault for what happened was not yours! No man would have acted differently."

Garret fixed his gaze straight ahead. Though he heard Henry's words, he refused to listen to them, to heed their meaning. The man's breath was wasted.

Henry seemed to know as much. "Come here." He pulled out the chair he had sat in moments earlier and gestured toward it. "Sit and finish undressing," he stated firmly.

Wordlessly Garret went to the chair, unbuckling the leather straps which fastened the tops of his *chausses* to a waist belt. As he sat to remove the leggings, Henry took the chair beside him.

Lowering his voice, he continued. "Garret, listen to me. 'Tis as normal for a woman to want a man, as 'tis for a man to want a woman. Whilst you ache with the need to bury yourself within her, do you not think she aches with the need to have you there? You are no inexperienced squire. Why else, think you, she grows wet to ease your way—then swells around you, to sheath you once she has been entered?"

Garret felt his earlier arousal strengthen. As if the sight of his wife's unclothed body were not sufficient to break his control, he now had to listen to Henry's whispered erotic descriptions! "His Majesty has missed his calling. Mayhap he should consider a position as panderer in a house of ill-fame."

There was no humor in Henry's answering laughter. "I

shall overlook your insolence, for I know the depth of your torment. However, the time for talk has passed. Stand up and cease your dawdling. Hose and breeches off—now!"

Garret stood, his hands going to the tie at his waist. As he undid the knot and slid the final article of clothing down his hips, Henry nodded in satisfaction. "All the way, Garret. Be quick about it."

From her position in the bed Taryn watched as Garret's jaw clenched in silent fury. Obeying his king, he mutely bent at the waist and stepped out of the remainder of his clothing. Straightening, his hand rose to rake back the hair that had fallen across his face. Tall and proud, he stood glaring at his lord.

"All right, Garret. Join your wife."

The pale eyes narrowed. "Does His Majesty intend to order me to bed her as well—that he may watch?" His voice was weighted with sarcasm.

Taryn looked to Henry in sudden fear. Garret's words were so preposterous she paid them no heed. What clutched at her heart like an icy hand was the rancor she heard in her husband's tone. Surely with such irreverence he risked the man's fury?

To her surprise, Henry stood, smiling. "Oh, you would like that, would you not? You could go ahead and take her, feeling neither guilt nor responsibility. Nay, Garret. I shall order you to do naught but remain in that bed, beside her. I know your belief that in this marriage there is no love or passion. 'Tis your actions, however, which shall prove that conviction."

As Garret strode toward the bed, Taryn kept her focus on Henry. He appeared most pleased with himself. Catching her eye, he smiled. "Your letter stated that he felt naught for you, lady. Already I have seen proof of that untruth."

"What you saw, Sire, was what he allows himself to feel for his whore—not his wife."

Henry shrugged. "Then I am indeed perplexed. 'Tis a fortunate man who can have in one woman both a wife at his side *and* a whore in his bed."

"Not according to my husband. To his thinking a wife does not experience pleasure." She ignored the silent warning she sensed from the man approaching and concluded softly. "And if she does, she is wanton—hence he feels no desire for her, and lies instead with others."

Henry laughed softly as he started for the chamber door. "I know not who those 'others' might be. For in the three weeks he was at court, the ladies did naught but lament his disinterest."

Taryn looked at Garret. From the black look on his face, she knew he was not pleased with this revelation of Henry's. She, however, was filled with elation—especially when Henry betrayed even more.

"I know his habits as well as my own, and a renowned wencher does not choose a path of celibacy without cause. And I believe, lady, that cause is *you*. However . . ." He paused and opened the door. "By morning we shall know the true state of this marriage. I shall not wait to see you both abed. I have made my will known and trust it shall be obeyed."

The door closed behind him, its latch falling into place with a haunting click of finality.

"Would you be so kind, madam, as to move to your side of the bed."

Chapter Nineteen

With a sharp intake of breath and a silent oath, Taryn turned her attention from the door to the naked man standing beside the bed.

"I repeat, madam. Will you move to your side?"

Taryn forced herself to meet Garret's penetrating glower. "Surely you do not intend to . . . to actually participate in this madness?" she asked, her voice quaking with emotion she was loath to reveal and yet powerless to check.

"I intend to obey my king. Now . . ." He reached for the coverlet and with a quick jerk tossed it back. "Lest you intend to take your half of this bed out of the middle, will you move?"

Anxiety swiftly yielded to anger. Proudly she tossed her head, indignant at his display of arrogant possessiveness; had it not been for her tight-fisted grip she would have lost her draping. Clutching the bed covers tightly to her, she eased over, staring straight ahead. She felt his weight settle beside her and could not, despite her ire, resist a sideways glance.

Garret tugged the coverlet free from her grasp and arranged it over the lower half of his body. With a loud, drawn out sigh of disgust she knew was for her benefit, he lay back. As he pillowed his head upon his arm, his elbow came within inches of striking her. Yet when she attempted to put more distance between then, she found she could not. A long length of her hair was caught beneath him.

Could he not feel it? she thought in furious frustration. But rather than ask him to sit up, she tugged the tresses free, wincing silently at the pain. "This shall be a very long night," she muttered beneath her breath, rolling over onto her side and facing pointedly away from him.

To her surprise his rich laughter greeted her proclamation. "Madam, your gift for understatement is truly astounding."

She rolled back over to glare at him. "I fail to see *any* humor in this ludicrous and, might I add, repulsive attempt to encourage mating!"

As she watched his expression harden, she suddenly realized the candles had not been extinguished. She thought to mention her observation, then quickly decided against it. In his insufferable arrogance he would simply command her to out them. Besides, it was not as if their light would keep her from an otherwise peaceful slumber!

"Be of good cheer." His cold voice put an abrupt halt to her private musing. "This night of discomfort shall be a small price to pay for your freedom. Now move back to your side of the bed."

With his words she realized that in rolling over she had indeed moved closer to him. She realized, too, the sudden strained quality in his tone. The need to taunt him, to strike back at him was suddenly overwhelming. "Does my closeness so threaten you, my lord?" In spite of her modesty, she sat up, letting the bed sheet fall away. "Or is it my nakedness which disconcerts you?"

Immediately he turned his face.

"Look at me, Garret. Are you afraid to? Are you afraid you cannot control your arousal—the passion you claim with word and deed to be dead?"

He stared straight ahead, the only clue to his fury a

small twitching in his jaw muscle. "I am familiar with your appearance, madam. There is no need to flaunt yourself like a whore—nor is there need for you to speak as one."

She reacted without thought. But the hand she raised to strike him was wrestled to her side in an instant. She found herself flat on her back, with him leaning over her.

"Do not test me, Taryn," he growled. "I could wring the very life from your shameless body in a heartbeat."

She raised her other hand, and it, too, was intercepted and pinned to her side. But in doing so, he had forfeited his balance and now lay atop her. She struggled to escape his hold. "Curse you!" she cried. "I am no whore—nor am I shameless. I have given myself to only you."

The feel of her warm flesh writhing against his own tore a cry from Garret's throat. If he did not distance himself from her, he would succumb to the mastery of his body over his mind and will, acting upon his desires and losing all control. "Taryn," he gasped, "if I release you, do you stop fighting me?"

She nodded and he removed his hold. No sooner did he sigh in relief, than his gut tightened anew. Though she lay quiet beneath him, there was no doubt as to the cause of the shudder he felt go through her body. She was crying.

He felt his anger wash away as an earthen dam in a spring rain, just as had happened that night in Kirdford. "Why do you cry?" he demanded in exasperation, sitting up and thereby putting precious space between them. "In a few hours' time you will have what you desire."

"You do not have the . . . the . . ." Suddenly she began to weep in earnest. ". . . the slightest inkling of what I desire."

Garret steeled himself against her sobs. "Your letter served adequate notice," he muttered.

She looked at him in wide-eyed, albeit watery, wonder. "Think you that is what I truly desire?"

"'Tis what you requested," he retorted hotly, reacting again in anger to the emotional threat he felt.

"You are a beast!" She sobbed even harder. "You know naught of how I feel—what I feel—the sense of failure. I tried. I truly tried to be what you wanted. I listened to Maite—did as she said. All it earned me was your contempt."

"Maite? What has Maite to do with this?"

The confusion in his tone seemed to dry her tears. She sat up and studied him for a moment before replying. "She told me that first night I should not be afraid, that I must not show fear. I should encourage you, for 'twas very important that you believe I enjoyed our lovemaking. And I did." Despair entered her voice anew, and with it, resentment. "But 'twas not what you wanted! When I found pleasure, you accused me of wantonness and called me whore."

Garret stared at her in shock. "Maite told you those things?" He saw her nod of affirmation, but did not note it. His thoughts had already raced to others. "That second night—you heeded her words as well?"

Again she nodded, and he cringed, remembering his deliberately rough and callous taking of her. No wonder she had not protested his treatment of her—she had been cautioned not to struggle! "And yet you found pleasure that night, despite my . . . my . . ."

"I have found pleasure with you each time." A faint and tender smile formed at the corners of her mouth. "But not because I am without shame."

"Then why?" With his tone he made it very clear he found no other feasible explanation.

"Because . . ." Two small teardrops that had clung to her lower lashes escaped and rolled down her cheeks. "Because I love you," she whispered.

Her words knifed him. Like a swordthrust he never saw coming, her unconstrained admission rendered him defenseless.

Taryn did not see the flash of agony which lighted his

eyes for the briefest of instants. Until this moment she had not admitted or recognized herself the emotion to which she had just confessed. Yet once said, the words seemed right. The confession gave her a curious sense of strength. She did not care what his reaction would be. She knew only that she had to tell him. "I love you," she repeated. "Blessed Mother, help me, but I do."

"You . . . you have a strange way of showing love, madam." Garret struggled to gather his wits, his defenses. He did not know how to react to this profession of love except to refute it. "You claim love as the reason for your unbridled response? Yet whilst you trembled still in pleasure from our bedding, you expressed interest in being with other men!"

"Other men?" Taryn looked at him horrified. "I ne'er said such a thing! Forsooth, I have ne'er even considered the possibility!"

"Indeed? Then for what purpose were your questions about men and women? Why did you ask if a woman might feel the same kind of pleasure with any man who bedded her?"

Suddenly she remembered the conversation of which he spoke. *Dear God! Was that how he had interpreted her question?* "You do not understand," she replied, squeezing her eyes shut, unable to endure the accusation she saw in his. "I asked that only because I feared you would otherwise know the true intent of my question."

She knew she would never convince him if she did not look at him. She forced herself to open her eyes again. "I asked about men and women because I wanted to know if you had felt the same with Geneviève Flambard as you did with me." She heard the bitterness of jealousy in her voice, but could not stop it anymore than she could stop the rise of new tears. "I wanted so much to believe that what we had shared was different than what you had known with other women. I wanted it to be more with me—"

Her voice cracked, and she had to draw a deep breath to

continue. Embarrassed, she finished weakly. "I wanted to mean more to you."

"You were not asking about other men?"

"Nay."

Her reply was so soft he barely heard it. He would have laughed out loud were this not so serious. Her confession made sense—but how ridiculous her doubts had been! She was jealous of those faceless, nameless women he had bedded without so much as a second thought! "Taryn, Geneviève and the others . . . they were taken in mere fulfillment of physical need—just as I eat to satisfy hunger and drink to quench thirst. No more than that have they mattered, and none of them did I make my wife."

"But that was not of your choice," she cried. "I had no way of knowing I meant aught to you other than a responsibility and duty forced upon you. You admitted you felt no love for me. What else could I have thought?"

"You might have asked," he growled.

"I ne'er had the chance! You stormed from the room, and from that moment on you only ignored me. For weeks you slept at my side and ne'er once touched me. And then, after what happened with the serf, you turned me out completely."

"Which was when you turned to d'Orléon." His dying anger surged with new life.

"I turned to him for friendship, no more! He was kind to me when all others were barely civil, for they followed your lead. Only Simon was not afraid to treat me with compassion."

She drew a deep breath and continued. "I was wrong to have lied about the date of the boy's disappearance. I know that now. My actions held you up to ridicule from your men, and you were justified in your response. But my motive was not to shame you, or to defy you. Can you not forgive me?"

She touched his arm and he flinched as if struck. Her hand instantly recoiled.

Garret struggled with his emotions. He respected her for her admission of guilt, and had long since forgiven her. But what had driven them apart could not be resolved so simply. "There is more than that incident which divides us," he stated, his voice harsher than he would have liked.

"Then you truly hate me?"

"I do not hate you. But you are too much of what I cannot understand or accept. I have lived my life firm in the belief that women are either whores or wives. And you, madam, do not act as a wife."

"By your definition! Why are you so convinced I am wanton? I have given you no true cause to doubt my faithfulness. Aye, I am outspoken and stubborn. I possess a temper akin to the Devil's own, and I do not know my proper place."

"A thorough listing of your faults . . ." Despite himself, Garret smiled. ". . . save one."

She colored slightly. "And too, I did find pleasure in our coupling—a fault in your eyes. But 'tis a pleasure I want with no other man. Even Henry said a man was fortunate to have that in a wife."

Garret's good humor vanished. "Henry would have done well to have kept his opinions to himself. Too much of what he said had no right in being uttered."

She remained silent for a moment, then spoke again. "Garret, why did you help me that morning—with Charles?"

Her question caught him off guard, and he replied without thought. "Because of your tears, the fear I saw in your eyes. It reminded me of another's. Her fear I could ne'er take away."

"Of whom do you speak?"

He looked away, realizing he had already said too much. All this dredging up of Henry's of the past must have affected his mind!

Taryn reached out and touched his arm again. Though he did not flinch this time, or physically pull away, he was suddenly very distant, staring unseeing straight ahead.

"Your wife? Clarissa?" she prompted gently.

"Leave it," he whispered hoarsely. "Leave it alone."

Instinctively Taryn knew she had met her enemy. With only what Henry had revealed to guide her, she proceeded. "That you may continue to blame yourself? That is what Henry said, is it not? Garret, she is dead. The past is dead. Whatever happened, happened when you were young. Henry said the fault was not yours. You cannot—"

"You do not know what happened!" He grabbed her wrists and forced her flat. His menacing face, only inches from hers, was wracked with pain. "She died, driven to insanity by my actions! I cannot bury that guilt as easily as I buried her body. It lives here!" He pounded his chest. "And here." His fist went to his forehead. "It lives in my memory and haunts my dreams. That night . . ."

"What night? Garret, please!" With his hold released she scrambled from beneath him to her knees. "Tell me." She touched his cheek. "Please."

He stared at her in silence. Could he believe in the trust he felt in her voice? Did it exist in her eyes, in her soul? Suddenly he could not keep imprisoned the demons within him. He had never discussed in detail with anyone what had happened. Not even Maite knew the entire story. Was it Taryn's confession of love which made him want to tell her? Or did he hope by revealing his sin to her, she would be repulsed, leaving him to his private Hell? Whatever the reason, he found the words forming.

"My first wife, Clarissa, was sixteen when we married. Of the ways of men and women and of life she was totally ignorant. As Henry said, she had been raised in a convent, her mother having died in childbirth, and there being no female kin . . ." His voice faded as he gathered his thoughts. "I was twenty and had already known years of battle. I knew about women, as well. Serving wenches, whores, women at court. Married and maid alike, they had all warmed my bed. But ne'er had I been with a woman less experienced than I. On our wedding . . ."

He clenched his fists and drew a deep breath. The blame he felt had never before been expressed aloud. There had been no one to whom he could tell it. ". . . at the banquet following the ceremony I drank more than was my habit. Later, when I went to her she was terrified. But because of my drunkenness I ignored her fear. She was not prepared, and in my inexperience I took her without . . . without realizing the pain the breaching would cause. She screamed and I panicked. I dressed and left her bleeding, sobbing in terror."

Again he paused. When he continued his voice was a flat monotone. "After that she would not let me near her. A few times I tried. She would pretend to be willing, at first, believing 'twas a wife's duty. Then her fear would return. She made no secret she thought the act to be terrifying and vile."

"Mother of God," Taryn whispered. In her breast her heart wrenched with his pain. "I said those things to you. I said that 'twas a reflection of the man were a woman to believe thusly—that he be not gentle, but deliberately cruel, finding pleasure in inflicting pain. Forgive me! How my words must have hurt you! No wonder you stormed from the room."

"You did not know," he stated dryly, laying his head back upon the pillows. "Later I realized that, and my anger abated."

She looked down at him in silence. So many things now made sense: Maite's cautions, his hesitation the first time, even his dismissal of her the night they had played chess. When she had reacted to his touch in fear, he must have felt as if the past were being reenacted! How could he be faulted for not wanting another wife? And how could he not think, with that memory of his first wedding night haunting him, that she was wanton in her response?

Her heart swelled with compassion. Tears gathered in

her eyes. Ten years he had been tormented by this guilt. Surely he had heard the cruel rumors, as well. Grounded in truth, how could he have denied them? His actions *had* driven his child bride to insanity.

"You did not know either," she whispered. She edged closer and laid her head upon his chest. Beneath her cheek his pounding heart belied his stoic exterior. Within him a private war raged. Yet what he had told her had not lessened the love she felt. If anything, it was stronger. Like a chink in armor, his pain provided her a means to touch the man beneath. "You had no experience with virgins. You did not hurt her with intent and could not have known the path of escape her mind would take."

He shook his head. " 'Twas not that night which drove her to insanity. After several weeks she moved out of the chamber we shared. She took the room you were given when you arrived. She began to withdraw inside herself, participating in naught which happened around her. I thought if I could provide her with an interest, she might regain the sanity she seemed to be losing. For a while it appeared to be working. She began to decorate her chamber, ordering furnishings made and stained glass. She turned the room into a chapel-like sanctuary—then refused to leave it. The vows she took were to be my wife, yet beneath my roof she lived as a nun."

His voice cracked, and Taryn lifted her head. Though his eyes were focused upon that other time, there was no mistaking the anger which blazed in the pale depths. Suddenly, to her surprise, his arm went around her shoulder, and he brought her back against him. She accepted his embrace and again laid her cheek upon his chest.

Several moments passed, and yet she did not prompt him. She knew when he was ready he would tell her the rest.

Hesitantly, he began to speak, still in the emotionless tone which seemed to serve as a way to distance himself from the pain. "Finally, my pride could withstand the snickered comments behind my back no longer: the lord of Jaune was not man enough to make his wife a wife. I went to her and demanded she fulfill the responsibilities of her marriage—*all* of them. I was convinced if I took her again and proved to her the experience would not be painful a second time, she would return to my bed. I forced her to hers. She lay like stone beneath me. This time there was no sobbing or pleading. I thought her willing to . . . to submit. But when I touched her she screamed with such terror I released my hold. She pushed her body from mine and then got to her feet. She had screamed only that once. Frozen, she stood there until I moved. I saw her hand go under the folds of her robe, and as I attempted to stand, she withdrew the knife and lunged toward me. I grappled with her before I felt the blade bite into my flesh. She was like a wild thing, twisting, thrusting, kicking. Her eyes were wide with an agony of fear—like an animal's—and they carried no sign of recognition or sanity. That knowledge, that the line had finally been crossed, tore at me in a way the dagger she wielded could not. Finally I handled her as harshly as I would a man. I struck my fist against her chin, and her body fell limp to the bed."

Taryn forced herself to lie still. She feared if she moved or spoke, he would withdraw from her. The only response she gave to the horrible tale he told was the dampness of tears she knew he did not even feel pooling beneath her cheek.

"I summoned Maite and had her send a rider to the abbey at Portchester, to prepare the abbess for Clarissa's return. Then I ripped a strip from her robe and tied her hands together should she wake on the way. I carried her downstairs. By that time Richard had been wakened. He held her whilst I mounted my horse. What hour I arrived at the abbey I do not know. But I remember there was a lantern burning above the door. I pulled the rope which would sound the bell within the convent's walls. Almost at once three nuns shrouded in black and white appeared.

Clarissa had awakened on the journey, but she never spoke. I told her I was taking her home, and she seemed to understand. They led her away. I ne'er saw her again. She died by her own hand six months later, on her seventeenth birthday."

Taryn lifted her head, meeting his eyes focused questioningly upon her. "You were not to blame. What caused her to see you as an enemy, your love as danger and your touch as threat was not of your doing. Henry spoke the truth. She was sick."

A wry smile twisted the corners of his mouth. "You, Maite and Henry, you all sing the same tune."

"Then is it not time to believe it? Garret, you are *not* to blame. There is naught evil within you. You made me your wife—in every meaning of the word—yet I did not go mad or grow to loathe you. I grew to love you."

"As I stated before, you have a peculiar way of showing love, Taryn. You petitioned for an annulment."

Taryn smiled, hearing in his voice his control regained and strength returned. The past had been laid to rest. It was time to deal with the present, and the future—their future—together.

"Because you would not give me what I truly wanted."

His brow lifted in confusion.

"I wanted a marriage," she replied in soft response to his unspoken question.

"You *asked* for an annulment."

"I *wanted* a marriage," she repeated adamantly. "And I still do."

He grasped her shoulders and sat forward, sitting her up as well. "In spite of all you have just learned of me?"

She shook her head. "Not in spite of, but because of. Garret, I *want* to be your wife. What has divided us has ceased to be insurmountable—if you can believe 'tis love which allows me to respond as you think a wife should not."

Without replying Garret gathered her back into his embrace. He did not know that he believed in the existence of this emotion she professed. Yet before Henry had told him about the letter, he had decided to try and end their estrangement. His weeks in London had proven to him the importance she held in his life. She was willful and sharp-tongued, and too intelligent for a female—a flaw which surely attributed to her inability to accept a woman's proper place. Yet something bound him to her. And now, more than ever before, he recognized the void she filled.

"Garret?"

"Aye?" He looked down at the woman in his arms and felt an unexpected sense of tenderness.

"Will you give me the chance to be a wife to you?"

"Aye . . . though I fear you shall have a devil for a husband."

"I think not," she replied, snuggling contentedly against him, "for I could not love a devil."

Chapter Twenty

Henry mounted the final stair. Here, unlike the darkened stairwell at his back, there was no need for the torches still burning in the iron wall sconces. The small corridor into which he stepped was more than amply lit with early sunlight entering through the single narrow window at the hallway's end.

He took a half dozen paces forward, stopping at the heavy oaken door upon his right. From within the chamber he could hear no sound. At least they were not at each other's throats. It could be a good sign; his plan might have worked despite his having had little more than suspicions as to what had driven Garret and his bride apart.

Without hesitation he laid his ear to the door's rough planks. Like a common servant, the King of England, Duke of Normandy and Aquitaine and Count of Anjou, listened for the goings-on in the room beyond. Still nothing.

He smiled. It appeared his instincts might once again have served him in good stead. The flame-haired siren was just what Garret needed. They belonged together, of that he was convinced. Certainly no one who had known Garret d'Aubigny as a youth could have failed to see the change that had occurred within him after his first wife's death. A part of him had died with her. Not until the advent of Taryn Maitland had Henry seen that life, that flame of passion, reborn. And a body would have to be blind and deaf not to recognize the embers of love burning in the wench's eyes.

Garret's bride no more wanted an annulment of their marriage than did Garret. When his vassal had learned of her request, Henry had seen the flash of pain and the anticipation of loss Garret had fought to conceal beneath his anger. Yet his response was not without logic. For a man such as Garret d'Aubigny anger was a far more accessible emotion than love. Still, with the proper guidance it could serve a useful purpose—firing the blood, and hence, fueling the flame.

Confident, Henry straightened and raised his fist to pound upon the chamber door. Mid-air he checked the blow. Upon second thought, he would not announce himself . . .

The heavy door swung open and slammed against the wall. The thunderous crash elicited a male shout of fury and a feminine cry of fear.

From his vantage point in the doorway Henry could see but a scramble of naked flesh and a flurry of billowy bed sheets tugged and hastily tossed into place. "Good morning!" he shouted.

Garret's eyes blazed; the identity of the intruder mattered not to him, nor did the jovial greeting.

Henry smiled, respecting the man's right to outrage. "Mayhap I should have first knocked."

"Indeed."

Henry ignored the terse rejoinder gritted through clenched teeth and turned his focus to the woman half-hidden from his view beneath her husband's kneeling form. "Lady Taryn."

"Sire," she answered weakly. If possible the stain of color in her cheeks deepened.

Henry pursed his lips. It was unfortunate he had entered at the moment he had, thereby interrupting the couple. Still, his previous night's aim had obviously been achieved. He allowed himself a nod of satisfaction. "'Twould appear, lady, that there is mutual passion and desire in your marriage after all. I am pleased indeed, and satisfied."

"Would that I were of a like sentiment," growled the man still poised above her.

"Oh?" Henry returned his gaze to his vassal. "Do I take your words to mean that this . . . er . . . matter . . . has *not* been resolved?"

"Resolved, aye," Garret snarled. "But thanks to Your Majesty's poor timing . . ."

Henry laughed and waved a regal hand of dismissal. "You'll have time aplenty later for a proper consummation. Right now your presence is required downstairs."

"I am required here," Garret countered, his anger still strong and shadowing his judgment, for a behest from his king was not to be ignored or refused.

Henry let this insolence pass, however. Were he in the man's position he would feel no different. "In that case, the request becomes command, liegeman. Your king requires your presence downstairs and his need is, at this moment, more urgent than your wife's. The watchmen have spotted Maitland's banner on the horizon."

Startled by Henry's announcement, Taryn looked at Garret to see his response.

His entire demeanor changed at once, his features hardening as cold control and calm replaced his anger. "So the coxcomb comes to repledge his oath."

Henry shrugged. "To arrive at dawn's break, he obviously has ridden through the night. He comes to deliver something—whether or not 'tis his vow of fealty, we shall learn soon enough. Get dressed. I will meet you at the stables so that we may ride out to greet him."

As Henry closed the door behind him, Garret hurriedly disengaged himself from the sheets tangled about his legs. To Taryn's consternation she realized that in spite of his amorous mood only moments earlier, he now seemed to have forgotten her very existence.

"Garret?" She touched his arm hesitantly. A dozen questions swirled in her mind, not the least of which was the reason for her half-brother's arrival at Jaune.

By way of an acknowledgment he dipped his head swiftly, brushing her lips with a soft kiss. "I am sorry, Taryn. Though this must wait, know that I would prefer to stay."

He then rose from the bed and crossed the room to where his clothes lay in a heap from the night before.

She watched him dress in silence. Once clothed from the waist down he went over to the wash basin and quickly wetted his face and neck. Towel in hand, he returned to the side of the bed where he stared down at her for a moment.

"I can read the questions in your eyes as easily as you read a parchment," he stated gently. "You have no cause for concern. The reason for Charles' arrival has naught to do with you. Your brother did not respond to Henry's summons to London, hence Henry has ordered him here, along with several other barons who shall be arriving later today. Henry desires that they reaffirm their vows of fealty to me, and to him."

Taryn nodded, indicating her understanding. She knew the practice of having a vassal repledge his loyalty and reenact his homage was a common one. The more recently made, the more likely the oath was to be effective.

Was that the case now with Charles, she wondered. It had been upon their father's death over a year ago that he had taken his oath.

"You are deep in thought." Garret's voice drew her from her reverie. Dressed, he stood at the door belting on his sword.

"I do not trust him," she stated quietly.

"Nor do I." A smile of shared understanding and reassurance tipped the corners of his mouth. "Dress and come below. And remember, you are no longer his sister, but my wife. He shall know that, and guard both tongue and action accordingly—or answer to me."

She smiled hearing his protective tone and nodded. With her marriage Charles' control over her *had* ended. Perhaps there merely needed to be a passage of more time before her fear and distrust of him faded.

She watched as Garret left, then rose to do as bade. She washed and dressed without haste, allowing herself to reflect upon what Henry had interrupted. Last night they had not made love, each sensing the time was not right. She had been content just to lie in his arms. But upon waking, he had reached for her, and she had responded eagerly, wanting him as much as he did her. Her newly acknowledged love for him let her understand the urgency she felt in his touch, the hunger. He needed to take her to put aside the past and to start anew.

Henry's untimely intrusion, however, had precluded that from happening. And while she accepted that Garret's duty to his king must come first, acceptance did not make her disappointment less, though Garret's clear reluctance to leave her did.

Like a tender embrace, that thought warmed her as she went to the window and looked down onto the bailey below where through the inner curtain wall less than a score of riders now passed. Despite the distance she was easily able to make out the identity of the three men who rode at the column's head. Charles' fair locks contrasted sharply with Henry's red hair and Garret's dark waves.

Deliberately she waited several moments more, until she was certain that Charles' entourage and their escort had dismounted and entered the keep.

Annoying thoughts gnawed at her as she descended the stairs. Charles never travelled at night, nor had she ever known him to travel in the company of less than forty knights. Given the animosity he felt for Garret, this humble pilgrimage of his to repledge his fealty seemed out of character. Whether commanded by Henry or not, she was certain this visit was not what it appeared to be.

At the entrance to the great hall she paused and

allowed herself to view the gathering of men. Many were Jaune's own men-at-arms arrived for the morning meal. Others, whose features were unknown to her, wore the king's colors. Surpisingly, those who bore the Maitland azure and sable were men she recognized. For some reason, Charles had seen fit to exclude from this escort the German mercenaries that had swelled the ranks of his private army during her last six months at Wynshire.

Her uneasiness building, Taryn's focus settled upon the trio moving toward the dais. Henry, Garret and Charles appeared deep in conversation. Hesitant to interrupt, she scanned the room for a familiar face. Spying Simon just inside the doorway, she moved to his side.

Though he nodded in greeting to her, his attention, too, appeared fixed upon the three men now mounting the platform. "Proud as a cock on a dunghill," he stated softly, as if to himself. "You'd never know by looking at him that in coming here he's had to tuck his tail betwixt his legs."

Taryn regarded him in surprise, his remark confusing her. This man was not of Charles' acquaintance, yet he spoke as if he knew him. "What do you mean?"

Simon turned to look at her, his features suddenly blank. "Naught, my lady. From what I heard at court, I simply don't care for the man. My outburst meant no more, and for it I apologize. I know he is your half-brother."

She shook her head. There was more to Simon's "outburst" than a comment made out of turn. "I do not believe you, Simon," she stated firmly. "Nor do I trust him." She glanced over to the dais, noting that while Henry and Garret had seated themselves, Charles remained standing. "What do you know about this? Is there a reason for Charles to be here other than the repledging of his oath?"

Simon laughed tonelessly. "He's come to repledge all right . . . since he was left no choice in the matter once

Henry saw fit to reject his petition."

"What petition? What are you talking about?" As her floundering suspicions found solid footing, Taryn felt an uncomfortable tightening sensation in her stomach. She laid her hand upon the knight's arm, thereby forcing him to meet her gaze. "I have the right to know. Please, Simon. Tell me."

For a brief instant she feared he would refuse. But as she watched the play of emotions upon his face, she saw his reluctance yield—first to hesitation, and then to concession.

"Very well." He nodded, and with his mouth set in a grim line that told her he still questioned the wisdom of this decision, he took her elbow.

Leading her away from the doorway, now in steady traffic with servants entering and exiting the hall, he guided her to a small alcove which housed the cupboards containing the keep's store of extra linens and trenchers. Though private, the spot still left them in clear view of those gathered in the main body of the room.

"What petition?" she asked, giving him no time to change his mind.

"The one your brother made to Henry, the one in which he requested permission to renounce his oath of fealty to Lord Garret."

Taryn shook her head. "I don't understand. You and Garret both have said he is here to repledge—not to renounce."

"And so he is, for according to the talk at court, Henry would agree to grant only half his petition. Your brother was free to renounce his vow as long as he forfeited the lands he currently holds as your husband's vassal. Henry rejected the half which would have deeded those same properties to him as compensation."

"Compensation for what?"

"It has to do with the grounds for the petition. He claims Lord Garret broke faith with him—hence the fault is not his, and he should, therefore, be permitted to keep the lands. At any rate, Henry refused. He sent a message—"

"How did Garret break faith?" she interrupted. It was clear that on this issue Simon was being vague.

He hesitated, and when he finally responded, his reply was quiet and reluctant. "Rumor has it that he cited Lord Garret's interference in your marriage contract with Baron Lynfyld, lady."

"Then Garret lied? He told me Charles' presence here has naught to do with me."

"And it doesn't . . . really. Most at court believe this business with Lynfyld was but an excuse to accomplish what he has wanted since the title of Earl of Wynshire fell to him. He wants to free himself from Lord Garret's authority without forfeiture of his holdings. But Henry saw through the charade. As I started to explain, he sent a message informing your brother that unless he was agreeable to losing those lands, he had best get himself to Jaune, resolve his difference with his liegelord and reaffirm his loyalty—before Lord Garret exercised his right to bring the matter to a sword reckoning."

Taryn smiled wryly. Charles was a coward who paid others to fight his battles. At all cost he would avoid mortal combat with Garret. She nodded in satisfaction and private relief. This made sense. Charles' humble pilgrimage was humble after all. "So he does this unwillingly," she murmured softly.

"Can there be doubt?" Simon laughed. "Look at him, lady." He gestured to the man still unseated on the platform. "I would wager a year's pay that beneath that smile plastered on his face, his teeth are clenched. Every word he's uttering tastes like bile."

"But he'll swallow it to keep the lands," she murmured.

"Aye."

Suddenly, as if he had heard their voices, the man they studied looked up and caught sight of them. Excusing himself, he departed the dais and made his way through the rows of trestle tables to where they stood.

"Taryn." With a cool half-smile Charles bowed his head in greeting, then turned a haughty eye to the man beside her. "Sir Knight, I should like a private word with my sister."

Simon did not move. Toe to toe the two men stood, silently appraising one another. At last Charles spoke.

"The man who makes this request is the *Earl* of Wynshire, knight."

Simon's gaze narrowed. Clearly the pointed reference to their stations did not intimidate him. He looked to Taryn. "Is it your desire that I leave, lady?"

Though she preferred he did not, Taryn nodded. It was clear whatever Charles had to tell her would be told only if she were alone with him. "'Tis all right, Simon."

She watched as the man withdrew a respectful distance, then turned a wary eye to her half-brother. "What do you want?"

Charles lifted his hand to his breast in gesture of feigned pain. "Your harshness wounds me, sister. I want only to inquire about your well being. After all, so much has happened, and I am curious—did you find your love match? From what I hear, the lord of Jaune's preference was to bed you without the bond of marriage." He sneered. "That is, until Henry forced him to honor you."

Waves of the familiar old enmity washed over her. "You know naught of honor," she retorted, steeling herself against his insult. "Forsooth, were I Garret or Henry, I would trust little in any oath you made this day—even were it to be rendered whilst you stood knee-deep in the Saviour's own blood!"

"I think you would prefer the blood were mine."

His smug, mocking voice caught her aback and she winced at the naked animosity she suddenly saw in his eyes.

"So," he continued, "you do not answer my question. Mayhap you do so intentionally? Mayhap you now regret marriage to that Devil's spawn?"

"You would do well to speak of your liegelord in a more respectful tone."

He laughed, amused at her attempt to taunt him with his position. "'Tis a regrettable, but alas, necessary situation. One, however, which appears to have served you well enough." His affable smile transformed into an ugly fleer as his eyes travelled her length with unabashed scorn. "From mistress to countess . . . I must congratulate you, sister. Indeed, I underestimated you. I did not think that what you had betwixt your legs was worth so much."

With a soft cry of rage Taryn raised her hand to slap the jeering face before her.

Charles blocked the blow and snagged her wrist in one practiced move. "Do not," he snarled, "raise your hand to me. I am still your blood kin, and should something befall the devil you call husband, 'tis to my control you would return!"

In his words Taryn heard the truth. She realized a flutter of panic and tried desperately to ignore it. With a confidence she did not feel she drew herself up to her full height, wrenched her arm free and turned to walk away—thereby stumbling promptly and blindly into the tall figure that had reappeared at her side without warning.

"Lady, are you all right?"

"Simon!" She gasped in relief and instinctively slipped into the protective refuge of his encircling arm.

"Is there a problem," he asked, drawing her safely to him as his gaze slowly raked her half-brother.

Charles glared at the stranger who had with his actions now made himself his enemy. "My sister and I are not yet finished."

"I think that you are." Without taking his eye from his adversary, Simon offered a deep, mocking bow. "Earl."

Taryn shuddered. Simon was at least a head taller than Charles, massive in proportions. With his wide, muscled shoulders firmly set and his legs slightly apart, his entire stance suggested the violence of which he was capable. And though his hand did not go to his sword, she felt his unspoken challenge.

Charles felt it, too. He swallowed loudly, then wheeled toward the keep's exit.

"Come, lady." Simon stepped away from her and extended his arm. "Your place is with your husband."

From the dais Garret watched the confrontation between his vassal and Maitland. He had seen little which had preceded it, his attentions having been focused upon Henry. What he had seen, however, was Taryn's obvious distress and he had been in the act of standing when d'Orléon stepped forward. Even from where he sat there was no doubt in his mind that the embrace he had witnessed had been one of a protective nature only. D'Orléon had seen her to be somehow threatened and had reacted to disarm that threat.

Garret leaned back in his chair. Indeed, the man now escorted her to him. He rubbed his jaw. He owed d'Orléon a word of thanks, and mayhap, too, an apology, given the previous night's revelations. Taryn regarded him with no more than friendship. Henry was probably right. His vassal had had no knowledge of the letter's contents. In delivering it he had merely provided his lord's wife service—no different than what he had just performed now by protecting her from possible harm.

Still, acknowledgment of misjudgment and apologies did not come easily to Garret. He would speak to d'Orléon later, in private.

He turned his attention to Henry. "What say you, Sire, to a hunt? Our other 'guests' will not be arrived until late this afternoon. Certes, the thought of spending the remainder of the day within these walls makes my flesh crawl—especially given the company available." He inclined his head in the direction of Charles Maitland's departing form.

Henry regarded him with a questioning expression. "You know I have no greater passion, Garret," he answered. "And God knows I do not sit idle when given choice. However, Maitland has been in the saddle for better than two days. I scarcely think he will be of either the mind or body to participate."

Garret shrugged and smiled. "So, how runs your taste, Sire? Deer . . . or boar?"

Henry laughed. "Boar."

"Maite, is aught wrong?" Taryn looked up from the tapestry she stitched. The intricate handiwork had done little to take her mind off the morning's events. Charles' presence at Jaune had unsettled her greatly, as it had apparently Maite as well.

As the day had worn on, the old woman had grown increasingly quiet, and her mood more strange. Never had Taryn seen her in such a restless state. Maite had never been known to spend but a moment or two in the wool room, yet now she paced the chamber nervously, going repeatedly out onto the balcony. Somehow, Taryn doubted she did so to take in the warm summer sunshine. She appeared almost to be watching for something—or someone. Yet Garret's hunting party would not be returned until sunset.

"You should have said something to keep him here," Maite murmured at last, her reply to Taryn's question no reply at all.

"Men will have their sport, Maite."

In acknowledgment of Taryn's gentle reproach, the old woman emitted a derisive snort. "Boys—in men's bodies! If they are not in combat with one another, they wage war upon the creatures of the forest, and call it sport!"

Taryn felt the eyes of the several women in the wool room upon her. Several were futilely concealing grins of amusement as they attempted to gauge their mistress' response to Maite's inexplicable anger.

Admonishing them with a stern gaze, Taryn looked back to the frail form still pacing. Maite had been in such a genial mood that morning, Taryn had been certain she knew in her peculiar way that Garret and she had mended their rift. What could have caused this change?

Suddenly, without warning the woman spun toward the door. "Something is amiss. I see blood."

Like an icy hand closing about her throat, a sense of irrational fear gripped Taryn, and she pushed aside the tapesty frame to stand. She knew of Maite's ability to see what others could not, and against logic and reason she now believed in whatever premonition the old woman had seen.

She followed her from the chamber down into the great hall, deserted save a few servants carrying in fresh rushes through the keep's open doors.

Suddenly, there erupted from outside the sound of shouting. Fear and urgency shrilled the voices, but one word was clear: *Garret.*

Taryn swayed as the strength in her limbs seemed to flow from her like sand poured through a sieve. Cold with dread, she rushed unsteadily after Maite who already raced toward the doorway. Before she reached it, the sunlight streaming in was blocked by the forms of several men.

Through the dizzy haze which had become her vision, Taryn recognized one of Garret's squires.

"Lord Garret has been hurt," he gasped. His young face was flushed, beaded with sweat and streaked with dirt and tears.

"Is he dead?" Maite demanded.

"There—there was no time—" The youth stammered weakly. "I tried . . . but the boar charged before I could react."

"Dwell upon your guilt later, boy!" Maite's sharp voice was a slap. The youth's tears ceased instantly, but she did not stop to take satisfaction in her action. "I asked after your master's well being. Your only thought should be of him. Does he live?"

"Aye," he nodded listlessly.

Maite sprang to action "You there! And you three . . ." She pointed to the two men in the doorway and then to the servants. "Shove one of those tables over here where I'll have some light."

As Maite barked her instructions, Taryn felt a numbing sense of calm, and found her own voice. "Squire, go to the kitchen and tell the cook we shall need boiled water." Without waiting to see that her command had been obeyed, she turned to the pair of women who had followed her downstairs. Once she had hoped never to need Moira's training, but now she strove to recall every detail. "Nora, Louise, return to the wool room. I shall need a needle sharp enough to pierce flesh, and strong thread." She paused, remembering all she had been taught. "Also clean linens ripped into strips."

Several more servants appeared, and the orders continued: a fire, to be built in the hearth should the wounds require the searing of a heated knife blade; rope, should restraints be necessary; the white of an infertile egg for application to deep gashes; Maite's herbs and healing potions, to be brought and laid out in readiness.

Through the flurry of activity a curious sense of order prevailed. Taryn paused to look at Maite and caught her eye.

In acknowledgment of their shared prayers and common aim, the old woman nodded. There was no time now for tears or weeping. When the hunting party arrived, they would be ready.

Almost in response to that silent thought, a great clamor was heard. The blasts of hunting horns mingled with the shouts of men and the hoofbeats of horses.

Chapter Twenty-One

Taryn took a faltering step forward, only to be halted by Maite's hand upon her arm.

"They will bring him, lady. 'Twill be of more help that you keep out of their way."

Reluctantly Taryn acquiesced to the old woman's logic. Trembling, she watched as the hunting party reined in their mounts at the base of the wooden stairs. She saw Garret's form slumped over his saddle and experienced an agonizing sense of dread. Had his squire been wrong?

The two men on either side of his horse hastily dismounted, and together they eased his limp body to the ground. Two other men jumped forward to aid them. Dimly she noted that one of the men supporting his head and shoulders was Simon. It was his voice she heard issuing calm instruction as they carried Garret up the stairs.

At first the bodies of the men who supported his feet and legs blocked her view. But then, as they neared, Taryn caught clear sight of the man whose weight they bore with such tender care.

Garret's *hauberk* was torn and bloodied, but it was his right leg which caused her to choke in fear. The entire limb was crimson. She felt herself sway, and fearing she might faint, she leaned weakly against the door frame.

The men passed by her, laying their previous burden upon the table which had been readied. And though Maite stepped forward at once, Taryn found herself unable to move.

"Lady, mayhap you should leave." Simon's soft voice and gentle touch upon her shoulder shattered her trancelike state.

She blinked in an effort to focus upon the man who, having delivered his lord, now stood before her.

"He is in good hands," Simon continued. "The wound is not as serious as it appears. 'Tis a clean cut. Come. Let me take you out into the fresh air."

"I'll not go. My place is here." She looked up at him fiercely, daring him to challenge her decision.

A gleam of what might have been surprise glinted in his eye. He inclined his head in a gesture indicating he would offer no further argument and then took up a protective stance at her side.

The reason for his actions escaped her until she followed the direction of his gaze. There, standing in the doorway between the hall and the anteroom, stood Charles.

His eyes darted about the great room, taking in what was happening. Taryn was struck with the image of a rapacious wolf, lying in wait for its hapless prey. His face alive with anxious interest, he skulked forward to stand at Henry's side.

The same blood as his flowed through her veins, and her own primal instincts surged. Like a she-wolf ready to do battle to protect her mate, she left the safety of Simon's side and moved toward the predator.

"Your presence is not welcome here," she stated coldly, putting herself between her half-brother and the table, thereby blocking his view.

Charles looked at her in feigned aggrievement. "Certes, you misinterpret my motive, sister. As your kinsman I am here only to offer you support. Should your husband—and my lord—die, we should share equally a common grief."

"What we would share would be his holdings, for if I were a widow, you would control Arundel. For this you lie in wait, your eyes bright with greed."

Charles stiffened, and his gaze flitted to Henry.

Though the man's attention seemed focused entirely upon what was taking place at the table, Taryn had no doubt he listened to their every word. Charles had to know it as well, as his nervous glance revealed.

"I shall forgive and ignore this unjust and wholly undeserved attack, Taryn," he answered glibly. "Forsooth, fear for your husband's life has rendered you irrational."

Suddenly a weak laugh could be heard from the table. "Come here, wife," Garret's voice sounded, "that you may see for yourself that your fears are groundless."

Taryn moved at once to his side, taking his hand into her own. Despite his reassuring squeeze, her stomach lurched at the sight of him. His entire body bore evidence of the boar's attack: numerous ugly and jagged cuts across his upper arms and chest, deep bite marks upon his forearms—not to mention the leg she could not bring herself to look upon. Under Maite's orders several men peeled off his *chausses*, another worked to strip him to the waist.

"Now . . ." he murmured, "pull in your claws and stay by my side—where you belong." He smiled faintly and closed his eyes.

Thinking him to be blessedly unconscious, Taryn turned her attention to the actions of those who attended him.

Seeing at last what was laid bare, she gasped. His right thigh had been slashed to the bone. She looked back at his face, noting for the first time how gray his color was. His eyes fluttered open as the jarring to finish removing the leggings again roused him. Weakly he tried to sit up and was promptly held down by a man who grasped his shoulders.

"Becket," he gasped. His speech was suddenly slurred and his lucidity of the moment before gone. "Where is Becket?"

"The dog is being cared for," Henry spoke up, stepping forward to the table's edge. "Lie still, man."

Taryn looked at him in confusion. "Why does he call for the dog?"

"No doubt because he values its life above his own," Henry muttered in a curious mixture of grudging respect and anger. "Of all the want-witted acts . . ." He shook his head in disgust. "But for that damned dog he would not be here—lying in a pool of his own blood."

"I want him brought to me," Garret insisted anew, again attempting to rise.

Henry clapped his hand upon his shoulder, forcing him down. "Lie still, man. The hound was brought back. Do you not remember? You would not let us put you on a horse until the dog's wounds had been bound. He will be attended to, I promise you. Maite will see to him herself as soon as she is done with you. Is that not so, Maite?" Henry looked at the old woman, bidding her with a silent nod to confirm his vow.

But Maite only grunted and impatiently gestured for a cup of wine to be held to Garret's lips.

Weakly he turned his head away. Refusing the wine and the pain-dulling herbs it contained, he focused upon her. "Ere I drink one drop of your brew, old woman, I will have my dog attended to! I did not suffer this to lose him."

Taryn heard Henry growl in fury. "Ere you die of bloodloss before my eyes, liegeman, you will do as ordered. Drink or I shall have it poured down your throat!"

"Sire, please! You attempt to reason with a man who is beyond its capacity." Taryn leaned forward into Garret's field of vision. She clutched his hand to her and gently touched his cheek. "Garret . . . if I have Becket brought here and tend to him until Maite is finished, will that satisfy you?"

He nodded, and this time when the cup was put to his lips he did not turn away.

Taryn straightened and turned her gaze to the squire waiting white-faced at the keep's entrance. "Have the dog brought at once," she ordered. As the boy jumped to do as commanded, she looked back at Henry and nodded.

Without waiting for his reaction, she shifted her eyes to Maite and watched as the woman cleaned the blood from the leg to better gauge the treatment needed. Even to Taryn's inexperienced eye, the wound was too deep to be seared. It would have to be sewn.

"How did this happen?" she asked, voicing her silent question.

Seemingly from far away she heard Henry respond. "I was not there, but from what I can gather, Becket chased a boar into underbrush too thick for the horses to enter. Garret and his squire rode around the thicket. They heard the beast squealing and knew Becket had it cornered. Garret shouted for the dog to stand down, but stubbornly, like its master, the damned hound instead held his prey. By the time the horses found entrance to the clearing, the boar had attacked. Garret threw his lance, and the boar went down. Then the fool dismounted to see to his dog—without first seeing that his mark had been true."

"The mark *was* true," Garret gritted through clenched teeth. "It should have been fatal."

"Obviously, 'twas not!" Maite spat, looking up from her ministrations for the first time. Her anxiety was clearly manifesting itself in anger.

"Hold your tongue, old woman," Garret growled, "forsooth, 'tis sharper than the needle you would stick into me."

"It cannot be done elsewise," she snapped. Lifting her head, she issued a command to one of the many servingmen standing about. "Bring a stick of thumb's width, that your lord might bite down upon it should the pain be too great."

"I require no stick!" Garret countermanded to the faceless servant. He looked at Maite and smiled tautly, albeit weakly. "For I will not cry out from any pain wrought by a woman's hand. Do what needs be done."

Henry chuckled. "I think, Maite, that you could cut off his leg and he would not give you the satisfaction of a whimper."

Taryn glared at the man standing at her side. "In your own words my husband lies in a pool of blood, his flesh ripped open to the bone. I can scarcely see the cause for your humor, Sire."

Amusement flashed in the regal eyes. But before Henry could reply, Taryn heard a noise behind her. She turned to see the squire enter the hall, the bay hound cradled in his arms. The unconscous animal's legs hung limply; his tongue lolled from his bloody muzzle. Swathed in a clumsy attempt at bandaging, Becket bled no less freely than his master, the pulsing wound the only evidence that he was not already dead. His entire left flank appeared to have been ripped open by the boar's teeth and tusks. She pointed to the second table that had been set up to hold Maite's array of herbs and potions. "Lay him there."

Garret lifted his head and watched as the dog was gently placed, then looked to her. "You will tend to him?"

Taryn noted his voice was stronger, his color better. Whatever herb or root Maite had put in the wine was taking effect. He was clearly in less pain—though no more lucid in his thoughts and concerns. "Aye," she promised, squeezing his hand before she released it.

She moved around to the table's far side in order to allow Garret to watch.

At once Simon appeared next to her. "You will need help."

Taryn nodded, grateful for his presence.

Spent, but satisfied that his wishes had been honored, Garret lay back. He looked at the man beside his wife and smiled. "I owe you my life, Simon d'Orléon."

"Then let us not lose it for your stubbornness, my lord." As if he were embarrassed with Garret's acknowledgment, Simon swiftly set about the task of unwrapping the dog's bandages. "Are you ready, lady?" he asked, drawing Taryn's attention to the injured animal and giving her little chance to think further of the exchange she had just witnessed.

"Aye." She tried to concentrate on what she was about to do and not upon the other table. Despite these efforts, she saw Maite gesture to the men now standing in readiness on either side of Garret.

"Hold him down. If need be, tie him."

Taryn felt her stomach lurch, and when she heard Garret moan, she tasted her fear. Knowing Maite had commenced and needing to concentrate on something besides the muffled grunts she could hear each time Maite's needle entered and exited Garret's flesh, she turned her attention to Becket. Dipping a scrap of clean linen into the bucket of warm water that had been brought and set upon the table, she began to clean the dog's wounds. From the corner of her eye, she looked at Simon. "Tell me the rest of what happened."

"There is not much to tell." Simon shrugged. "When the boar attacked Becket, Lord Garret attacked the boar. The beast went down; unfortunately, it did not stay down." He shook his head. "The hunter became the hunted, lady. There is no more to the tale."

"But there is, Sir Simon!" the youth at his side exclaimed. "You must say how you killed the boar and saved Lord Garret's li—"

Taryn looked up at once, too late to actually see the penetrating look with which Simon had silenced the youth midword. Remnants of it, however, still lingered upon the man's face and in his voice.

"The boy exaggerates, lady," he answered tightly, in

reply to the question she had not yet asked. "The tale is done."

"I think not," she stated quietly. Puzzled by his reaction and uncharacteristic loss of composure, she studied him in silence before turning again to her task. When Garret had expressed the debt owed, Simon had been uncomfortable then, too.

Suddenly, from his position between the tables, Henry spoke. "Squire, as Sir Simon is apparently too modest to offer a proper telling, why don't *you* continue? I, too, should like to hear the end of this tale which quite obviously is not 'done.'"

Helplessly the youth looked at Simon. As loath as he was to garner the man's disfavor, he could not refuse this behest made by his king.

Simon seemed to realize as much and reluctantly nodded the approval the boy sought.

A smile of relief broke out immediately upon the youthful face. Now fair bursting with the desire to tell his story, his words tumbled out atop one another in a rush. "'Twas like His Majesty has said. Becket had this beast cornered. He had to have had the weight of two men, lady, for he was monstrous, huge—black as night—and as fierce a beast as I've ever seen."

Several restrained but audible snorts of derision greeted this proclamation, as many around the tables reckoned the youth's years and found him lacking in experience.

Ignoring their jibes, the squire continued. "Well, he was holed up in this thicket, squealing. We knew he was about to attack, but Becket wouldn't stand down . . ."

Taryn took up a needle and forced her mind to ignore the fact that what she was about to sew was not fabric. "Go on," she prompted, as she hesitantly took her first stitch to close the deepest of the dog's wounds.

As she did so, Simon pressed together the edges of torn flesh. The squire moved forward helpfully to wipe away the blood still oozing from the gash. All the while his voice recounted the events of the hunt.

". . . just as we broke through, we saw the boar catch Becket with his tusk and toss him into the air. Before he even hit the ground, Lord Garret had thrown his lance. Indeed, the mark *was* true—right through the neck and shoulder. The boar went down, and Lord Garret dismounted to see to Becket. Surely he was dead, I thought, chewed up like he was, bleeding, not moving. I . . . I sat there and watched Lord Garret try . . . to stop the bleeding. I should have been watching the boar . . ."

For the first time since beginning his tale the youth's voice faltered. Hearing in his hesitation his shame and guilt, Taryn gently urged him to proceed. "Go on."

"I didn't hear him rise, or see him until he charged. I tried to throw my lance—I did! But by the time I had aimed, he had attacked. Then I couldn't throw it, not without hitting Lord Garret. They rolled on the ground, blood everywhere. I couldn't tell if it was the boar's or my lord's. I couldn't move. And . . . and then this horse came through the thicket and a lance flew through the air. 'Twas Sir Simon. He jumped off his horse, grabbed his lance whilst it still stuck out the boar's neck, pulled it free and drove it through the heart. I never saw such a deed." His voice lowered in awe. "If it hadn't been for him, my lady, Lord Garret would surely be dead. Why, you should have seen him—Sir Simon—when the boar attacked Lord Garret, he just appeared out of nowhere."

Taryn turned her head to look at the man beside her. For a brief moment, as she beheld the face of Garret's deliverer, the control she fiercely fought to maintain wavered. Her eyes rimmed with tears. "I owe you a great debt," she said softly.

He smiled grimly. "The boy exaggerates, lady."

"I think not," she whispered. "Would that I possessed the words to thank you for giving back what was nearly taken . . ."

She broke off and silence descended, as all in the room contemplated the loss of life averted by the man's unselfish bravery.

"What a splendid tale." Charles' unctuous voice interrupted the heavy silence. "A heroic deed, indeed."

Taryn's head snapped up. She had forgotten her half-brother's presence. To be reminded of it by his almost sarcastic comment instantly rekindled her protective instinct. She looked anxiously to the other table, noting that Maite had completed her task and was applying a poultice to the wound to draw out any infection. Garret's eyes were closed. Had he lost consciousness from the pain, or was this the effect of the potion he had drunk?

"He will sleep and feel naught—at least until nightfall." Catching her eye, Maite cast her a reassuring nod as she proceeded to wrap the leg in clean linen.

"Then he will live?" Taryn breathed fearfully.

"Aye, he will live."

From the corner of her eye, Taryn saw Charles turn furiously toward the keep's exit. She had no time to revel in his defeat, however.

Brushing a strand of gray hair from her forehead, Maite stepped back from the table. "Come, see that he is put to bed whilst I look at that damned dog. Surely there will be the Devil to pay if he awakes and finds the animal dead."

Simon watched as Taryn gratefully surrendered her needle into Maite's capable hands and went to her husband's side. He felt his heart wrench, seeing her longingly gaze down upon the still form, touching the lips with her fingertip in a gesture of poignant intimacy. Knowing now that Garret would live, she had let down her guard, and to all who looked upon her face, her love was revealed.

Simon looked away, unable to bear the sight. The love he had longed for all his life had come to him at last, and it had come too late. She was not his. She belonged to another—to a man he had come to respect above all others.

All around him men now touted his selfless bravery in

whispered words. Only he knew the truth. It was not respect or loyalty, or even instinct, which had caused him to act. It had been selfish cowardice that had sent his lance unerringly to its mark. He could not have faced her tears, knowing that his act could have spared her that anguish. Would that the thrust which had stilled the boar's heart had stilled his own as well!

He looked down at the tiny woman at his side. "Can you manage?"

Maite nodded, and he stepped from the table. Taryn never noticed his withdrawal. Though engaged in conversation with Henry, her thoughts were clearly only of Garret.

Her voice followed Simon to the doorway. "He is not strong enough! The ceremony should be postponed."

With rare patience Henry responded. "Know the value I place upon his life, lady, and know I would do naught to risk it. He will need only to sit in bed and accept the pledges."

Realizing the reenactment of homage would still proceed, Simon smiled. He knew of one who would not be pleased.

At the doorway he paused and looked back a final time. He should leave this place. Until he had come here, he had called no man friend and loved no woman. No life had he ever placed above his own. To all he met, he had remained a stranger, allied with neither crown nor cleric, his sword for hire to the highest bidder.

Wearily he passed his hand across his brow. What was he doing in this place, feeling what he felt for these people? Love and loyalty? Loyalty was a commodity to be bought and sold. Obligation ceased when the silver did, and devotion was not for sale at any price. Devotion involved emotion; like love, it marred excellence because it evaded control. Having lived his life thusly for better than twenty years had proved a wise path.

Aye, he should leave. But to leave now could cause those he cared for more harm than if he stayed. He must remain for a time to protect them. He owed them that much for having come into their lives a betrayer cloaked as a friend.

He passed through the open doors and descended the stairs.

"So . . . he will live?"

Simon turned at the sound of the low, snarling voice at his back. Cautiously his gaze searched the yard for any of Jaune's people who might bear witness to this clandestine meeting. "Aye," he answered slowly, "he will live."

"Thanks to you!" Charles Maitland stepped from the dark recess beneath the keep's wooden stairs. Remaining in the shadows, he, too, let his eyes wander the bailey. "Tell me, Simon d'Orléon," he hissed, "do I pay you to save my enemy's life?"

"Do you pay me not to?" Simon swiftly countered. He felt his loathing for the man before him rise up in his throat like the bitterest of bile. He swallowed it, as well as his anger, and arrogantly regarded his accuser. "I remind you of the terms of our agreement: I was to enter d'Aubigny's service, earn his respect and gain his loyalty. To accomplish that end I had to make a solemn vow to protect his life."

Coolly he tossed off his next comment, knowing the challenge his words contained. "Your 'enemy' now owes me a great debt. A cunning man would be pleased."

"I would be more pleased had your lance been off its mark and he were dead."

Simon's gaze hardened in contempt. "'Twould have been too easy. When a man's enemy does not see who wields the blow that destroys him, the victory is hollow."

"Of course." Maitland's scowl lifted at once into a smile of smug understanding. "My apologies, d'Orléon. You *are* as good as your reputation. I should have realized as much this morning after our confrontation in the hall, when you came so gallantly to my sister's aid. 'Twas a masterful stroke to have thought to gain her confidence as you have. Through you she will do whatever I want."

Simon's fists clenched at his sides. "Leave her out of this."

Maitland's brows shot up. "Do you forget to whom you speak? I own you, d'Orléon. You have been bought and paid for—like a whore. And like a whore, you *will* perform the services for which you accepted payment."

"Thus far you have no complaint."

"See that it remains so! Do not even think to cross me, for I would not hesitate to betray you. The esteem in which my sister holds you would turn quick enough to hatred, and the fact that you have this day given him his life would not stop d'Aubigny from taking yours. You are good, mercenary, but he has killed men as good—men who had two eyes!"

He turned to leave, then whirled on his heel to offer a final threat. "Give me cause again to doubt your loyalty and—"

"And you will do naught, for you would risk more than you are willing to lose. Make no mistake, *Earl* of Wynshire, we are equally bound to one another in this unholy alliance."

"It has been a week since your belongings were brought back into this chamber, yet you still do not share my bed. Why?"

Taryn pointedly crossed the room to set down the tray she held in her hands before answering. Garret's strength had been steadily increasing the past few days. His fever was gone, and he was completely lucid, awake much of the time now. Perhaps that explained why she had felt strangely shy in his presence the last day or two. He watched her constantly as she moved about the room, and when she caught him staring, he did not even bother to look away or disguise his intent. Was he merely bored with his confinement and in need of distraction?

"You require rest, my lord," she answered evenly.

"*My lord?* 'Tis not enough that you choose to keep at a

distance, now you become formal with me as well?" Though his voice was harsh, his pale eyes reflected more amusement than anger. "A week ago you had no difficulty in addressing me as Garret, nor were you so demure in your demeanor."

She smiled sweetly and proceeded to pour a goblet of wine from the flagon she had brought to accompany his evening meal. "That was before you were injured. Mayhap you have forgotten that you have suffered a grievous wound which might have killed you."

"Mayhap *you* have forgotten that I am very much alive and hence do not care to be treated as an invalid at death's door. Put down that cup and come here."

She complied and went to the bed, sidestepping in the process the prone form of the bandaged dog lying in her path. The bay hound lifted his head and weakly thumped his tail against the floor. In spite of herself Taryn smiled. She was sure the animal was stronger than he appeared. Once recovered, Becket would lose this preferential treatment and be relegated back downstairs. As if in response to her thoughts, the dog emitted a heart-rendering whimper of pain.

"Well done, Becket," she chided softly, grinning as she walked over to the bed. Catching sight of Garret's unrelenting stare, her light-hearted mood abruptly fled. Nervously she stood beside the bed, clasping her hands and lowering her eyes.

"Look at me," he commanded. "I do not relish this change in you, wife. You are far too meek for my taste. Indeed, I have grown used to, and rather fond of, the sharp-tongued wench I married. I would see her returned."

Taryn flushed in pleasure at his words. "When your strength returns, so shall she. Then I fear you will sorely miss the meek and dutiful wife who has been at your bedside this week past."

Garret smiled slyly. "Whilst I was ill I may have needed you *beside* my bed. Now that I am nearly recovered, I want you *in* it." He lay back and settled himself into the pillows. "Therefore, dutiful wife, 'tis time you performed your duty. Take off your clothes and lie with me."

"I do not think that is wise, my lor—" She broke off, seeing his brow furrow into a scowl.

"You disobey me?"

"Nay," she whispered, her heartbeat quickening. She turned from the bed toward the mantle to extinguish the candles burning there. His voice stopped her.

"Did I tell you to out the candles?"

"Nay, but I thought since we shall sleep, there would be no further need for their light."

"I said naught of sleep." Again the same sly smile appeared.

She felt a surge of anticipation and hastily drove it back. "You are not yet ready for any activity but sleep," she stated firmly, forcing a stern tone.

"You challenge me, madam," he announced tauntingly, "and I am a man who prides himself upon his ability to rise to meet a challenge."

She giggled, recognizing the double meaning of his statement. "I've no doubt of your ability to . . . respond, husband. But I fear your desire exceeds your strength. You can not yet put weight upon that leg, hence your brave and boastful words are impotent."

"Try me," he stated quietly.

She shook her head. "I'll not endure Maite's wrath should those stitches tear open."

"Then you refuse me?"

"Only for a little while yet."

"Very well. But lie with me anyway. I am tired of sleeping alone."

She nodded, happy in her victory, yet wishing he had not given in so easily. Perhaps he had realized his weakness after all.

She extinguished the candles and removed her clothing. Gingerly she climbed into the bed beside him, careful not to jar or touch him. Her efforts, though, were wasted, for the moment she laid her head to the pillow, he reached out for her. Thinking he desired only to embrace her, she permitted his touch. It did not take her long to realize her error.

With her head resting upon his chest, his arm encircled her shoulders, his hand coming to rest upon her breast. At first he only caressed her gently, as though reacquainting himself with her softness. But then his touch grew bolder. His fingers concentrated their effort upon her nipple, rolling the nub between thumb and forefinger. She felt a most pleasant swelling sensation, and as the stimulation continued, she experienced a tingling deep within the core of her.

As if knowing the reaction he induced, he slipped his other hand down the length of her, coming to rest between her thighs. Locating the most sensitive part of her, he teased her woman flesh in a most delicious manner.

Lost in the sensuality, Taryn moaned softly, arching against his hand.

"You see, wife, there are other ways of pleasuring a woman which do not require the strength you seem to think I lack."

Garret's voice jolted her back to sensibility, and she attempted to pull away. He held her fast. "Lie still, or I shall be forced to mount you properly."

His threat, coupled with her growing pleasure, obliterated her desire to struggle. Telling herself she did so in order not to tax his strength, she permitted his touch. Soon she writhed in need and realized he was intent upon bringing her to complete fulfillment. Almost at the same instant the thought was formed, she felt the heated wave of her passion crest. She shuddered and cried out at the intensity of the feeling washing over her. And as she floated in the wondrous aftermath, she paid no heed to his hands, which had moved to encircle her waist and lift her to straddle him. Languorous, she did not realize the purpose of his actions, nor did she care, until she felt his penetration. Her eyes flew open.

Beneath her Garret grinned as he lowered her onto him. "There are other ways to pleasure a man as well." In conjunction with his words, he showed her with gentle pressure upon her waist how to move forward and back, keeping her weight from his thighs with a slow sliding action which somehow still served to thrust him deep into her.

His breathing quickened, and with a groan she feared was not wholly born of pleasure (for despite her care she still exerted weight and pressure upon the bandaged limb) he took his release. "Well done," he whispered hoarsely. Bringing her mouth down to his, he kissed her, then eased her from him. "*Now* we will sleep."

Chapter Twenty-Two

"I say again, as I have for months now, this reconciliation makes no sense!"

"And I contend it does—if you consider all aspects. All who witnessed their meeting at Fréteval in July concur in the mention of Henry's unusually good mood."

"And you believe Thomas Becket would take a mere mood change to be a change of heart? Suddenly he is content with a promise of friendship and fair dealing, without the ratification of the Kiss of Peace? Any time during these last six years he might have had exactly those terms. Why would he now be so easily satisfied?

Taryn turned her head and concealed a smile—only to start an instant later as a goblet came down hard upon the table.

"By the saints! Are the reasons not clear? Alexander's desire is strong for peace with the King of England. Do you not know 'tis he who forces Becket's actions? The only way to restore order to England is for Becket to return to Canterbury, regardless of the price to his pride."

Taryn shook her head. For nearly two months, ever since Henry's return to Normandy and his meeting with the exiled archbishop, she had listened to this same argument. Garret and Simon never seemed to tire of it.

She cast a discreet gaze at the dark man seated beside

her husband, then looked at Garret. In each of their faces the same expression was mirrored: conviction that his stance was true and steadfast determination to sway the other. But beneath the outward passion fueling their beliefs and words, lay an emotion of a different sort.

The hunting accident which had nearly taken his life had left Garret with two lingering effects—an added scar upon his body and a new openness in his heart. Between him and the man who had saved his life there had formed the strongest bond of friendship; they had become as brothers. And like brothers, they goaded and challenged one another as equals. To a casual eye the line between lord and vassal was barely perceptible.

Again a goblet meeting the table with force intruded upon Taryn's thoughts.

"For a mercenary you *are* a naïve man!"

"And for a Great Earl you are a short-sighted one!"

"And for grown men, you *both* are acting as children!" Taryn suppressed another smile as the heads of the men swiveled toward her.

Taking advantage of their startled stares, she plunged ahead. "Is there truly naught else you can find to discuss? And I *am* being kind when I say 'discuss'. 'Tis October already, with winter around the corner. There are matters aplenty at Jaune which would benefit greatly from such attention. Blessed Mother, how my head pounds from your fruitless, endless blusterings!"

Garret's gaze slipped to the man beside him. "Did you invite the wench to speak, Sir Simon?"

"Certes not, my lord. Did you?"

"Indeed not. And a sharp tongue she possesses, would you not say?"

"You would know, my lord. She *is* your wife."

"And so she is. 'Tis fortunate, therefore, that she possesses other attributes which outweigh her rough disposition."

Simon looked briefly away, as if unable to continue the game further. "As I said, my lord," he laughed awkwardly, "you would know."

"Very amusing," Taryn snarled, feeling a rise of color. But the anger she sought to muster would not materialize. And how could it—with naught to fuel it? In the past four months she had known such happiness and contentment! Her days had been filled with the duties Richard had gratefully relinquished to Arundel's Countess, her nights spent in learning of the man who was her husband.

What had been born between her and Garret the night he had told her of his past had continued to strengthen and grow. In his arms she felt loved, though she was not so naïve as to believe he had come to feel the same toward her. But in gaining at least a part of of him, she was able to make herself believe it was enough. He never professed love, yet his desire for her was strong. When he pleasured her, and she, in the throes of passion, proclaimed her love, he did not seem displeased. She belonged to him completely. Was there aught else a wife could hope for?

Mistaking the silence of her private thoughts to be a withdrawal from further comment, Garret and Simon resumed their argument.

"If all is well and Becket has consented to return, why does he still delay his journey? Why does he remain in France?"

"I have offered you reasonable explanation. You are simply not reasonable enough to accept it. 'Tis hoped Henry will spend Christmas in England—hence Becket has decided to return with him, so that they might make this new beginning together."

"And thus the exile is forgiven?" Garret grunted. "I will believe it when I see it, and not before."

Though this was where their argument normally ended, Taryn pushed back from the table and stood.

"Do we drive you away, wife?" Garret looked up at her and grinned.

"Not at all, my lord. But while *you* may see fit to waste

away the day, *I* have duties to which I must attend." Without waiting for his reply, she turned her focus to the man beside him and nodded. "Sir Simon."

With a warm smile Simon acknowledged her leavetaking.

Taryn left the dais and headed abovestairs. Her words of reproach to Garret had contained as much truth as teasing. With winter's approach there were many tasks which needed to be undertaken.

Daily now the air was filled with the song of the woodcutter's ax. Not only did stores of wood need to be laid in for the dark and cold months ahead, but oak bark must be brought down from the forest as well, to be added to firechips swept from the woodshed and old rushes cleared off from the hall floor—for soon the skies over Jaune would be clouded with the smoke of drying fires as meat was cured for winter keeping.

That responsibility was Richard's, as well as the manor's other needs for the changing of seasons: the preparation of the outbuildings against rough weather, the purchase of winter supplies, and the storage of the harvest. Once grazing ceased, livestock which was not to be wintered over and fed must either be sold off into the towns or slaughtered.

Taryn's responsibility was solely for the keep. This day she planned to oversee the cleaning of the tower structure's numerous fireplaces. Each would be swept, since winter's constant fires might set a dirty chimney alight.

Perhaps it was the anticipation of the black soot and ash inevitably to be breathed in that made her step suddenly falter. She leaned weakly against the stairwell wall and struggled to overcome an all too familiar wave of nausea. For a week now she had experienced this same sensation. The first time she had simply attributed the ill feeling to something she had eaten. But as the dizziness and nausea continued to be nearly daily occurrences, she found that excuse less plausible.

More reasonable was the possibility she dared not yet fully grasp. She knew little of such things, and her monthly rhythms were not regular. Still, for the past few days she had entertained a private hope—that the cause for these spells might be a joyous one.

"My lady, are you all right?"

Taryn smiled in apprehensive recognition of the feminine voice. "Aye, Maite. I . . . I . . . just stumbled. I think I must have stepped on the hem of my gown."

"You should take more care. These stairs are not well lighted."

Despite the woman's even reply, Taryn sensed that her own explanation had not been believed. Immediately she regretted the lie, and for a moment she considered confiding in the petite figure now poised on the step below her. But this was not the place.

She turned and headed up the stairs. By the time she had mounted the fourth floor landing, her thoughts were only of reaching her chamber. The faintness had not passed, and she felt certain she would collapse if she did not sit for a moment.

With Maite at her heel, she opened the door and stumbled toward the settle before the hearth.

Maite looked at her strangely. "Are you certain you are all right, lady?"

Taryn nodded and tried to draw a steadying breath. "Normally it does not last so long."

"Normally? Then this has happened before?" With more than concern narrowing her eyes, the woman scrutinized her. "For how long?"

Seeing the glint of suspicion turn suddenly bright, Taryn lowered her face. "For a week now. I . . . I think I may be with child," she confessed softly.

With her admission finally made, she felt a nervous giddiness and sense of elation. Not until this moment had she put the hope into words. She felt somehow embarrassed. It was a normal enough occurrence when a wife lay with her husband, but was it too soon? They had been married only five months, and reconciled barely four.

She remembered the joking comments Moira and the other serving women at Wynshire had once made when one of their own made a similar announcement only a few months after marrying. "Poking you right regular, is he?" they had chortled, reveling in the poor girl's crimson color and stammered reply before embracing her warmly.

Thinking back upon that embrace and the resultant squeals of delight and well wishes, Taryn was now confused at Maite's silent pursing of her lips.

"*He* does not know." Her question was more a statement of fact.

"Nay," Taryn replied, feeling suddenly more hurt than confused by the woman's unemotional response. "I . . . I wanted to wait until I was absolutely certain."

"That is wise." Maite nodded as if to herself. Then sensing or perhaps seeing Taryn's disappointment, she offered a slight smile. "How far along are you?"

At first Taryn did not understand the question. "Far along? Oh! Well . . . I am not sure. I think a month or two."

Again the woman nodded. "Then we must wait another month to be sure."

"I should tell him then?"

Maite's face took on the strangest of expressions. "Nay," she answered almost sharply, though she then hesitated to make amends for her curtness. "What I mean to say is . . . lady, the seed often does not plant itself firmly in the womb. In the first three or four months the babe can be lost very easily. Ofttimes in fact, a woman will not even know that she is carrying a child when it is lost—especially when 'tis the first breeding."

"I see," Taryn murmured, suddenly frightened by the warning. She drew another deep breath. "Then we shall wait until I am sure the seed is planted, and planted firmly. *Then* I may tell him?"

Maite hesitated. "Men are different than women, lady."

"This I have noticed." Taryn laughed uneasily. Maite's odd behavior was upsetting her more than she wanted to admit.

"The differences are more than what can be seen, lady," she chastised gently. "There are differences beneath the surface, differences in how they think and regard certain things. Childbirth is one. As they are not the ones to bear a child, they can be impatient. Though they know that a seed must grow to fruition, once a woman announces that she carries a man's child, he expects the babe to pop out in short order. He grows weary of waiting, especially when 'tis months before he can see any evidence of the life he has sown. A woman such as you, who has not yet borne a child, and who is wide of hip, may not swell out until the fifth month."

Taryn listened carefully to what Maite was telling her. Moira had always made a point of keeping such knowledge from her, believing it was unseemly for a chaste maid to know about such matters.

"'Twould, therefore, be best if you waited until then to tell him, and even then the months he must wait will seem interminable."

Taryn nodded. Certainly in having delivered both Garret and his father into the world the woman possessed the knowledge and experience to know of what she spoke. She accepted Maite's reasoning. And yet she felt certain there was more . . .

Suddenly a thought came to her. "Maite, he will be pleased to learn I carry his child, will he not?"

Maite smiled gently. "Aye, lady. He will be pleased, but . . . but it may also bring back painful memories. For that you should be prepared."

"Memories? What sort of memories?"

"Of another child. One that was lost."

Taryn looked at her. "His child?" Thoughts swirled in her mind with such speed she could not at first grasp hold of them. "Clarissa's child? Is that why you caution me to wait before I tell him? Did Clarissa lose a child in the first months—the seed you spoke of not firmly planted?"

"Nay." Maite's voice was strained and hushed, as if some force were somehow strangling her.

"But you said—"

"I know what I said. And mayhap I should not have said it." She looked away for a moment. "But 'tis time you learned of it. Garret has told you about Clarissa—and the night she left?"

Taryn nodded, feeling her own throat tighten so that she could not reply in words at first. "He . . . he took her to the convent, ne'er to see her again. She died there six months later by her own hand."

"Aye."

"Was it there she lost the child? For that loss did she take her life in grief?"

"'Twas there that the child died, aye. And mayhap in grief she did take her life. But the child was not lost—'twas murdered."

Taryn felt the room swim before her. Though she was seated she gripped the arm of the settle and bent her head, fearing otherwise she would fall into the darkness rising to swallow her. "What?" she whispered. "Who? Who would have killed—"

"Clarissa." Maite's voice was like death's own knell.

Weakly Taryn lifted her eyes, feeling the darkness begin to subside. "Clarissa? How? *Why?*"

Maite stepped closer to her. "At Jaune no one knows of this but Garret and I. What I tell you now must stay in this room. Do you understand?"

Taryn nodded, and in a flat, emotionless voice the woman began her tale.

"No one knew Clarissa was with child. In her inexperience and ignorance she might not have known it either at first. At any rate, she did manage to conceal her condition from the nuns. 'Twould not have been difficult to do. She remained in her chamber, ne'er leaving, even to take meals. She took to wearing the habit of the order, and beneath its folds her secret was well hidden—and safe, until one night. Alone there in her cell, she gave birth. Only God can know what went on in her tortured mind, what led her to do what she did. Mayhap she thought it to be His will, a sacrifice to Him like Abraham of old."

Maite's voice grew softer until Taryn had to strain to hear it.

"She strangled the child, probably in its first minutes of life, for when 'twas found with her rosary about its tiny neck, 'twas still covered in blood."

"Dear Mother of God!" Taryn sobbed.

Her outcry evoked no reaction from Maite. She continued almost trancelike, and Taryn realized the depth of the old woman's pain. To hesitate, even for an instant, in the telling of her tale would be to succumb and drown in the anguish of the past.

"She dragged herself from her cell, went up to the chapel's bell tower, and threw herself from it. Mayhap her reason returned, and she could not live with the knowledge of what she had done."

Taryn wept softly, as Maite still continued. "The nuns buried her and her child in the convent courtyard and then sent word to Garret. In the same breath he learned of his son's life . . . and death." Maite's voice finally cracked with emotion, yet she went on. "I wanted him to bring his son back to Jaune, to give him a name and to bury him at what should have been his home. He refused, and since that conversation he has ne'er spoken to me of it. But I know it haunts him—the guilt. If he had not gone to her that night, she might not have lost her mind. He would not have had to take her away. She would have been here. We would have known she carried his child, and when he was born, he might have lived."

Maite paused. For several moments she stood in silence, as though wrestling with the fingers of pain tight around her throat and her heart. "Do you understand now, why 'twould be best not to tell him that you carry his child? He will be reminded of the past and may even fear God will see fit to take away this child as well. Waiting a few more months until the most tenuous time has passed may mercifully spare him pain should you be unable to carry the child now growing within your womb."

"But what if the child is lost later—after he learns of it?" Taryn raised her tear-filled eyes.

"If you carry to Christmas, we shall know the seed is healthy—as will be the child you birth in the spring."

"'Tis so far off," Taryn murmured. "Winter is not yet arrived, and we speak of spring!"

"The time of rebirth," Maite reminded her with a reassuring smile that at last revealed a glimpse of her joy. "You will see, lady, the time will pass quickly."

More for the old woman's sake than her own, Taryn returned a tenuous smile. But the confidence she forced was false. How could she carry this knowledge, yet continue in her daily life as if nothing had changed? Garret would know something was wrong; she was not so skilled in concealing her emotions. Still, what other choice was left her? At all cost she must keep this secret. She could only pray that Maite were right, that the time *would* pass quickly.

That night as she sat at Garret's side for the evening meal, she was reserved, but adequately composed. Garret gave no indication of having marked a strangeness in her behavior, and when they retired abovestairs she found her confidence increased.

As was his nightly habit, he stepped to the chamber's window and opened its wooden shutters. Goblet in hand, he watched as the guards upon the battlements took up their positions.

Taryn undressed and donned a bed robe. Sitting before her table and mirror, she unbound her braided hair from the coil in which she now, as a married woman, wore the plaits.

Involved in her task, she did not hear Garret close the shutters and step away from the window. He came up behind her noiselessly. She saw the movement in the mirror just as she felt his hands come to rest upon her shoulders.

He caressed the crook of her neck. "You are very quiet tonight."

Taryn forced herself to turn slowly, her gaze travelling his bare torso to his face. "I am only tired." She offered a teasing smile. "But not too . . ." Hoping to dissuade him from further questions, she let her fingertips trace the narrow line of hair running from his chest to his waist.

Garret frowned and stilled her hand. "What I see in your eyes has naught to do with weariness. Give me your honesty, Taryn. Surely, you did not take this morning's teasing to heart?"

"Of course not!" She laughed in immediate relief—it was to that he attributed her silence! "Over these last months I have grown very used to the both of you, and your antics."

He lifted her to a standing position and let the knuckle of his forefinger tenderly stroke her cheek.

She knew the glint in his eye, the gentle, yet firm insistence in his touch, and inwardly trembled at it.

"Then what?"

"Naught," she murmured, staring past him to the wall behind him.

"Taryn . . ."

His voice was uncompromising, and as she transferred her gaze to his face, she found him staring down at her. His expression was suddenly dark and unfathomable.

"I will have an answer," he stated, with a calm she had learned was deceptive.

"It . . . it makes me . . . uneasy—when I hear you question this reconciliation between Henry and Thomas. It makes me fear that there are troubled times ahead."

His soft laughter contained both amusement and relief. "That is why politics are best left to men. We follow the course we know to be true, regardless of such irrational and emotional thoughts." Clearly appeased, he laid his mouth to hers and kissed her. "I think, madam, that we should turn your thoughts to those more womanly—and wifely—in nature."

Taryn nodded and happily surrendered herself to the strength of his arms. He lifted her, turned and was headed toward the bed when a hesitant yet persistent knocking sounded at the door.

With her still in his arms he faced the portal. "If I deem this could have waited, by God you will have wished you had!" he threatened to the nameless, and as yet voiceless, person beyond the oaken planks. "Enter!"

Taryn struggled to escape his embrace. Reluctantly he set her down as the door opened. His icy gaze directed toward the unwelcome intruder required the accompaniment of no words.

"Your pardon, my lord." Richard took a reluctant step into the chamber and bowed.

"This had better be important."

"I would not disturb you elsewise. It cannot wait until morning, my lord."

Impatiently Garret raked his fingers through his hair. "Speak."

As if torn by his need to obey and the desire to be courteous, Richard hastily looked to Taryn. "Lady, my apologies."

Taryn drew the folds of her bed robe closer to her. "'Tis quite all right, Richard." Then, sure that the man's discomfort exceeded her own, she bestowed upon him a reassuring smile.

Richard turned his attention to Garret. "A letter from His Majesty has just arrived by messenger."

"And?"

"His feud with Becket has resumed, my lord. The reconciliation, if 'tis not already dead, is in grave danger."

What Taryn saw in Garret's eyes surprised her. She

would have expected complacent satisfaction; his suspicions and doubts these past months had been proven true. She saw instead disappointment and regret.

"Does Henry say what happened?"

Richard nodded. "By trickery the Archbishop attempted to gain the Kiss of Peace."

"I knew it!" Garret growled. "I knew he could not let it lie. How? When?"

"Last week, whilst Henry was in Tours for a conference with Count Theobald of Blois. Thomas followed him to Castle Amboise where the meeting with Theobald was to take place. He entered the chapel just as Mass was about to begin. His plan was surely to step forward at that point in the Mass where by custom Henry should bestow a kiss on the most important member of the congregation. Clearly he figured that would be himself. He would thereby obtain what Henry has refused to give. However, the royal chaplain was able to see ahead, and proposed to Henry that he give the order for the priest to say instead a Mass of Requiem."

"In which the words 'May the Peace of the Lord be with you always' are not said—hence the Kiss is not given." Garret chuckled softly. "I knew Nigel was clever . . . and self-serving. After all, he holds one of the Archbishops's prebends. The inevitable loss of that stipend, were this reconciliation to take place and restitutions carried out in full, surely sharpened his wits. So, how did this end?"

"When the Mass finished, Thomas approached Henry and directly begged him to grant the Kiss. Henry answered that 'twas not a suitable occasion. He said instead that he might grant it later on, at some festival when there would be great men aplenty present to bear witness to it. Thomas did not take his refusal well. Some say they heard him state that Henry is still his foe. He left Amboise immediately for Sens and is now preparing to cross to England without waiting for his king."

Richard scanned the parchment he held as if to make

certain he had omitted no detail. "Henry concludes his letter with a summons. You are, my lord, henceforth ordered immediately to Normandy to offer counsel."

"Normandy?" The word escaped Taryn's lips before she could stop it. "For how long?"

Garret and Richard exchanged furtive looks not lost to her. Then, with a barely discernible shake of his head, Garret warned his steward against reply. "See to the preparations. I will leave at first light."

"And your escort?"

"Twenty men."

"Shall I inform Simon—that he might choose those to accompany you both?"

"Aye, have Simon select the men, but inform him that he is to remain here."

This declaration stunned Taryn, as it did Richard.

"My lord?" he asked, arching a brow.

"You heard me, Richard. Simon shall remain at Jaune. In my absence Arundel is vulnerable. There is not a more qualified and skilled knight in my service, nor any man I trust more to protect what is mine. I have entrusted d'Orléon with my life, now I do so with that which I value far more."

Taryn wondered at the underlying meaning of Garret's words. Was she to be counted among the possessions he valued?

Lost in her thoughts, she neither heard Richard's withdrawal nor Garret's approach. Resuming what had been interrupted, he drew her into his embrace. "Will you miss me?" he teased, his lips seeking hers.

She nodded wordlessly, determined not to betray her anxiety over his leaving. He could not refuse a summons from his king. "We . . . we should go to bed. You must rest for your journey."

"Forsooth, bed *is* my goal, madam," he responded, his husky whisper sending a quickening sensation through her as he swept her up into his arms, "but not for the purpose of rest."

Chapter Twenty-Three

Taryn shivered and drew tighter the fur-lined cloak draped about her. At her back the cold, biting November wind beat the balcony doors against the keep's stone wall with a rhythmic, crashing force. The fierceness of the gale stung her eyes and she blinked, releasing warm tears which instantly turned icy upon her cheeks. She should go inside, into the comfort and warmth of the wool room and its blazing fire.

Yet she did not move. Her focus remained upon the horizon lined with trees long decloaked of their autumn foliage of color. Through the bare, brittle branches the gray sky gave promise of the first snow—and nothing else.

She knew the earth was now too hard-packed by frost to yield the rising clouds of dust which in summer would indicate approaching riders. Still, as she had since Garret's departure a month ago, she watched for a sign of his return: a flash of movement, a glimpse of color, or a fleeing deer, startled by man's entrance into its forest domain. But there was nothing, only the heavy, lifeless sky and the dead trees.

A sudden noise from within the chamber drew the attention of the dog standing at her side. Becket pricked his ears and turned his head toward the open doors, but did not move from his stance at her side.

Taryn smiled. Unless she gave the order, the bay hound would remain where he stood. Unlike his master's injuries, Becket's had left him impaired. His easy, loping gait was now marked with a limp. With difficulty he went from a standing to a lying position, and once down, rose only upon command. His hunting days were over, and Garret had overridden her decree that once recovered the dog would return downstairs.

Having grown attached to the animal, she indulged her husband's soft-heartedness, failing to point out that if the dog's condition were so limiting he should be unable to ascend the flights of stairs with the ease with which he did. Indeed, Becket now had run of the entire keep, though since Garret's departure he had remained constantly at Taryn's side. He followed her in the overseeing of her household tasks and lay at her feet whenever she was seated, whether at the high table for meals or at her loom. And as the nights had grown colder, he had abandoned his sleeping place on the floor beside her bed in favor of the bed itself—a habit that she had instructed him would cease once his master returned.

The dog turned his eyes to her and wagged his tail.

"Aye," she answered. "I hear the knocking. We have visitors." With a wave of her hand she gave the command he awaited, and followed him into the room.

The three men waiting respectfully just within the doorway bowed nearly in unison at her entrance.

"My door was closed," she stated tersely.

"The fault is mine, lady," Simon replied. "You did not answer the knock."

"I did not hear it," she lied.

"Forsooth, 'twas drowned out then by the wind's howling." Simon regarded her with an amused expression.

Self-consciously Taryn brushed her fingertips beneath her eyes, sure even as she did so the precaution was too late. Simon had seen her tears. "What did you want?" she asked brusquely, turning to Richard.

The steward gestured to the man standing between himself and Simon. "This is Sir Robert, lady. He has just arrived with news of Lord Garret."

"Garret?" Taryn focused on the knight. "What news have you? Is my husband well? Is he safe?"

"Aye, lady. Well and safe, and back in England."

"Thank God," she murmured. "But why does he not return with you?"

"Of this I can say naught, lady." The man bowed and offered her an encouraging smile. "However, Lord Garret bids you greeting and extends to you his hope that in a fortnight's time he will be again in your presence."

"Where is he now?"

"I can say only that he is under his king's orders. But his thoughts are of you, lady."

Simon stepped forward. "Lady, the mood of things may not permit Lord Garret to offer more in this message."

"Of course," she nodded numbly, her old fears rising anew. For a month Jaune had had no news at all of the events taking place upon the Continent. At least now she knew Garret was returned. "Richard, would you see to Sir Robert? I am sure after his journey he must be wanting of a tankard of stout ale and a hot meal."

"Thank you, lady." The man bowed in gratitude, and for the first time Taryn was aware of the lines of fatigue etched upon his face. Clearly he had ridden long and hard to deliver his message, and in foul weather, too.

"I offer you my thanks, Sir Robert, for having brought to me this word of my husband. Now, let me delay you no further from partaking of Jaune's hospitality."

The man flashed a grateful smile. "Lord Garret was right. His lady wife is most gentle and gracious."

Taryn swallowed the lump in her throat evoked by the man's compliment and her own emotions. That Garret's retainer should be here—and not Garret himself—tugged at the fringes of the anxiety which had steadily grown and strengthened with the weeks of his absence.

Garret's greatest value to his king lay in his battlefield experience. It did not require great insight or a knowledge of politics to know why he was not yet returned. Henry, if he did not already anticipate civil war, was at least preparing for it.

Sir Robert bowed and turned to leave. Richard followed.

Simon, however, made no move to exit, even when Richard paused at the doorway and looked back at him questioningly.

Taryn caught the slight flicker of reproof in the steward's eyes. She knew he felt that Simon often overstepped his position. He disapproved, perhaps even resented the trust and faith Garret had placed in the knight after such a short acquaintance.

"Simon, would you remain a moment?" Though she told herself she made the request solely to ease the tension between the two men, she suspected her underlying motive. Her position as Arundel's countess did not afford her the luxury of weakness, for in their lord's absence Jaune's people looked to her for strength. She must portray only bravery and stoic confidence, but with Simon she did not have to sustain the lie, nor did she need to. With him she felt a sense of comfort, and it was from that and his own strength that she drew hers.

After Garret's accident, she had not had the need of Simon's friendship and acceptance, so fulfilling was her new relationship with her husband. Without her conscious perception, her friendship with the dark man had waned. Now that she was again alone, he was once again her mainstay—anticipating her emotional needs almost before she was cognizant of them herself.

"Lady?"

"I am worried," she blurted. "I sense ill times approaching, and I fear what shall come to pass." She turned to go back onto the balcony .There her tears could at least be attributed to the cold and wind, and not her womanly weakness and faint-heartedness.

She heard Simon follow, yet could not bring herself to look at him.

She felt him set around her shoulders the marten skin which had lain upon his own. Through her cloak she felt the added weight and absorbed the warmth of his body still contained in the garment. She nuzzled the fur against her cheek. "I'm sorry," she whispered, turning to look up at him. "I am a coward."

"I think not." The gentlest of smiles appeared and he stepped closer, his hand reaching out to pluck from her hair a wind-blown leaf.

It was all the impetus she needed. As her weakness sought his strength, she fell into his embrace, her head coming to rest upon his chest. He raised the fur over her head to shield her face from the wind. Enveloped by his strength and warmth, and sheltered by the marten skin, she wept.

Simon let his arms fall to his sides. The feel of her against him had sent a rush of emotion through him for which he was unprepared. Overpowered, he set his head back and gulped a lungful of air. He could not have met her eyes had she lifted them.

His head was reeling, his heart aching as he strove with cold logic to crush the madness that had come upon him. She had stepped into his arms only to seek the comforting embrace of a friend. Whatever love she felt for him was the love for a brother. No more. Thoughts of one man only filled her mind and agonized her soul. Save for the purposes of warmth and support, she had forgotten the one who now comforted her. Were she to know or guess what lay buried in his heart, she would be appalled.

He looked down at her. Surely for one moment he could know the joy of holding her? But the arms he would raise were like dead weights. It was Garret whom she loved; Garret who had entrusted her to him in faith and friendship. To touch her suddenly seemed a profanation. Not even to know the torturing bliss of clasping her, could he betray that trust. The calm he had lost came back, and gently he set her from him.

Below the balcony, crossing the inner bailey, a solitary figure paused. Richard looked up at the dark platform jutting out from the keep's walls. Through the balustrade of enclosing stone columns he saw two shadowy forms blend into one.

Suspicion, like a seed bursting from its pod, took flight upon the wind.

In the great hall's massive fireplace, flames blazed up merrily. Spaced between the chairs and gaming boards which were set in a semi-circle before the hearth, a dozen hounds dozed in the fire's warmth, as oblivious to the raging snow storm beyond the keep's walls as were Jaune's human denizens. Better than a week had passed since their lord had sent word of his return to England. It was now December. Winter had arrived, and with it the long and cold nights which drove even those with no interest in gaming to linger in the hall after the evening meal had ended.

With a watchful eye upon her opponent's hand poised above his bishop, Taryn slipped her feet under Becket's belly.

Immediately the dog lifted his head in sleepy protest.

"If you are going to lie at my feet, you might as well prove useful," she chided the animal affectionately as she watched the onyx bishop move diagonally to take a strategically placed ivory pawn.

"I fear he fancies himself still a great lord's prized hunting dog and not a lady's footwarmer." Laughing, the man seated across the chessboard from her picked up her pawn and set it beside those pieces already lost.

Taryn grimaced at Simon's taunting smile which promised his imminent victory. "'Tis hardly chivalrous to flaunt your impending triumph, Sir Knight. Would you not agree, Richard?" Of late Jaune's steward had been rather quiet and sullen. How the poor man seemed to suffer under the inactivity of winter! In hopes of drawing him into their conversation, she now leaned forward in her chair and sought to catch his eye.

Pondering his own backgammon game, Richard did not bother to look up. "I think there have been changes about which Lord Garret will not be pleased," he grumbled.

Taryn's surprised gaze collided with Simon's. She knew he sensed the same rancor as she; both Richard's tone and words had contained more than a little sarcasm. "What do you mean, Richard?" she asked curtly.

Richard looked up. A dull red stain of uneasiness was creeping into his face, and though he laughed, it was a forced laugh. "Lord Garret may well be furious, lady, when he sees to what his dog has been reduced."

Almost as if he understood what had been said about him, Becket lumbered to his feet. Then his entire body went rigid, from his pricked ears to the hair rising upon his back.

"I think Becket has taken offense at your disparagement, Richard." Simon grinned. "Look with what pride he now holds himself."

"Nay," Taryn whispered, her speech muted by the sudden and frantic beating of her heart which echoed in her ears. "'Tis something else. I have seen that stance . . ." She followed the direction of the dog's attention to the keep's doors. Stumbling to her feet, she stared at the closed twin portals and gasped in startled fright as the one on the right suddenly opened, flung wide by the force of the outside wind. At first the doorway was filled only with a flurry of snow, white against the darkness of the night. Then, slowly, through the swirling flakes, a figure emerged.

Forgetting the chessboard in her path, Taryn took a faltering step forward. Oblivious to the toppling pieces and the sudden stinging pain in her shin, she stared at the man who had turned his back to the room in order to close the door. He was wrapped head to foot in a snow-covered cloak of fur, yet to her and to the dog quivering at her side, his identity was clear. The set of his wide shoulders, the air of absolute possession as he stepped forward, as though claiming what was his . . .

"Garret!" The whispered cry left her lips the instant a shrill and familiar whistle left his. Becket bounded forward with no trace of limp in his gait. Though she wanted to, Taryn dared not let herself display the joyful abandon of the dog. She forced herself to remain where she stood, to wait as a dutiful wife should for her husband's acknowledgment.

His stride unhurried, his mien one of utter control, he made his way toward the hearth. A shiver raced down her spine as she realized how hauntingly reminiscent this homecoming was of the first time she had seen him. Indeed, she had forgotten the handsomeness of his chiseled features and the look of power about him, power granted to the title but exercised by the man.

And then he was nearly within arm's length. He had flung aside the furred skin and was standing before her, tugging off his mail coif. As was his wont, his celadon stare revealed no trace of his thoughts. He pulled the leather binding from his hair, and the dark waves, longer than she remembered, fell free—well past his shoulders. His unshaven face at last exhibited a smile.

The man at her side immediately took a step backward, thereby allowing Richard to be the first to greet his lord. Once welcomed by Jaune's steward, Garret turned to Simon. As brothers, each clasped the other's forearm.

"'Tis a fine night you picked for your return, my lord," Simon remarked, the scar on his face crooked by the wide smile he offered.

"Aye, the hounds of Hell would not venture forth upon such a night as this," Garret agreed as he finally allowed his focus to settle upon Taryn. He had been aware of her presence from the instant he had entered the hall, yet had purposely delayed greeting her. He had told himself he did so because he was a man disinclined to public displays; theirs should be a private exchange. With this one look at her, though, the truth broke through that lie like a battering ram through a door of rotted planks. He did not know *how* to greet her.

She was his wife, aye. But the feeling went beyond obligation and responsibility. Away from her, his every idle moment had been filled with thoughts of her. Other women had held no interest for him. At Henry's court in Normandy, as had been the case before in London, there had been no shortage of seductive offers, offers which at another time would have inflamed his senses and awakened his lust. He need not have remained celibate, but had chosen to, realizing the meaning of that choice. He had found more pleasure with his wife than he had ever found with the likes of Geneviève. In the four months of his convalescence, he had taught her the intimacies of men and women, finding not only a renewed delight but a greater joy in lovemaking than he had ever believed possible.

There, he had admitted it! No longer did he desire any woman but her. He had missed her greatly, but had she felt a like sentiment? Clearly she looked also to be at a loss for a response. Nervously she stood, only paces from him, making no move either to speak or come forward.

A frown drifted into his expression. Might his absence have given her cause or opportunity to examine their relationship? In the face of their separation, the love she had professed for him might even have fled. In a woman's eyes, could two months be too long a time for a man to be away from his home and wife?

"Yours is a poor welcome, wife, for a husband gone so long," he stated quietly.

She blushed fiercely, a light previously absent in her eyes appearing. Responding to the nature of his greeting, she offered a quick retort. "Had you given us warning, husband, I would have practiced womanly hysterics in advance. Then I might have greeted you with a proper show of tears, mayhap a swoon as well upon first sight of your face."

Garret laughed. "I see that winter's confinement has done naught to blunt your tongue, madam. 'Tis reassuring indeed to know the wife I left has not changed in my absence."

Richard cleared his throat. "My lord, what news have you?"

"None that is good," Garret replied. He turned his gaze from Taryn and beckoned forward one of his squires. "Help me out of this mail."

As the youth hastened to unfasten the *hauberk's* buckles and leather bindings, Taryn summoned a passing serving maid. "Bring a cup of warmed wine for your lord, and a trencher as well."

She realized he must have heard her when, in drawing the coat of mail over his head, he paused to grin at her. "That will satisfy two of my needs." Then, growing suddenly serious, he looked to the men awaiting his report. "Thomas Becket is back in Canterbury."

"We had heard," Richard replied.

Taryn's head snapped around, and she glared at Garret's steward in silent fury. Purposely this news had been kept from her, and no doubt with Simon's complicity. She redirected her glare to the knight, but her effort was wasted. Simon's attention remained upon Garret, who had resumed speaking.

"By the time I arrived in Normandy, Henry had already decided to allow Becket's return. I think he finally realized his power over him would be greater if the Archbishop were at Canterbury, and further from the Pope and no longer under the protection of Louis. Above all else, for the peace of England and the strengthening of his son's title, Henry needs Becket to perform the second coronation in the spring."

Spring. Taryn's heart hammered in her breast. But the significance of the date was unknown by the men. All attention was riveted upon Garret, now peeling off the wet leather tunic worn beneath his *hauberk*.

"Several days after my arrival in Normandy, Henry learned why Becket had lingered so long in Sens before continuing to Wissant on the coast. As it came to pass, he was waiting to receive from the Pope certain letters that he had requested. These would suspend the Archbishop of York and place the bishops of Salisbury and London under ban of excommunication for their part in the unsanctioned crowning. In granting him these papal bans, Alexander apparently authorized Becket to make use of them at his own discretion. They are still as yet unpublished. Thus, Henry decided I was to return to England and regain my men, whom I had left waiting in Dover. We were to intercept these letters with the help of the forces of Ranulf de Broc, Reginald de Warenne and Gervase, Sheriff of Kent."

"All bitter enemies of the Archbishop," Simon noted.

Taryn looked at him, surprised that in having been such a short time in England, the man should know so much about the players in this political struggle.

From the darting look Garret directed toward his vassal, it was clear the same thought had occurred to him. "My orders were to use these combined forces to place armed bands in all ports. As soon as Becket landed, his baggage was to be searched and the papal censures confiscated before they could be published."

He tossed the leather tunic aside. Dressed now only in woolen shirt and *chausses,* he stepped toward the fire, stretching his hands out toward its warmth. "Becket is naught if not a clever man, however. Somehow, he learned of the waiting forces and sent the letters to England by messenger the day before his own crossing. Then he sailed, not for the King's port of Dover, where I awaited him, but for Sandwich. Somehow, too, he allowed his change of destination to become known. According to Gervase and the others who stood in arms at the dock, a vast, cheering crowd awaited his arrival on shore. Many of the throng even rushed into the icy water to welcome him." He shook his head in dismay and frustration. "Obviously our forces could do naught against him. The next morning he set out for Canterbury upon a road lined with his adoring faithful. 'Twas said some prostrated themselves before him, or tore off their clothes to strew along the way—that he need not touch the frozen ground."

With a grimace of disgust Garret paused, drawing a breath before continuing. "With our mission failed, and fearing an uprising of the masses, Henry ordered all forces withdrawn."

"What of the letters?" Simon asked.

"You are not alone in your concern." Garret laughed dryly. "Upon learning of their existence Roger of York and the others crossed over to Normandy to complain to Henry. I've heard it said that their ship actually passed Becket's own. But to answer your question, as yet, no attempt has been made to publish them. Nonetheless, as long as Becket has them, I fear Henry shall have little choice but to allow him some latitude. There are too many who support him, and not just the peasants. Many barons also side with him for they believe in doing so they side with God."

"Not to mention those who would use this rift to their own benefit," Simon murmured softly.

Again Garret looked at him strangely, yet merely nodded in agreement. "At all cost Henry must preserve peace and unity, and his son's title. Fortunately, Becket seems thus far content to remain quietly in Canterbury."

Apparently now warmed sufficiently, he moved away from the fire and settled himself into the closest chair. Though he waved aside the trencher of food, he did accept the goblet of wine, downing the cup's contents in a single draught before speaking again. "Having no immediate need for my services, Henry released my forces to return to Jaune, at least for the time being." Then, with his gaze fixed solely upon Taryn, he smiled. "Hence, I am home."

Distracted to find herself now the sole object of his

attention, she nervously took her seat in a chair which faced his own. "If the venison was not to your liking, I could have something else prepared. You must be hungry."

He shook his head and smiled, and with a start she realized that she heard his thoughts as clearly as if he had spoken aloud. *My hunger is not for food.* However, out of respect for the men in whose hands he had left the running and safety of Jaune, and who now waited to make their reports, he must deny himself that fulfillment—at least for a few moments longer.

She looked away hastily, and still felt his gaze upon her. The knowledge of his desire incited her own, and she stirred uneasily in her chair. Like a new bride's, her heart pounded at the thought of his lovemaking. Surely what was so apparent to her must be felt by every person in the hall—his silent arousal and her aching anticipation? As casually as she could manage, she rose to her feet. "Your leave, my lord?"

The smile he bestowed upon her was as intimate as a kiss. "I shall join you . . . soon," he promised, the perfunctory tone of his voice belied by the double meaning of his words and the lust in his eyes.

Garret kept his promise. The cold bed had scarcely warmed with her body's heat when she heard his entrance into their chamber. With the curtains drawn against drafts she could not view the scene, so concentrated instead upon conjuring a mental picture from the sounds she heard: the thudding of boots falling to the floor, chain mail clattering to a like destination, and the familiar clicking of Becket's nails wherever rugs gave way to stone.

As she expected, the dog headed straight toward the bed. He poked his head through the slit of an opening in the curtains and laid his head upon the extra coverlet folded at the foot. "Nay," she whispered sternly, waving him down as he set one tentative paw upon the mattress. "This night you sleep on the floor."

"I scarcely think so, madam," Garret answered, pulling open the bed curtains. Already stripped to the waist and working to unfasten the breech string at his waist, he presented the very essence of virility. Strength rippled from every corded muscle shining bronze in the firelight. And if she had thought to have seen lust's glow in his eyes downstairs, what she saw now was the full blaze of passion.

"I . . . I did not mean you," she stammered, unable to pull her gaze from him. "'Twas Becket," she finished weakly.

He did not seem to have heard her. He reached out and, without warning, yanked the covers down. For an unnerving moment he only stared, and then one knee came down on the bed. His long hair fell forward across his shoulders as he leaned toward her. "Tonight I reclaim what is mine."

She didn't know if he meant his bed or her body, and she didn't care. If possible, the deep timbre of his voice had stimulated her even more. He could take her at this moment, and she would be ready.

And that was exactly what he intended, for without bothering to finish undressing, he climbed atop her.

Bearing out his unspoken desire, his mouth sought hers hungrily. He positioned himself above her and parted her thighs with his knee. He fumbled with his clothing for an instant and was inside her the next. By his third thrust she had matched his rhythm, but not his urgency. He seemed to realize as much. To aid her and to bring her with him to the edge, he slipped his hand back between their bodies. His skillful fingers instantly plunged her into a sea of stimulation. Higher and higher he brought her, until with one final thrust the heated wave crested. From far away she heard his low groan. For the longest time he remained within her, shifting his weight only slightly to allow himself access to her breast.

"For two months I have thought of this," he murmured, lowering his mouth to tease the still peaked bud. "I thought to have memorized every inch of you, and yet . . ." His hand slid down the length of her. "Clearly I have been gone too long—or my memory is enfeebled. Forsooth, I do not remember such softness." Then, with a moan she was sure was of pleasure, he brushed his lips across hers in a tender kiss and withdrew. Rolling on his side, he pulled her to him.

Taryn held her breath and waited for him to say more. Despite her languid state she had the presence of mind to realize the significance of his comment. As long as she was clothed, the outward signs of her condition were not evident. Her belly was still flat. Nevertheless, Garret had noticed the slight thickening of her waist and the new rounded fullness to her breasts, though he appeared quite satisfied with his own explanation as to the cause. Should she tell him the truth and reveal her secret, or should she continue to let him think time and distance had served to alter his memory? By month's end she would be well into her fourth month. But surely there could be no harm in waiting until Christmas week to present him with what she hoped would be an occasion of joy. What more perfect time could there be, or better way to usher in the new year?

Content with her decision and this hopeful prediction of a future which appeared bright and happy, she snuggled closer to him, squirming until her backside lay nestled against his thigh and his arm had come around to encircle her waist.

"Lie still, wench," he murmured into her hair, "or you shall find yourself again sleeping with Becket—in *his* bed."

Taryn giggled. "Now that you are returned, he has no bed."

"My point exactly."

"'Tis time. Will you announce the toast, my lord?"

Taryn watched as Garret nodded in response to

Richard's prompting. Though he did not break off his conversation with Simon, he did indicate with a raised hand he would comply presently. She flashed the steward a grateful smile. Jaune's great hall was filled to capacity, its villeins and castlefolk alike having gathered for this celebration of the coming year. The din and confusion generated by the throng in attendance had worn upon her nerves. Besides, she was anxious to have her husband to herself at last. Weeks earlier when she had chosen the eve of the new year as the night she would share the news of the child she carried, she had certainly not pictured the scene she now viewed.

Unlike other lords, Garret d'Aubigny extended his hospitality not only on Christmas Day, as was customary, but also on the last day of December. Just as on Christmas Day, every man upon the manor had the right to four places at his lord's tables for members of his family. He was entitled also to white bread, had a trencher and mug, and was allowed to eat off a cloth. Afterwards he was permitted to sit drinking in the hall.

It was this drinking which had for her, and apparently for Richard as well, worn thin. The meal, which had commenced with a course of boar's head decorated with branches of rosemary and carried into the hall with great show and ceremony, had concluded long ago. Yet until Garret made the final toast, the evening would not be considered ended. No doubt the steward was keeping a running tally in his mind of the barrels of ale already consumed and had decided enough was enough.

Taryn glanced about the huge room bedecked for the occasion with boughs and garlands. Heathen emblems, Father's Gregory's voice whispered inside her head. She smiled. Indeed, Wynshire's priest would be no less offended at the reminders of earlier and pagan times than had been Jaune's village priest. Of the hundreds in residence upon the manor, he had been the only one to decline Garret's invitation. Even Simon, who had absented himself for several days after Garret's return, had kept his promise to be back in time for the celebration.

At least the new year was the reason given for the feasting. She was more convinced it was for the purpose of needling the village priest that Garret held the celebration. A body would have to be a fool not to note the blatant allusions to beliefs and traditions against which the Church had never ceased speaking. Yule logs burned in remembrance of those pre-Christian days when, during the darkest month of the year, the Saxon month of "yole," fires burned to keep away the demons who roamed forest and field to snatch up careless souls. Then too, the celebration of the advent of a new year was really a celebration of the imminent return of the sun, another pre-Christian tradition.

Garret's chair scraped upon the wooden platform, and despite the noise of the hall, the insignificant sound elicited almost immediate quiet. All eyes turned to their lord.

Garret raised his goblet. "To the successful consummation of the old year—and to the new."

"To the new!"

As the echoing cry resounded from all directions, Garret brought the goblet to his lips.

Of all who watched him, only Taryn was near enough, or intent enough, to note that he did not drink. She saw the hard, square line of his jaw become more so, and he set the cup down, its contents untouched. Seeking to discern the cause of his sudden displeasure, she followed his narrowed gaze to the keep's doors.

In spite of the cold, they stood open, allowing the press of humanity to spill out onto the steps and the bailey. Through the crowd two men emerged to push their way into the body of the hall.

Taryn recognized only one of the men as Garret's. The other wore colors unfamiliar to her, but clearly not to Garret. She could tell from the rigid set of his shoulders that he knew, the allegiance, if not the man. With no word of explanation to her or to the men at his table he stepped off the dais and headed toward the approaching pair.

She turned immediately to the man seated beside Garret's vacated chair. Simon's gaze was also riveted upon the encounter taking place among the lower tables. "Do you recognize those colors?" she asked.

Simon shook his head slightly.

Taryn was positive he lied. But why? She glanced back to the three men now deep in conversation, and her breath caught in her throat. Garret's face was white, and he was no longer speaking. Fear welled up within her. "Richard?"

Her plea to the man beside her was barely a whisper, yet he heard her and understood. "The de Brocs, lady. He wears the colors of Ranulf and Robert de Broc."

Her eyes darted back to Simon, and she suddenly felt as if her breath had been cut off completely. The look on Garret's face was mirrored in Simon's. *He knew!* a silent voice inside her screamed. He had recognized the colors and suspected the man's purpose even as Garret learned of it. But how? And what? What could bring that look of shock and horror?

"Lady." Richard's voice jolted her from frantic thoughts.

She looked at him, but he was staring straight ahead. She followed his gaze.

With the stranger at his side Garret approached the platform, stopping abruptly at the table nearest to it and directly to her left. Taryn knew the men seated there were his most battle seasoned knights. A rapid exchange ensued—orders issued, brief questions asked, and even briefer answers given—and then the entire table of better than forty men stumbled to their feet and hurried toward the keep's exit.

Only when the first had disappeared from his sight did Garret turn to face those seated upon the dais before him.

"Thomas Becket is dead—murdered."

Chapter Twenty-Four

"*Sweet Jesú,* help us!"

Taryn didn't know which of the men at the high table had made the divine entreaty. For an instant after the utterance they all sat in mute horror, deaf to the raucous sounds of the celebration around them, and then the questions came—fired like a volley of arrows at Garret and the man with him.

"How?"

"Who?"

"Where?"

Garret worked his mouth as if the words he must speak were bile. "Two days ago, in the cathedral at Canterbury."

A collective gasp greeted his response, and Richard voiced the common thought. "What manner of man would have the hardihood to violate the sanctity of the Mother Church of England—to commit such a crime?"

Garret's face darkened with the effort of keeping his emotions in check. "Four knights from the King's court."

Again a shocked silence descended. Regardless of the politics which had set Thomas Becket at odds with his king, his murder was a sacrilege.

"Did they act upon his orders?" Only Taryn dared to ask aloud the question they all considered, yet knew would be a tantamount to treason to utter, bound as they were to Henry by oaths of fealty.

Garret shook his head. "When I left him, he did not thirst for Becket's blood. Nay. I would give my life in the belief that these men did not act upon his command."

"By what names are these men known?" Simon interjected, sitting forward and focusing upon the messenger.

"Reginald FitzUrse, William de Tracy, Richard le Breton and Hugh de Moreville," came the nervous reply.

Only Taryn noted how Simon looked down at the mention of the last name. The eyes of the others at the table remained fixed upon the stranger.

"And how is it you came by this information?" Garret demanded.

"These four knights arrived at my lord's castle, Saltwood, the day before they committed the deed, having taken ship from four different ports in Normandy."

"Odd behavior for men who either acted upon the King's orders or who expected afterward to be rewarded," Simon remarked, studying the stranger. "Why did they come first to Saltwood? Did your lords not question the purpose for their arrival, as well as the secrecy?"

"Indeed." The stranger bristled at the thinly veiled accusation that the de Broc family might be considered involved in the Archbishop's murder. "The barons told them that they were come on the King's orders to arrest Becket. Ranulf and Robert de Broc will swear a holy oath they believed he was to be seized and brought to Henry for justice—no more."

Undaunted, Simon continued in his attack. "Did your lords ask to see the royal writ?"

"Nay," the man murmured uneasily, color draining from his face. "But they accompanied the barons to Canterbury the next morning to see that all was carried out in a seemly fashion. They could not have forseen

Thomas' flagrant disavowal of his duty to his king. When he was confronted, he refused to surrender the letters of censure and threatened to excommunicate the barons as well. And when told that the King demanded he leave England, he refused. The barons left but returned at the head of an armed force, hoping to frighten him into submission. Meanwhile, Thomas had taken refuge inside the cathedral."

"Who comprised this force?" Garret asked. Clearly he had realized the direction of Simon's questions and now sought to follow it.

The man reddened instantly. "We were . . . are . . . men whose fealty is sworn to the de Broc family."

"And so, *you* were there?" Garret replied, answering Simon's darting look toward him with a curt nod of understanding. "Continue."

The stranger swallowed loudly. "Only the four barons entered the cathedral. We were stationed outside to—to prevent the Archbishop's escape and to keep out the townsfolk, who were arriving to attend vespers."

"So you do not know what actually occurred inside?" Garret interrupted a second time.

"I know they intended only to seize him—not to kill him!" The man looked from Garret to Simon, then back at Garret. "You can ask any man who was there. He will say the same: Thomas was bent on martyrdom! He hurled insults at the four meant to madden them and refused to surrender—even when FitzUrse struck with his sword. 'Twas only a warning blow, which merely knocked the cap from his head."

Garret and Simon exchanged glances. "A trained swordsman could hardly miss a stationary target so completely," the latter admitted quietly.

Garret nodded in agreement. "He intended to take him prisoner."

"I don't understand." Though it was not her place to speak, Taryn could keep silent no longer. There could be no denying the common posture of thought and unspoken communication between Garret and his vassal. Each played off the other—like a succession of planned moves in a chess game. For that purpose Garret had no doubt brought the man forward to complete his report in Simon's presence. But this was not a chess game, and their strategy was one she could not follow.

Garret spoke to her in patient indulgence. "When a knight is captured in the field, the victor grasps his helm in a symbolic gesture of vanquishment. Then, if he has not the time to lead his prisoner to the rear, he removes the helm. A bareheaded man has no hope of escape amongst the swords of battle—hence he does not even try. Becket was a trained soldier. He would have understood FitzUrse's action."

The stranger nodded. "As I told you, he chose death and he courted it. Why else would he have continued to hurl insults at FitzUrse? Then he seized him by his *hauberk*, nearly throwing him to the ground. That was when the barons knew they would ne'er take him alive! In anger and desperation, they set upon him with their swords."

"How is it, man of de Broc, that you know so much about events to which you were not a direct witness?" Simon asked.

"Because I was a witness to the barons' report to Lord Ranulf," the man answered defensively.

"And we are to believe this account?" Simon pinned the stranger with a cold and penetrating stare. "We are to believe *you,* man of de Broc?"

"I would have no cause to lie, knight of Jaune. I have been sent here to tell the truth, and to ask the Earl of Arundel for aid in preventing an armed uprising of the people. You do not know the mood in Canterbury. The monks and townsfolk already call the Archbishop 'saint'—to the extent of having collected the blood and brains scattered on the pavement as holy relics! They throng into the cathedral to view where he fell. They even call for the overthrow of the King! Word of the tragedy has been sent to him, of course, along with documents seized from Thomas' private rooms. These will prove he plotted against his king. But by the time Henry can bring that proof to light, or refute the charges of murder, it may be too late. The present threat of civil war is real."

"What is real is that *your* lords may have had a hand in the murder of the highest churchman in England, and now, fearing the people's retaliation against them, they have called upon *my* lord, requesting that he come to their aid." Simon glared at the stranger, daring him to deny the charge.

"Rein in your outrage, Simon," Garret stated, his voice so low Taryn barely heard it. "I know you seek to protect me, but my aid is not rendered to the de Brocs. My men and I ride tonight in defense of my king and the integrity of his realm."

"Tonight?" Taryn gasped, realizing the meaning of his words and the cause for the withdrawal from the hall of his best men. "You will not wait at least until the morrow?"

"Nay. Tonight is already too late. There are many who will believe Henry ordered the murder and others who will not care if he did or not. This is the opportunity for which they have waited. They have cause for revolt and will do so, unless presented with a show of force and armed opposition."

"Which you intend to provide." Suddenly numb, she could barely form the words. "You are speaking of war!"

"I am speaking of loyalty." His tone brooked no further dissent. He turned his attention to Simon. "See that a hundred men are armed and supplied, and ready to ride as soon as possible. Once again I must ask you, friend, to remain."

"Allow me to go in your stead, my lord. Or at least at your side. This business reeks of conspiracy and teems with self-serving thieves who have put their own backs against a wall."

Garret shook with head. "I want you here. Until my return you are lord of Jaune, and your orders shall be obeyed as if they were mine." He looked at Richard as if challenging him to protest.

The steward did not, however, and Garret smiled in grim satisfaction. "Richard, keep the others inside the hall, ply them with drink and keep them content. I do not need panic."

Taryn sat in stunned silence. The sounds of the new year's celebration seemed suddenly deafening, and Garret's caution unnecessary. If any reaction had been wrought by the events of the last moments, it was merely curiosity. For none but those who had heard the conversation at the high table had the mood of the evening changed.

Garret left the hall, as did the others at the table. She did not know how long she sat there. Finally one of Garret's squires approached, telling her that Garret had requested she come out into the yard. She followed the youth who led her from the keep to the middle bailey, lit with torches and filled with horses and men. The confusion and tension in the air were palpable, and she shivered in response.

Mistaking the cause, the squire offered her his own mantle, gallantly laying it upon her shoulders as he pointed to where Garret stood, now dressed in the full panoply of war.

Catching sight of her, he immediately left the company of the half dozen men gathered about him and crossed the distance between them. He led her away from the worst of the noise and disorder of the rapidly assembling army.

"I am fated to leave you once more," he stated softly, pulling off his glove of mail to cup her chin in his hand. "Each time I find the leavetaking more difficult." But as his thumb wiped away a tear sliding down her cheek, he suddenly seemed at a loss. He stared down at her and appeared to search for the words to express his thoughts. "Taryn, I . . ."

But whatever he had begun to say was destined to remain unsaid. A shouting erupted from the center yard as a war horse trained to rear and strike out with spiked front hooves broke free of its handler. The ensuing mêlée of men scrambling to dodge the slashing spikes seized his focus momentarily. Turning back to her, he bent his head and kissed her hard, clasping her to him for a brief moment. And then she was alone, watching him as he strode to his waiting destrier and mounted. He raised his arm and a hundred men placed foot in stirrup.

Suddenly, from out of the darkness, a tiny figure emerged to stand at Taryn's side. "You did not tell him," Maite stated softly, her gaze also locked upon the departing column of mounted men.

"Nay," Taryn whispered, her voice breaking. "I did not."

In the weeks following Garret's departure news and rumor arrived at Jaune steadily. Whether carried by pilgrim, traveler or peddler, the information all conveyed a common theme of strengthening forces, clearly drawn sides and impending war.

All Christendom reeled in shock at the murder of Thomas Becket. In Normandy Henry vehemently proclaimed his innocence, stating that his knights had set out of their own accord to arrest the Archbishop. That their actions had ended in murder was not his doing; he had not condemned his old friend to death. Still, he realized few would believe he had not contrived the crime. With the immediate necessity of staving off excommunication for himself and interdiction on all his lands, he hastily went off to Ireland where no papal messengers could reach him. To his loyal followers in England he left the task of maintaining unity and putting down revolt. Entrusted with that command was his most favored tenant-in-chief: Garret d'Aubigny, Great Earl of Arundel.

At Jaune, Taryn languished in a state of constant foreboding. Despite Richard and Simon's efforts to shield her from worrisome or disturbing reports, she still learned of each small battle that broke out between baronies yet loyal to Henry and the growing armies of usurpers. Many of the uncommitted barons waited only for the Pope to act. Should Alexander indeed excommunicate Henry, they were prepared to accept the action as God's permission to seize more power for themselves.

The threat of outright civil war and fear for Garret's safety compelled her to irrational behavior. As her belly began to swell with the child he might never see, she refused to celebrate the new life. Beneath many layers of winter clothing, she continued to conceal her precious secret from all save Maite.

And still the weeks passed, turning into months. Henry remained in Ireland. He even launched an invasion of that "uncivilized" region, obstensibly for the cause of faith. He hoped to bring the Irish back into the fold of the Roman Church, thereby restoring the remnants of his reputation. Becket's murderers, in learning they would not be rewarded for their crime, had fled north, where Scotland's king had taken great pride in sheltering these criminals from the justice of his hated English overlord.

At last March arrived, and with that blustery month all news seemed to dry up. Taryn's condition had progressed to a point where the secret she guarded would surely soon be common knowledge. The movements of the child growing in her womb were strong, and she knew she carried a son. But her joy was bittersweet and the ironies acrid. The last heir of Arundel born had not lived to see his father; this time the father might not live to see the son. How could she take pleasure in the feel of the tiny being within her?

She grew ever more reclusive and saw no one but Maite. The old woman's concerns for her health and that of the child she nurtured revealed themselves in persistent nagging about her lack of appetite and refusal to leave her chamber to take exercise. Finally, in an attempt both to escape and appease her, Taryn took to walking in the garden each afternoon.

It was there on a particularly windy day that Simon found her.

"This is a strange place to seek refuge, lady," he stated gently. "'Tis barren and lifeless . . . melancholy. Might not the company of your weaving maids before a cheerful fire better lift your spirits?"

Taryn seated herself upon a cold stone bench and absently stroked the furred head which instantly found its way into her lap. Becket's soulful eyes looked up at her and he wagged his tail.

She smiled and directed her attention to the man before her. "'Tis the barrenness which attracts me. In spite of the apparent absence of life, I know it exists. Beneath the frozen ground it sleeps, awaiting the spring." Unconsciously her hand slipped from Becket's head to her belly.

The acton did not escape Simon's note. Could it be . . . Her voice prevented his thought from forming into the complete substance of words.

"My husband's obligation of military service to Henry is forty days, is it not?"

"I could not say for sure, lady. But, aye, forty days a year is the average length of service owed by a vassal to his lord." Simon guarded his expression. She would know as much without asking. The reason for her question had to lie elsewhere. "However," he offered, "that is the service required on summons to an offensive war. What has taken Lord Garret from Jaune is a defensive campaign. His requirement is bound to be greater than forty days."

"This year he has been gone thrice that amount," she stared flatly, the message in her unspoken words clear: Defensive action or not, he had been gone longer than was his obligation.

She raised her eyes to him, and he flinched, seeing their rimming of moisture. "Is it a choice of his making, Simon? Is war such a tantalizing mistress and peace such a boring wife?"

"Lady . . ." He sat down beside her and searched for an answer. The fates were cruel—to have put him in this position of defending to the woman he loved the actions of the man who possessed her heart. Might he not tell her she gave her love to a man unworthy? By his absences he was no husband to her. Indeed, were Simon in his place, he would not have left her side for a day. But to tell her these things would only hurt her, and betray the man he called friend. This path was one he could not pursue.

"You ask the wrong man," he answered, his mouth twisting into a wry smile that tugged at the scar upon his cheek. "I am a man who has lived his life mesmerized by that same mistress, following her from continent to continent and across the seas."

"Peace holds no lure for you? Nor home nor wife? Do you not grow weary of war?"

Though she asked the questions of him, he knew it was of another she wanted to know. He shrugged. "'Tis what I am." He traced the tight, raised line upon his face. "How I am."

"And your lord, my husband . . . is he also such a man?"

"The truth, lady?" Simon hesitated, torn by the selfishness of his thoughts. At last he replied. "A knight's honor is his most important possession. Above title and land, and even a woman's love, he holds it dear, for without honor he is not a man. What Lord Garret does, he does for honor, for the pledge he has made to his king."

"You defend him, and yet I have the sense you do not agree."

"He is a man of great honor, lady."

"And you are not?" She smiled with tender fondness. "I know differently."

"Nay, lady, you do not." His voice grew harsher as his emotions threatened to surface. "You do not know the man I am."

She looked at him in confusion, and he hastened to continue. "To kill for crown or cause, aye, I have done that. But to die for the same? Nay. I have ne'ere found cause nor crown worthy enough to die for, or even to sacrifice for. Hence I have chosen to be a mercenary, and a man without honor, a coward in service only to himself."

Taryn shook her head slowly. His words confused her. At Jaune he was no mercenary. He had made a vow to protect Garret's life at risk of his own, and had done so. Surely he had merely erred in his phrasing, erroneously making what had been the past sound like the present. "You give yourself too little credit, deliverer of my husband." She leaned toward him and gently brushed her lips against his cheek. "I know differently," she insisted.

An inward breath, loud in the silence between them, sounded from behind her.

Taryn looked up, but the greeting she would offer to the man poised several yards away just inside the garden gate never passed her lips.

If she had any doubt as to what Richard had witnessed or as to how he viewed the innocent kiss, she had only to look upon his face. His narrowed eyes swept over them coldly before settling upon her. She felt such naked recrimination emanating from the man that she lowered her gaze in shame and drew back from Simon, who stood immediately.

"Richard. I . . . we . . ." she stammered.

The steward interrupted sharply, "There have been banners spotted upon the horizon. I thought you would want to know—the colors are your brother's."

He turned on his heel, giving her no opportunity to respond either to his silent accusation or to the news he delivered. And indeed, her mind now grasped Charles' arrival to the exclusion of all other thoughts. Her frantic logic could conceive of only a single explanation. If something had happened to Garret, Charles would, as her kinsman, come into immediate control of Arundel until Henry either appointed another to act as overlord or married her off.

She rose unsteadily, inadvertently laying her hand upon Simon's arm for balance. "Why would Charles come here? For what purpose? Is it Garret?"

At first she thought he had not heard her. His gaze remained upon Richard's departing look. Finally, when the man had disapperaed through the gate, he turned to her and removed her arm. "I do not know. Go back to the keep, lady."

She trembled, seeing the fierce, cold set of his features, an iciness reflected also in his voice. She looked to his right hand and saw the fist rise slowly to the sword at his side. "Simon?"

Almost roughly he seized her arm and propelled her toward the gate. "Go, lady."

"Nay!" She twisted from his hold and then took a defiant step toward him. "From this you cannot protect me. If 'tis news of my husband I will hear it firsthand."

Charles Maitland shifted his weight in the saddle and patiently waited for the heavy iron gate to rise. Just beyond the portcullis he could see a dozen knights taking up defensive postures within Jaune's outer bailey. Without looking upward he felt the presence of the score of archers he knew were strategically placed upon the battlements, their bows trained not upon him or even the half dozen men positioned on the drawbridge at his back, but upon the fifty mounted men waiting just across the moat.

Silently, he grinned. Jaune's men-at-arms would piss buckets if they knew of the additional hundred German mercenaries awaiting his orders from the cover of the forest.

Unable to help himself, he indulged a soft chuckle. D'Orléon's reports of Jaune's depleted force appeared to be accurate. With that fact now visible firsthand, he was more confident than ever of the inevitable success of his plan.

Indeed, he had given this scheme great thought. The forces still in support of Henry were strong, and they were strengthened by d'Aubigny's leadership. As long as the Great Earl of Arundel remained in the field, so would the barons he commanded. But were that central leadership to be taken away, the barons' petty jealousies and power struggles would weaken their alliance, if not destroy it entirely. Then Henry's armies in England would be easily defeated by the rebel forces.

Garret d'Aubigny had already honored his forty-day commitment of service and hence could legally withdraw his aid of men and supplies. And if d'Orléon's assessment of the situation were true, the disappearance of his wife from Jaune would be adequate inducement to cause him to do so. If she were held by rebel forces, so much the better. Then d'Aubigny would have just cause for leaving the battle to wage his own personal war against those who had broached his castle and taken his property. With Charles' spy conveniently in charge of Jaune's men-at-arms, the abduction should be easily accomplished. The only possible obstacle might be his fiery-tempered half-sister.

Still, even for this he had a plan. In d'Orléon's reports he had made mention that for better than a month Jaune had had no news of the revolt's progress. Charles needed only to convince Taryn that the tide had turned against Henry.

With a final loud creak the gate reached its uppermost position. Charles spurred his horse forward toward the waiting reception party. He recognized Jaune's steward among the group and fixed an insincere smile of greeting upon his face. He was of neither the mood nor inclination to deal with d'Aubigny's man. Where was d'Orléon?

Almost in answer to his silent question the man

appeared, rounding the corner of the gatehouse. At his side was the cloaked figure of a woman. Upon sight of Charles she put back the hood from her hair. The glint of the late afternoon sun upon the russet tresses proclaimed her identity more loudly than any fanfare of trumpets would have.

Charles smiled widely. This was almost too easy! He had not expected her to meet him in d'Orléon's company. With the mercenary here to confirm all Charles would tell her, the plan was guaranteed of success. Hastily he dismounted and crossed the distance between them. "Taryn, sister, my greetings to you."

"Your purpose, Charles," she answered curtly.

Charles fought to keep his smile from slipping. The wench was as sharp-tongued as ever—more so with her one-eyed warrior at her side. Well, soon enough she would learn where the bastard's loyalties lay! Careful to maintain his expression, he looked to the black-haired knight. "I must speak with my sister. Please feel free to remain, but as this is an urgent and private matter, I must ask that we move from earshot of the others."

D'Orléon met his gaze in mute understanding, and Charles' confidence increased. When the mercenary had reported to Wynshire at Christmas time, Charles had warned him this day might arrive. At the time, however, Charles had told him nothing of his and de Moreville's plans. Still, d'Orléon was astute enough to have figured out Charles' role in Thomas Becket's murder: it was Charles who had contrived the murder, convincing de Moreville that their cause needed a greater rallying cry than to overthrow Henry for the mere sake of seizing power. That the Archbishop had unwittingly aided Charles by continuing to rile Henry had been an unexpected stroke of good fortune.

"Lady." D'Orléon obligingly propelled her back around the gatehouse wall—well out of hearing distance of Richard and the others.

Confident that what he would say could now be said without witnesses, Charles spoke. "I want you to come back to Wynshire with me, Taryn."

She looked at him, speechless and confused. "Are you serious?" she hissed at last. "For what possible reason would I leave what is now my home, and return to your control?"

Charles ignored the bitterness in her voice. "For your protection."

A derisive sound escaped her. "I am quite safe here—not that I believe for a moment you care a whit for my safety. Now, what is the *real* reason, Charles?"

Without acknowledging her accusation he switched strategies. "Have you had news of the revolt?"

Her face instantly drained of color, and he knew he had struck a nerve. "It does not go well for the forces loyal to Henry," he stated, quickly seizing the opportunity presented. "Our victory is imminent."

"*Your* victory!" Taryn reeled at the meaning of Charles' words. "You are allied with those who oppose the king?"

Even as the blond head bowed in affirmation, she formed her response. "You traitorous bastard!" she spat, feeling a new loathing for him.

But her outrage garnered no reaction other than a calm and complacent smile. "Spare me your righteous indignation, Taryn, and listen. We are within weeks of victory. Our cause is just and sanctioned by Alexander himself. Henry and all those who support him act against the holy Church. They have already been excommunicated, and that is not the end of it. If he dares to return to England, Henry will be executed, as will those closest to him. *That* will include your husband, I can promise you!"

Taryn shook her head, fighting to deny the truth of what he said. "Nay! I don't believe you!"

"Believe me, sister. There is one way and one way only Garret d'Aubigny can escape death—and that is if I convince my allies that his loyalties were mixed. I can do that only if you return with me now to Wynshire. Hence I have the argument that the Great Earl would not otherwise have sent his wife to the enemy camp, unless he wished to join us."

Taryn felt as if the ground had shifted under her feet and a great chasm had opened up. She teetered on its edge, fighting for balance between reality and madness. "I don't believe you. This makes no sense. You seek to harm him somehow, not save him—and I'll not be a party to it! I'll not act against my king and my husband!" She tore her gaze from his smug face and looked to the man beside her, beseeching him to speak. "Simon, please," she whispered. "Tell me that he lies!"

But the man she addressed in desperation only stood silent, refusing even to meet her eyes. Helplessness surged within her. She looked back to Charles and fought to order her thoughts. "Why? Why should I trust you and believe you would save Garret's life?"

"Because in spite of everything, you are still my sister."

Taryn shook her head and squeezed her eyes shut. The chasm was widening, and the dark madness within rising. Reality was fading, her grasp of it weakening. *Think!* she silently screamed. He would have sold her to Lynfyld. There was no loyalty of blood betwixt them. His loyalty was to himself. He did naught unless 'twas for his own benefit. But why would he risk revealing himself to her unless he *were* assured of victory?

With her eyes shut she did not see the look exchanged between Charles and the man at her side.

"Lady . . ." Simon's voice caused her to open her eyes, and she looked up at him numbly.

He waved Charles back and then moved to stand before her. "You must do as he says."

"Nay!" she gasped. Her eyes filled with tears as she realized he had forsaken her. "Simon, how can you ask this of me? You—more than anyone—you know I do not trust him."

"Do you trust me?" he asked quietly.

"With my life," she whispered.

"Then you must do as your brother says. If there is the

slightest chance that what he says is true, Lord Garret's life may depend upon your actions."

"Simon, how can you believe he acts to save Garret?"

"Even if he does not . . ." Simon paused, and for the first time since Richard had brought the news of Charles' arrival, he met her gaze squarely. "You must think of another's life, that of the child you carry."

Taryn gasped in shock. "How did you know?"

He smiled gently. "I was not certain, until this moment. Lady, listen to me. If Charles and his side are victorious and they act to eliminate those who have fought against them, do you think 'twill matter to them that Lord Garret's heir is a mere babe in swaddling? If God sees fit to grant them victory, they will kill a boy child who, when later grown to manhood, might seek to avenge his father's death."

"Blessed Mother!" Taryn pressed her hands to her belly. Simon was right; the rebels would never let Garret's son live.

"Taryn." Charles' voice sounded from behind Simon's back. "I must have your answer."

Taryn looked at Simon. She didn't have the strength to fight Charles. It was as if the life she nurtured had tempered her and made her vulnerable, unable to trust her own instincts. "Tell me what to do," she whispered.

"Go with him."

She nodded. Not for what Charles had said did she do this, but out of the consummate faith she had in this man who had saved Garret's life once before.

As Charles approached, Simon turned to face him. "She will go with you, but so shall I. I am bound by an oath to protect her."

"Very well. But we need to go back to the others. Your steward is growing nervous."

At the mention of Richard, Taryn's resolve faltered. She looked to Simon. "What will we say to Richard?"

Before Simon could reply, Charles spoke. "Tell him that Moira is gravely ill. She is not expected to live, and I have come to take you back to Wynshire that you may be with her."

Taryn nodded mutely. She could not very well tell Richard the truth.

They returned to where the anxious steward waited. "Lady, are you all right?"

"Aye," she answered. "I . . . I have just received news that my old nurse is very ill. I must go to Wynshire. On the morrow?" She looked at Charles, who nodded.

"Lady, I must protest! 'Tis not wise for you to engage in travel without Lord Garret's permission."

Taryn strove to keep her voice even. "Since when has Jaune become my prison, Richard—that I require my jailer's permission to leave it? Wynshire is my home and a woman I care for deeply may be dying."

"But, lady—"

"Enough, Richard." She heard her own voice strained and shrill, and drew a steadying breath. "My brother has brought an ample escort. My safety shall be assured. There is no cause for concern, especially as Simon shall accompany me."

At this revelation Richard's features instantly clouded and unvoiced hostility shadowed his eyes. He turned his protest upon Simon. "What of the orders left you by your lord? He entrusted you with the protection of Jaune, yet now you would leave it undefended?"

"My absence hardly renders Jaune without defense, Richard." Simon smiled coldly. "Though I am flattered you think so highly of my prowess. Regardless, I shall return in a week's time."

Richard's only reply was an arched brow. Taryn knew he disapproved of the entire matter, yet was powerless to do anything but speak his reservations. This he had done, to no avail. Still, his responsibility had been met. It was now to others that fault would fall.

"And what of Lord Garret?" he asked. "Shall he know of this?"

"Of course," Charles answered smoothly. "I shall

send word to him myself."

Taryn turned to Simon. She could not bear the lies any longer. "Please see to the arrangements and to the needs of my brother and his men." She turned to head back toward the keep.

Simon watched her go. He heard Maitland speak briefly to Richard about food for his men's horses, while informing the steward that his men would make camp outside Jaune's walls. Then, as Richard withdrew to comply with his request, he turned to Simon. "Well done, d'Orléon. I did not think at first you could convince her. Tell me, what did you tell her?"

"That she should trust me."

Charles burst into laughter. "My compliments, mercenary! You betray them with their own trust."

Simon looked at him speculatively. "And if I had not been able to convince her, how many men have you lying in wait in the forest to see your plan through had I failed?"

Charles continued to laugh. "Enough, mercenary, enough. But thanks to you they are unneeded—though they will not withdraw until we are well gone from Jaune."

Simon nodded, having gained his justification. If he had been unable to convince Taryn to leave willingly, her brother had been prepared to lay siege to Jaune. Despite the self-disgust which now seized him, he had acted prudently. What he had told Taryn, he almost believed himself. At least thinking so assuaged his guilt—or did it? Could he have ordered at attack upon Maitland? What if it had failed? Simon had to remain within the man's confidence. Only then could he know what manner of foe he fought—the form of attack Maitland would bring against Garret.

"See to your men, earl," he stated quietly, willing with extreme effort a passive and indifferent expression. What was done was done. He had to keep her safe. This was his most immediate aim, and he could not reveal to Maitland any wavering loyalty or weakness.

Charles nodded and crossed to where the dozen riders who had followed him through the gate still waited.

Simon watched him mount, then lead his men back through the gate. Once they had passed beneath the raised portcullis, Simon waved to the gateman, ordering the iron grating again dropped. He turned to head toward the barracks—and was met halfway by Maite.

He had no doubt the old woman had come in search of him. Nor did he have doubt as to why. "Maite."

His greeting went unanswered. "You are letting her go with that bastard she calls brother. Why?"

Simon looked down at the frail form. In her peculiar way Maite knew what no earthly being could, and that knowledge was more a threat to him now than the skill of the most worthy of knights. To lie would accomplish nothing and only gain him a formidable enemy. His only hope was the truth. "There was no other way, Maite. You must believe me. I do this to protect her and the unborn life she carries."

If Maite was surprised he knew of Taryn's condition, she did not show it. Her eyes bored into him as though to read the thoughts he would keep from her. She finally replied, "For that very reason I am going with her. She will be in the company of better than fifty men. Without an attendant 'twould be unseemly and appear odd. Then, too, I fear for them both."

"You think I would let harm befall her?"

"You tell me, Simon d'Orléon." Maite took a single step back and folded her arms across her chest. "Does she have aught to fear from you? Or does my lord?"

"'Tis to protect them both that I do this. Maite, you know me."

"Aye, I know you. But from the first day of your arrival I have felt for you the most peculiar pairing of trust and distrust. Know this well, mercenary. Should harm befall her, the child she carries, or my lord, I will personally drive a blade through your black heart."

Chapter Twenty-Five

"We shall reach Wynshire by noon tomorrow." Charles swept aside the flap to his tent, then stepped aside, beckoning Simon to enter before him. "'Tis the old woman's fault—troublesome hag! I should have left her on the road. Without her our pace would have been twice what 'twas, and a two and a half day journey would have brought us to our destination."

He followed Simon into the tent, lit well enough with several hanging oil lamps, and pointed to one of two kegs meant to serve as chairs. A pallet for sleeping completed the spare accommodations.

"Sit."

Simon declined the offer with a shake of his head. "I've been sitting a horse for three days." He moved back to the tent's opening and lifted the flap. He hated the confinement of a tent. Even when fighting in Tripoli he had forsaken the huge desert marquees for the open sky. A man could not breathe in a space scarcely tall enough for him to stand.

His gaze went across the camp comprised of a dozen or more tents and settled upon one set apart from the others. At its entrance stood a pair of guards. No light was visible from within the tent to cast shadows of movement upon its walls so Taryn and Maite were asleep already. The journey from Jaune had been difficult for them both.

Fortunately Maite's age had provided a feasible excuse for the slow pace Simon had insisted they maintain. Basking in his victory, Charles had been indulgent enough to allow the frequent rest stops he had also requested. Thus far Taryn's condition remained undiscovered.

"You seem distracted." Charles spoke from the tent's interior. "Tell me, d'Orléon, does your conscience trouble you? Is duplicity bitter to swallow, or does silver act as sweet wine to make the taste more palatable?" He laughed softly. "Mayhap a bonus would make the taste sweeter still?"

Simon heard a rustle of movement accompanied by the chink of coins hitting the ground at his feet. He turned to look down at the small leather pouch.

"Take it. You've earned it." Charles' handsome face sneered in triumph.

It was all Simon could do to keep his sword at his side. "I have long lived my life in accordance with a personal code. Once I have taken payment, I perform the service. What compels me now to see this through is my own honor. Keep your forty pieces of silver."

"*Honor?*" Charles regarded him with an amused expression. "'Tis a strange word to be spoken by a spy and a traitor. I think mayhap now you find yourself at odds with your 'code,' mercenary." He stepped forward and swiftly bent to retrieve the purse. "I think you may have found payment of another sort." He straightened, and the leer returned. "I've been watching you—and her. I think your 'service' to the husband has become service to the wife—or mayhap I should say servicing of?"

Immediately Simon stiffened, and yet he managed to control his emotions and respond calmly. "I will see no harm befall her," he avowed in neither affirmation nor denial of the lascivious speculation.

Tucking the pouch of coins beneath his belt, Charles offered a nonchalant shrug. "Whether you have or not is of little interest to me personally." A sudden gleam appeared in his eyes. "However, there may be an element of some import. Mayhap she does not know of your real service—to me?" He peered at Simon shrewdly. "Well, does she?"

Simon turned his head to conceal the torment induced by Charles' question. He would do almost anything to keep from Taryn the knowledge of his betrayal—and Charles now knew it. It gave the man an edge Simon was loath to endure.

"So, it does guarantee our alliance and insure your loyalty to me, after all." Laughter filled his voice as he continued. "You have naught to worry about, valiant knight. My plans are not to harm her. I simply need her to act as the lure."

Simon struggled to keep his features blank. At last Charles would reveal his scheme! "For . . . ?" he asked, slowly facing his adversary. Charles Maitland was too pompous to exercise caution; his arrogance would impel him to boast.

The man took his time before answering, settling himself down upon one of the kegs. "My plan is twofold," he replied at last as he tugged off his gauntlets. "My first concern is to remove d'Aubigny from the field. Once we are at Wynshire I shall send word to him of his wife's situation, along with a threat he cannot fail to perceive. He will depart immediately, probably with a veritable army at his back, and my first objective shall be met. Without the central leadership he provides, disunity will quickly reign and Henry's support and our opposition shall crumble. The victory which is now within our grasp, will be in hand! And as for d'Aubigny . . . my Germans will be lying in wait for him. He will ne'er reach Wynshire alive!"

Simon stared at Charles. No sign escaped him of the hell he was enduring. Within that stalwart silence his loyalties hung in the balance. The vow of fealty he had once uttered as mere words to a stranger had grown to hold great meaning. And yet with Garret's death he could have what he wanted. He could have her and love her, accepting her child as his own. But what of his guilt? What happiness could he realize in knowing its price? Were he to let a man he had come to call friend be led to certain death, would he ever be able to look upon her—or himself—and feel aught but self-condemnation?

Nay, this he could not do! He had coveted what was not his. To act upon that urge would make him no better than the base coward who sat before him. He could live without the respect of others, but never without respect for himself.

For a final time he thought of what might have been: *to love her and accept her child as his own.* And then, as the desire that could never be died within him, his thoughts took a new turn. Somehow he must deter Charles from the realization of his insidious plot. Suddenly a wild and improbable plan began to take form. "Is his death what you truly desire?" he asked, his voice quiet even in the silence.

"I want him destroyed!" The vehement and reckless statement was accompanied by a glare of sudden suspicion.

To assuage it Simon smiled and moved casually toward the empty keg. He shifted the sheathed sword at his side and sat. "There are different forms of destruction . . . and all manner of dying—some worse than death itself."

"What are you talking about?"

"Killing an enemy is a pleasure quickly passed. Do you merely want yours dead, or do you want to *see* him die, slowly, and in pieces?"

Charles's eyes burned as if with fever. The idea clearly intrigued him. "To see him first suffer . . . aye . . . but how? How do I 'destroy' him in the manner you speak?"

"Strip a man such as d'Aubigny of his pride and you cut out his heart. He becomes a broken man, dying from the inside."

Charles leaned back with a puzzled frown, and Simon

recognized instantly the cause. The concept of pride was incomprehensible to him. A man without honor could not possibly grasp its meaning or see its loss as a mortal blow. Simon sought to explain. "Honor drives d'Aubigny. 'Tis what he lives for. Look upon his current actions. He has naught to gain by defending his king, and everything to lose—his title, lands, position, even his life. And yet he fights on, unable to be aught but what he is."

Though by his expression Charles showed his doubt, he sat forward. "I might be inclined to accept this as truth if I knew how it could be done. What is the rest of it?"

Simon shook his head. "There is a price to that answer, earl, and to my aid—for without me the scheme will not work."

"What price?" Charles demanded, distrust hardening his features. "I have already offered you silver. What more do you want?"

"I don't want your silver."

"Then what?"

"I want Taryn and the old woman taken not to Wynshire, but to a convent, where they will be protected and safe." *And beyond your control,* he thought silently.

Charles' brow furrowed. This was not a prospect he had considered. Certes it deviated from his original plan, and yet he was not unpleased with the notion. He had feared d'Orléon would ask for land or titles, yet his price was one of no actual cost to Charles. Then too, did he really want Taryn back at Wynshire, underfoot and causing trouble? "I would hear your idea first," he stated, without capitulation.

Simon nodded. In utter certainty he knew what he was about to propose would save Garret d'Aubigny's life—and at the same time destroy him. They were alike. Simon knew what Garret had given up to make the commitment he had to her. For a warrior to love, he must give up that absolute freedom to risk his life. In and of itself that was a sacrifice of strength and manly pride. But more, it was an admission of weakness and a concession to vulnerability.

The irony was bitter. Simon had also avoided involvement, and its cost. Yet he had found in himself a like desire for this same woman, and would have gladly paid the same price. How could he not know what it would do to Garret now to learn his sacrifice had been for a commitment that was false, in the name of an emotion that did not exist? A man could not know, or render, a greater pain than love's betrayal.

There was no other way, and yet that knowledge did little to ease the anguish within him. Simon met the eyes studying him, drew a breath and began. "Your sister is with child. However, her condition was unknown by any at Jaune save the old woman. Given the extent of d'Aubigny's absences and the fact neither have told him of the life conceived, 'tis possible he may not believe the child is his."

Simon paused and steeled himself for what must come next. "When he arrives at Wynshire to affect her release, you need only to tell him her flight from Jaune was willing, the reason being that her child was fathered by another, and thus she could not face him in the knowledge of her adultery."

"He would believe this?"

"He would—if he is told the child is mine."

"Is it?" Charles eyed him speculatively, a slow grin pulling at the corners of his mouth.

Simon looked away. His lie would defile her honor, but assure her life and her child's—and her husband's as well. If given the choice, was the price one she would be willing to pay? "Aye," he whispered hoarsely.

The small tent echoed with Charles' immediate laughter. "You are a piece of work, d'Orléon! I send you to betray the man, and you do so in the most consummate fashion—by bedding and impregnating his wife! Aye, the knowledge of her faithlessness, that she not only laid with a man he believed to be a friend, but now carries his bastard, will surely strip the arrogance from him. Yet what makes you so certain this will finish him?"

"Because I know him as I know myself," Simon reaffirmed quietly.

Charles ran the back of his hand along his jaw. "I am still not convinced this will have the effect you profess. Of course, I can always order his death at a later time, after I have watched him suffer. What troubles me more is a lack of understanding as to why you will do this."

"'Tis as you have already guessed. I would make her mine. And I ask for one more condition." Simon stood and looked down at the man whose trust he now needed to maintain above all else. "When the time comes to kill him, let it be my sword."

With a sinister grin, Charles rose to his feet, clapping his hand upon Simon's shoulder. "Very well, my 'David', when the time comes to win your 'Bathsheba', you shall have the pleasure of slaying her husband."

Through the early morning mist the battlements of Wynshire Castle rose like an island in a swirling gray sea. From their position atop a neighboring hillcrest four hundred men viewed the objective not an hour's ride in the distance. Between the line of mounted warriors and the island lay a narrow valley shrouded in the same veil.

"It has the look of a trap, my lord. A thousand men could be hidden in that fog, and a body wouldn't know it until he heard their arrows sing. I say we wait until the sun burns off the vapour."

Garret nodded—but only in mechanical response to the man's voice. Despite the accuracy of his second-in-command's assessment and the soundness of the recommendation, he had no intention of heeding either. Since the moment he had received Maitland's messenger, he had been as a man possessed. Like a wound grown putrid to eat away at healthy flesh, his festering rage had steadily eroded rational thought.

Beneath his mail coif his square jaw clenched as he relived the moment he had learned of her abduction. No ransom demand had accompanied the message, no terms for her release—because her abductor did not intend ever to release her. In a brazen move made in advance of his believed victory, Maitland had "reclaimed" his kinswoman. With her in his possession he would hold lawful title to Arundel upon the event of Garret's defeat, or death.

A lance thrust through him could not have induced a greater sense of helplessness or pain. The threat to Arundel meant nothing compared to the threat to her. The knowledge of her peril had torn down the last vestiges of an emotional barrier he had been unable to cross. For until that moment when he was faced with her loss, he had not admitted he loved her.

Even when he had taken her into his arms that last time at Jaune, his fear of vulnerability and attachment had held fast. He could not utter the words his heart had yearned to speak though the preceding months had been the happiest he had ever known. She had become necessary to him, a part of him, as he had never before believed it was possible a woman could be. No greater joy had he known than to hear her profession of love as their bodies entwined and joined.

And even though he had been gentle with her and affectionate those weeks following his return from Normandy, gentleness and affection were not profession of love, nor was the act of making love, which with his moods had been either passionate or careless. He had prized her so lightly! How could he not have known how much she meant to him? Why could he not have conquered his fears and admitted to himself—and to her—that fragile emotion which now rooted itself so deeply in his heart?

Taryn. Her name whispered in his mind and the pain echoed in his very soul. The longing to hold her was almost unbearable, the thought of losing her unendurable. He would not lose her!

The silent vow burned within him and the pale gaze that was fixed upon the distant target suddenly narrowed. On either side of the helm's nasal the light green eyes deepened in color to blaze like emerald fire.

The man at his side watched the abrupt transformation. A decade in Garret's service had taught him well that look. He cast a quick glance to the men mounted nearest to them. To a man they all nodded; the unspoken question asked and answered.

He cleared his throat to gain his lord's attention. "Then again, 'tis unlikely Maitland will have anticipated a six day ride to have been made in four—not by a force of a size worth reckoning. Move we now and use the mist as cover and our approach will go unnoted. We will be at that whoreson's gate before he has broken his fast."

For a brief instant Garret's focus turned to his men. Many of the men who rode with him now had been with him for years, through countless campaigns. But they had never known him as he was now. The threat of harm to the woman he loved had stripped from him the savage, dispassionate and methodical control he had always maintained, leaving in its stead a cold fear which drove him to her aid. He rode with a reckless lack of judgment apparent to his men. He had seen this recognition in the sly exchanges of furtive glances, though he knew at this moment they stood ready to kill or be killed upon his command, so fierce and inexorable was their loyalty to him.

"If she has been harmed in any way, there shall not be two stones left standing atop one another," the man at his side stated further.

Garret nodded. A fortnight she had been in that bastard's hands! The how did not matter. What mattered was that what was his had been taken from him, and he would now take it back. If need be, he would see Wynshire reduced to dust and every male of battle age sent to Hell!

He raised his arm, and in a silence marred only by the creaking of leather harnesses and the muted jangle of accoutrements, half of his army spurred their war horses forward.

Those left upon the crest united in a common wish: would that they, too, could be part of this first onslaught! Nevertheless they reined in their nervous mounts; a reserve force was crucial, both to conceal their true number and to provide reinforcements should they be needed. And so they watched in envy as their comrades descended into the sea of mist to be swallowed up by the haze as if they had never been.

"He is here."

The man seated at the high table lifted his head from the bosom of the serving wench sprawled across his lap. Without taking his eyes from the rosy mounds, he responded with no emotion other than annoyance that his entertainment had been interrupted. "Who?"

"D'Aubigny."

Simon reveled in the unguarded, albeit brief, reaction elicited by the name. An unmistakable glimmer of fear passed across Charles' face—and then it was gone, replaced by a sneer of arrogant bravado.

"He cannot have brought any army then. My messenger only returned yestereve himself. 'Twould be fair impossible for a mounted body of men to cover such distance in less than five days."

Simon arched his brow. "Mayhap you would care to repeat that statement to the men who ride under his banner? A good two hundred are less than a hundred yards from your gate, though . . ." he paused for effect, ". . . I'd wager there are probably at least that number again lying in wait."

Charles jumped to his feet, unmindful of the girl who, in the process, tumbled to the floor. Her squealing protest of pained indignation was silenced instantly by a swift and brutal kick. As she crawled from the dais, her assailant redirected his rage upon its true target. "Damn you, mercenary! If this plan of yours fails and he attacks, I'll have your bastard cut from her belly and their carcasses tossed to the wolves!"

Despite the baleful threat, Simon smiled grimly. Taryn was safe from Charles' vengeance, as was her child. That much his betrayal *had* accomplished. "The plan will work, and the size of his army is inconsequential. Once he learns that her 'abduction' was a willing flight—and the reason for it—he will withdraw to Jaune."

"So you have said." Charles growled, settling himself once again in his chair. ". . . we shall see. Send a single rider out. Tell the Great Earl that I will receive only him; his army is to remain outside Wynshire's walls." Suddenly he hesitated, as if in doubt of the order. "Think you he might *not* enter alone, anticipating a trap?"

"He will enter," Simon stated quietly. "Driven as he is by pride of possession, and love, he would enter the very gates of Hell—as would his men should he not exit alive."

The subtle warning brought an immediate and snarling retort. "I am not such a fool as to kill the man whilst his army camps at my door! Send the rider and then return here. I want you there . . ." He pointed to a small alcove just off the main body of the great hall. The alcove and a man standing in its dark recesses would be nearly invisible to anyone facing the high table. The snarl on his lips became a grin of utter evil. "You shall remain there until you are . . . summoned."

Summoned to announce 'twas he who had sired the child Taryn carried. Simon turned away lest Charles see his anguish. His true mettle was about be tested as it had never been before. Had he the courage? From the corner of his eye he saw the man lean back in his thronelike chair.

"One thing else . . ." Charles' voice drifted across the

distance between them. "Make certain he is well escorted."

Simon wheeled and leveled a taunting glare. "To guard him, or to protect you?"

"Tighten your tongue, mercenary, and loosen it only when you are told! Or do you forget the interest you share in this scheme—and the prize to be won?"

"I have forgotten naught—least of all the reason for my actions."

The creaking of iron hinges and the sound of footsteps announced him.

Simon laid his back to the stone wall, unsure his presence would remain concealed by the alcove's darkness as Garret passed its opening.

Yet upon entering the hall, d'Aubigny looked neither right nor left. He strode without fear, bothering not even to sweep aside the mantle from his shoulder should he have need to clear his sword from its scabbard. The contrast between the fire in his eyes and the calm on his face was remarkable.

In a silent acknowledgment of admiration Simon bowed his head to the man who could not see his tribute.

Garret stepped toward the dais, the four helmed knights who flanked him remaining several paces back yet cautiously within sword's reach.

From his location Simon had no view of the high table where Charles had positioned himself, nor was one needed. Garret's piercing glare and the descending silence told him what he could not see. The foes were face to face.

"Your arrival is early, d'Aubigny," Charles spoke first. "Expected, but early."

"Release her to me now and I will let you live," came the icy response.

At once the four knights moved forward, but halted—no doubt in reaction to a signal from Charles, whose complacent chuckle rang out. "At five to one, the odds are scarcely in your favor."

"Once more . . ." Garret's low growl was barely audible. "Release her and you live."

"Your arrogance knows no bounds, d'Aubigny. But you will not attack and risk her life. Hence the size of your army means naught. You are in no position to make demands."

Again there was silence, at last broken.

"Then make yours—what price?"

With those words Simon flinched. At the cost of his pride Garret would now humble himself before his enemy, and concede to bargaining, so great was the value he placed upon her.

Charles sighed in a pretense of helplessness. "Alas! I must confess, this places me in a most awkward position. As you have correctly surmised, her release might have been bought. Our coffers have rapidly emptied under the burden of supporting our cause."

"You mean paying for the swords you raise against the king in treason." Garret's tone revealed no surprise at the confession just made. The revelation of Charles' alliance with the rebels was betrayed only by his eyes, narrowing in contempt of the traitor before him.

"As we are on opposite sides, I do not expect our outlook to be the same. What you call 'treason,' I call 'justice'—the seizing of power from a tyrant no longer fit in the eyes of God and man to hold it! However, this is not the issue which brings us together. My sister, herself, has made ransom an impossibility. You see, Earl of Arundel, your wife does not desire to return to you." He sighed again as if unaware of the shocked reaction induced by his proclamation. "And in all good conscience I cannot force her to go with you when she desires to stay. Then, too . . ." he continued, a soft chuckle accompanying his words. "I must confess, I find it more than a little strange that you *want* her back. After all, few men would desire the return of a faithless wife—especially one whose womb now swells with the seed of another man."

Simon saw Garret's hand move to his sword. But the folds of his mantle hampered his efforts. Before he could draw the blade and address the charge of adultery with cold steel, his guards had positioned themselves defensively between him and the table and reached for their own swords. Simon moved to the alcove's entrance in time to see Charles rise as he ordered, "Sheath it, d'Aubigny. You have entered under a flag of truce."

Charles' cold and confident arrogance rang in the hall. Simon watched Garret's face, knowing he would honor the truce. Slowly he released his grip. "Bring her forth," he whispered hoarsely.

"She betrayed you with another! Would you save her? Or take her back?"

"I would hear it from her," he gritted between clenched teeth, taking a single, threatening step forward.

Charles shook his head. "That will be unnecessary, as there is another already present whose words you will surely believe. Dare you face the man who had of her what you believed to be yours and yours alone?"

"Let him come forward and face *me,*" Garret declared with a bold arrogance, so firm was his conviction that no man would be so foolhardy at the expense of his own life.

In a single stride Simon left the darkness.

At first Garret only stared. In his eyes a silent battle raged. "I want to believe your presence is out of the vow you made to protect her life," he finally stated quietly. "Tell me this is so, and I will believe you, my friend."

Simon hardened his heart against the agony which clasped about it like a fist to rip it from his chest. And then the words came, delivered with the swift mercy of a death blow. "I cannot."

His vision blurred, and in Garret's face he saw the mirror image of his own turmoil, twisted with pain and grief. A glance to the man's right hand revealed mute evidence of the rage consuming his soul. The fingers, returned to the hilt of his sword and again wrapped about it, were white.

Garret looked at the man before him. That Simon could not even meet his gaze drove home the truth: the child she carried could only be one man's—this man whom he had trusted above all others, and the only man who could have been his rival. Both had betrayed him! With a sick feeling in the pit of his belly, he knew he had known it all along. It had been there for him to see: their closeness and the private meetings. But when had the act of ultimate betrayal been achieved? While he was at Jaune, or while he had been gone—and which time? He had to know. "When?" he choked.

As if pondering the reason for the question, Simon hesitated. Had he guessed the importance of one answer over another? "When you left to lead Henry's armies."

Garret relaxed his hold and his hand fell to his side. Like the shield he had raised so often in battle to protect himself, his pride now instinctively rose. No man would see his pain or know his loss. "I have called you liegeman, friend and brother—everything but what you are. And yet the one whom I once considered wife is not worth even *your* blood, mercenary. I will not lift my sword in defense of a whore."

Simon winced at the epithet attached to Taryn, yet bowed his head in acceptance of the affront directed at himself. He could expect no less than what he had just received—the supreme insult one warrior could bestow upon another: Garret's refusal to fight him.

Wordlessly Garret turned on his heel and stalked out, ignoring the four knights standing with drawn swords. Simon watched his exit in a mixture of relief and grudging admiration.

Charles folded the sheet of parchment he had just received. Setting it aside on the table before him, he leaned back in his chair, closed his eyes and reveled in the heady sensation rushing through him. He had prevailed!

Beginning with d'Aubigny's removal from the field and ending with the awaited confirmation of this missive, every step of his plan had enjoyed flawless success. The Great Earl's withdrawal of men three weeks ago had been enough to turn the tide of battle, giving the rebel forces a decisive victory. And with that victory Charles and his allies had been able to launch the next stage of his plan, waging a war more specific in nature by attacking the baronies and individual properties of those still loyal to the crown.

Loud in the empty hall, his contented laughter rang out. Was there any wine more intoxicating, or pleasure intense, than vanquishing one's enemies? He sat forward and reached once more for the letter, the tangible proof of his triumph, and his ultimate victory! He who had once posed the greatest threat now posed none at all! The rumors filtering out of Arundel were true. The proud lord of Jaune, favored vassal of the King of England, sat sodden in his castle, too drunk to leave its walls or to stop his men's desertion. Without d'Aubigny's leadership Henry's support was nearly gone and his army next to nonexistent. In the last two weeks alone seven barons who had lent men and arms to their beleaguered monarch's cause had withdrawn their aid for the purpose of defending their own interests. They had retreated to their homes to preserve what had not yet been lost. Unlike the Great Earl, however, they remained a minor threat to be dealt with in due time. But d'Aubigny? D'Orléon had been right: the knowledge of his wife's betrayal *had* destroyed him!

"D'Orléon," Charles grumbled aloud, a sudden frown crossing his brow. Mere thought of the name cast the one dark shadow in an otherwise bright picture. Since the confrontation with d'Aubigny, d'Orléon's hostility toward Charles had been unrestrained, his contempt outright. Soon he might be uncontrollable.

Charles sighed. Though he had hoped to enjoy d'Aubigny's suffering a while longer, his course was clear. He must make final use of the mercenary and order d'Aubigny's death.

"Conar!"

His shout brought his hefty steward forward in moments, grease dripping from his chin and a leg of mutton half concealed behind his back.

"Milord," the man choked, hastening in the same breath to swallow and speak.

"Your fondness for the kitchen can quick enough put you there permanently." The threat to his station instantly drained Conar's face of color, but Charles was of no mind to either notice or enjoy the man's discomfort. "Find d'Orléon and bring him to me."

"I . . . I don't know as I can do that, milord. I seen him at the stables a bit ago. He be having the looks of leaving. I thought 'twas by your order."

"I gave no such order, you lackwit!" Charles jumped to his feet, hastening for the keep's exit. He took the stairs two at a time and crossed the bailey in heated strides. Rounding the corner of the barracks, he paused to catch his breath and summon a trio of passing knights to his side. Flanked by the men, he approached the solitary figure leading his horse out from beneath the stable's lintel. "What matter of treachery is this? Without a word you would skulk off into the night?"

"'Tis the full light of day, earl, and had you waited but moments more you would have been informed of my decision." Without glancing over his shoulder to look at Charles, d'Orléon shifted the reins to his left hand and moved to his horse's side. After giving the girth strap a stout jerk with his right hand, he finally turned. "Our alliance is ended. Hence, I am taking my leave." Once more presenting his back, he slung the saddlebag from his shoulder across his horse's neck and gathered the reins more tightly. "Consider yourself informed."

Charles seethed at this exhibition of arrogance. Still, he stepped to the man's side. "What of your unfinished business with d'Aubigny?" he hissed. "You vowed to kill him."

With a grim smile, d'Orléon set his foot in the stirrup and mounted. Once firmly in the saddle, he looked down upon Charles in utter loathing. "I took no payment to do the deed in your name. My service to you has been fulfilled. *I* own my soul, now, and d'Aubigny is solely my concern."

Suspicion flared within Charles, finding expression in the selfsame instant. "You greedy, covetous bastard! You want it all! You think to kill the husband, wed the widow and lay claim to what would otherwise have been mine. This—this was your aim all along!" Beside himself with rage, he choked on his words, yet still possessed the presence of mind to wave the three knights out of earshot. "No wonder you wanted her hidden," he whispered, "you intend to pass off your bastard as Arundel's rightful heir, defying my claim!"

"I am no threat to your 'claim'. I don't want Arundel."

"And her?" Charles shrilled, past caring what his men might hear. "You think still to have her? Once I might have given you the wench, but now you'll rot in Hell before you set eyes upon her again!"

D'Orléon stared at him for a moment, his mouth twisting slowly into a smile that contorted the disfigured face into a hideous mask. "As well I know." Then, setting his heel to the destrier's flank, he urged the animal forward.

Charles stood, watching the man and horse galloping across the bailey toward the outer gate. He heard footsteps approach and wheeled to the trio of knights, their gazes also locked upon the lone rider. "Follow him. I want to know where he heads. Once you discover his destination . . . kill him."

Chapter Twenty-Six

Garret reached for the pitcher before him, his hand shaking as he lifted and tilted it. Ale sloshed over the table and into his cup. He swore silently and hurled the now empty vessel across the room. The earthenware smashed upon the floor, the noise instantly rousing the dog lying at his feet.

Becket rose and laid his head upon his master's lap. But Garret was beyond comfort, and angrily pushed the animal away. What he truly wanted to force aside, he could not. Even in his drunkenness she haunted him! Her image was alive in this empty room and he could not exorcise it—as he could not release her from his thoughts. Helpless to prevent it, he drew memory to him and lashed himself with each detail of tormenting recollection: the taste of her kisses, the sway of her hips, the sound of her voice.

Only inebriated sleep ever accorded him a semblance of peace. And yet when he awoke, the pain was still there, and the hurt returned. That part of him which she had touched would stir and awaken and grow stronger until he reached again for the mind-numbing ale.

If he could only break the hold she maintained upon his heart and shatter its mastery of his mind and will . . . if he could only act against his longing, he could regain control. But he could not. He could not forget. She had betrayed him, and though he hated her, he still loved her.

Sweet venom, Flambard's words, knifed at him. Never did he think to understand or feel the selfsame pain of love's betrayal. How he had tried to deny to himself the truth of what he had learned at Wynshire. But upon his return, Richard had readily dispelled those fragile and foolish hopes. With his own eyes the steward had seen what Garret had prayed was lie. And now he knew Flambard's suffering, the humiliation of a faithless wife. The only disgrace Garret was spared was that neither Richard nor anyone else at Jaune had known of the child she carried. And yet his dishonor remained. He saw his people's knowing looks and heard their rumors. Though none dared utter in his presence any expression of mockery, he could not face the shame. He had retreated to his chamber these past two weeks and saw no one but the serving wenches who replenished the ale. Once or twice in the beginning, he had taken one to his bed, but he had been unable to function as a man. She had taken that from him as well!

He lowered his head into his hands, but a sudden noise at the door caused him to look up. In brittle silence he stared at the man standing there. Rankled that Richard had not bothered to knock before entering, his jaw tightened. "You no longer see a need to announce yourself, steward?" he growled, lowering his gaze in prompt dismissal.

"You have a visitor, my lord."

Garret lifted his eyes enough to catch a glimpse of the cloaked figure Richard ushered into the chamber. The man's head and face were covered by the garment's cowl-like hood, raising no recognition within him. He returned his gaze to the goblet cupped in his hands. "I am of no mood to receive visitors. Whatever he wants, see to it."

"My lord . . ."

Richard's voice held an anxious tone, but the effort to lift his pounding head once more was too great. "Be gone, damn you!"

Unseen by Garret, the cowled figure nodded to Richard and motioned him toward the door. Richard inclined his head in obedience and with a final look to the man slumped at the table, he exited, closing the door firmly behind him.

"Do you no longer see a need to stand in the presence of your king, liegeman?"

Garret's head snapped up—more in response to the voice than to the words spoken. Through the blurry haze that was his vision, he tried to focus. Reason battled senses. It could not be . . . "Sire?"

His hoarse whisper caused the man to draw closer, removing the hood from his head as he crossed the distance between them. "I see the rumors are true." He shook his head sadly.

Finally realizing this was no drunken illusion—that he was in fact in the presence of his king—Garret stumbled to his feet. Swaying, he reached for the table's edge for balance. "And what rumors would they be?" he asked, his voice heavy with drink and sarcasm.

Anger instantly leaped to Henry's eyes. "That the man I once respected above all others has been reduced by a woman's betrayal to a whimpering knave, drowning in self-pity and ale. Look at yourself! The sight of you makes me want to retch."

"Then don't look," Garret snarled. He knew Henry attempted to provoke him with this goading and was not about to succumb. And yet like a lance that found its mark, the scathing censure pricked at his innate pride. Henry had drawn blood. In a gesture of blatant defiance he moved to sit.

Immediately Henry rounded the table and hooked the leg of the chair with the toe of his boot, yanking the seat from beneath him. Garret fell to the floor, and Henry stepped back. "Stand up! And if the wench has taken your backbone as well as your self-respect, then remain on your knees and crawl, you pitiable cuckold!"

The name he had once attached to Flambard ripped through his drunken consciousness. Through Henry's eyes he finally saw what he had become. Anger and pride surged, and he stiffened. He lifted his head, raked back the hair from his forehead and slowly climbed to his feet. At first unsteady, he held on to the table's edge as he drove back the numbness brought on by the ale—which was on only a surface level, for he could not drink enough to deaden the pain so deep within him. And then he released his hold, his stance again firm.

Unblinking, he looked once more at the man before him, now seeing him clearly. He took in the other's manner of dress and started. Even for Henry the attire was shabby, poor-spun wool near the quality of that worn by the lowliest of serfs. The hooded cloak he wore was patched and torn. The hood . . . upon his entrance it had been worn in such a peculiar manner . . . "Your presence in England is not known," he stated softly in sudden understanding.

Henry's face split into a wide grin. "Even sotted, you possess more wits than any hundred men." He reached for the chair he had pulled from Garret and without extending either gesture or spoken invitation for Garret to do the same, he sat. "As you have correctly surmised . . ." he plucked at the coarse fabric of his *bliaut* in disdain, ". . . I do not travel as England's king. My return has been a guarded secret. Only the dozen men in whose escort I travel know of it. My enemies think me still in Ireland."

"Where you have successfully avoided excommunication," Garret reminded him. The ale's effects still upon him, he struggled to order his thoughts, "You risk much by this return, Sire. Should Alexander or his messengers learn—"

"They will not learn," Henry interrupted. "Why think you I am clothed as I am, and my escort disguised as landless knights? Even the horse I ride is but a cart-horse with a saddle."

His liege's love for fine horseflesh was well known, and Garret smiled wryly at the image of the man upon such a mount.

"Take amusement if you will, but know there is serious reason behind my actions. If you are sober enough, I will explain further."

Garret's smile vanished. "Sober enough."

It was Henry's turn to smile. "I have returned to put down this rebellion and to see my realm once more united."

Garret shook his head, then winced at the dizziness the sudden movement induced. "The battle has changed. Your enemies wage war singly upon each lord now." Ignoring Henry's startled gaze, he stepped away from the table and crossed the room to a small table that held a wash basin. Drawing a deep breath, he plunged his head into the cold water. The shock upon his senses sobered him additionally, and as he straightened and reached for a towel, he continued. "There is no single great army to defeat."

"I do not intend to defeat an army," Henry answered, watching Garret's actions in droll approval. "This rebellion is as a beast with a hundred hands fisted about swords. But I have learned the identity of the traitor who acts as its head. Captured rebels in the north, desperate to save their necks from the hangman's noose, have betrayed his name. He has turned the others against me and emptied his coffers of silver to pay for the armies now attacking my allies. And while his mercenaries fight, he sits comfortably in his castle, waiting for such time as he is able to claim the prize—my England! But the rebels are factioned and they grow weary of warfare. Once the head of the beast is severed, the revolt will die. Then I shall seize back what has nearly been wrested from me."

He quieted suddenly as Garret returned to the table, towel still in hand. "I am not a good man—not even a good king," he resumed, "but goodness has less to do with ruling than strength and determination. My success or failure depends on whether or not the barons and earls will obey me once this beast is dead. But first I have need of you, Garret, and your army—if they have not all deserted you by now."

Garret grimaced at the pointed remark. Bowing his head, he flung the towel around his neck. It was no thanks to him that he still possessed even a single man-at-arms. "Ronald has been a loyal second in command. The integrity of Jaune's garrison remains, as well as better than half of those who were with me in the field."

"How many men?"

"Better than three hundred."

Henry nodded. "Then ready them to ride. We leave at dawn."

"Leave for where?" Garret asked, realizing Henry had not yet—and perhaps purposely so—revealed the name of the traitor.

"Wynshire Castle."

Garret sucked in his breath. "Maitland?" The name immediately brought back his pain. For several moments he had been free of her. She had faded from his thoughts. Now she was returned. The hands hanging at his sides clenched.

"Aye, your vassal and brother-in-law." Henry studied him intently. "I know 'twas in his escort that your wife left," he then stated quietly, "along with the mercenary, d'Orléon. The chance is great she is still at Wynshire . . ."

There was no need for him to continue. Garret knew what had been left unsaid; a siege could claim innocent lives. Within him anguish churned. "I care not what fate befalls her," he growled in denial of his emotions. He owed her nothing—not even her life! "But Maite went with her—'tis the old woman I would not see killed during Wynshire's siege. Maitland will fight a good fight—his life depends upon it. Wynshire will not fall easily." He drew a deep breath, his commitment made. "Have you a plan?"

Henry smiled. "Forget you my reputation? You were a squire at my side when I took Thouars. 'Twas reputed to be impossible to take—yet 'twas reduced in three days. We shall have little difficulty, for indeed I have a plan and have already mapped our attack."

He withdrew from inside his *bliaut* a crinkled sheet of parchment and smoothed it out upon the table, continuing. "When Maitland's father was alive I visited there often. The old fool would ne'er accept my suggestions for refortification, and hence I know its weaknesses. Unlike Jaune's, the footings of Wynshire's keep and walls are not cut into rock, but merely earth." He gestured Garret closer. "A filling of the outer moat here, followed by mining underneath this wall here . . ." He stabbed at the crude drawing. ". . . then use of a trebucket against the weakened wall will gain us entrance into the outer bailey. This latrine tower will lead us into the keep itself."

Garret nodded slowly. "Laborious to be sure, but it may work."

Henry grinned and snatched up the map. "Not 'may'—shall. Together we shall send the traitorous bastard to Hell, where he belongs!"

Garret turned away. And her? Could he bear to set eyes upon her? For that encounter he would need a plan of his own—but none came to mind as yet.

"Countess?"

Taryn opened her eyes, reluctantly surrendering the peaceful half-sleep evoked by the soft spring breeze and warm sunshine. Recognizing the black and white figure before her, she smiled. "Allow me to guess, Sister Magdalena. As I missed vespers yestereve, you've been sent to fetch me that I might endure yet another of the Reverend Mother's tiresome lectures?"

The young nun who had become Taryn's only friend at the convent of St. Anne's giggled and shook her head.

"This time you are only half right, my lady. Reverend Mother wishes to see you, but not for the reason you state."

Intrigued more by the animated tone in Magdalena's voice than her words, Taryn tilted her head and arched a brow. "And what might the reason be then?"

"I shall not say. 'Twould spoil the surprise." Again she giggled and extended her hand. "Come. I promise you will be pleased."

Her curiosity now truly piqued, Taryn glanced across the garden to where Maite's tiny form knelt amidst an array of herbs. Reassured the old woman was too occupied to miss her company, she placed her right hand flat upon the stone bench and reached for the nun's with her left. With Sister Magdalena's grasp providing balance, she commenced the arduous and awkward task of standing. Feet apart, back arched, and belly first, she lumbered to an upright position.

"Are you certain the babe is not to arrive for another month?" the younger woman asked, her eyes wide in wonderment. "Forsooth, I have ne'er seen such . . . such girth!"

Taryn laughed at her choice of expression. "And to be sure you've had occasion to see many a pregnant woman at St. Anne's?"

"Of course not!" came the shocked response, followed by yet another giggle.

In warm affection Taryn patted the girl's hand before releasing it. Six weeks had passed since her arrival, and in that time she had had no word of the outside world. Boredom and worry had consumed her days, and only the young nun's friendship and blithe nature had staved off depression.

Magdalena was fascinated with Taryn's tales of her life at Jaune, and Taryn found that in speaking of Garret and her home she was not only able to keep the memories from fading, but to draw comfort from them as well. Though the anxiety and fear for Garret's safety were not eased, she maintained hope, and even found her own pleasure rekindled by the younger woman's excitement over the unborn life she nurtured. For the first time since Garret's leaving she eagerly anticipated the birth of their child. Together with Sister Magdalena, who in her cloistral naïveté thought the couple's separation to be terribly romantic—akin to that of star-crossed lovers in a minstrel's song—she prayed for his safe and speedy return.

"Hurry, my lady!" Magdalena called to her over her shoulder as she stopped to allow Taryn to catch up.

"Won't you tell me what this is about?" Taryn gasped, realizing the cause for her shortness of breath. While she had been lost in her thoughts, they had crossed the breadth of the inner courtyard and were, in fact, now poised outside the garden door of the convent's parlor.

The younger woman shook her head. Summoning a serene expression, she quickly straightened her veil and then knocked. At the sound of a voice bidding entrance, she opened the door. "The Countess, Reverend Mother."

Taryn stepped forward. "Reverend Mother."

With a slight nod St. Anne's stern-faced prioress acknowledged Taryn's greeting. "Countess d'Aubigny, you have visitors. I believe you have the acquaintance of these people?"

Taryn followed the direction of the older woman's haughty gaze, but found that in entering from the bright afternoon sunlight her vision was momentarily dimmed. Then, too, positioned to receive the morning sun, the parlor was now ill-lighted.

From the room's darkest corner a pair of silhouettes emerged.

Taryn blinked in disbelief. "John! Moira!" she cried, running to embrace each. From behind her she faintly heard the prioress' exit.

Moira met her halfway, throwing her arms about her in joy. "Taryn!" she sobbed, holding her close then setting her gently back. "A babe," she murmured in awe. "We did not know." She laid her hand tentatively upon Taryn's swollen belly. Through the tears welling in her eyes, she beamed. Suddenly her features hardened. "That swine! At such a time he left you here—without the comfort of so much as a familiar face. What know these 'Brides of Christ' of the ails of breeding?"

Taryn was not sure if the "he" Moria denigrated with such vehemence was Charles or Garret. Did she know the true circumstances of Taryn's coming to St. Anne's? "I have not been ill, Moira," she stated gently, seeking to ease the woman's distress. "The babe grows well. Besides, I have not been alone. A woman very much like you accompanied me from Jaune. You shall meet her. But first you must tell how you have come to be here—both of you."

She reached out to take John's gnarled hand into her own. "We heard rumors of an attack made against Wynshire. If the war is so near, surely 'tis not safe for you to travel?"

John smiled. "'Tis clear you know not the whole story, milady. 'Tis true enough Wynshire was attacked. The siege lasted but two days before the outer walls were breached."

"Breached? In two days? 'Tis not possible!" Taryn exclaimed.

John's smile widened into a grin. "Aye, 'twas the strangest thing, milady—what brought it about. In the middle of the night, whilst one of the serving maids distracted the gatekeeper, some old fool cracked him over the head and raised the portcullis."

Taryn fought a smile. "I think I know the old fool, but which of the maids would possess such daring?"

"You would not know her, milady. She came to service from the village about the time of your marriage. Be the truth told, 'twas she that come to me with the plan. Mighty odd, too, for a maid to have such pluck. Goes by the name of Rose, she does."

The name meant nothing to Taryn. "And once the gate

was opened?"

John shrugged. "Once inside the attackers made short work of storming and taking the keep. Charles had sent off most of his Germans to join the rebels, keeping only a few dozen of Wynshire's men-at-arms. Overconfident he was safe, thinking good men who'd been devoted to your father would follow him with like dedication against the Crown. Those not caught still abed laid down their arms the moment they realized who and what they would be raising sword against."

"And Charles?" Taryn felt her throat tighten as she realized the import of this news.

"He'll hang for his treason, milady."

Taryn squeezed her eyes shut and breathed a prayer of silent thanksgiving. No longer would he be able to threaten or harm her. Suddenly a broader realization dawned. Excitement rose within her. "Then the rebellion has died if Henry's forces have taken Wynshire!"

John's expression instantly changed. He glanced at Moira, then back to Taryn. "They were your husband's men, milady—not the king's."

"Garret's? Are you sure?" Her excitement mounted and she clutched at the old man's hand.

"Aye, milady. 'Twas the Great Earl. Rode right up to the keep's steps he did on a fine war horse. Three hundred knights he had at his back all bearing Arundel's colors. I seen the yellow falcon on his shield myself."

Suddenly Taryn's initial joy evaporated in confusion, and her anxiety returned. Garret had attacked and seized Wynshire, and yet not come for her, or even sent word? Blessed Mother! Might he have been injured, or killed? Surely Simon would have told him of her whereabouts? But perhaps Simon had been killed in the attack . . . still he would have told Garret—unless he had never returned to Jaune? It was possible Charles could have had him killed! And if Garret had not gone first to Jaune, he would have no way of knowing she had left. Then too, if he knew, he might not be able to come for her himself.

That must be it! In his stead he had sent John and Moira.

She looked at the two dear servants who had been as family to her. Of course he would have sent them! Chastising herself for her foolish thoughts, she turned her concern to practical matters. "Does my husband desire that I return to Wynshire or to Jaune? If he must still be away—" She broke off seeing the stricken look upon Moira's face. "What is it?" she demanded, a sudden fear clutching her. "Has something happened to Garret?"

Moira took her hand. "Nay, Taryn. 'Tis not that."

"Then what?" she cried.

"Taryn, your husband . . . he . . . thought you were at Wynshire. Once the attack was over and Charles captured, he demanded to see a woman called Maite. When he was told neither she nor you were in residence and that Charles had placed you here, he . . ." She wiped at the tears now flowing freely. "He said 'twas where you belonged—just imprisonment for your crime of betrayal."

"Betrayal?" Taryn gasped, her breath leaving her. "That I left? That by going with Charles, he thinks I betrayed him?" A cold numbness descended, and she reeled in shock.

Moira reached out and took her arm. "You must sit, lady. Think of the child."

Taryn shook her head. "Nay! This cannot be so!" Frantically she grasped for reason and logical thought. If Garret had thought her at Wynshire, then he could not have spoken to Simon. *Simon!* she cried in silent relief. He could explain to Garret her reasons for leaving—that she had sought not to betray her husband, but to protect him. She squirmed from Moira's hold and turned to the man beside her. "John, I must send a message to Jaune, to one of my husband's vassals. He is a tall man with black hair and beard, and a scar." She gestured to her left cheek.

John looked at her in bewilderment. "Milady, you

describe the mercenary, d'Orléon."

Taryn started. "You know of him?"

"Not 'of,' lady, but know in fact." The old man's eyes, always so warm and gentle, hardened. "One of the bought wretches, he was, in service to your half-brother—until his leaving a week ago."

Taryn felt as if all the strength had left her. "Nay," she gasped, swaying weakly into Moira's arms. "This cannot be!"

"I swear 'tis so, milady. I first laid eyes upon him last Christmastide. He stayed only a day, then left. Next time I saw him he was riding through Wynshire's gate with Charles and the men who brought you here from Jaune. Strange 'twas, though—betwixt him and Charles. They were clear enough enemies and yet he followed Charles' command until he left."

"Nay!" Taryn shook her head weakly. John's face was blurred through the tears that suddenly filled her eyes. Simon in alliance with Charles? Her body rebelled against the onslaught, and she shuddered convulsively.

"See what you've done!" Moira's voice sounded. "She is not strong enough to hear this now. My lady, please, I beg of you. Sit."

Taryn stood rigid, resisting Moira's attempts to push her toward a chair. "I must go to him. Garret must know."

Moira laid her hand gently on Taryn's cheek, forcing her to meet her gaze. "Taryn, look at me. I saw the look in his eyes. There is no forgiveness in his soul. You cannot go to him."

"I must!"

"You cannot! He spoke of betrayal and crime for which there was neither forgiveness or repentance. Taryn, listen to me. He wants ne'er to lay eyes upon you again. As far as he is concerned, you are dead!"

Taryn shrank back trembling. A rush of tears blinded her, and Moira's face, filled with despair and sorrow, dissolved in a mist. Yet her voice remained.

". . . But as Wynshire is now yours, he said he would not prevent you from returning there. Taryn, please, let us take you home."

Taryn shook her head. "I cannot go with you. I have no right or claim to Wynshire."

"What are you saying? Of course you have right—and entitlement!"

Taryn closed her eyes. Suddenly she was conscious only of an overwhelming weariness, a longing for rest that would still the aching emptiness within her. "You need protect me from the truth no longer, Moira. I know of the circumstances of my birth. Charles took great delight in informing me of my illegitimacy when he was preparing to sell me to Lynfyld."

"Illegitimacy?"

The shock in Moira's voice caused her to open her eyes and add in a dull whisper, "You did not know my mother's first husband was still alive when she and my father were wedded, hence I was bastard-born?"

"Not so, milady!" John spoke up furiously. "Had I known Charles had told you of this, I would have told you what he did not. Right before you were born your father learned of the tinker's death. He and your mother were wed then and there, legal and proper. I know, because I witnessed the vows myself. Legitimate you were, when you entered this world—and I defy any to say different!"

A fragile joy sparked within her, but quickly died. Of what import was it to have regained what she believed lost when she had lost so much more! Suddenly a sharp pain cut through her. She bent at the waist and gasped, clutching at her belly.

Moira's arms were about her instantly. "The babe?"

Taryn shook her head. "'Tis too soon." She drew several rapid and shallow breaths, and the pain subsided. Slowly she straightened. For Moira's benefit she tried to force a reassuring smile, though in truth, she was frightened by the intensity of the pain. She had never felt such before. "'Tis just my son's way of making his presence known. Mayhap he wants to insure that his mother does not forfeit his inheritance out of ignorance and foolish pride. You are right. Wynshire is my home. As soon as I am delivered of this babe, and we are able to travel, I shall return to it."

As Moira nodded contentedly, Taryn caught sight of John gesturing toward the parlor door which was opening abruptly.

"Your pardon, Countess," the prioress spoke, stepping without invitation into the room. Her insincere apology was then followed by an impatient and lengthy sigh. "This seems to be your day for visitors. There is a monk here, arrived from the monastery of St. Swithin. He claims to be in possession of a letter addressed to you and insists he must deliver it personally. Will you receive him?"

At Taryn's nod of affirmation, the woman withdrew, returning almost at once with a man robed in the familiar garb of the brothers of St. Swithin's.

"Lady." With an utterly inexplicable smile of recognition, the kindly man took in her condition as he bowed his head in greeting. From the leather pouch about his ample waist he withdrew a folded length of parchment. "Forgive my intrusion, but I swore a holy oath . . . to place this letter in no hand but yours. 'Twas dictated to me by a knight found wounded on the road near—"

Taryn heard nothing else of his words. A second pain, as intense as the first, sliced through her, and she cried out.

Moira took hold of her firmly. "You must sit, my lady. Reverend Mother, would you fetch some wine, please?"

Leaning weakly against Moira, Taryn allowed the woman to lead her to a narrow settle. Her thoughts raced. Who would dictate a letter but a man who could not read? *Garret had been wounded!* Icy fear deadened the pain within her. In that instant she knew, despite everything Moira had told her, that she still loved him! "Please, brother . . ." She looked up at the monk. "This knight, by what name is he known?"

She noted the flicker of apprehension that appeared in the man's eyes as he lowered his gaze from hers.

"If . . . if you will allow me to read aloud his letter, lady, I think your questions will all be answered."

Taryn hesitated. Might knowing be worse than not knowing? "Read it," she whispered.

With a marked nervousness in both his hands and voice, he broke the letter's seal and began to read. "'My lady . . . If you are reading this, then I will have failed in my effort to right the grievous wrong I have wrought against you and our lord.'"

Our lord! Taryn repeated. Joyous relief washed over her. It was not Garret! Then who . . . ?

Through her silent questioning the monk's voice continued. "'As you have surely learned by now, it was as Charles Maitland's spy that I came to Jaune.'"

A new emotion struggled within her. *Simon!* John's report of him had been the truth! And yet a nagging in the back of her mind refused to be stilled. Shifting uneasily, she tried to listen intently to the monk.

"'Before acquaintance of the man I was to deceive, I was untroubled by guilt or remorse for the planned deception. But once I came to regard as friend the man I was to betray, and even, God forgive me, love the woman he called wife, I could no longer carry out the insidious scheme. And yet to have left Jaune would have only placed you both in greater danger. Maitland would not have been daunted from his aim to destroy his foe. He would have merely replaced one betrayer with another.'"

Abruptly the monk stopped reading. "Shall I continue, lady?"

Taryn stared up at him blankly. His words—Simon's words—confessing betrayal and professing love? She closed her eyes against the dizzying numbness descending. She felt Moira's hand slip into her own, squeezing in comforting reassurance. Without opening her eyes, she nodded.

At first she had difficulty hearing him, for his voice came thickly. "'Heinous though my crimes be, know, beloved lady, everything I have done has been to that one aim—to protect you and those you love. I helped convince you to leave your home only to avert the attack your brother was prepared to launch against Jaune if you resisted. He had a plan to draw our lord from the field, and you were the lure. But once you were under his control, I could not let you remain in his hands, and so I persuaded him to bring you to St. Anne's. For this I beg your forgiveness, lady: I claimed Lord Garret's child as mine. There was no other way I could convince Maitland. As Arundel's heir, the unborn life within your womb was a threat to him and all he would obtain. Though you and your child were then safe, the danger to our lord remained, as Maitland intended to murder his foe.'"

The meaning of what she was hearing wrenched a cry from her, and again the monk stopped, lifting his gaze questioningly. "Lady?"

"Go on," she whispered.

"Mayhap this is not wise, Taryn," Moira spoke gently.

Taryn pulled her hand from the older woman's clasp, clenching it in her lap. "I said proceed!"

Though it was the monk's voice that resumed, it was now Simon's that she heard. "'Only by knowing the details of his scheme could I thwart it. But the cost to Lord Garret was dear, and a price he would not have paid if given the choice. I convinced Maitland to content himself not with Lord Garret's death, but with his complete debasement. When he stormed Wynshire demanding your release, I continued the lie. I swore to him that our adultery had produced a child. Thus Lord Garret left Wynshire and returned to Jaune. But he returned alive, lady. You must believe me when I say that otherwise this would not have been so. Still, I have been unable to live in the knowledge of what I have done. Gladly I would have given my own life to keep even a shadow from your path, yet now you are despised by the man you love. That thought and all it implies eats at my soul, as does the destruction at my hand of the only man I have ever honored and called friend. I left Wynshire, headed to Jaune to remove the epithet upon your name and the sin from your pure soul, when I was attacked by Maitland's retainers. Two I sent forthwith to Hell; the third escaped gravely wounded. But in the battle I was also wounded. The good brothers found me and took me in. However, their ministrations and prayers are futile. I am certain the time nears that I must atone for my sins. But I fear neither death nor God's justice. My only regret is that I must speak these words to you through a letter, and yet I do not know if I would have had the courage to face you with these truths. I could not bear to see in your eyes the hatred you must bear me. Forgive me, Taryn. What I did, I did for love—the love of a woman and the love of a friend.'"

The monk looked up. "'Tis signed 'Simon,' my lady."

"I know," she whispered. Through her burning tears she watched as he carefully folded the parchment with such finality that further questions were pointless. And yet, she had to know. Slowly she stood. "When?"

"Before dawn two days ago. After dictating this letter, he slipped into unconsciousness. He never awoke."

A flash of pain shot through her. She doubled over, heard Moira's frightened cry and felt her touch. And then there was nothing.

Chapter Twenty-Seven

The clumsy two-wheeled cart hit still another hole in the pitted highway, the impact sending its occupants lurching sideways.

"Can you not avoid just one of those ruts?" Maite demanded. Righting herself, the old woman glared at the cart's driver. "'Tis not goods for market that you have back here!" Hissing an expletive beneath her breath, she turned to the woman seated across from her. "My lady, are you all right?"

Taryn smiled. Maite had always used her name in conjunction with the title "lady" or just the title alone. Not until a month ago, when she had placed Taryn's newborn son in her arms for the first time, had she used the word "my." Each time Taryn heard it, she felt the same glowing warmth of final and total acceptance—recognition earned with the bearing of Arundel's heir.

She looked down at the sleeping infant at her breast. He'd not even stirred. She touched the tiny soft cheek, and her heart swelled with the love she had felt at first sight of his dark hair and light eyes, so like his father's. He had inherited Garret's strength as well. A month early he had entered the world, and yet according to Maite's proud and no doubt prejudiced proclamation, he was as large as any babe birthed full term.

"We are fine," Taryn replied quietly in response to the

question she thought Maite might have forgotten having asked.

But the old woman hadn't forgotten. Despite Taryn's reassurance, a cross frown descended upon the wrinkled brow. "No thanks to that fool driving this box on wheels!"

"I heard that, you tiresome hag," John retorted, turning to glare over his shoulder at his accuser. "Think that you can do a better job, and I'll give you the reins."

"Humpf!"

Maite's reply brought an instant smile to his face. "I thought as much."

Taryn brought a hand to her mouth and laughed softly. Ever since leaving St. Anne's it had been so. For some reason John and Maite had been in competition with one another. Both were old, and in their ways firm in their devotion to Taryn, so to each the other presented some sort of threat—or curious attraction. At times their bickering was almost like that of children who knew no other means of expression. Regardless of its cause, after two days their heated feuding had reached the point where their escort of twenty of Wynshire's knights now drew lots to determine who would have to ride in hearing distance of the constant sniping and arguing.

"I still think this trek might have waited a few more weeks," Maite muttered, now turning her ire upon Taryn.

"We've been through this, Maite. The babe is strong enough to travel, as am I. Besides, we are nearly there."

"My lady." One of the knights riding as forward guard reined in his horse to match the cart's slower pace. Leaning from his saddle, he was able to peer into the tent-like covering to address her. "The castle has just come into sight." He raised his arm and gestured to the horizon ahead.

Taryn quickly surrendered her son into Maite's arms and crawled forward. Past John's shoulder she stared, narrowing her eyes against the bright orange rays of the setting sun. Dark in the distance she saw Jaune's battlements. With a rush of unexpected emotion her heart started to pound. Suddenly a part of her wanted to turn back. Other options, a week earlier entertained and summarily dismissed, now appeared so much wiser. Why hadn't she returned instead to Wynshire? From there she could have sent word to him or she could have sent Maite. Maite could have told him of Simon's deathbed confession. He would have believed her. But then he might have come, not for Taryn, but to claim his son.

His son. She glanced over to the baby still slumbering in Maite's gentle embrace. Even without Simon's letter there was no way Garret could look upon her child and still doubt this was his son. But what if her absolution from the sin of adultery did not matter to him? The very reason for their marriage had been to produce Arundel's heir. Now that she had, what further need did he have of her?

His words, spoken in the wool room the day he had proposed marriage, suddenly came to mind. *I cannot promise you love, for I do not love you.* As hard as she might try to deny it, no other words had passed his lips to refute that statement. In the few months of happiness they had shared, not one utterance had ever been made alluding to love on his part. And in regard to her love for him, what value could he have placed upon it when he had been so quick to believe her faithless? From the very beginning he had believed her capable of it—endowed with a whore's lust. In view of all of that, why would he want her back? Regardless of her reasons, her leaving would always appear to some as proof of an involvement with Simon. No man as proud as Garret could hear the whispered rumors and ignore them. She had shamed him and caused him dishonor. Ever he would be called upon to defend her honor.

The truth she did not want to face, and had therefore buried, now broke free and rose within her thoughts:

there was no reason for him *not* to cast her aside! She was a fool after all, to be making this trip.

Nay! She could not let herself believe that. She loved him, and she would not quietly disappear from his life, as much as he might prefer it. If he wanted her gone, he would have to tell her so himself—and not in a message delivered through her nurse! Her innate pride rebelled against passive surrender or acceptance of guilt of whose taint she was undeserving. She would not only defend herself, she would fight back—armed with the two weapons against which Garret had no defense: Simon's letter tucked into the hem of her sleeve and her son nestled in Maites' arms. She crawled back, intending to retrieve her sleeping child.

Suddenly the curtain at the back of the cart parted, revealing the helmed face of the captain of her men-at-arms. "We approach sight of their sentries, lady. They will soon spot our colors. Shall I have the men cloak their shields and strike the banners? 'Twould give us an element of surprise, and, as we are a small party, we might be able actually to cross the moat before we have to identify ourselves and beg entrance."

Realizing what he was saying, a curious sense of strength came to her. With an abrupt clarity of purpose, she met his gaze. "I am the Countess of Arundel, captain, by legal right of marriage. I will not 'beg' entrance to my own home, nor will I conceal Wynshire's colors in shame. Display them. Display them proudly!"

Beneath the helm's nasal a smile flashed. "By your command, lady."

He wheeled his horse to the right and spurred it forward to the column's head. Though the band was a small one, he took pride that each man was a long-time, loyal retainer of the Wynshire household. All the German mercenaries he had so detested had fled even before Charles' death.

Within the cart his lady had no view of what he did. But if she had, she would have seen him issue to each man he passed the same order, eliciting the same response. Backs straightened and shoulders squared, the message of their lady's words was clear. With Charles Maitland's treachery the name Maitland might have ceased to be an honorable one. Yet the honor of his sire was a legacy not so easily blackened. His daughter would see that service to Wynshire gave no man cause to bow his head, but to hold it high.

Taryn leaned back and closed her eyes. She listened to the rumbling of the wheels upon the mud-packed road, waiting for the change in sound which would tell her they were upon the drawbridge. After several moments it came—the smooth and even reverberation, without the jarring of the uneven roadbed.

The cart lurched to a stop. Above the wheels' sudden silence, voices rose—men arguing. Taryn recognized her captain's voice immediately, but not the other. She moved forward to look out. "What is it, John?"

"We've a problem, milady. The sentries refuse us entrance."

"Do the fools know who we are?" Maite demanded, looking out as well.

"Aye. 'Tis why they won't let us pass."

Taryn flinched as if struck.

"Take your son, my lady."

Before Taryn could either react or protest, Maite had pressed the babe into her grasp. At last awakened, he began to whimper softly, turning his head and moving his mouth in search of her. Taryn placed her finger against the roof of his mouth to soothe him. She could not suckle him now.

Maite crawled to the back of the cart and flung aside the curtain. "Help me down!" she commanded to a mounted knight who stared at her in mute surprise.

Despite her anxiety, Taryn smiled, seeing the mail clad warrior hasten to do the old woman's bidding. Shifting her weight to her knees, she moved up closer to John and watched as Maite appeared in front of the cart.

"Where is Richard?" she demanded, approaching the sentry.

Even in the now fading light of dusk his astonished expression was evident.

"Well?" she repeated sharply. "Have you lost your tongue as well as your wits, man?"

"Nay," he murmured, looking helplessly for aid from the two men who flanked him. When none came, he shrugged. "Fetch the steward."

His order, however, was unneeded, for at that moment Taryn caught sight of Richard rounding the gatehouse. Clearly word of their arrival had spread, for he was accompanied by no less than a dozen men-at-arms.

Cautiously the men of Taryn's escort laid hand to sword hilt and closed ranks. Taryn shrank back into the darkness provided by the cart's covering, out of view of the approaching men.

"Go back to your mistress," she heard the captain order Maite.

The old woman's derisive snort sounded above the stomping of the nervous horses. Defiantly she stepped forward in clear view of Jaune's men.

"Maite!" Richard's cry of recognition was immediately followed by a command to his guard to stand down. Swords half cleared of scabbards were instantly sheathed.

"At last a bit of reason," Maite noted in sarcastic approval. "Now, let us pass."

"I can't do that," Richard replied quietly. "She who sits in that cart may not enter these walls. The orders are not mine, Maite. Hence, I cannot belay them—even if I wanted to."

"She 'who sits in that cart' is the mistress of these walls, you ignorant heeder of gossip! And in her arms she holds your lord's heir."

Richard's mouth gaped, and Taryn knew then that Garret had told no one of Simon's claim to have sired her child—or that she had even been pregnant.

"Will you risk that babe's life," Maite continued in unrelenting confidence, "merely to keep his mother from entering these gates?"

Taryn held her breath and clutched her son close. The sudden action startled him and he let out a whimpering cry.

Had she at that moment peered out from the curtain, she would have seen Richard's face drain of color. Instead she only heard his voice, tight with conflicting emotions. "Let them pass."

Without bothering to dry the moisture from his body, Garret wrapped the towel about his waist and stepped from the wooden tub. Raking the wet hair from his forehead, he walked to the settle before the fireplace and sat. Wearily he leaned against the hard back, wincing at his muscles' protest. Nowadays, he pushed himself to the brink of exhaustion—not that it much helped.

He passed his hand across his eyes. With the day's activities done, the night had begun, and with it the loneliness he was able to keep at bay only as long as his mind and body remained occupied. Despite the passage of time, the pain within him was still alive, though he had gotten beyond raw agony to the dull ache of emptiness and grief.

How long? How long would she continue to live in his thoughts? Would the love she had inspired never die and release him from this life without her, which was less than life? A hundred times in the past month his pride had embroiled itself in battle with his heart. Once, at a particularly weak moment, he had even issued the order for a man to ride to the convent to do no more than verify her continued presence there. But then reason had rallied, and he had rescinded the order.

What purpose was there in knowing if d'Orléon, having left Wynshire before its attack, had retrieved her? Did he want to torture himself even more with the thought of them somewhere together? And if she had gone with her lover, what difference did it make? He could never take her back to his bed knowing she had given herself to another. He was not Flambard. His heart could neither accept her betrayal nor pretend it did not exist. His love for her might still be alive, but his trust in her was dead. Never would he be able to forget—or forgive.

He stared into the empty hearth, remembering the first night she had come to him. He had been sitting just where he was now, but then there had been a fire burning. The flames had been set to dancing in response to the draft created when she had opened the door, alerting him to her noiseless presence.

Unconsciously reliving the moment, Garret looked to the door, blinking in disbelief as the portal suddenly opened. He had been sober since the attack upon Wynshire more than a month past. Hence, the figure before him could be no drunken delusion. And yet there she stood.

His heart leapt in his chest and his hands clenched the seat's edge. She could not know the struggle within him—the longing to take her into his arms and the desire to choke the very life from her. With a single blow he could kill her. He was being torn apart, and yet he could do no more than stare at her as she slowly crossed the room to where he sat. She seemed at an equal loss for words. She stood before him mute, as his eyes took in her appearance in a single cold and sweeping glance. A protective shield of pride rose. He must conceal his emotion from her, else she would see the weakness and turn his pain, now scarred over, once more into an open wound.

Taryn forbade herself to tremble, and yet his silence terrified her. Were his fury, his rage at her believed betrayal, his hatred of her so great, he refused even to speak? Before his silence, her pride shredded, and finally her tremulous whisper shattered the silence between them. "My lord."

His voice came like the crack of a whip. "Did you lose your bastard, madam? Forsooth, by now I would have thought your bitch's belly to be swollen with the whelp of that mongrel cur."

Instinctively she reacted to his attack. Everything she had planned to say, each carefully conceived point of logic rehearsed a hundred times in the last month, fled from her mind. She seized the remnants of her pride, donning her dignity like a cloak, and drew her hand back. Then, as she saw the fierce warning flash in his eyes, she stilled and checked the blow.

He marked her action and smiled cruelly.

But the fight within her remained. "'Tis no way to speak of your son, my lord."

"My son?" He stumbled to his feet, wordless and shaking with anger.

"Aye." She lifted her chin and met his accusing glare straight on. "Healthy and thriving, your son is. He awaits below in Maite's arms to be presented to his father."

"No babe torn from the womb at five months could live," he challenged viciously.

"But one at eight can, and has."

A son. Garret struggled against the conflicting thoughts and emotions raging within him. D'Orléon had lied! The affair must have begun even before Becket's murder! But, nay, Maite would bring no bastard to him and proclaim it was his. And if it was his . . .

He whirled on her, understanding of her aim cutting through his jumbled thoughts. Somehow she had lost her lover and now sought, with his son as lure, to regain the position she had tossed away! "If you bring my son to me," he snarled in pain, "in belief my welcome will include the whore who is his mother, you have made a grievous error in judgment!"

"Damn you!" she gasped, fighting the traitorous tears filling her eyes. She refused to cower before his rage. "Had I done what you believe, I would deserve your loathing. But I am innocent and will not suffer your contempt! Jaune's lowliest serf is allowed to offer a defense before he submits to your justice. I demand the same right!"

Her outcry elicited nothing. He stood before her as if he had turned from a being of flesh to one of stone. Still she continued, fumbling to retrieve the letter before his control snapped and he threw her bodily from his sight. "This arrived at St. Anne's the day our son was born. In fact, Maite insists 'twas the shock of its contents which brought on the early birth." She looked at him. "Will you hear my defense?"

When his eyes revealed neither a command to cease nor permission to proceed, she seized the latter and tore open the parchment. "'My Lady . . . if you are reading this . . .'"

As she read, she continually looked up from the parchment to watch for any reaction the letter's contents might provoke. The revelation that Simon had come to Jaune as Charles' spy struck the first nerve. It was barely discernible, but Garret's granite composure weakened just a bit. It opened even further with Simon's profession of love—then cracked as she revealed Charles' intent to murder him. As alike as the men had been, and able to know the other's thoughts without benefit of speech, Taryn was certain Garret had grasped far more of the letter's contents than what she had thus far read.

She knew she was right when he abruptly turned his back and hunched his shoulders, as if what he heard was not words but the unsheathing of a sword whose imminent blow he was helpless to prevent. She glanced at the words she had just uttered: *the price he would not have paid if given the choice.* With her attention distracted, she searched for the place she had left off. "'I swore to him that our adultery had produced a child.'" she read, her voice breaking with emotion as she saw Garret lower his head into his hands. The low cry of pain which escaped him seemed torn from his very depths.

"Finish," he whispered.

She ended the letter with difficulty, barely able to see through the tears in her eyes. She folded it slowly, unconsciously, in the same manner as had the monk, and replaced it in her sleeve. "The . . . the monk to whom he dictated this, said that he died the following morning."

As she had guessed at Simon's fate, so did Garret now. He nodded wordlessly, but did not turn.

Suddenly the anger that had fueled her fight was gone. And though she wanted desperately to touch him, she could not. Her pride would not let her take that single step which would physically close the distance between them. "I know that it seems I betrayed you by going with Charles," she admitted slowly, "and if that was abandonment, I ask your forgiveness for it. But that was my only sin. That, and loving you, for the two cannot be separated. Were it not for that love, I ne'er would have left Jaune. But it seemed the only way to save your unborn son's life, and mayhap yours, if the rebels won."

In hopeless despair Taryn stared at the back still turned to her. "There was no adultery; I know you believe the letter. I can feel your pain. For your life, and your son's, Simon gave his own. You were alike, the two of you." Her tears began to fall and this time she let them. "But so are you and I. Despite his sacrifice, our pride can still destroy what he sought to preserve. I will not let that sacrifice be in vain. Since I have naught without you, I strip away my pride and stand before you naked, clothed only in love."

Garret would never know what made him turn. There was no whisper of sound to have alerted him to her action. Yet there she stood, her gown pooled at her feet, her body bare.

She gave him no chance to speak. "'Tis thrice I have stood thusly before you. Twice you dismissed me. If it be your will to dismiss me again . . . I shall relinquish all claim to our child—for no man should sire two sons and have no heir—and I shall return to Wynshire. But know this: I will ne'er stop loving you." She lowered her gaze, unable to look upon him as she awaited his answer.

"Taryn. Look at me."

He watched as her head slowly lifted and her eyes widened. As she had done to him, he gave her no chance to speak. "Before you I stand, my lady, equally naked and stripped of pride." He stepped forward, took her in his arms and then turned her face up to his. "Clothed only in love."

He touched his lips to hers, and in their trembling response was the forgiveness for which he had not yet asked. A hard sob broke from him, and he kissed her fiercely. Later he would put into words what now needed none: for what he had done to her, he would beg her forgiveness. And he would tell her, too, what he had learned. That as a knight was nothing without honor, so was a man nothing without love.

Epilogue

Without drawing any notice, she passed through the crowd and approached the huge destrier and its rider. Tilting back her head, the tiny woman shaded her eyes against the summer sun's rays reflecting upon the man's helm, and frowned.

"This is not wise," she chided. "You risk much by this appearance."

"Still sharp as steel, eh, Maite?" From beneath the helm which covered the man's face, amused laughter sounded.

"And just as dangerous," she retorted, "if I believe one I love is threatened or in danger."

"I am neither threat nor danger."

"I know that," she answered softly, a gentle smile erasing her frown. "But others may not. Let not that silver which purchased your messenger's silence be for naught. You must go before you are recognized."

"Just tell me she is happy."

"Judge for yourself. Look at her." Maite turned and pointed toward the stairs leading up to the village church.

He caught sight of her immediately. Like molten bronze her hair shone in the sunlight. Indeed, her face told him all he needed to know. Her smile rivaled the sun for brillance, and when the dark-haired man beside her slipped his arm about her slender waist and lowered his head to whisper something into her ear, her laughter rose above the noise of the crowd like the sweetest of music.

"I must go back," Maite stated. She laid her hand upon his knee. "If the observations of an old woman mean aught, the black heart is no longer black. No greater love will they ever know than yours. God speed, Sir Knight."

As Maite disappeared back into the crowd, he returned his focus to the couple now poised in the doorway of the church. The man reached out and took the small bundle cradled in the woman's arms. With her accompanying nod of approval, he held the infant aloft.

"My son!" he proclaimed. The crowd went wild with cheering.

Taryn blinked back the tears of happiness which sprang to her eyes as she beheld the pride and joy reflected in Garret's face. She looked from him to the throng of villagers and castlefolk assembled. Apart from the main body of the crowd she noted a solitary rider. His face was concealed beneath his helm, and he wore no colors to distinguish allegiance. However, there were many strangers present this day, knights in service to Garret's invited guests and mere curiosity seekers. Still, this one particular man seemed strangely familiar . . .

But it could not be! She shook her head and quickly brushed the sudden wetness from her cheeks.

"Taryn?" Garret's voice drew her gaze back to him. "We must go inside. 'Tis time for the christening."

"Of course." She took her son into her arms and looked a final time toward the tall rider.

He seemed to know she was staring at him. Slowly, and ever so slightly, he inclined his head in apparent acknowledgment.

Taryn felt her heart swell with hope. Perhaps she was being foolish, refusing to accept truth as fact. But in the midst of the happiness she now knew, a small sadness had remained—until this instant.

She brought her fingertips to her lips. If this man were truly the one she had known, he would know the gesture was meant for him.

Beneath his helm, Simon d'Orléon smiled.